BLESS YOUR HEART

BLESS YOUR HEART

A NOVEL

LEIGH DUNLAP

NEW YORK

Books should be disposed of and recycled according to local requirements. All paper materials used are FSC compliant.

This is a work of fiction. All of the names, characters, organizations, places and events portrayed in this novel are either products of the author's imagination or are used fictitiously. Any resemblance to real or actual events, locales, or persons, living or dead, is entirely coincidental.

Copyright © 2025 by Leigh Dunlap

All rights reserved.

Published in the United States by Crooked Lane Books, an imprint of The Quick Brown Fox & Company LLC.

Crooked Lane Books and its logo are trademarks of The Quick Brown Fox & Company LLC.

Library of Congress Catalog-in-Publication data available upon request.

ISBN (hardcover): 979-8-89242-163-8
ISBN (paperback): 979-8-89242-271-0
ISBN (ebook): 979-8-89242-164-5

Cover design by Heather VenHuizen

Printed in the United States.

www.crookedlanebooks.com

Crooked Lane Books
34 West 27th St., 10th Floor
New York, NY 10001

First Edition: August 2025

The authorized representative in the EU for product safety and compliance is eucomply OÜ Pärnu mnt 139b-14, 11317 Tallinn, Estonia, hello@eucompliancepartner.com, +33757690241

10 9 8 7 6 5 4 3 2 1

For Farrell.
No finer person ever existed.

PROLOGUE

"Did you just call my son an asshole?"

Birdie Milton was fed up with these rednecks. She rose from her prime seat in the middle of the bleachers, ten rows up, and faced a woman who had just called her son, Freddie, that very thing. Birdie had short, blonde hair the color her hairstylist called Golden Sahara and was, by Buckhead standards, an unacceptable size fourteen, which made her bigger than the woman in every way. Bigger size. Bigger wedding ring. Bigger bank account.

Eleven-year-old Freddie Milton, wearing the teal and purple uniform of the home team Vikings, stood on second base, refusing to concede an inch of ground as the coach for the opposing Macon Mudcats, who bore more than a passing resemblance to a velociraptor, screamed bloody murder from his team's dugout. Freddie had slid into second base, cleats first, and accidentally (maybe) had used his spiked shoes to move the second baseman out of the way. It had all gone down in a flash of flailing arms and legs and a cloud of dust. Blood was seeping from the puncture wounds Freddie left behind.

"He slid into my son on purpose," the cursing woman said. "He should be thrown out of the game."

"I don't know how you conduct yourselves at baseball games in Macon," Birdie told her, "but here in Atlanta we don't call eleven-year-old boys assholes. You redneck piece of shit."

The bleachers were filled with a mixture of Buckhead parents and the parents of the Mudcats, who had made the two-hour journey north to Chastain Park to take on the Vikings, a team filled with boys aged eleven or twelve, none of whom would ever be a professional baseball player. Many in the bleachers, though, seemed to think they were at the World Series, rather than a Little League game between preteens. That level of competitiveness, more so among the parents than their children, caused normally rational suburbanites to turn into screaming banshees.

Birdie was about to go on and say and do who knows what to the unfortunate woman from a place that unfortunately wasn't Buckhead, but stopped when she heard someone call her son's name.

"Freddie! You're out of the game. Come on in."

Birdie watched as Freddie kicked second base in frustration and glared at the bloodied Mudcats player. Freddie was short for eleven but also big for eleven. He led with his shoulders when he walked and looked more suited to football than baseball, but Birdie wouldn't let her sons play football. Not *her* boys. Football was too dangerous. The threat of concussions—of possible *brain* damage—was too great. Birdie was nothing if not a ferociously protective mother.

Birdie came down the bleachers toward the field in a huff, stepping over and sometimes *on* other parents. She wanted to stop herself, but she couldn't. She never could. Birdie felt like she was the voice of reason and the enforcer of rules and the only sensible person in almost any situation. Birdie didn't "do" polite. "Tact" was not a four-letter word in her arsenal. She sometimes went to sleep hating herself, but at least she *could* sleep at night. Unlike lesser women who cared what people thought of them.

Marcus Wiley, the Vikings assistant coach, a tall and muscular Black man who still looked the part of the revered football star he once was, stood impatiently near third base. Birdie thought she saw him roll his eyes at her. How dare he! Birdie wasn't a fan of Marcus, either as a football player or an assistant coach, and he wasn't a fan of hers, either as a team mother or as a person. There was an unspoken agreement between the two of them to simply avoid one another, so Marcus waited this one out and let Birdie do her Birdie thing.

"Anderson Tupper!" she yelled as she reached the fence that separated (or maybe contained) the parents from the field. "Don't you dare bench my son!"

Anderson Tupper sat on a bucket of balls at the entrance to the Vikings' dugout. His tanned legs (even in spring) were stretched out before him and his Vikings baseball cap, with an embroidered approximation of the god Thor (whose younger brother Anderson could have easily passed for), was slightly askew. He eyed Birdie warily. He seemed to constantly be looking out for the mothers. He turned his attention back to the game and his team. That team of boys fidgeted on the bench awaiting their turn at bat and stifled laughs as Freddie marched off the field in a squall of anger and joined them, even as his mother screeched from the other side of the fence.

"You should sit back down, Birdie," Anderson told her.

"I signed him up for this league so he could *play*," she said.

"It's not like he's benched forever. Just until we can have a talk about sportsmanship."

Sportsmanship? Birdie thought that was a ridiculous word. A loser word. She didn't want her son being taught that the real world operated under some kind of chivalric code where doing the right thing mattered. Because it didn't. The people that got ahead in life did so by crushing namby-pamby do-gooders who moaned about fairness—and *sportsmanship*. Birdie lived by a motto she had picked up from Douglas MacArthur (or maybe it was Jennifer Aniston): *Life's tough. Get a helmet.*

"My team," Anderson tossed out as he joined his players in the dugout. "Not yours."

Oh, how Anderson Tupper annoyed Birdie. He was so handsome. He was so rich. He was so charming. He just *was*. He didn't have to earn it. He didn't have to marry for it. All his many gifts came out with him when he was born, as if God had packed them up himself in a little Louis Vuitton diaper bag and sent them along through the birth canal.

"I swear to God, Anderson Tupper," Birdie spit out, "you'll regret this!"

CHAPTER

1

After the Murder

SHAY

IT WAS POISON. A fine powder the shade of yellow you might find on the walls of a baby's room or on a sympathy card left with flowers at a funeral. It looked harmless but was like a serial killer masquerading as the kindly next-door neighbor. Ted Bundy in a lemon sherbet windbreaker. It attacked your eyes and your airways, leaving you crying and choking for breath and wondering if taking your own life wasn't the more merciful way to go. Some said it was the heat in the South that caused people to act a little crazy. Shay couldn't prove it, but she was certain it was the *pollen*.

It seemed to Shay that spring brought out the worst in Atlantans. There was no escaping the pollen. It hung as a cloud over the city, covered cars until they too were yellow, and ran down the streets in rivers when it rained to form a paste along the grates of storm drains. It was in the air and in the people and Shay observed that in spring the citizens of Atlanta became somewhat unhinged. Maybe even murderous. Perhaps the pollen had gotten to Shay.

Maybe spring was the same as any other time of year. Maybe pollen wasn't the crazy-making villain she had always thought it to be. As she stood over the bloody body, however, Shay was more convinced than ever that her theory was correct.

"He's a good-looking guy," Shay said as she shined a flashlight across the body. She was, officially, senior homicide detective Lt. Resa LaShay Claypool, known to everyone but her mother as Shay. She looked down at a very dead white male. Despite his bashed-in skull, she could still see that he was handsome. Or had been. Shay had encountered enough dead bodies to see through blood and bruising and all forms of gruesomeness to the person beneath.

"I don't see it," said her partner, Dub Rattigan (he had always been and would always be just Dub). He was ten years older than Shay but was her subordinate. Junior detective to her senior. Sergeant to her lieutenant. Not that he seemed to mind.

"Don't be jealous, Dub. It's not his fault he's pretty."

"I mean, I literally don't see it. Not with all the blood."

The body of the handsome but dead male lay in a fetal position in the dirt. Shay and Dub kept a respectful distance to preserve the crime scene. They wore gloves and even had white sanitary booties over their shoes. A police photographer, also wearing gloves and booties, carefully stepped around the body. The flashes from his camera lit up the night in blinding bursts as he took pictures for the final pages of the photo album of a man's life. All their care to leave as little footprint as possible, however, probably wouldn't matter. The body was in the dugout of a Little League baseball field and who knows how many cleats had trod through the dirt that day.

"You should wear a mask," Shay told Dub. "Don't want you sneezing all over the crime scene."

"Have you heard me sneeze once today?" Dub asked. "Debbie got me some newfangled allergy medicine and it's actually working. It's natural. Made from roots."

"Roots of what?"

"No idea. I don't ask questions. I just do what the wife says."

"Murder weapon?" Shay asked.

"Nothing yet."

"From the looks of it, it was something big."

"Big and blunt," Dub agreed. "He was definitely beaten to death."

Shay walked to the entrance of the dugout and knelt down to get a different angle on the man's body, the beam from her flashlight slowly scanning from his feet to his head. Every bit of him was covered in blood that had already dried on his body or was congealed in puddles around it. As the flashlight moved up his arms, the beam caught a glint from the watch on his wrist. It was gold, and Shay could just make out the diamonds on the face beneath the blood splattered crystal. If Shay had been looking for something to steal, that would have been the first thing she would have taken. Which led her to one obvious conclusion.

"It wasn't a robbery," she said. "Don't see a wallet, but he's still got his watch. That's a Rolex. It costs more than your car."

"Everything costs more than my car."

Shay turned away from the gruesome scene but not because it disturbed her. She'd seen far worse. Hell, in South Atlanta she'd once come across a parked car with two suspects sitting inside. When she'd approached, she realized that the two men had been decapitated, their heads placed back on opposite torsos, burritos sticking out of their mouths, and Taco Bell bags carefully placed on their laps. But that was South Atlanta, with its gangs and drug deals gone bad. This was Buckhead. The Beverly Hills of Atlanta. Murders here tended to be a little more high class.

Shay and Dub left the dugout and walked toward home plate. They both wore fedoras, the signature of the Hat Squad of police detectives in Atlanta. Shay couldn't remember a time in her life before she became a detective that she had ever worn a hat. Yet she wore this hat with pride and thought she looked good under its wide felt brim. It gave her authority. Other detectives and police officers worked around the field gathering bits and pieces of this and that and putting them in bags for cataloging. There wasn't a lot to gather, however, because the field was so pristine. It was part of a complex of other pristine fields at Chastain Youth Baseball. This was where the boys of Atlanta's most prosperous area used the best equipment money could buy to battle for small plastic participation trophies.

The dew in the perfectly manicured grass shimmered under the field lights as Dub pulled his jacket, a sale purchase from Burlington Coat Factory, a little tighter against the chill of the spring night. "Good Lord, they probably have baby goats cut this grass," he said. His Southern accent seemed to be getting thicker by the moment. "You should have seen the fields I played on when I was a kid. They didn't have to mow the grass because there wasn't any."

Shay had heard these types of stories from Dub hundreds of times in the three years they had been partners. She had grown up in Atlanta. *In* Atlanta. Not a suburb or in a one light, one policeman, one filling station town in South Georgia. Not like Dub, who was from Pitts, Georgia, which was south of, well, nowhere. They made for an odd pair. Shay was Black, while Dub was so white he didn't even have freckles. Shay was a city girl and Dub was a country boy. Shay was liberal and Dub was conservative. It didn't take Shay long to realize, though, that they had kindness and decency in common, and that's all that really mattered. They liked each other just fine.

It was the middle of the night, and they were both tired. This area wasn't their usual beat, but cutbacks and the luck of the draw had made this their case. Shay would have liked to have stayed home in bed. She wasn't a fan of the drive to North Atlanta or the area. It was only when she spent time among the mansions of Buckhead that Shay lost some of her abundant confidence. Even though she was a single mother who'd managed to send her son to college (the Ivy League, at that, and damn it was expensive, even with the scholarships), had bought her own home and paid it off, and rose through the ranks of the Atlanta Police Department to become a senior detective, being in Buckhead made Shay feel like she had somehow failed in life.

The idyllic quiet of their murder investigation was spoiled by the appearance of a man in a baseball cap with CYB embroidered above its visor. He hovered off the first base line, nervously watching the many police officers trod across the field.

"Excuse me," he called out to Shay and Dub, "but could y'all possibly not step on the grass?"

He actually said that.

"Sir," Shay said in her best mom/detective tone, "did you not see the dead body in the dugout? Unless you're here to make a confession, and we can wrap this up right now, we'll be walking wherever we damn well please."

This wasn't the type of man who tolerated women speaking to him that way. Even though he was wearing a ball cap and a sweatshirt, Shay couldn't miss the Gucci loafers below the hem of his professionally distressed jeans. He was used to being in charge and respected, if not for any other reason than his existence.

"I'm Dr. Lamar Burrows," the man said. He looked uncomfortable as Dub wrote the name down in one of the small notebooks he always carried with him. "I'm on the board of CYB."

"They have a board?" Shay said, sort of to Dub and sort of to the cosmos. It seemed so ludicrous. It was *Little League*.

"Were you the one who found the body, Mr. Burrows?" asked Dub.

"It's *Doctor* Burrows . . ."

"Is that Burrows with a U or an O at the front?"

"Burrows with a U, obviously," Lamar Burrows said condescendingly, as if Dub were a simpleton. "And no, I didn't find him. The groundskeeper did."

"We're going to need to talk to him," said Shay. She looked across the field. Signs for sponsors from Morgan Stanley to Delta Airlines to Coke hung along the fence. No Chico's Bail Bonds here. She turned back to Burrows-with-a-U. She didn't like people who were rude. Especially if they were rude to Dub, who was the nicest man she knew. She decided from now on the Doctor would be known, in her mind at least, as Burrows-with-an-FU. "Did you know the victim?"

"Of course," said Burrows. "It's Anderson Tupper."

"He's a Tupper," sighed Dub, shaking his head. He closed his notebook.

"Tupper?" Shay asked. "Like, *the* Tuppers?" Shay didn't need an answer. Of course, it was *the* Tuppers. They were one of the richest families in Georgia—after Tyler Perry, the guys who started Home Depot and the people who sold the chicken sandwiches Dub loved so much. Shay knew that there would be no wrapping this up on this night. Even if the murderer ran out now, covered in blood and screaming "I did it!" there wasn't going to be anything easy about this case. Shay rubbed her eyes. She was already exhausted. "It's the pollen. Makes people crazy."

CHAPTER

2

Fourteen Days Before the Murder

KIRA

There was mumbling among the parents as Kira approached the bleachers. She watched as a woman, whom she would later know as Birdie Milton, stomped her way up the bleachers and back to a seat in the middle of the spectators. There was a collective feeling of embarrassment in the air. Kira had heard the woman make some kind of threat against one of the coaches, but honestly, Little League tended to bring out the worst in parents. Kira had once seen a father slash the tires of a coach's car because the coach hadn't let his son pitch in the third inning of a game between six-year-olds. That was in Los Angeles, where Kira was from. Surely such things didn't happen in Atlanta.

Kira quickly scanned the scene. She was good at details. She could size a man up by looking at the shoes he wore (if he didn't take care of the shoes on his feet, he wasn't going to take care of the woman on his arm) and size up a woman by the bag she carried. The men in the stands wore fashion sneakers in brown or blue suede with white soles or leather Gucci loafers adorned with gold horse bits. Many of the women, at least the ones who were cheering for the home team Vikings, had insanely expensive, waxy-coated Goyard bags at their side. No one appeared to have the same color. It was like they had called one another in the morning to make sure they didn't match. Kira herself carried a Paul Smith handbag. It was expensive but not showy. It was the same but different. Like Kira.

Kira paused at the bottom of the bleachers and searched for a place to sit. She wanted to make the move quickly. Entering a new place like this with its new people and their different customs was always a fraught exercise for her. She was disappointed to discover that as you got older you never lost that *new kid* feeling. Kira was in her early forties, but today she felt like she was walking into the middle school cafeteria on the first day of school. She knew that the second she stepped up into the bleachers the judgment would begin. Everyone judged everyone else, even if they said they didn't. It was human nature.

There was an empty space about three rows up and conveniently near the end of the bleachers. It was perfect for a quick escape. Kira waited as the players from the Vikings ran out of the dugout and took the field. She had one eye on them as she climbed into the stands and quickly sat down. It was a small accomplishment.

Kira scanned the field and finally spotted the eleven-year-old who belonged to her. Out in right field, Kolt Brooks fiddled with a glove that seemed too big for his small hand. His brown hair poked out in random tufts from beneath his cap. Kira thought his hair was too long. Why hadn't his father taken him to the barber shop? She'd reminded him so many times.

Kira waved, trying to get Kolt's attention. She was excited to see him. She wished she could run out onto the field and hug him and not let go until he was properly horrified by her momness. Kolt finally looked over in Kira's general direction and spotted her. There was no smile. No excitement. Just a little wave of the oversized glove and he was back to the business of standing in right field, where no ball ever seemed to go.

A Black woman a few feet down the aluminum bench turned Kira's way. She had long honey-brown hair and eyes that were either brown or green depending on how the light caught them. Unlike Kira, who had never been comfortable with her beauty, this woman owned hers. She was as confident as Kira was not.

"Is that your son?" the woman asked.

"Yeah, he is."

"So, you're the mysterious Mrs. Brooks."

Mysterious? Kira wasn't sure this was a good way to be described.

"I'm Venita Wiley," the woman said as she scooted over a little closer to Kira. That gesture alone made Kira feel more welcome. She could already sense it. This woman was going to be her friend. After all, she held a Gucci backpack on her lap. It was printed with the small Gucci double-Gs, but also had a very hip red and brown growling tiger across its front pocket. It was fearsome. Venita, she could tell, was also the same but different.

"I'm Kira."

"Our sons are friends," Venita said as she nodded in the general direction of the field toward the only Black boy on either team. He was already, at eleven, noticeably taller than the other boys. "Wade."

"Wade!" Kira said. "I've heard so much about him. Thank you for being so welcoming to Kolt. It's not easy being the new kid."

"No matter how old you get," said Venita, as if she was reading Kira's mind.

The sound of bat hitting ball focused their attention back to the field. The opposing player at the plate, a little guy with mighty power and speedy legs, had hit a missile and it was headed straight toward Wade in left field. Kira relaxed. She thought what a lot of Little League mothers thought—please don't let any ball be hit anywhere near my hapless son.

Venita was not so lucky. Wade had been counting blades of grass when the ball was hit and in no position to field it. It was already rolling by him and headed toward the fence by the time he attempted to intercept it. He chased it down and made an awkward, errant, throw in the general vicinity of second base. Unfortunately, the batter was already crossing home plate at the time.

The other team's parents cheered while the Buckhead parents sat in silence. They weren't looking at Venita, but their silent judgment was overwhelming. Venita threw her arms up in frustration as she caught Wade's attention in the field. He just shrugged.

Marcus Wiley, who as well as being the team's assistant coach was also Venita's husband, kicked over a bucket of balls. He looked up in the stands at Venita like it was all her fault. It must be *her* sub-par genes that created this unathletic boy!

"Your husband?" Kira asked.

"For the moment," Venita said. It was hard to tell if she was serious or not.

A sweet Southern accent rose above the chatter in the stands behind them. "Venita, I have a question . . ."

Venita barely took her eyes off the field as Sutton Chambers came down the bleachers and sat behind them. She was a petite blonde who was incredibly fit and would have been the perfect spokeswoman for athleisure wear. Kira thought she resembled a blow-up sex doll with her inviting round red mouth and exaggerated proportions.

"What can I do for you?" Venita asked.

"You said you'd donate one of Marcus's shirts to the auction," Sutton said. "We have to have everything photographed for the catalog, so I need it, like, yesterday."

"It's a *jersey*, not a shirt, and the photographer already picked it up, so I think we're good."

"Thank you, Venita!" Sutton said with more enthusiasm than Venita seemed comfortable with. "You're the best."

"I know," Venita replied. "This is Kira, by the way."

"Hey," Sutton said dismissively. She didn't seem interested in Kira and wasn't finished with Venita. "I just wanted to check, did Marcus autograph the shirt?"

"Yes, he autographed the *jersey*."

"Right. Okay, great. Like I said, you're the best."

"Any time, Betty," Venita said as Sutton headed back up the bleachers.

"Nice to meet you, Betty," Kira called after her. It seemed the polite thing to do. Sutton, however, looked back at Kira with a frown as Venita smiled.

"What?" Kira asked.

"Her name is Sutton," Venita said. "I called her Betty as a joke. You know, the Buckhead Betties? It's not a compliment."

Kira glanced back at Sutton, who was now seated with the loud woman who had threatened the coach and another woman Kira heard Sutton call Amelia, who was accompanied by a pint-sized Little Leaguer in a bright orange Miami Marlins jersey. Unlike the other mothers, Amelia had a deep brown crocodile Hermes Birkin bag at her side. It was the Mount Everest of handbags, the ring in *The Lord of the Rings. One bag to rule them all.* The little boy, no more than four, tugged on the sleeve of Amelia's flowered dress until she pulled a juice box out of the Birkin bag and handed it to him.

Kira was sure the women were talking about her. After all, she had called one of them Betty! She hadn't been there ten minutes and she had already insulted one of the Mean Girls. This thought, true or not, would haunt her for the rest of the day. In fact, she'd probably have trouble sleeping.

"So, your husband was a baseball player?" Kira asked Venita, treading into new territory.

"Football," Venita replied assertively, as if Kira should have known that. Then she seemed to catch herself. Maybe not everyone knew who Marcus Wiley was. "He played for UGA. The University of Georgia? And the Falcons for a few years. Before he was injured. He won the Heisman."

"And now he coaches Little League?"

"He's a *volunteer*," Venita said with emphasis. "The coaches aren't paid here. Seriously, it's Little League. We own a Ford dealership. The biggest in the Southeast."

Kira was starting to feel like she had made another faux pax. She was about to start babbling to try and get herself out of this, to explain that she didn't think all Venita's husband could do in life was coach Little League, that of course that was ridiculous, and that she was utterly embarrassed and should probably just go off into the woods and *die*—but instead opted for door number two.

"So, what do you do?" Kira asked, hoping to God that Venita didn't say she was a *housewife* and make it seem like Kira was rude for assuming that wasn't a real job. Because, of course, Kira thought it was. She was a terrible housewife and whatever it took to be a good one was a skill beyond her abilities.

"I'm a lawyer. What do you do?" Venita asked.

"I'm a writer."

"Oh, really? What do you write?"

"Books, mostly," Kira replied.

"Anything I'd know?"

"It's YA stuff. Young Adult."

Kira always had to navigate this part carefully. She didn't want to come off like she was better than anyone else, but it was difficult to dance around the fact that she had written a series of books for teenagers that were so popular even adults knew of them and had often read them themselves. She had even sold the movie rights and the latest hot young actress was slated to star.

Kira finally relented. "I guess my most popular things are *The Star Runners* books."

"Well, damn," Venita said. "I guess Marcus isn't the only famous person here."

VENITA

The game had mercifully ended. Venita didn't even know what the final score had been. She had learned from her years of being first the girlfriend of a college football star and then the wife of a professional football player that it was best not to worry about the outcome of a game. Some games would be triumphs, but more would be disappointments. She had her standard blank game face either way. Win or lose, life would go on.

"Okay, guys, let's get packed up," Marcus said as the boys ran or walked or dragged themselves back to the dugout. "Let's not leave any garbage this time. I'm talking to you, Cash." A very blonde boy with long eyelashes the envy of any woman nodded. Wade was the last one in from the field, having lumbered under the weight of his large feet. He was going to be as big as his dad. They had the same build, and Wade could easily be cast as a young Marcus in some cheesy inspirational movie about an impoverished, small town football player who battled the naysayers, married an actress who looked a lot like Halle Berry, and triumphed against all odds. Wade, however, wasn't poor, wasn't born in the country, and never had to battle for anything in his life. He was just like all the other kids in Buckhead.

Venita and Kira stood at the gate to the dugout and waited for their boys. Venita thought that Kira seemed nervous. She had heard enough about their family history from Kira's son to understand why.

Wade dragged his equipment bag through the dirt and presented himself to his mother. "I sucked today," he said.

"You did your best," Venita told him as she placed a reassuring hand on his shoulder and gently rubbed it. "That's all that matters." Venita didn't really think that doing your best was all that mattered. Lots of people did their best and those people tended to work at 7-Eleven. Wade, however, was already down and now was not the time to pile on.

Marcus joined his wife and son. He was usually camera-ready and armed with a perpetual smile and a lighthearted veil of congeniality. Although his business was ostensibly selling cars, his real job was being Marcus Wiley, sports legend. Today, however, he had on his coaching hat and wore a look of disappointment. It was bad enough that his son had chosen to play baseball instead of football, the sport that had made his father famous and paid for the little-used, insanely expensive bats that filled Wade's equipment bag, but there was the added indignity that Wade had, indeed, sucked.

"We should go directly to the batting cages and get in some practice," Marcus told Venita.

"You're not going to the batting cages," Venita said. "Wade has homework to finish." Wade's shoulders, which were already slumped, slumped a little bit more. He was practically melting into the ground. "This is Kira," Venita continued, introducing her husband to the newest Buckhead resident. "She's Kolt's mom."

"Marcus Wiley," he said as he shook Kira's hand and his car dealer/football star smile appeared in all its glory. "Nice to meet you. We sure do like your son."

"Nice to meet you," said Kira. "Congratulations on the Heisman."

"Well, they gotta give it to someone," Marcus said.

There's my husband, thought Venita. That's the man I married. Not the grumpy Little League volunteer assistant baseball coach. This season couldn't end soon enough. In her head, Venita was already practicing the speech she would give both father and son about how they should never do this again. It obviously didn't make any of them happy, and Wade obviously was never going to make the highlight reels on *Sports Center*. This baseball experiment was just setting him up for failure, and Wileys never failed.

KIRA

Kira watched as her son Kolt came through the field gate lugging his equipment bag like a weary soldier returning from the trenches of Verdun. He shuffled along slowly, and rather than meet his mother with a smile and cheerful greetings, he said, "What are you doing here?"

"Well, hello to you too," Kira responded. She tried not to show how sad her son's lack of enthusiasm made her. It was a punch to the gut. "No hug for your mom?"

Kolt reluctantly leaned in and gave Kira a pathetic little side hug. An entire undiscovered Shakespearean manuscript was being played out in their subtle gestures. "Where's Iris?" he asked.

"I don't know," Kira said. She should have known where her daughter was, but Kira was no longer privy to the movements of the seventeen-year-old. "I called and texted her, but she didn't reply."

"She doesn't look at your messages."

First a punch to the gut and now a stab through the heart. Kira had just driven across the country. She had made the five-day drive from California in four days just so she could get to her children sooner. Now she was regretting that she hadn't stopped off in Bentonville, Arkansas, to go to the Crystal Bridges Museum of American Art. Or at least stopped to see the world's biggest ball of twine. She had thought back to when she had driven cross-country with her parents when she was eight. "Dad, it's the Petrified Forest!" she said then. He told her it was "just a bunch of dead trees." "Dad, let's go to the Grand Canyon!" It was "just a hole in the ground." Her father was always hurrying to get back to work, no matter where they were. Kira was a lot like him.

Just as Kira was blowing up the imaginary balloons for her own little pity party, a man's soothing voice brought her back to reality. It wasn't a redneck, Boss Hogg, *Deliverance* kind of southern accent. It was deep and resonating and, well, kind of sexy.

"Welcome to Atlanta, Mrs. Brooks."

Kira turned to find Anderson Tupper standing behind her. She had caught glimpses of her son's coach from her perch in the bleachers, but they hadn't prepared her for the full picture. Anderson was a storm of sexuality blowing around pretending to be a man. At any moment, anyone could be struck down by one of his lightning bolts. Kira certainly felt the storm front approaching. She unconsciously began fiddling with her wedding ring, twisting it around and around her ring finger.

"I'm Coach Tupper," he continued. "Anderson Tupper. You're Kolt's mom."

"I am," she said. She wasn't sure if that had come out as a statement or a question. I am! I am? "I'm Kira."

"Nice to meet you, Kira." Anderson held out his hand and Kira shook it. Her hand was cold and the warmth of his caught her off guard. She held on a little too long. If Anderson noticed, he was too polite to let on. "This a fine boy you have here."

Kira gathered herself. She was an adult, damn it, not some quivering, awkward teenage girl with a crush. She was a mom. A *wife*. This was her son's baseball coach, not some guy she was meeting in a bar. "He's great. I think I'll keep him." Ugh. She couldn't believe that was all she could come up with.

Kira was about to offer up some better chitchat when she sensed the approach of her daughter. She could always feel her coming before she saw her. Judgment, shame, and a whole lot of attitude were making their way toward her in the form of Iris Brooks. She was wearing too-short jean shorts, some God-awful chunky boots that made her feet look two sizes larger than they were, and a crop top that was an inch shy of just being a bra. Never mind that it was spring and Kira herself was wearing a sweater.

"Hey," Iris said. She was void of enthusiasm. Kira had bypassed the Barbed-Wire Museum in Texas for this?

"Hi!" Kira said with way too much enthusiasm. "I tried calling you, but you didn't pick up."

"Sorry. I was busy."

"Hello, Iris," Anderson said. He didn't seem to be fazed by the family dynamic playing out before him.

"Hey," Iris said in return. Kira was sure she was doing this just to annoy her. She had lectured her daughter before on the insufficiency of the word "hey." It was a throwaway word that lacked any charm. "Hey is for horses" was how Kira's father would have put it. Iris already looked halfway to a frown and close to an eye roll, and Kira knew now was not the time for lectures.

"Why don't we all get some lunch?" she asked. Then she realized Anderson Tupper was still there. "Why don't you join us?" she said to him. She really wished he would.

"Thank you, but I've got to finish up here," Anderson said. "But I appreciate the kind offer." He was so polite. Why hadn't the manners of the south rubbed off on her children yet? They'd been there for months.

"We always get pizza after games," Kolt said. He looked at Iris, not his mother.

"I love pizza!" Kira said. Again, with too much enthusiasm.

"Actually, it's kind of our thing," Iris clarified. Just to make it clear. Our thing. Not Kira's thing. "But, um, we'll see you at home, right?"

"Right," Kira said. She smiled but didn't want to. Her son and daughter had never been particularly close. Iris had enjoyed being an only child and had made it clear, at age five, that she didn't appreciate the fact that Kira had gotten pregnant. Everyone called Kolt the *surprise* baby, but he was anything but. Iris was just like her father, both in looks and temperament. Kira was looking for allies, so she created one. Now Kolt, who had always been her ally, was allied to another. Kira wasn't interested in getting pregnant again. She would have to seek new allies elsewhere.

She watched as Iris and Kolt walked off together toward the car Kira had purchased for her daughter as, well, a bribe. Here's a seventy-thousand dollar BMW so you'll love me again. It didn't work. Maybe there weren't enough luxury German cars in the world.

"Listen," Anderson said. He moved a little closer. "Kolt seems like a really sensitive kid. I've just, well, I've been trying to build his confidence. A boy can't have enough male role models. I hope it's okay that we've been talking."

Kira felt her body turning to stone. Her own weight was pushing her into the earth. She could no longer even pretend to be light. What did this man already know about her?

Anderson seemed to sense that he had crossed a line and redirected. "I mean, I think being a new kid at school has been kind of rough for him. We just talk about guy stuff. Like standing up for yourself and making friends. Things like that. I just wanted to tell you that I'm there for him. And you. If you ever need anything."

"Thank you," Kira said. She knew they were talking about something else, but she appreciated that he hadn't said what that something else was. "Well, good game."

"We lost."

"Still a good game," said Kira. "It was nice meeting you."

"Very nice to meet you," said Anderson as Kira headed toward the parking lot.

She looked back over her shoulder. He was still looking at her. She couldn't tell if he was pitying her, checking her out, or just *looking*. It was hard to tell because he seemed able to do all those things at the same time.

SUTTON

The most famous person Sutton Chambers had ever met (not including Marcus Wiley—who as far as she was concerned didn't count, because who cared about football anyway?) was Dolly Parton. Sutton almost passed out when she saw the real-life Dolly at Dollywood, the singer's amusement park in the Smoky Mountains. It was on one of the few trips Sutton's family had taken when she was growing up. Dolly Parton. Imagine that. As a girl from rural Alabama who dreamed of living in far-off exotic places like Tampa Bay and Myrtle Beach, meeting Dolly made Sutton realize anything was possible. At age thirteen, Sutton was petite and flat as a board, something that didn't change when she hit puberty. It was the country icon who inspired Sutton to get the impressive breast implants she now possessed.

First Dolly Parton and now Kira Brooks. Not that Sutton really knew Kira's name. When Venita told her, though, that Kira had written *The Star Runners* books, Sutton almost started hyperventilating. Almost passed out right there in the Chastain Park parking lot.

"Oh, Sutton, calm the fuck down," Birdie told her. "I bet you haven't even read the damn books."

It was true. Sutton had never particularly enjoyed reading, but she was a fan of audiobooks. Especially those that promised listeners a better life through manifestation. They had guided her at age twenty to leave Alabama and head to the big city of Atlanta. She would listen to her inspirational books as she drove around town, looking for a better life. Sutton would often park in front of one of the many mansions of Buckhead, in front of the house she thought was the most beautiful, and dream of what it would be like to live there. As instructed by her many manifesting gurus, she thought of every last detail, from the four-tiered crystal chandelier in the foyer to the soft pink marble in the master bathroom.

To make your dreams come true, you needed to "set your intention," and Sutton intended on one day living in Buckhead. So Sutton got a job in Buckhead, at the place where the richest Buckhead folk gathered—the Peachtree Driving Club. The club was made up of two parts. There was a *city* club that was in downtown Atlanta and was for everything except golf, and there was the *country* club that was east of the airport and was for all things golf. Though neither club was technically *in* Buckhead, they had planted their flags on foreign soil, like U.S. Army bases surrounded by razor wire in the center of Kabul.

Sutton secured a job at the pro shop at the golf course at the PDC, as members referred to the Peachtree Driving Club. As it mostly required her to be pretty and personable, things Sutton excelled at, she was a star employee. But Sutton wanted more. If she was going to be good at her job, she knew she would have to learn about every man who came to the pro shop to check in for his round of golf. Good employees went the extra mile!

She scoured the membership directory and memorized every name. She looked up their addresses and drove by their houses. The more she learned, the more she felt like she was a part of their world. Like she was one of them. She wasn't just the girl at the desk. She was their *friend*.

And then the most miraculous thing happened! Sutton drove through the streets of Buckhead to one of the homes of one of the PDC members and found herself in front of the same mansion she had often sat in front of and dreamed of living in. What were the chances? It was fate, of course.

She had manifested it.

She would learn later that the mansion had a name. It was called Azalea, and it was owned by one Charles Chambers. Chuck! She knew Chuck. He was so nice. He always flirted with her (didn't they all?) and would jokingly say, "I think we're destined to be together, honey." He was old. Well, he was *older*. Oh, what difference did it matter how old people were where love was concerned? And Sutton could love him. In fact, she was pretty sure she was *already* in love with him. So what if he was married? Obviously, he wasn't happy, or he wouldn't be flirting with her. None of that made any difference because it was all meant to be. As destiny decreed, Chuck traded in wife number two for wife number three, and Sutton Varney of Alabama became Sutton Chambers of Buckhead. And now here she was, years later, in the center of the Buckhead cabal.

"Kira is famous," Sutton said to Birdie and Amelia as cars came and went in the Chastain Park parking lot. "I googled her. She has over a hundred thousand followers on Instagram."

"The Ayatollah Khamenei has almost a million followers," Birdie shot back. "Doesn't mean I want to play pickleball with him. Besides, look at her daughter. What kind of mother lets their daughter dress like a prostitute?"

"That's how all the girls dress," Amelia said.

"Yes, that's how all the girls dress when they're visiting their boyfriends in prison," said Birdie. "Freddie has a crush on the girl," she added. "I don't need him liking women who dress like whores. You should be worried about your son too, Amelia. He may take after his father."

Sutton waited for Amelia to get a dig back at Birdie, but as usual she kept quiet. Amelia's ex-husband had the annoying habit of sleeping with prostitutes. Sutton was sure Amelia had known about it and put up with it because she was too timid to speak up. Sutton had never even heard Amelia raise her voice. Maybe she had been timid in bed too, and that's why her ex-husband had strayed.

Kira came up from the fields and Sutton waved her over. "Oh, my God," Sutton said as she grabbed Kira's hands in hers. "Venita told me you wrote *The Star Runners!*"

Kira smiled shyly. "I did."

"I loved those books!"

"I'm Birdie Milton," Birdie said.

"Nice to meet you."

"Amelia Tupper," Amelia said, offering her slender hand for Kira to shake.

"Tupper?" Kira asked. "Are you the coach's wife?"

"Sister-in-law," Amelia said.

"*Ex*-sister-in-law," Birdie declared emphatically.

"I had the best idea," Sutton said as she clapped her hands together as if to congratulate herself. "Kira should donate a lunch to the Steeplechase. People would pay a fortune to meet you."

Kira looked utterly confused, and Amelia stepped in to clarify. "The Peachtree Steeplechase. It's a horse race for charity. We're on the auction committee."

"We *are* the auction committee," Birdie added. "And I'm not sure anyone would bid on having lunch with a writer. No offense, Kira."

"People do it all the time," Sutton said. "I googled it. Someone once paid twenty-eight thousand dollars to have lunch with Suzanne Collins."

"Well, Kira's hardly Suzanne Collins," Birdie said. Sutton thought Birdie could be so rude. Birdie had a cabinet full of custom-made Jenny McCartney prayer vessels, but seemed to think God should pray to her and not the other way around. She could at least pretend to be nice like everyone else.

If Birdie's comment bothered Kira, though, the writer didn't show it. "She's right," Kira said. "I'm no Suzanne Collins."

"Well, I'd pay to have lunch with you," Sutton declared. "It's a done deal." There would be no consulting Kira on it.

"So, Kira, where have you been all these months?" Birdie asked.

"That's *her* business," Amelia said. She seemed to be trying to reel Birdie in.

"Oh, it's okay," Kira said. "I had to stay behind in California to deal with the sale of the house. And to do some work things."

"Huh," said Birdie. Just huh.

"Since you're donating a lunch, you don't even have to get a ticket to the Steeplechase," Sutton told Kira. "You're going to love it. You get to be involved and you get to hang out with us—"

"Don't scare her, Sutton," said Amelia.

"I'll text you the info. You're in the KP directory, right?" Sutton said, referring to Kensington Preparatory Academy, the school their sons attended. Kira confirmed that she was and then was on her way. Sutton watched as Kira headed off to her car. It was a red Mini Cooper and had retro black and yellow California license plates. Sutton thought it was incredibly cool. As she grabbed her son, Cash, and headed for her Maserati Grecale, she thought maybe she should get a Mini Cooper too.

AMELIA

Anderson's *ex*-sister-in-law. The *ex*-Mrs. Chatham Tupper. *Ex*-wife. *Ex*-this. *Ex*-that. Amelia never thought she'd acquire this prefix. It meant she *used to be*. Like she *used to be* rich. Like she *used to be* important. She knew it was all over for her when she was put on the snack roster for the Little League games. The Team Mom shockingly asked her to bring fruit roll-ups. Before, when she *used to be* the wife of one of the richest men in Buckhead, no one would dare ask her to bring fruit roll-ups. But this is what her life had come to.

Amelia wasn't supposed to have been Mrs. Chatham Tupper. She was supposed to have been Mrs. Anderson Tupper. That was what her *ex*-mother-in-law, Tilly, had intended. Tilly Tupper was the woman behind Edgar Tupper, the man who created the Tupper empire. Some said it was actually the other way around, but Tilly was too much of a Southern Lady to ever suggest such a thing—in public at least. Tilly was a tiny little scorpion of a woman and held the reins to vast holdings. There was the grand Tupper manor, Mayfair, in Atlanta, that took up seventeen acres of prime Buckhead real estate and hosted parties that crowned governors and senators alike. There were private jets (three), a yacht in the Bahamas, a pied-à-terre in Paris, a three-million-dollar "cabin" in the mountains, a six-million-dollar "farm" in South Georgia, and a fourteen-million-dollar Sea Island "cottage" (there were no houses on Sea Island, only cottages) off the state's southern coast.

Sea Island. The West Coast has Coronado and Napa Valley. The Rockies are home to Aspen and Telluride. The Northeast has Martha's Vineyard and the Hamptons. These are the places the rich go to take their bank accounts on vacation. In the South, it's either Highlands, North Carolina, for that old-money, multimillion-dollar cabin vibe, or Sea Island, Georgia, for that old-money, multimillion-dollar beach shack vibe.

At the Sea Island Resort, you could rent bikes and ride past understated vintage mansions and oak trees with large limbs that hung low to graze the surface of jade-green lawns. You could go skeet shooting at the Sea Island Shooting School and hone your skills for an upcoming dove hunt, ride horses, go boating, or work on your golf game on a course beside the sea. No activity, however, was as exciting as the daily parade of privilege at the Beach Club. You went to the Beach Club to be seen. The men, most of them middle-aged and pale, walked around in their Vilebrequin swim trunks with cocktails in their hands, putting in the requisite family time between rounds of golf. The women, in an array of Missoni and Zimmermann swimsuits, reserved the best spots on the beach under green and white umbrellas and pretended to watch their children build sandcastles while secretly watching each other. One had to watch to make sure one wasn't being gained upon.

It was at the Beach Club that Amelia first met her ex-husband-to-be. Years before, Amelia's mother, Brindley, had brought her daughter to Sea Island to help her get over a bad breakup. It was with some guy in Knoxville that Amelia barely remembered. At the time, though, it seemed like her life was over. There's nothing like a millionaire, however, to mend a broken heart.

Brindley subscribed to *Atlanta* magazine and *Birmingham* magazine and *Town & Country* and was well acquainted with the pieces on the Sea Island chessboard. There were Coke millionaires and cable billionaires and everything in between. The family that caught her particular attention were the Tuppers. They built the largest timber company in the country and had not one but *two* unmarried sons just about her daughter's age.

Brindley placed Amelia on a lounge chair by the pool for all to see. And she certainly didn't go unnoticed. On night three of Brindley and Amelia's Sea Island holiday, Tilly Tupper invited Brindley to her table in the dining room at the Beach Club. An invitation from Tilly was just the seal of approval Brindley had been hoping for.

"I've never seen you here before," Tilly said. It sounded more like an accusation than a statement, but Brindley played along. She told Tilly of her daughter's breakup and how only a mother's love could mend her.

"Bless her heart," Tilly said with honey-drizzled sincerity. "Your lovely daughter needs to meet my son. He's just come back from Thailand. Oh, speak of the devil."

Brindley turned to see Anderson Tupper enter the dining room. He was leisurely tying the knot on a tie the maître d' had thoughtfully provided and was all smiles as he glad-handed and backslapped his way across the dining room. He was a walking Ralph Lauren ad with his glorious blond locks and perpetual tan.

"This is our new friend, Brindley," Tilly told her son. "She has a darling daughter you must meet."

"Does she now?" Anderson asked.

For a moment, Anderson was the most eligible bachelor in the room. What young woman wouldn't want to be introduced to him? Or have sex with him? Marry him? Have his children? Spend his money? It didn't get much better than Anderson Tupper. Unless you were Chatham Tupper, Anderson's older brother. He entered the dining room and all heads turned. It wasn't because he was better looking than his brother. Because he wasn't. It was because he was more powerful than his brother. He was the first born. He was the smart one. The hard-working Tupper. He was the heir apparent.

Chatham didn't have to arrange for a tie from the maître d' because he was already wearing one. It was an orange Hermes tie with blue details that only on very close examination were revealed to be small exploding frogs. Chatham didn't stop to greet people along the way as much as they rose to greet him. He wasn't yet thirty years old, but he commanded respect.

Chatham didn't kiss his mother hello and didn't acknowledge Brindley's presence. He took a seat at the table and waved a nearby waiter over. "Gin and tonic." The waiter was off as fast as his feet could carry him, and Chatham sat back in his chair awaiting entertainment.

"Hello, son," Tilly said.

"Mama."

"This is my other son, Chatham," Tilly said to Brindley. "It seems he left his manners in Atlanta."

Chatham either felt bad or feared his mother's wrath and half rose from his chair and shook Brindley's hand. "Chatham Tupper."

"Brindley has a daughter Mama wants us to meet," Anderson said to his brother.

"No, she has a daughter I want *you* to meet," Tilly corrected Anderson. Amelia was for *him*. "I saw her at the beach this afternoon and she is just lovely."

Said daughter duly appeared as Amelia scanned the dining room for her mother and finally spotted her at the Tupper table. Amelia took in the scene. There was an older woman sitting next to her mother. She looked like the kind of woman who had her hair done every day. She also wore a diamond ring the size of Bermuda. And then there were the two men sitting with them. A vague resemblance to the woman led Amelia to deduct that they were family.

The blond one was handsome in an obvious way. Too handsome for Amelia. She never went for the obvious.

It was the other one her gaze lingered on. His hair was darker and his skin paler, like he didn't have as much time to lounge in the sun. Everyone except him was smiling as she approached. He looked like he couldn't give a damn. He was Amelia's kind of guy. Even though he was respectable and wasn't wearing a motorcycle jacket or sporting tattoos, she could feel it. Chatham Tupper was a Bad Boy.

Despite the efforts of Old Lady Tupper and Brindley, Amelia and Anderson failed to spark. However, the sexual chemistry lab was brewing up a concoction of attraction between Chatham and Amelia that was undeniable. After an awkward dinner of small talk, Amelia and Chatham escaped for a walk on the beach. There would be no romantic lovemaking that night. Instead, Amelia found herself restrained to a lounge chair with Chatham's Hermes tie and its exploding frogs secured around her wrists. Chatham fucked Amelia the old-fashioned way, then spun her over and fucked her as her face pressed against the canvas of the lounge chair. No, this was not lovemaking. This was most definitely fucking, and Amelia had never been so fucked before.

Ex. Used to be.

Now, all these years later, while standing in the Chastain Park parking lot with Birdie, Amelia realized she had left the fruit roll-ups at home. By the way the remaining members of the Vikings, including her son Hampton and Birdie's son Freddie, were running around the lot with an abundance of energy so unique to young boys, Amelia was certain that there must have been plenty of other things for them to eat besides fruit roll-ups. Maybe the Team Mom would think twice about putting her on the snack schedule in the future.

"Who is *that*?" Birdie said very pointedly.

As a line of SUVs drove past and cleared the view, Amelia saw Dan Milton, Birdie's husband, leaning against the rear end of his vintage convertible Jaguar. Dan was handsome in a Don Draper kind of way with a nice head of hair he would never lose. He was slim and stylish like his car. The "*that*" that Birdie had referred to was a younger woman Dan was talking to. She was dressed in tight gray leggings with lime green stripes down the sides and a tiny matching lime green sports bra.

"I don't remember her name," Amelia said.

"Didn't she used to date Anderson?" asked Birdie.

"I don't know. Probably." Amelia may not have dated Anderson, but it seemed like almost every other woman in Buckhead and the surrounding zip codes had.

"Dan!" Birdie shrieked so loudly that Amelia flinched. Her call shook the entire parking lot. Dan and his companion looked over, and, spotting Birdie, the woman with the iron butt ran off on her merry way.

"She better run," Birdie warned.

"I think one fight is enough today, Birdie, don't you?" Amelia asked.

"One fight? I haven't met my daily quota yet," Birdie said as she headed her husband's way. Amelia tagged along, if for no other reason than to see the second fight on the day's card.

"Where have you been?" Birdie asked her husband.

"I left to go hit some balls," he told her, though by the look on her face, this seemed to be a woefully inadequate response.

Birdie looked off in the direction of the younger woman, who was now running gracefully down the jogging path that circled the park like she was a Lipizzaner stallion prancing around a ring. "Who was that?" Birdie asked.

"Oh, that's Brit," Dan said. "Or Britney. I'm not sure. She's one of the spin instructors at Flyte Time."

Birdie called across the parking lot to her son, and Freddie dutifully left his friends, grabbed his equipment bag, and came to join them.

"You need to take Freddie home," she told Dan.

"Why can't you?"

"Amelia and I are going to ADAC to pick up some wallpaper samples." The fact that they were going to the Atlanta Decorative

Arts Center was news to Amelia, but she remained quiet. The mysterious machinations of Birdie Milton were best left unchallenged.

"I just got new old-stock carpet installed," Dan whined. "Freddie's going to get it filthy." New old-stock carpet. That meant that Dan replaced the carpet in the Jag with carpet that had been made in the 1960s and never used before. Amelia thought that was a very Dan thing to do. Amelia had always believed that Dan had chosen Birdie as his wife because of her place in Buckhead society. He would certainly choose the carpet for his car just as carefully.

Freddie arrived covered in dirt and blood and mustard from the hot dogs one of the other team moms had brought as a snack. If only Amelia had brought the fruit roll-ups, Dan might not have been looking at his son with alarm.

"Freddie! Take your shoes off," Birdie told her son. Birdie turned her attention back to her husband. "I'll take his bag and shoes. He's not that dirty." In fact, Freddie was filthy.

Dan gave up the fight. His adversary was too formidable. "Let's go, Freddie," he told his son. "Try not to touch anything."

"How am I supposed to do that?" Freddie asked. Freddie tried to lower himself gingerly into the passenger seat, but there was no chance the new old-stock carpet would get out of this unscathed.

Dan got into the car and put on a retro, beige and black, tweed driving cap. Amelia thought he looked dashing. Birdie appeared to think otherwise.

"For God's sake don't wear that stupid hat," she told him. "You look like a retired accountant from Boca Raton." She leaned down and kissed Freddie on the head. Dan didn't get so much as a nod from his wife before he peeled out of the parking lot and sped all of twenty feet before joining the traffic jam on Wieuca Road.

"I didn't know we were picking out wallpaper today," Amelia said.

"We're not," Birdie replied with a sideways smile of satisfaction. "I'm going to Diptyque to get some candles. The ones Dan's allergic to."

With that, Birdie marched off to her SUV. Amelia wondered how Birdie could survive the stress of the constant self-imposed battle that was her daily life. Sometimes Amelia also wondered how she survived the stress of being Birdie's best friend. Maybe it was because it was better to have Birdie as a friend than an enemy. She wasn't someone you wanted to encounter in a dark alley on a stormy night. You might get shivved.

Amelia wasn't in a position to give up any friendships, no matter how difficult. She didn't need any more *ex* anythings.

KIRA

Kira sat in the postgame traffic surrounding Chastain Park and looked at the world around her. So this was Buckhead. She had hoped to keep a low profile and stay out of the social fray, but she was already in the thick of it. In a manner of minutes she had agreed to sell herself for charity and go to some sort of horse race. She had successfully crossed the Buckhead Rubicon, though, even if she hadn't made it through the trial unscathed. There were psychic wounds to attend to. She felt that maybe she hadn't been friendly enough or confident enough and had probably insulted someone, somehow, but she had survived. Just.

There was one overriding question she had yet to get an answer for, however. What, exactly, was a Buckhead Betty? She pulled out her iPhone and consulted the *Urban Dictionary*.

BUCKHEAD BETTY—A catty and pretentious female living in the Buckhead area of Atlanta who comes from money or marries into it. The Betty tends to be insufferably entitled and stubbornly closed-minded. Totem: A Goyard bag. Catchphrase: "Bless your heart!"

CHAPTER

3

After the Murder

SHAY

THE CIRCUS HAD come to town. News vans from the local Atlanta stations lined the road above the baseball fields at Chastain Park. Reporters from WSB-TV and Fox5! and 11Alive! and even the big guns, CNN, competed for space along the sidewalk with Lululemon-wearing Buckhead housewives out for a Sunday morning stroll in the sunshine.

A parade of SUVs jammed the roads around the park as parents, not yet clued in to the murder, made their migration to the field for the now-canceled Sunday games. There was much honking and a little bit of swearing, though there was much honking and a little bit of swearing every weekend at Chastain Park when the crush of the Little League contingent collided with the rush of golfers and walkers and weekend equestrians.

As the sun warmed Atlanta, Shay shed her coat to reveal the slightly too tight blue sweater beneath. She had recently (and painfully) started a plant-based diet, but lately it had been one thing after another. Her water heater broke and flooded the laundry room. The IRS was hounding her about taxes she didn't even owe. Her mother was fighting her about going into an assisted living facility. She was disappointed with herself at how long it had been since she had exercised. She was determined to get back on track. Tomorrow.

The two piping hot cups of coffee she was carrying threatened to burn her hands as she passed the police and the yellow tape surrounding the field. Several reporters fired a barrage of questions at her as she walked toward the crime scene, but she ignored them all. Some detectives loved the limelight. They were eager to talk to the press, like they were the stars of *CSI: Atlanta* or *NCIS: Atlanta* or *911: Atlanta*. Shay didn't crave the limelight.

One of the reporters peeled away from the pack when he saw Shay. His name was Chris Odi. Shay had seen him on television before. He had once been the host of an Atlanta morning show where he and his size two, IQ of two, buxom cohost did cooking demonstrations and covered light local stories like the one about a Great Dane from Jonesboro that gave birth to sixteen puppies. Shay would never forget the look of terror in the poor mama dog's eyes.

Chris Odi was fired for sexually harassing his cohost (which he vehemently denied) and now covered crime for another station. "Detective Claypool," he said. "Can I get a minute?"

"No," said Shay. "And how do you know my name?"

"One of the officers said you were in charge," he told her. And then he said what she hoped he wasn't going to say. "Is it Anderson Tupper?"

Jesus, Shay thought, word travels fast. She had given everyone strict instructions not to discuss anything with anyone. Especially not the press. And least of all some guy who looked like a Newscaster Ken doll.

"I don't have any information for you," Shay said. She kept walking and he kept following.

"Cops are all over his house right now," Odi informed her. "It would be great if you could confirm that it's him. I'm not trying to be difficult. I'm just doing my job."

"You want to do your job?" Shay asked. "What about the Anita Moss case?"

"What case is that?"

"Anita Moss was killed last week in Lakewood Heights," Shay told him. "Found her behind a Circle K with her throat slit. There were five murders in Atlanta last month, but y'all only want to talk about the one in Buckhead." Shay paused for a moment but didn't break eye contact with the reporter. "I have a deal for you. I'll be happy to talk to you about the Buckhead murder when you're ready to talk about all the other murders in other parts of the city too."

Shay moved on from the reporter and headed toward the scene of the crime. In the parking lot on the edge of the fields, she passed a group of parents gathered around their SUVs. Along with Teslas, SUVs seemed to be the official mode of transportation in Buckhead. There were no Dodge Caravans in sight. A lot of women who looked very anxious (though that seemed to be a general trait of Buckhead women on any given day) gathered, speaking in hushed tones, while a group of men huddled separately, impatiently waiting for updates from the field.

Dozens of loud and floppy-haired children ran around the parking lot, lost in their own little social circles. There were miniature Yankees and Red Sox and even the politically incorrect Indians. (There was no way they were going to change their team's name, damn it. This was America!) A contingent of Vikings chased each other around one of the many Cadillac Escalades (this one in Satin Steel Metallic with 4WD that would never ever be used). Although the boys were playing like any other eleven-year-olds, with a mixture of laughter and good-natured roughhousing, there was extra tension in the air. Every so often one would look toward the field or toward one of the parents. They had heard enough words ("Murder," "Coach," "Bloodbath") to know that something was very wrong. The fact that no one was telling them anything was a clear sign that whatever was wrong was very, very wrong.

A brigade of uniformed officers guarded the crime scene, and Shay noticed that one of them was talking to a bystander in the parking lot. Unlike all the other men milling about, this bystander was Black. And unlike all the other men, who wore what appeared to be the standard Atlanta suburban uniform of khaki pants and golf shirts, this man was wearing athletic shorts and a T-shirt with the *G* logo of the University of Georgia Bulldogs on the front. It was just like the logo for the Green Bay Packers. Shay knew this because she had once seen the Packers former quarterback on *Jeopardy*. The man before her now was very large. He must have been six foot three or more, and other than the beginnings of a slight belly visible beneath the T-shirt, he was in impressive shape.

He looked vaguely familiar, but she couldn't quite place him. She was pretty sure he was an athlete but had no idea which sport. Shay didn't like sports. Not like Dub, who lived and breathed the Braves and the Hawks and especially the Falcons. He even cried when the Patriots beat the Falcons in Superbowl LI. Or was it Superbowl XLIX? Shay didn't like sports or Roman numerals.

As the big man returned to the other parents, Shay approached the police officer with her patented stone-cold stare of death. "I told y'all not to talk to any civilians," she scolded him.

"But it's Marcus Wiley," he weakly protested. Of course, it was. Shay should have recognized him from the commercials he did for his car dealership. "I don't care who it is. There's no talking to anyone about what's going on here. You keep making my job harder and I guarantee you'll be transferred to traffic duty!"

Shay left the chastised cop behind and found Dub sitting on the lowest bench in the bleachers. He was going through his notebook. Its pages were now filled with handwriting. She handed him one of the coffees and sat down next to him. They looked out at the game being played before them. The police officers keeping the onlookers and press at bay. The detectives doing their detective things and the forensic people doing their forensic things.

"I spoke with the groundskeeper," Dub told her. "He said the last game at the complex ended just before ten. He found the body when he was locking the gates at 11:45."

"Narrows the timeline down," Shay said. "I'm sure you saw Marcus Wiley over there."

"Now, don't tell me you knew that was Marcus Wiley."

"I knew he was someone."

"His son was on Tupper's team," Dub remarked. He held up a printout of the team roster with all the parents and contact numbers listed. "He was the assistant coach. Left the team, though. We'll need to figure out why."

"Yes, we will."

"Oh, and big news," Dub said with a conspiratorial lift of his right eyebrow (something Shay was unable to do—and it annoyed her to no end). "Someone threatened Tupper during a game two weeks ago."

"Hooray! Case solved," Shay said sarcastically.

"It was one of the mothers."

"Oh, good God." These Buckhead people were shameless. "Which one?"

"Birdie Milton."

"Seriously?" Shay asked. "Her name is Birdie?"

"Her name is Birdie."

BIRDIE

"I wasn't threatening to kill him," said Birdie. "I was thinking more like spreading a rumor he had gonorrhea."

Birdie sat at a table across from Detectives Claypool and Rattigan in what she assumed was an interrogation room but seemed more like an office they had taken from the human resources manager. There was no swivel lamp on the table to shine in Birdie's eyes and no video camera to record her confession. It was an innocuous space with a cheap oil painting of the Chattahoochee River hanging on the wall and a worn-out gray loveseat Birdie could imagine Detective Rattigan taking a nap on with a half-eaten Egg McMuffin laying on his chest.

"How well did you know the victim?" Claypool asked.

"Victim?" Birdie scoffed. "Just because he was murdered doesn't make him a victim. He was a spoiled rich guy with no wife and no kids. And he was a terrible coach. I mean, I guess it's sad in a general murdery kind of way, but he's hardly a *victim*."

"But you were friends?" Detective Claypool asked.

"Yes, we were friends."

"If he was your friend," asked Detective Rattigan, "why did you threaten him?"

Birdie stared at the detective for a long moment as she pressed her lips tightly together. Rattigan shifted uncomfortably in his seat. "You think I killed a man because he *benched* my son in a *baseball* game?" she asked as she leaned across the table, seizing territory like she was annexing the Crimea. "Don't you think that's more than a little ridiculous? I'm not some cheerleader's mom who wants to murder someone because my daughter was cut from the junior high squad. This is Georgia, for God's sake, not Texas!"

"These are just questions," Detective Claypool said. "Could you tell us where you were at the time Anderson Tupper was murdered?"

"I don't know what time he was murdered," Birdie replied.

"That evening."

"Early evening?" Birdie asked. "Twilight? Dinner time? Cocktail hour?"

"How about you just tell us where you were that day," said Detective Claypool.

"I was at the Steeplechase."

"The horse races?" Detective Rattigan asked.

"At Crabapple Plantation," Birdie confirmed. She noticed Detective Claypool grimace when she said the word "plantation." "Terrible word, isn't it?" Birdie continued. "I mean, we don't call places *concentration camps*, do we? *Oh, we're going to a carnival at Auschwitz on Saturday.* Crabapple Plantation . . ."

"Do you remember what time you left?" Detective Claypool asked.

"I was there until 8:45."

"That's a very specific time," the detective said. "I'm surprised you remember that."

"Had to get back for the babysitter," Birdie told them as she looked at the Cartier Tank watch on her wrist. "Anderson was there too."

"Did you notice anything odd about him or anyone else?" asked Detective Claypool. "Did anything of note happen?"

"Well, my horse lost," Birdie said. "So that was a bummer."

"Do you know when Mr. Tupper left?"

"About the same time I did. It was all winding down at that point. They had closed the bars, so everyone was leaving."

"What did you do the rest of the evening?"

"Before or after I murdered Anderson?"

"Mrs. Milton . . ." said Detective Claypool in a weary tone that reminded Birdie of her own mother.

"I was at home. If you're going to charge me with murder, you should speak to my husband," Birdie said. "He's a lawyer, by the way."

"We're just logging the facts, Mrs. Milton," said Detective Rattigan. "You're not a suspect."

"Good," Birdie said. "Because I'm late for a hair appointment and you know how traffic can be. I'm sure you have my address if you want to arrest me. You should probably talk to Kira Brooks. No one was dead before she came to town."

Birdie marched out of the Atlanta Police Department like she was leading an elite Green Beret battalion into battle, instead of going to get highlights. If it was only being bitchy that made someone a murderer, the streets of Buckhead would have run red with blood.

CHAPTER

4

After the Murder

SHAY

EVERY TIME DEPUTY Chief Henderson said the word "family," Shay could feel a few more of her brain cells dying, like they were lemmings throwing themselves off the cliff of her cerebral cortex. The detectives were not a "family," although Shay considered Dub to be a brother. The rest of them were colleagues. She had no desire to hang out with her coworkers at after-hours events or join therapeutic office WhatsApp group chats about things like "morale" and "feelings" and, yes, "family."

Henderson was a very fit man, the kind of guy who did two workouts a day. He had a perpetual smile and had been brought in from Utah to head the detective unit a year prior. Shay didn't know there was a lot of crime in Utah and thought he was an odd choice to lead them. He came from the Tony Robbins school of management, where there were no problems, only obstacles to overcome. He had turned their weekly meetings into rah-rah, high-fiving, team-building exercises and insisted on calling everyone "cousin" because, of course, they were a "family."

"Cousin Claypool, Cousin Rattigan," Henderson said as Shay and Dub sat across from him in his office. "We have a family crisis." A few more lemmings leapt off the cliff. "You know the good people of Buckhead want to secede from our city and take all their tax revenue with them. That wouldn't be good for the citizens of the less prosperous areas, and it wouldn't be good for us, would it?"

Every few years, a group of residents in Buckhead would get riled up and start a movement to leave the city of Atlanta and form their own government. They didn't feel like they got value for the obscene amount of taxes they paid, and Shay thought they were probably right. Taking that revenue away, however, would cripple the rest of the city. The push for Buckhead to divorce Atlanta usually amounted to nothing but this year had taken root and was a serious threat. Making Anderson Tupper's murder all the more relevant. One of theirs had been killed in their own backyard. The Free Buckhead movement was already touting Tupper's death as their latest and best reason to pull the trigger and leave Atlanta.

"The governor has been talking to the mayor who has been talking to the chief who has been talking to me," Henderson said as he flexed his enviable biceps. Or at least Shay imagined he did. "Everyone is very eager for this murder to be solved."

"We're eager for that too," Shay said.

"We need to find out who killed Mr. Tupper before the secession vote," Deputy Chief Henderson said. "The people of Buckhead need to know that we're working hard for them too."

Henderson ushered Shay and Dub out of his office saying things like "You're invaluable members of the family" and "Superheroes come in all shapes and sizes, don't they?" as they went. She liked their old boss who just used to tell them to do their damn jobs. She wanted to tell Henderson that she treated all murders the same, North Atlanta or South Atlanta, but she knew that the Tupper murder wasn't the same. The future of the city might depend on them solving it.

"Man, they got a lot of pretty people in Buckhead." So remarked Anthony Oakley as Dub peeled off to get them some coffee and Shay entered the War Room, a conference room at headquarters that had become their command central. Anthony was one of *the Kids* who worked behind the scenes at Atlanta PD. They were all good with the technical aspects of detective work like computer forensics and video surveillance and helping Shay learn how to navigate the latest iOS update for her iPhone. Anthony was looking at eight-by-ten blown-up driver's license pictures of Birdie Milton, Kira Brooks, Lamar Burrows (that's *Doctor* Lamar Burrows to you!), and Marcus Wiley all taped to the wall and circling a photo of Anderson Tupper. They would add more photos as they discovered more suspects. Even in unforgiving DMV photos, they all looked like they had been photographed for Italian Vogue.

Along with Anthony, two more Kids worked at computers around a large oval table. Hannah Delgado typed away at her laptop at a million strokes per minute with bright pink nails that annoyingly clicked across the keyboard, and the youngest of the Kids, Farrell Davies, worked away in his own seat surrounded by files and a mess of paperwork. He was the kind of guy who wore glasses even though he didn't need them. He relished his standing as the office nerd.

"So, what've we got?" Shay asked her young charges. "Do we have the final autopsy report yet?"

"The coroner is still working on it," Hannah said. "Though he did say they found skin underneath Tupper's fingernails." She paused her typing for a moment. "Someone else's skin. Not his."

"I do love a bit of DNA," Shay said. "Did we get Tupper's phone records yet?"

"We're working on it, boss lady," Anthony told her. "I put in a request. They said it would be a few days."

This frustrated Shay to no end. "Don't they know we're investigating a murder? What about the security cameras?"

"The ones at the fields didn't work," Hannah told her. "They were getting new ones."

"Of course they were," Shay said. "Let's pull everything from the area. I'm sure those folks in Buckhead have security cameras up the wazoo." She looked at the photo of Anderson Tupper on the wall. He seemed so clean-cut and wholesome. He was the standard sun-kissed prom king, the kind of guy who no one had a bad thing to say about, who recycled the bottles left over from his expensive wine, and who volunteered as a youth baseball coach so he could relive his own glory days. He was too good to be true. Which meant—*he was too good to be true.*

Shay noticed Farrell was sitting patiently, smiling at her with a look of self-satisfaction.

"What?" she finally had to ask.

"I have the toxicology report," he said as he waved a piece of paper around in front of the other Kids.

"Alright, let's have it," Shay said.

"Well, I can tell you that Mr. Tupper's last meal was Asian food," Farrell told them. "I'm guessing it was Thai. He seemed like a Thai kinda guy. He had also been drinking that evening, but not excessively . . ."

"And?" Shay asked. She wanted him to get on with it.

"Gamma-hydroxybutyrate," Farrell finally said.

Shay would have placed a bet on marijuana. It seemed like everyone in Atlanta used that. She would have believed it if Farrell had said cocaine. That certainly wasn't out of the question. But GHB? The date-rape drug? What was a thirty-five-year-old businessman doing with a drug in his system that was usually reserved for unsuspecting sorority girls and unfortunate women at bars?

Before Shay could ruminate any more on the toxicology report, Dub stuck his head into the War Room, interrupting them. "The new girl is here," he told Shay.

The new girl in town. Maybe she would have some answers.

* * *

Shay noticed Kira Brooks's handbag before she noticed Kira. It was from the British designer Paul Smith. Shay had fallen in love with all things Paul Smith when she took her son on a celebratory high school graduation trip to London. She told Darron that he could pick anywhere in the world as long as it didn't require more than two flights to get there. He spent a good three days trying to find a way to get to Antarctica with only one stopover, but finally gave up and picked London.

They had walked past a Paul Smith shop in Covent Garden, and Shay had instantly fallen in love with the multicolored swirl pattern that was on so many of the Paul Smith things, from shoes to wallets to bags—like the one Kira Brooks was holding in her lap. All Shay could afford that day in London was a Christmas ornament decorated with the swirl. A bag? Well, that was a dream for another time when her son wasn't in college and didn't have an UberEats account that was eating *her* alive.

Kira was sitting at the table in the interrogation room and Shay thought she looked like the girlfriend in every Hallmark movie. All-American and pretty and nonthreatening. She also had the nervous expression of someone who didn't like to disappoint people. Kira Brooks looked guilty whether she was or not.

Dub, the good Southern gentleman that he was, pulled out a chair for Shay and they both sat across from Kira. Their pleasant introductions hardly seemed to calm Kira's nerves. She sat, wide-eyed, and fiddled with the strap of her bag. She finally offered a slight smile, an almost apologetic one, and took a deep breath.

"How can I help?" Kira asked.

"Well, obviously we want to talk about Anderson Tupper."

"Okay."

"You knew him," Dub said.

"I did."

"Any idea who murdered him?" asked Dub. Straight to the point. He didn't care about the Paul Smith bag.

"No."

Okay. I did. No. Shay recognized these types of answers. They were the types of answers people were told by their lawyers to give in depositions. Shay had been told this when she had to give a deposition in her divorce. *If they ask if you know the color of the sky, just say, "Yes." Don't say, "Yes, it's blue."* Never give them more than they ask for.

Shay looked down at the notes scribbled on her yellow legal pad. She was determined to get multisentence answers from Kira Brooks. "You just moved here from California?"

"Yes."

"But your husband and children moved here in September?"

"To start school," Kira said. "I stayed behind to get our house sold and finish up some work."

Two sentences! Shay was making progress. "You're a writer?"

"Yes."

"My wife loves your books," Dub said. "She was real excited that I'd be meeting you today."

"Thanks."

Oh, this could go on all day! Shay dove back in. "Tell us about your relationship with Mr. Tupper."

The word "relationship" seemed to rattle Kira. She grimaced like the word had flown over and stung her. "He was my son's baseball coach. I barely knew him. He was nice. Seemed like a good person. I don't have much to offer. I mean, I saw him at the games and saw him at the Steeplechase the day he was . . ."

"Murdered?" Shay offered.

"Yes," Kira continued. "But other than that I couldn't tell you much about him. He was just . . . my son's coach."

"So, you only knew Anderson Tupper for a few weeks before he was murdered?" Shay asked Kira.

"If that."

"What time did you leave the Steeplechase?"

"I don't know," Kira said. She paused like she had to really think about her answer. She was making a show of it. "Sutton Chambers," she finally blurted out. "I think she's a drug dealer."

Shay and Dub both looked up from their notes at the same time. Shay had a little bit of motion sickness from the sudden swerve in the conversation. "Sutton Chambers? One of the team moms?"

"Yes."

"Do you think drugs may have played a role in Mr. Tupper's death?" Shay asked.

"I don't know," Kira said.

"Well, you must think it's important because you just threw one of your friends under the bus there," Shay told her.

"She wasn't a friend," Kira said. "None of them were."

"Them?"

"The Buckhead Betties."

CHAPTER

5

Eleven Days Before the Murder

SUTTON

SUTTON WAS GIVING the world's worst blowjob. The Olympic judges would have given her a three out of ten. She worked the flaccid penis in her mouth like a professional, but her heart just wasn't in it. Sutton's knees were getting sore. She knew they'd be imprinted with the pattern of the carpet when she was finished. It was the last wife who picked out this coarse beige carpeting. Sutton had wanted to replace it but had already gone over her renovation budget. Now she was cursing every last polyester fiber.

Her mind was drifting away to thoughts of the calories in a Starbucks white chocolate mocha and an upcoming appointment with her gynecologist (at least *she* got something out of that), when she felt a hand push her head back and the limp penis pull out of her mouth. Five one-hundred-dollar bills floated to the floor beside her. One was almost torn in two.

"It's a thousand dollars," Sutton said. "It's in the prenup."

Her husband, Chuck, walked away without looking back at her. She was still on her knees on the cut-rate carpet. "You didn't finish the job," he said gruffly.

"No, *you* didn't finish the job," Sutton replied in a voice barely above a whisper.

Chuck Chambers spun around. He was eighty-three years old but still commanded a room. "What did you say?" he asked. Or accused. He mostly spoke in an accusatory tone, as if someone, usually Sutton, had done him wrong. This seemed to be common among the powerful multimillionaires of Buckhead who had already made their fortunes but now found themselves with demanding second (or third, in this case) wives and a second set of young children who didn't realize these men had once *been* someone.

Sutton scrambled up from her knees and slid the hundred-dollar bills into the pocket of her short silk robe. She wasn't wearing a bra, and her large, expensive breasts threatened to escape the confines of the nightgown she was wearing. Usually, her breasts were distracting enough and got her out of all sorts of trouble, but this situation also required a humble smile.

"I didn't say anything," she said. She slunk away past Chuck and his bad temper and escaped to the bathroom. It was bigger than most apartments and what walls were not covered in pink marble were lined with mirrors trimmed with gold accents. It was every poor girl from Alabama's idea of a rich girl's bathroom.

Sutton cupped her hands and filled them with water from one of the gold-colored taps at the double vanities. She drank the water in, swished it around, and then spit it out. Spit *him* out. She hung her head over the sink for a good while. When she finally looked up at her reflection, it was with self-loathing.

Chuck Chambers had made his fortune by growing the biggest fertilizer company in the country. He had literally built an empire of shit. It turned out Chuck would need every dime he made to pay off his first two wives. Wife number one, Martha, was the one he still referred to as his "good" wife. She was his childhood sweetheart. She was the one who convinced him to expand his business at just the right time. The one who said they should move to Atlanta and talked him into buying a rundown old mansion and renovate it into the showplace of Buckhead. Chuck loved Martha. Even when he was having an affair with his secretary, Paige, he was still singing Martha's praises. Even when Martha divorced him and took half his money and all the kids, he still said she was the best wife a man could ever ask for.

Chuck worked hard to make back the money he had lost in his divorce and married that secretary, Paige. But as the British billionaire Jimmy Goldsmith once said, "When you marry your mistress, you create a job vacancy." It wasn't long before Chuck met a pretty young woman at the PDC. She had little breasts and a big smile and looked at him like he was the sexiest man alive.

Sutton became the new Mrs. Chambers and moved into the house she had manifested. As stipulated in their prenup, her rich but cheapskate husband gave her a small monthly allowance (that she supplemented with a drug-dealing side hustle), one thousand dollars for every blow job, and an extra five million dollars if they remained married for fifteen years. There was also a broadly defined *morals clause* that Chuck added to ensure his new wife never did anything to harm his reputation. (Never mind *his* affairs and the three wives thing.) Sutton didn't give it a second thought when she signed the prenup. Of course, they would be married for fifteen years. Maybe even fifty years! Happily married.

Now, however, as they approached their fourteenth anniversary, she just hoped she would outlive him.

VENITA

Their morning family run was, to be honest, Venita's idea of what the fifth ring of hell might look like. All those demons running around in circles when they should have been in bed getting their beauty sleep. Marcus, however, insisted that the family exercise every morning. Together. They would all be healthier and stronger for it.

So at six AM on almost every day of the year, Venita dragged herself out of bed, then dragged her son out of bed, and they joined Marcus for a loop around Buckhead.

When they first started this routine, it made for an odd sight. Not only because they were three Black people running around the predominately white enclave but also because they were a *family* running. It wasn't something you often saw, and an old white woman who lived on another block once called the police on them. Once the officers saw that the alleged criminal was the illustrious Marcus Wiley, however, the police were on their way with an autograph and a story to tell. When the old woman died, Venita bought her Baccarat wine glasses at the estate sale. She loved the idea of the woman rolling in her grave as Venita sipped Cabernet from the old biddy's crystal.

On this chilly morning, Marcus, as usual, led the pack. He ran ahead of Venita and Wade, waving to people who stopped to gawk at the great Georgia football star, always with a smile. They could be future customers, after all. Venita noticed her husband wasn't as fast as he used to be. He noticed too. He was getting older. He didn't move the same way. It frustrated him that what had come so easily before was now difficult. His temper was shorter too, and he lashed out when he was frustrated, something he had never done before. Venita remembered her father being the same way as he aged. Women fought aging with plastic surgery. Men fought it with six AM runs and fury.

As they jogged past their neighbor's mansions, with Marcus waving to people and Wade struggling to keep up, Venita would quiz her son on whatever subject he was studying at school. He would call out answers to questions as he tried to catch his breath. Marcus and Venita Wiley were the Apache helicopters of helicopter parents.

Venita grew up in Gainesville, Georgia, a medium-sized town about an hour north of Athens, where the University of Georgia and its iconic Sanford football stadium with its famous privet hedges stood. Growing up in this average town best known for its abundance of chicken farms, Venita never would have imagined how much of her life would end up being defined by what went on *between the hedges* in that stadium in Athens.

The Cummings family lived in a small brick house with white shutters that didn't close. There were matching white flower boxes beneath the windows filled with plastic pansies and lilies year-round. Venita's mother, Dorothea, thought fresh flowers were a waste of time and money. You could achieve the same thing with plastic ones, and you never had to water them. They just needed to be dusted off every so often.

Dorothea and her husband, Lonnie, didn't think much of anything was worth the time or money except money itself. Dorothea and Lonnie held money above all else. It was magical. If you accumulated enough of it, most of your problems disappeared. When Venita, who had always been strong and opinionated, once asked as a surly teenager if maybe, just maybe, happiness was more important than money, her father told her: "Make money so your grandchildren have the luxury of being happy."

Not too long after that, in high school, Venita declared that she had figured out what she was going to do in life. She would be a paralegal. Dorothea gave her daughter a familiar look of disappointment. Dorothea herself had worked her entire life as a receptionist at a textile mill. Lonnie had risen through the ranks at a chicken processing plant from plucker to packer to supervisor. They hadn't sacrificed and saved for years so their dearest daughter could become a *paralegal*.

"The hell you are," Dorothea had told her. "Think bigger. If you can be a paralegal, you can be a *lawyer*."

Venita took that advice to heart. Her mother was right. She should think bigger. Because Venita wanted her grandchildren to be happy.

In order for Venita to someday have happy grandkids, she was going to need to have kids. That was something she and Marcus agreed on. They wanted lots and lots of kids. Marcus wanted a whole football team full of them. Four miscarriages later, Venita finally produced Wade. He was a tiny baby born a month early. Just let him survive, Lord. That's all Venita and Marcus wanted.

Wade not only survived, but he quickly made up for lost time and was in the 95th percentile on the growth chart. When he was five, he looked like he was eight. He inherited his mother's big brain and his father's big feet, but sadly none of Marcus's athletic ability. This was distressing to both Marcus and Venita. Wade Wiley was such a good name. The name of a sports superstar. They kind of wished they had saved that name for the next child. Unfortunately, there would be no next one. Venita would never again become pregnant. There would be no football team of kids. Marcus tried to fill up the half empty glass. Maybe his son wouldn't be a football star, but there was always tennis or golf (look at Tiger!) or baseball.

Wade may have lost an inch in height trying to live under all the pressure of being Marcus Wiley's son. He began wetting his bed at age seven. He developed an ulcer at nine. He bit his nails so far down, they bled. At one point he would only eat purple foods, which pretty much limited his diet to Power Purple Gatorade and Japanese eggplant. That phase was followed by his blue period of berries and blue corn chips and finally by orange, which at least made it easy for Venita to get him enough vitamin C.

Several child psychologists later, Venita and Marcus were told to just let Wade be. Don't pressure him. Don't expect greatness. Let him be happy.

Almost every morning by the time Wade could walk, they ran. And almost every morning by the time Wade could talk, they studied.

You make money so your grandchildren have the luxury of being happy. Venita had achieved. Her husband had achieved. By God, their son was going to achieve too.

KIRA

"You want me to make you a smoothie?" Kira asked, eager to please. "I could add protein powder. That's good for athletes."

"I'm not an athlete," Kolt replied without looking up from the plate of eggs he was playing with more than eating. He was wearing his school uniform of khaki pants and a royal blue polo shirt. A logo of a lion passant facing a reared-up majestic stallion graced the breast of the shirt. It was like something off a shield a knight would have carried into battle during the Crusades rather than the insignia of a private school in Atlanta.

They were in the kitchen of a very big and modern home that seemed bigger due to a lack of furniture. Modern houses were a rarity in Buckhead, which was, architecturally at least, steeped in the traditional, but they had grown in popularity as new people with their new money began to invade the staid old streets. Unpacked moving boxes were stacked along the walls and pushed to the side on countertops and tables. Boxes with *kitchen* scribbled in sharpie surrounded Kira and Kolt, and other boxes marked *dining room* could be seen in the room beyond. Her husband and children may have been there for months, but it looked like the moving van had just left.

"Have you guys unpacked the blender?"

"Ask Dad," Kolt said.

On cue, Dad walked into the kitchen. "Ask Dad what?" Kallan Brooks said as he headed straight for the red Nespresso machine and popped in a coffee cartridge. He was a compact, pleasant-looking man, shorter than average, and not as handsome as his wife was pretty. Looks-wise, at least, he had married above his station. He was dressed for work in a striped button-down shirt and dark-blue dress pants. Kira was surprised to see he was wearing brown Gucci loafers. He had already become one of *them*.

"I was looking for the blender," Kira said. She was embarrassed that she didn't know where to find it in her own house.

"I don't know," Kallan told her. "I just threw it in a box. We did the best we could."

"I know that."

Kira often wondered why she had ever married Kallan. She didn't find him particularly attractive. Sex with Kallan was something she endured, not enjoyed. He was a nice man, though, and he had loved her. In fact, he was the first man who ever did. He had been crazy about her. The totality of his love more than made up for the shortage of hers. Until it didn't. They had never been a good match. All Kallan wanted in life was to have sex and play golf. All Kira wanted was to be a mother and rule the world.

"Has Iris already left for school?" Kira asked.

"She's still sleeping," Kolt said.

"What?" Kira looked at Kallan for an explanation, but he offered none. It was Monday! Her daughter needed to be at school and, as a matter of fact, her husband needed to be at work. She hadn't spent seventeen years raising her daughter to have it all fall apart now. Why were the members of her family all acting like they were on vacation?

"I'll go get her," said Kolt. He began to get up from the table, but Kira stopped him.

"No, finish your breakfast," she said sternly, like the mother she had once been. Then she stopped herself and adjusted her behavior. Dictator mom had been deposed months ago. "It's okay," she said in a softer tone. "I'll check on her."

Kira headed off in search of her eldest child. As she moved down the art-gallery-white hallway that was devoid of pictures and across the wide-planked ash wood floor, she thought back to when she gave birth to Iris. She had never wanted a daughter. She had been one herself, after all, and she knew how difficult girls could be, especially for their mothers. Even though Iris was not the son she had hoped for, she loved her in a way she didn't know was possible. Kallan was shocked when Kira told him she loved their daughter more than him. She was shocked that it shocked him. Didn't all parents love their children more than their spouses?

Kira wanted to give her daughter a cute name that started with a K. They were Kira and Kallan so it only made sense. Kim? Kourtney? Khloe? Kendall? Kylie? Damn, all the good ones were already taken. She thought about Kristen, but it was so pedestrian. Maybe Kate. Maybe not. She finally settled on Kayla but her choice was dismissed out of hand by her husband. Their daughter would be named after his mother, a horrible woman who never liked Kira. Iris the Elder had died the week before her granddaughter was born. Kira was sure she had done it on purpose just to make sure the baby was named after her. Iris. Kira would have to wait for the birth of her son to get the K name she wanted.

After a long journey, Kira finally found the door she was searching for and knocked lightly. Timidly. When there was no answer, she opened the door to find a cave-like room with blackout curtains pulled tightly closed. It was like her daughter was in a sensory deprivation chamber. The sound of waves gently lapping the shore of a beach came from a machine that also offered up rain storms and crickets to sooth someone to sleep. Kira turned on the lights and almost gasped at the state of the room. Had she not known she was in Atlanta, in her daughter's room, she would have sworn she had made a wrong turn under a freeway overpass in Los Angeles and wandered into a homeless encampment. It was a good bet that the walk-in closet was empty because all of its contents covered the floor of the room along with what seemed like a thousand plastic cups from Starbucks, each with a different amount of leftover Frappuccino.

Iris peeked out from beneath her duvet and squinted at her mother in the bright light. "Oh my God, turn them off!" she screeched at Kira.

Kira quickly turned the lights back off. It was a relief for them both. "You're going to be late for school."

"There's no school today," Iris said from somewhere in the darkness.

"Why not?"

"It's a mandatory mental health day. Would you please just close the door?"

Kira did as she was asked. Iris went to an expensive all-girls school, and Kira was a little perturbed to be paying thirty thousand dollars a year in tuition for this mandatory mental health day.

When she was in high school, you were expected to be miserable. Deal with it.

Kira had heard once that it was the daughter who took care of you in your old age. This was exactly what now worried her. This is what she would inevitably lose sleep over. If Iris was in charge of Kira at the end of Kira's life, she was pretty sure that her daughter wouldn't hesitate to pull the plug.

SUTTON

Fourteen years of marriage brought Sutton and Chuck the two children who were now sitting at the football-field sized island of their kitchen at Azalea. Cash was eleven years old and Ally was five. They both favored their mother with their white-blond hair and cute little noses. The children were eating a hearty breakfast of sausage and tortitas de ejotes that had been prepared for them by their long-suffering Guatemalan housekeeper, Reyna, who was busy at the sink cleaning pots and pans. Sutton came into the kitchen in her daily uniform of Lululemon leggings (perhaps a size too small) and a crisp white T-shirt (ironed lovingly by Reyna) with a pink (her favorite color!) sports bra underneath. "Good morning, family!" she said as she kissed her children. Cash accepted her kiss with great reluctance, but Ally drank it in. She lit up every time she saw her mother. It was like seeing Cinderella in a parade at Disney World. Sutton was Ally's very own Princess come to life.

"Reyna, could you clean out the drain in my bathroom?" Sutton asked as she fiddled with a cappuccino machine that looked like it was built for the International Space Station. "It's clogged with hair."

"Yes, of course," Reyna replied.

"That's gross," Cash said.

"My hair is not gross, Cash," Sutton told him.

"Mommy, Reyna made us tortas de coyotes for breakfast," Ally said with a mouthful of spicy eggs.

"Tortitas de ejotes," Reyna corrected in her very pleasant Spanish accent. "No coyotes."

"Coyotes!" Sutton laughed. "Reyna is so funny, isn't she?" The cappuccino machine fired up with a racket. It was amazing how much noise was required to make a tiny cup of coffee. Sutton shifted from one foot to the next as she waited for the grinding and clanging to produce the desired result. Just as the coffee began to fill her cup, Chuck joined his family in the kitchen.

"Hi, Daddy!" Ally said. She waited for a kiss on the head, or even a tousle of her blonde hair, but it never happened.

Cash looked up with a fork full of fritters. "Hey, Dad, you gotta come to our next game. I think we're going to make the playoffs."

"Nope," Chuck said as he slid up behind Sutton. He wrapped one arm possessively around her. "You know those games are just too long for your old dad."

"You don't have to stay the whole time," Cash said. He was visibly annoyed. Chuck had never been to any of his son's games. Or really any of his anythings. No school things. No sports things. No orchestra things to see his son attempt to play the violin.

Chuck cupped his hand around one of Sutton's breasts. They were the breasts he had paid for, so he felt a pride of ownership. "I'm ready now," he whispered in Sutton's ear. He slid his other hand along her very tight bottom and reached his fingers between her legs. Cash had a full view of his father and mother, and Sutton could see he was embarrassed.

"I have to get the kids to school," said Sutton.

"What the hell do we have *her* for?" Chuck said angrily. He didn't even look at Reyna. Why would he look at *her*? She was there to cook for *them*. To clean for *them*. And also to drive his children to school if he needed to get a blowjob. He walked out of the kitchen. Sutton was expected to follow.

Sutton put her cappuccino aside and turned to her dear children with the sunniest of smiles. "*I'll* be taking you to school," she told them. "I'll be right back."

"We're going to be late!" Cash declared.

Sutton knew her son had witnessed his father's kitchen antics and also knew he felt bad every time Chuck chose not to spend time with him. She smiled at Cash, reassuringly. "We won't be late."

As someone (not Jimmy Goldsmith) once said: *When you marry for money, you earn every penny.*

KIRA

Kira had always hated the school run. It had been the black hole of her very busy days, sucking her valuable time into its vortex of the mundane. There was no car line when Kira was growing up in Los Angeles, yet somehow kids made it to school. Sometimes Kira walked the eight city blocks to school from the Mediterranean house with a perennially leaking roof that she grew up in, and sometimes her mother would drop her off on her way to work. Her mom would pull over to the curb at a nearby intersection, and Kira would jump out of the car as her nervous mother yelled "We're holding up traffic!" Kira's mother was always nervous. It was an unwanted trait that Kira inherited.

Children these days were evidently too valuable to dump at a nearby intersection. They couldn't be trusted to think and act for themselves and had to be dropped off like insured FedEx packages at the school door. Now, as her son sat in the passenger seat growing older by the minute, the school drop-off seemed a precious thing to Kira. She couldn't wait to do it again for the afternoon pickup.

A parade of cars lined up in the parking lot of the grand, chiseled stone buildings of the Kensington Preparatory Academy, or KP, as it was known to the locals. It looked like it had been there for ages and had educated kings and princes alike, when in fact it was built in 1974 and educated the children of Atlanta's one percent.

Kira pulled her car into the line of cars and had barely stopped when Kolt opened the door and jumped out. He was like a fugitive jumping from a moving train. She half expected him to roll across the pavement when he hit it, but instead he weakly waved back at her, without looking, and joined his waiting friends. They were some of the boys from his team. They gathered like brothers-in-arms and joined in the sea of royal blue flowing through the main door of the school.

The line of cars in the queue moved up, and Kira was about to follow the flow of traffic toward the exit when a familiar blonde woman began waving at her from the back of a Maserati SUV. Kira followed the woman's directions and pulled out of the line of cars to park. The tailgate of the Maserati was open, and there was a small crowd of mothers gathered there. Kira was pretty sure this wasn't allowed. It never was. There wasn't any parking in the drop-off line. That was a universal, if not a federal, law.

Kira's mind raced as she sat in her car for a moment trying to pull the woman's name out of a hat. This was the woman she had called "Betty." She was a Buckhead Betty. But no! That wasn't her name. Not Betty. *Not Betty.* Don't call her Betty! As Kira climbed out of the car, she finally got it.

"Sutton!" she said with great relief.

"Hi, Kira! Oh my God, y'all, this is Kira," Sutton said to the other mothers. Kira noticed that Sutton talked like an excitable teenager. Like a high school cheerleader in a teen movie from the 90s. "She's Kolt's mom. He and Cash are in the same grade. Cash and Kolt. It's so cute."

"You're the writer," said one of the mothers, a sour woman who introduced herself as Laura Cho. She had a pointy chin and reminded Kira of a pigeon.

"I'm *a* writer," Kira said, trying to play it down. She was not *the* writer.

Sutton jumped in. There was no need for Kira to talk. "She's a famous writer," Sutton told them. "Like J. K. Rowling famous. Everyone's read her books. I'm sure you guys have read them. If you haven't, you *have* to."

"What have you written?" Laura asked this new creature who had appeared in their midst.

"Um, I wrote a YA series," Kira said. "It's called *Star Runners*. I'd be surprised if you've read them."

"I certainly haven't," Laura told her. "Those books are on the banned list at our church. I mean, no reflection on *you*. Bless your heart, it's not *your* fault."

Well, Kira *did* write them, so she had to take some blame. Kira had heard that her books were banned by some churches. They felt that science fiction had replaced the good Lord and threatened to warp the impressionable young minds of the God-fearing youth of America.

"*The Adventures of Huckleberry Finn* and *To Kill a Mockingbird* have been banned too," Kira said. "At least I'm in good company." Kira instantly regretted having opened her mouth. She was about to denounce her own literary creations and apologize for being an ungodly heathen when she was mercifully saved by the appearance of a middle-aged potato of a man driving a golf cart with the Kensington Prep logo on the side.

"Let's move along, ladies," he said with a wave of his hand toward the exit.

"Okay, Mr. Murdoch, we're leaving," Sutton said. Luckily, he was looking at her breasts, which cut her considerable slack. "Thank you so much for doing such a good job. We really appreciate it."

The golf cart continued on its way, but not before Mr. Murdoch took one last lecherous look at Sutton. She waved and then turned to the others in disgust. "Jesus Christ, he's so fucking gross!" Laura gave Sutton a disapproving look. "Sorry, Laura. I didn't mean to blasphesize."

Kira wasn't sure what form of blasphemy Sutton was trying to come up with there. She watched as Sutton pulled open a compartment in the back of her SUV and took out three small ziplock snack bags filled with little orange capsules. She quickly passed them to the other women, and they just as quickly handed her cash. Kira knew what those little orange capsules were. They were Adderall pills, and they were used to treat ADHD—from which a suspiciously high number of children seemed to suffer. Adderall was the go-to drug of choice to calm down rambunctious children, as if being rambunctious was somehow a sickness that needed to be treated with amphetamines. Parents loved it because it helped their children focus. Teachers loved it because it kept their students quiet. Increasingly, suburban moms had grown to love it too—love taking it.

How else could these housewives handle the pressure of raising children *and* husbands? Of crafting perfect dinner parties and tight bodies? Just stepping out of the house was fraught with impossible expectations of perfection. Look good. Look happy. Look like your life wasn't an impossible task that would never be completed to anyone's expectations. Laura Cho was first in line to grab her bag of Addys. God may have not been much of a reader, but evidently he was an Adderall man.

The drug exchange was so casual Kira didn't know what to think. Had Sutton called her over hoping she would be a new customer? Should she say something? It didn't matter what she thought because Sutton closed her tailgate and business was done for the morning.

"So nice to meet you," Laura said to Kira. "I hope we have more time to get to know one another."

Beside a bonfire of burning books, perhaps?

"Nice to meet you too," Kira said.

"Oh, fuck, the Grinch is coming back," Sutton warned as Mr. Murdoch approached in his customized golf cart. "I'll see you later," Sutton told Kira.

The carpool attendant gave Sutton a stern look as she climbed into her SUV. Sutton gave Mr. Murdoch the middle finger in return (when he wasn't looking, of course) and drove away, cutting off another car and almost running over a group of teenagers as she went.

Kira quickly realized she was the only car left parked, and the gaze of the other parents and the totalitarian attendant were shifting her way. She climbed into her Mini and edged her way into the outflow of traffic. Kira just wanted to keep her head down, get her work done, and spend time with her kids. She'd only just arrived in town, and she was already running with the wrong crowd.

CHAPTER

6

After the Murder

SUTTON

"Are y'all sure I don't need a lawyer?" Sutton asked without waiting for an answer. "I mean, I have a prenup and I think there's, like, a morals clause. I wouldn't want anything to get out that might be misconscrewed." Sutton knew that was wrong. What was the word? She was too nervous to come up with it.

"You're welcome to have a lawyer present, but this is very informal," Detective Claypool told her. She and Detective Rattigan were sitting across from Sutton in an interrogation room. Sutton thought Detective Rattigan was nice. He reminded her of her uncle back in Alabama. He had a pig farm and would let her play with the piglets. Rattigan seemed easy to deal with. Detective Claypool was another matter. It was like she could tell Sutton was lying, and she hadn't even started lying yet.

"It's about the drug thing, isn't it?" Sutton asked. "It's just, it's not really drugs. It's not like I sell heroin, you know? I mean, it's not like I sell *anything*. Except supplements. For your health. I just . . . this is about Kira, right? She said something? I mean, I think she thinks she saw something, but she totally didn't. I volunteer at my kids' school. I, like, do a ton of charity stuff. I'm a respectable citizen."

"What about gamma-hydroxybutyrate?" Claypool asked. "Do you ever sell that?"

"I don't even know what that is."

That was the truth.

Detective Claypool seemed to be looking right into Sutton's soul. "You may know it as GHB," she said.

"I don't know what that is either," Sutton told the detectives.

That was a lie.

CHAPTER 7

SHAY

It was unseasonably cold for Atlanta, and no amount of layers could keep out the dampness that seemed to penetrate directly into Shay's bones as she attempted her first morning run in ages. She was determined to get back in shape. It was on a date, with a man she had met on one of those dating apps for *mature* people (seriously, what was she thinking?), that she realized the "little break" she had taken from exercising had lasted eighteen months.

"I'm relieved to see you don't work out either," her date had said. It was obvious he didn't work out. He was at least thirty pounds overweight. Shay's first thought was—how dare he? Her second thought was—he was right.

So, she ran.

Shay lived in an area of Southwest Atlanta called Venetian Hills. The name conjured up visions of Mediterranean villas, but the neighborhood was mostly filled with modest cottages and ranch homes. When Shay bought the house fourteen years prior, after a harrowing divorce that left her with little money and less sanity, the neighborhood wasn't quite as nice as it was now. A few years of carpetbaggers escaping California and New York for the lower prices and better living standards of Georgia, however, had improved the neighborhood and raised property values.

The last few feet of her run were the hardest. It was the climb up the four stairs to her front door that kicked her ass. Every time she climbed those stairs, she regretted her decision to buy a house with a porch. When she caught her breath, however, she stood on that porch and took a moment to congratulate herself on what she had achieved. Her house was lovely, though it wasn't the prettiest one on the street. That award went to the gay couple from Chicago who renovated a Craftsman cottage next door. It annoyed Shay at the time because it made her house look shabby in comparison, but in the long run she liked how one renovated house raised the bar and everyone, including Shay, upped their game. Shay added a two-person swing to the porch, and although she never used it, she loved the message it sent. It said whoever lived there cared enough about their house to put up a swing just for the heck of it.

Shay entered the house and put her key in a bowl on a table by the door. Mischievous cherubs were chiseled in the mahogany of the small table, and the legs were grapevines that twisted to the floor. Her home was filled with such follies. There were Polynesian tiki masks with wicked grins hanging on one wall and a Chinese ceremonial drum in a corner, waiting to be played. A collection of elephant figures, small and large, filled one of the shelves in the living room, and the cabinet in the small dining room was stocked with her grandmother's pink and green mapleleaf patterned china.

One thing, however, had changed since she left for her run that morning. A duffle bag with an airline baggage tag was on the floor in the living room. Shay recognized it immediately and her heart pounded a little faster in her chest. It belonged to her son.

"Darron?" she called out. She could barely contain her excitement.

"In the kitchen."

Shay hurried to the kitchen to find her son rummaging through the cabinets. She hugged him, and he pretended to bristle at the closeness but then hugged her back. He was nineteen years old but looked younger. He was skinny and appeared even more so in his baggy sweatpants and a faded, misshapen long-sleeved T-shirt with *Dartmouth* printed in green across the front. He and Shay shared the same eyes, but other than that they bore little resemblance. Darron was half Italian and looked more like his father than he did like Shay. He was a little shy, while Shay was anything but, and was a big-picture thinker, whereas Shay tended to get mired in details. He was more emotional than his mother and, she had to admit, more thoughtful and empathetic. No matter how different their personalities, though, they were as close as two people could be. They were mother and son and friends.

"What are you doing here?" she asked.

"Spring break."

"What happened to skiing in New Hampshire?"

"Global warming happened," Darron said. "No snow."

"No barbers, either, I see," Shay told her son as he sat down at the kitchen table. His curly black hair was sticking out in every direction like Sideshow Bob in *The Simpsons*. She was a mother. She couldn't help but comment on it.

"My hair's fine," he said.

"Next time you're coming home, warn me," she chastised him. "Send an email or a text with an emoji of a little plane or something."

"I will."

A book on the table caught Shay's eye. Darron had always been a voracious reader and was usually ambitious in his choices. "What are you reading?"

"Animal Farm," he told her as he ran his fingers along the spine of the book. "It's an allegory about revolution and how power corrupts." Shay nodded along politely. "Have you ever read it?"

"I'm waiting for the Netflix adaptation."

Darron banged his head against the table in exaggerated frustration. His long curls bounced around his head, only adding to the mock display of indignation. "Mom!" he whined. "You really have to expand your horizons. You should read more and watch less TV. It's rotting your brain!"

"Says the boy who spends most of his time on TikTok. Not to mention somehow I've managed to make enough money to send you to college," Shay reminded him. "Speaking of which, I'm late for work. I can't hang out with you today. I'm on an important case that needs to be solved yesterday."

"I don't need to be entertained."

"Are you going to see any friends while you're here?"

"I don't think so."

"Why not?"

"Because they all have different spring breaks than me."

"Maybe you should go to the gym. You could do the climbing wall. Or you could run down by the river. Or you could Uber over to the High Museum. They're having a show on Appalachian folk art."

"Oh, wow, sorry I'm going to have to miss that," Darron said.

"Then maybe you can get a haircut."

Darron ran his fingers through the overgrown chia pet on his head. "I'll think about it."

Which, of course, meant that he wasn't going to.

Shay was a forensics expert when it came to picking up the clues in her son's moods. She knew that he was hiding a problem somewhere underneath those unruly curls. "Is everything okay?" she asked him.

"Everything's fine."

Which, of course, meant that it wasn't.

CHAPTER

8

Ten Days Before the Murder

SUTTON

Sutton carried her daughter into the house. Her small backpack, decorated with a bedazzled unicorn, hung from Ally's limp arm, and her cheeks and eyes were red from crying. Sutton had been at her yoga class and was right in the middle of a bakasana pose when Ally's preschool called to say she was sick. Sometimes her excitable little girl pretended to be sick so she could be at home with her mother. She would have no such luck today, as Sutton said, "Why don't you go find Reyna? She'll make you a snack."

"But I want to be with you," Ally whined.

"You're on school time, not Mommy time," Sutton told her. "I had to leave yoga early because of you, and Mommy needs to get her exercise. Now I have to work out at home. We'll watch some TV together later. So go on. Get!"

Ally called out for Reyna as she shuffled off to the gallows. "Reyna!" she said again and again, weaker every time. She was a sad little sight as she dragged her backpack down the hallway toward the kitchen.

Sutton traversed the long hallway in the opposite direction toward the door to the basement. The hall was lined with Thomas Kincade oil paintings of the Rialto Bridge in Venice, Big Ben, and the Eiffel Tower. It had been one of Sutton's dreams since she was a teenager to own a Kincade painting. She had put a postcard with one of his works on her vision board. It was of a hobbit hut in a fairytale forest, and she thought it was the most beautiful thing she had ever seen. He really was the "painter of light." Someday she would own a Kincade, she declared then. Now she owned not one, but eight of the late artist's mainstream masterpieces. How far she had come.

The Chambers estate was in the aptly named Tuxedo Park area of Buckhead, where many of the mansions dated back to the Roaring Twenties and conjured up a *Great Gatsby* vibe of a time before pickleball courts and screening rooms. Not that Azalea lacked these things. Indeed, the ten-bedroom mansion had a screening room as well as a saltwater swimming pool, a putting green, his and hers home gyms and, yes, a pickleball court. Sutton worked out every day, staying in shape so she could keep her eighty-three-year-old husband happy but also so she could fit into the designer clothes that filled her obscenely large walk-in closet. Chuck worked out every day not to please his thirty-five-year-old wife but rather to hold back the sand in the hourglass that was marking his years.

As she approached the basement door along the hallway, Sutton could hear Chuck grunting somewhere downstairs. The sound was similar to the one he made when they had sex. It was also the same sound her father used to make when he mowed their lawn back in Alabama. She couldn't imagine that her father enjoyed mowing their tiny, parched lawn and wondered why Chuck never sounded like he enjoyed their (always) brief sex. It seemed like an awful lot of work for such a little bit of satisfaction.

Sutton opened the gym door and was surprised to find Chuck with their housekeeper. They were both on the floor, tangled together. Chuck was pantless and Reyna was topless. It was unlikely that they had been working out or cleaning. "Why aren't you wearing any pants?" she asked her husband. Chuck's penis was flaccid and his face was red, which was his usual state during sexual relations. But he didn't seem to be in a state of pleasure *at all*.

"Something's wrong!" Reyna screamed out.

"No shit," Sutton replied. She looked down at Chuck. He was gasping for air and clutching his chest.

"I'm having a heart attack!" he wheezed. "God damn it! I need help!"

Sutton turned to her traumatized housekeeper. "Well, go call 911," she said, more annoyed than alarmed. "Jesus, he's having a heart attack." She couldn't help but notice that Reyna had very nice boobs and that they were real. Reyna ran out of the room, and Sutton could hear her footsteps on the stairs as she hightailed it to a phone. Sutton looked back down at her gasping husband. She thought he looked particularly old.

"Why aren't you wearing any pants?"

CHAPTER

9

After the Murder

SHAY

"AMEN," DUB SAID. He was not so much praying as stating a fact.

Shay looked over to see who or what he was referring to. He was standing in front of a painting of a golf course. There was a stone bridge and pine trees and pink azaleas and the greenest of grass. It was probably what heaven looked like to an avid golfer.

"Amen corner," Dub clarified. Which was helpful since Shay had no idea what he was talking about. "Augusta National. The Masters?"

"Mr. Tupper's a member," said the woman who stood in the room with them. Her name was Johnelle Kale. She was about seventy-five years old and her coral-colored flower earrings matched the coral necklace around her tiny neck, which matched the coral pantsuit she was wearing. She was the kind of woman who had her hair styled twice a week and played bridge with her friends on

Thursdays. She looked like she was going to cry, but she held back the tears. "He *used* to be a member."

They were in Anderson Tupper's office in a nondescript brick building in Buckhead. There was a dental office next door and a title company across the hall. Tupper Investments was a small operation for such an illustrious Atlanta name. It consisted of two rooms—Anderson's office and the outer office where Johnelle manned a perfectly organized desk on which sat a calendar of daily inspirational messages from Joel Osteen.

"How long did you work for Mr. Tupper?" Shay asked Johnelle.

"A few years," Johnelle replied. "Since he came back from Colorado. I worked for his father before that."

"Do you mind if we take a look at his office?"

"No, not at all," Johnelle said as she led the way. "I've kept it just as it was when he was last here."

"When was that?" Dub asked.

"The day before . . ." Johnelle started but stopped. She composed herself. "The day before he died."

Shay stepped into Anderson's office with one thought. Why did such a rich man have such a crappy office? It was a one-man show. Anderson supposedly invested millions of dollars yet worked out of an office not much bigger than the one Shay and Dub shared downtown. His diploma from the University of Georgia hung on one wall and a painting of UGA's famous iron arch was hanging behind his desk. There were no family photos. No mementos. Nothing that said anything other than this person went to college and played golf.

Shay looked around Anderson's desk. There wasn't a whole lot to see. A white pad with inconsequential notes scribbled on it. A schedule of games for his Little League team. A three-year-old laptop computer that still had an Open Box sale sticker affixed to its black surface. "We'd like to take his computer in for analysis." Shay said.

"Whatever helps."

"Do you have his password?" Dub asked.

"Oh, no," Johnelle said. "Mr. Tupper was very careful with his passwords. He didn't even give them to *me*. He didn't want his clients' information to get stolen." She paused for a second. "*Hacked*. Hacked is the word."

"Yes, ma'am."

"Do you have any thoughts about who might have killed Mr. Tupper?" Shay asked as she worked to unplug the computer and Dub prepared a bag to carry it in. "Maybe a client who wasn't happy with him?"

"No," Johnelle said. "His clients loved him. Mr. Tupper was very conscientious. He always made sure he remembered everyone's birthday. Or people's anniversaries. We kept a list of all that. He would send Virginia peanuts on special occasions."

"Did Mr. Tupper get along with his family?" asked Shay.

Johnelle composed herself. "Of course."

"Even his brother?" Dub asked. "Anderson didn't work in the family business anymore, and there've been a few stories in the news about problems between them."

"That happens in family businesses, doesn't it?" Johnelle said. "Chatham wanted to sell the company but didn't think Anderson had the right to an opinion about it. Even though he was on the board!" Johnelle sat down in one of the two black maple captain's chairs in front of Anderson's desk. Each was engraved with the University of Georgia's logo on the top above the spindles. "I think the boys could have worked it out if it wasn't for that woman."

"What woman?" Shay asked.

"The sister-in-law. Amelia," Johnelle said. "For the life of me, I do not know why he thought so highly of her."

"But you didn't?"

"Born on third base and thought she hit a triple," Johnelle said. "Ever heard that?"

Dub chuckled. "I love that saying."

"So spoiled. She has stock in the family company too. I warned their father about that, but he gave her shares as a wedding present. Just enough to mess everything up. She's the one who convinced

Anderson not to go along with the sale of the company. I'm sure of it. And after Chatham and Amelia divorced, Anderson gave her money."

"Gave his sister-in-law money?" Shay asked.

"A *lot* of money."

"Any idea how much?"

"At least two million dollars," Johnelle said. "That's a lot of money."

Johnelle seemed to drift off into some other place and time. She could have been thinking about Anderson or she could have been thinking about playing bridge. In either case, she got up and walked out of his office without another word. Shay looked over at Dub and shook her head in wonder.

"Two million dollars," Dub said. "That *is* a lot of money. You thinking what I'm thinking?"

"It's almost always about drugs, sex, or *money*," Shay said.

* * *

"Hello, Mrs. Tupper. Thank you for coming in," Shay said as she and Dub sat down across from Amelia in the interrogation room. "Is it still Mrs. Tupper or do you go by your maiden name?"

"I still go by Tupper," Amelia said.

Shay watched as Amelia nervously rubbed the top corner of her Hermes bag. The leather there was worn, and Shay wondered if it was from this rubbing or from age. Amelia appeared to be worn too. Frayed around the edges. There was a sadness to her that surprised Shay. People often pretended to be happy when they weren't. It was a survival instinct. Unhappy people were weak. The woman sitting across from them seemed to have long ago given up the ruse of happiness.

"We're trying to establish a baseline here," Shay told Amelia. "We're just gathering information and the more you can help us understand certain things, the easier time we'll have with our investigation."

"Whatever you need. I want to find out who killed Anderson."

"He lent you a substantial amount of money," Dub said. "Is that correct?"

Amelia appeared visibly surprised the detectives knew about the money. "I . . . he . . . we helped each other out."

"With what?"

"With Chatham," Amelia said. "My ex-husband. Anderson's brother."

"Are you referring to the disagreements about the family company?" Dub asked.

"The company and, I don't know . . ." Amelia wavered for a moment. Shay knew that Amelia was weighing just how much she should say. "He helped me out with life. He knew what my ex-husband had done to me. He wanted to protect me."

"From your ex-husband?" Shay asked.

"Yes. Chatham was trying to bleed me dry and force me to sell my shares in the family company. He has first right of refusal. He needed my shares or Anderson's to have a majority so he could sell the company."

"Wouldn't that be a good thing?" Shay asked.

"Anderson thought Chatham was trying to cheat us."

"Why would he want to do that?" Dub asked. "No offense, ma'am, but I can understand why he might want to do it to you, but why would he want to do that to his own brother?"

"Because once you're Chatham Tupper's enemy, he'll do anything to destroy you."

CHAPTER

10

Nine Days Before the Murder

AMELIA

CHATHAM TUPPER HAD spent his life under the thumb of his domineering father, Edgar, the man who started the timber empire that would rule the South and beyond. He was a tough and humorless man and expected his eldest son to be the same. Edgar Tupper, however, was Mister Rogers compared to Tilly Tupper. She was the Generalissimo of the Tupper clan and loved nothing more than to tactically plan every aspect of her firstborn's life. Chatham started kindergarten at age three. He went to boarding school in New England. Like his father, he went on to university at Yale. Upon graduation, he started at the bottom rung of Tupper Timber and climbed his way up while carrying a backpack filled with expectations. Those expectations molded Chatham into a determined, uncompromising, diligent asshole.

Amelia knew Tilly Tupper never thought she was worthy of Chatham. Which was most likely the reason it took Chatham all of five weeks to propose to her. It was his way of letting his mother know he would be making his own decisions.

Tilly's counteroffensive began in the run-up to Atlanta's wedding of the century. She took control of the entire event (a dignified ceremony at Trinity Church followed by a lavish reception at the Peachtree Driving Club). She bought Chatham and Amelia a 1920s Buckhead Italianate mansion, Villa Rosa, as a wedding gift, and bought Amelia liposuction, to make her tummy just a tad flatter, and breast implants to make her boobs just a tad larger. "That's how my Chatham likes them," she told Amelia. In return, Amelia was to call Tilly "Mother" and ship her own mother back to Knoxville, where Brindley died three years later from cancer.

Or was it from a broken heart?

The girl from the humble suburbs of Knoxville, Tennessee, quickly learned to navigate the choppy waters of Buckhead. With a private jet at her disposal, Amelia began to crisscross the globe in search of the finest things to fill her new home. She purchased an eighteen-thousand-dollar Aga stove in England that was flown over along with the technicians to install it. There was Zuber wallpaper from France and silk Persian rugs, vintage Fornasetti butterfly tables, Hermes blankets and prized David Austin roses. Amelia loved every inch of Villa Rosa like it was a part of her.

The incendiary sex she had with Chatham ebbed and flowed, as it does, but soon produced their first child, Hampton, whom everyone called Ham. He was followed by Penelope, whom they called Poppy, and Augustine, who was called Auggie. The whole lot of them made for picture-perfect photo spreads in *Southern Living* and *Garden & Gun*.

It was Amelia's nose that finally ended their marriage. Returning home from a European shopping spree, she rolled her Rimowa suitcase into her bedroom and smelled something that wasn't quite right. Amelia had scents for every room, using candles and diffusers from Diptyque and Jo Malone to give every space its own unique fragrance. The kitchen smelled of Massa Lubrense lemons, fresh off a citrus tree on the Amalfi Coast. The library smelled of cedar, like the logs for the fireplace had just been brought down from a mountainside in Aspen. The powder room off the den had an alluring whiff of freesia and mandarin. The bedroom? For that space, she chose her favorite. Jasmine. Amelia loved how it always smelled so fresh and how every time she encountered jasmine in the outside world, it reminded her of passionate nights with Chatham in that very room.

Now it smelled of . . . what was it? Coconut? Their room smelled like cheap tanning oil. Amelia never used tanning oil. She stayed out in the sun just long enough to pick up a toasty brown hue and, even then, she used sunscreen. As she stood in her bedroom, a thought entered her mind. It was a thought that most people have at least once in a relationship. It was often an insidious little lie that caused nothing but anguish and heartache, but it was just as often the truth.

Was her spouse having an affair?

Of course Chatham was having an affair. He was actually having several. Although Amelia wasn't sure if *affair* was the right word. Nor was *liaison* or *fling* or *dalliance* or *hookup* or any other words like that in a thesaurus. No, Chatham was *screwing*. He was *screwing* prostitutes.

The ensuing divorce was the talk of Buckhead and beyond. Salacious stories of kinky sex and prostitutes (only some of which Amelia spread) filled the papers and lit up the blogosphere along with tales of Amelia's obscene spending habits. In the settlement, Chatham offered Amelia either her beloved house or primary custody of the children, thinking that she would choose the house. It was an act of cruelty. She chose the children. She would have been heartbroken either way.

After two years of fighting, Amelia walked away with the stock she had previously been given in the family company and twelve million dollars, one million for every year they were married. It seemed like enough money. But after buying a seven-million-dollar fixer-upper with property taxes of sixty-three thousand dollars a year, paying her lawyers, and paying Uncle Sam, Amelia was left with a Birkin bag filled with broken dreams.

Even though they had been divorced for almost two years, the fighting seemed to never end, and Amelia now found herself, again, in a courtroom with her ex-husband. Chatham was huddled at the table across the aisle from her with his divorce lawyer, a fifty-year-old woman in a gray suit named Margo Shands. Calling her a woman, however, was bestowing upon her virtues that she did not possess. She was a tormentor. A demon. She had been paid many millions of dollars to destroy Amelia and had made quick work of it.

"Mrs. Tupper, are we waiting for your attorney?" So said Judge Steve Merriman. He was an older man who had presided over courtrooms in Atlanta for thirty years. He was less than enthusiastic about being in this one now.

"I'm representing myself, Your Honor."

Judge Merriman sighed. Loudly. That was the last thing a judge wanted to hear.

"Fine. Let's get started. Ms. Shands, you want to fill me in?"

"Yes, Your Honor," Chatham's lawyer said. "As you see from our Motion for Miscellaneous Relief and Sanctions, Mrs. Tupper was required to vacate the family home, taking only items that were specifically agreed upon. Despite this, Mrs. Tupper removed thirty-five David Austin rose bushes from the grounds of the house that were not listed and has refused all efforts on our part to secure their return. This was flagrantly in violation of the divorce agreement, and we respectfully seek your assistance in this matter."

Judge Merriman looked to Amelia. She tried to look defiant, but she was already wilting. He turned back to Chatham and his lawyer. "Roses?" he asked. "I really hope this isn't about plants."

"They're very expensive rose bushes, Your Honor," Shands said. "They were cultivated over many years and won several awards. Their absence from the home has significantly affected the house's value and caused my client emotional distress."

"Emotional distress?"

"Yes, Your Honor. Mr. Tupper was very fond of the roses. He would often sit in the garden and meditate. He found that being among these very special roses offered him great solace during difficult times."

Meditate? Amelia couldn't help but let out a chuckle. She was the only one amused.

Judge Merriman wearily turned back to her. "Mrs. Tupper? Did you take the roses?"

"Yes, Your Honor," Amelia said. "They were *my* roses. I picked them out. I spent years taking care of them. Chatham never even liked them. I have a copy of an email he sent me." She picked up a piece of paper and prepared for her dramatic reading. "He said, 'I hope you die and are buried with your fucking roses.' He called them *your* roses. Would you like to see it?" Amelia held out the paper for the bailiff to retrieve, but the judge waved the whole affair away.

"I don't need to see it, thank you."

Margo Shands stepped forward again. She inched herself toward Amelia's side of the courtroom causing Amelia to step back. "Judge Merriman, my client has a deep love for these roses." She seemed to sense from the look on the judge's face that this wasn't the track to take and pivoted to another one. "But . . . regardless of whether he loves them—which he does—or hates them, they were part of the property of the house, and we respectfully ask that you order Mrs. Tupper to return them."

The judge looked between the two sides of the courtroom with utter disdain. "First, I'd like to make it clear that I find this matter to be a complete waste of the court's time. I really don't give a damn about your garden. What I think, however, doesn't matter. It's what the law thinks, and the law thinks that the damn roses were an improvement and a fixture that became part of the property. They were not on the list of items negotiated in the divorce and, therefore, Mrs. Tupper, you weren't supposed to remove them. So please return them."

"Your Honor, I can't afford to have them put back."

"Can you afford the ten thousand dollars a day I'm going to fine you if you don't?" the judge asked Amelia. Amelia dropped her head in defeat. She had lost another battle in the war of the roses. "You have three days to comply or face a fine and possible imprisonment."

"Thank you, Your Honor," Chatham said in a self-satisfied manner.

"Next time just buy some rhododendrons," Judge Merriman said as he left the courtroom.

"You're being such an asshole," Amelia told Chatham as he approached her side. "You don't even like the roses. You know, I'm going to tell the kids everything you've done. Everything. Ham and Poppy are old enough to understand now."

Chatham had a smile so smug Amelia wanted to slap it off his face. "First I took the roses," he said calmly. "Next I take the kids."

Amelia and Chatham's relationship had ended much as it had begun. With Amelia getting fucked.

CHAPTER

11

After the Murder

SHAY

Laura Cho sat across from Shay and Dub in the interrogation room. She was wearing not one but *two* gold crosses around her neck. The first was unadorned and long and thin. It was a simple token of devotion. The second was larger and studded with diamonds. The two probably represented her personal spiritual journey from humble Christian to self-appointed point person for Jesus in Buckhead.

"I was *conflicted* about calling you," Laura said. She emphasized the *conflicted* part like it took a prayer session for her to make the decision. Shay didn't think the woman was conflicted at all. She had called them and asked for an urgent meeting. She said she had vital information about the Tupper case. This woman was eager to be there. "I don't want to come off as a gossip," she continued. "I mean, if it hadn't been for the murder, I wouldn't have given her a second thought."

"Who?" Dub asked.

"Kira Brooks," Laura said rather ominously, as a villager might utter the name *Dracula* in a tavern in Transylvania. "I don't even think she had been in town a week before she went after Anderson Tupper."

"Went after?" Shay asked.

"It was obvious to everyone that she was attracted to him. And she's a married woman! Maybe that's okay in California, but it's not here. Married women don't cavort with unmarried men."

Cavort? Shay had to pinch herself on the leg to keep from laughing. Did people still cavort and did this woman really believe that the pious people of Buckhead *didn't* cavort? Shay knew very well that there was a lot of cavorting going on in Buckhead and everywhere else—including, she assumed, whichever church it was that this woman belonged to.

"Did you see something or hear something that led you to believe that Mrs. Brooks and Mr. Tupper were . . . *cavorting*?" Shay asked.

"I saw them at Fresh Market," Laura said. "I don't know if you have Fresh Market in your part of town—"

"I know what Fresh Market is," Shay said.

"Of course you do," Laura continued. "I didn't mean . . . anyhow, I saw them at Fresh Market."

"Uh-huh."

"*Together*. She had just arrived in town. She's a married woman. From *California*."

CHAPTER

12

Eight Days Before the Murder

KIRA

KIRA'S REFRIGERATOR HAD two items inside. A bottle of ketchup and half a container of mixed olives that had been in the car for three days and really needed to be thrown out. The pitiful contents of the fridge sent her in search of replenishment, which brought her to Fresh Market. It was the go-to market for Buckhead people, filled with things you needed and things, like truffle butter, that you never knew you needed. It was like a smaller, more expensive Whole Foods. If that was even possible.

The market gave off a strange vibe that made Kira uncomfortable. Everyone seemed nervous there. The women (and some men) hurried around with their half-sized shopping carts, racing from section to section like someone else might beat them to a better cut of meat or the last container of pimento cheese (and look better while doing it). And if that happened, if they failed to triumph in the aisles here, how could they compete *out there*? A trip to the market had ceased to be a simple excursion for groceries and turned into an existential crisis.

On her way through the produce section, Kira had passed by Laura, the book burner. Kira smiled and tried to catch Laura's eye, but the woman suddenly became enamored with a pile of watermelon radishes. Kira thought about going over to say hello but feared the woman might start speaking in tongues and try to cast out Kira's demons. In which case, they'd be there all day.

"Hello, Mrs. Brooks," came a voice from behind her. She had only heard it once before, but it was a memorable one. She turned to find Anderson Tupper standing before her. He was wearing a classy but casual Sid Mashburn suit and holding a sandwich wrapped in brown paper from the deli. Kira took note of the suit. He looked good in it. Of course, she thought he looked good at the baseball game too, in his T-shirt and shorts, but men always looked better in suits.

"Coach Tupper. Hi."

"It's Anderson," he said. "Only the kids call me Coach. Although a few have used saltier terms over the years."

"And I'm not Mrs. Brooks. I'm Kira."

"Hi, Kira."

"Hi, Anderson," she said. Her heart was beating a little faster. She could feel it flutter in her chest. Jesus, Kira. Get a hold of yourself, she thought. He's just a man.

But what a man.

"How are you settling in?" he asked. "Making any new friends? I mean, other than me, of course."

Kira couldn't help but smile. He was being charming and she wasn't immune to it. "I've met a few people. Mostly the team moms, I guess."

"Which ones? I know all the dirt."

She smiled again and searched the rolodex in her head. Come on! You can remember! "Venita," she finally said. "Wade's mom. And Sutton. She's . . ."

"Cash's mom."

Kira nodded as if confirming he was correct even though she had no idea. "And Birdie. Her son is Freddie, right? And... Amelia."

"My sister-in-law."

"Yes," Kira said. Though she wanted to say, "Your *ex*-sister-in-law."

"Her son is Hampton," he said. He cocked his head to the side like a dog when it hears a strange noise. It was adorable. He was so floppy. "So it sounds like you've become well acquainted with the Buckhead Betties."

"So they *are* Buckhead Betties!" It was out of Kira's mouth before she could stop it.

"If you're a rich woman living in Buckhead and you're anything other than Mother Teresa, you're a Buckhead Betty. So, sorry, you may be one too. You being a successful writer and all." He paused for a long moment, then admitted to that thing everyone does but no one confesses to. "I googled you."

He googled her? Kira was thrilled about that. Wasn't that the modern equivalent of looking someone up in *Burke's Peerage*? Anderson reached past Kira and pulled a bag of chips off a shelf. His arm brushed against hers and Kira became a little unsteady. That small connection sent a rush of blood to her head, and she blushed. If Anderson noticed, he didn't let on. "So, picking up some lunch?" she asked, then instantly regretted it. Obviously he was picking up lunch. He was holding a sandwich and potato chips.

"Uh, yep," he said. "Grabbing some lunch and getting a bottle of wine for a big date."

Kira tried to hide her disappointment. She was feeling a little jealous, though when she thought about it for a few seconds she realized she was jealous that her son's *Little League coach*, whom she didn't even know, was going on date with someone else she didn't even know. Kira wondered when she had reverted to being a thirteen-year-old girl. "Well, hope your date is great."

"Me too," he said. "You know, you're from California. You probably know all the great wines. Why don't you help me pick something out?" Almost before the words had exited his mouth, Anderson's demeanor suddenly turned dark. He stepped back from Kira and began fumbling his words. "I'm so . . . I'm sorry. I completely forgot. I . . . damn! What an idiot. I can't believe I said that."

If she wasn't sure when she first met him, she was sure now. He knew her secret. He knew why she was late in following her family to Atlanta, and she had to assume he knew everything else too.

"It's fine," she finally said. "There's no harm in getting a bottle of wine. It's only dangerous when you open it."

CHAPTER 13

After the Murder

SHAY

A LONG LINE OF people snaked out the door and into the parking lot of Taqueria del Sol. It was a hip Mexican restaurant in a redeveloped industrial section of Atlanta. The tasty food warranted the lines of Atlantans who waited patiently to order at a counter and find a seat in the airy dining room or on the patio. Shay used to go to Taqueria three times a week until she realized that her love for their jalapeño cheese dip was turning into a dark obsession.

Shay bypassed the line at the door and entered the patio, where she found Darron seated at the back. Red baskets filled with tacos and enchiladas and coleslaw and chips were laid out in a semicircle before him. There was only a slight possibility that some of the food was for Shay. Darron waved as she approached, but Shay didn't wave back. She had a stern look on her face that he would have recognized from his childhood. Either his mother had had a bad morning or Darron had done something wrong.

"It's not spring break," Shay said as she pulled one of the metal chairs out to join her son. It scraped across the cement floor. She sat down and tried very hard to look at her son and not the cheese dip on the table. This was serious. Darron leaned back in his chair. Shay could see that he was contemplating an excuse, but she didn't give him time to respond. "I looked at the school calendar to see when you had to be back, and it turns out that spring break isn't for two weeks. I've just been too damned busy to remember that. Want to tell me what's going on?"

Darron sunk in his chair. Whatever façade he'd been putting up finally dropped. He looked away for a moment like he was trying to gather strength that he no longer possessed, then turned back to his mother. "Dad's been calling me."

It seemed like such a simple thing. A father calling his son. This simple thing, though, sent a shockwave through Shay's body. "What? Well, did you . . . did you talk to him?" she stammered.

"No. Well, yeah. The first time he called. Because I didn't know it was him."

"What did he say?"

"He just said he wanted to talk," Darron said as his eyes began to fill with tears. "I hung up after that and I blocked his calls. I didn't know what else to do. I didn't want to be at school. I just, I couldn't concentrate. I couldn't do anything. I mean, what if he came to campus? What if he comes here?"

Shay reached out and grabbed Darron's hand. He tried to resist, but she pulled it closer to her. She looked down and could see a few inches of his forearm that had been hidden beneath the sleeves of the hoodie he was wearing. There were deep scars there that looked like a topographical map with lines of red and pink and white swirling across his skin. Scars from a burn.

Shay's thoughts went screaming back to fifteen years prior. She had tried so hard to forget she ever had a different life, a *before*, but her life would always be *before* and *after*. Before, she was a married woman living in Stone Mountain. It was famous in Atlanta for its beautiful park and infamous for the Confederate generals carved into the face of its granite mountain. It was a mountain that held tight to its history, good or bad. People had called for the carvings in the granite to be destroyed, but Shay thought that destroying history could also destroy the memories of the bad things that had happened. You couldn't change *before*, and you shouldn't forget it either.

In Stone Mountain, Shay lived in a two-story midcentury house with a slanted low-slung roofline. There was a pool in the backyard and a basketball hoop mounted above the two-car garage. It was a family home and Shay lived there with her husband Eddie and their son Darron.

Eddie was Eddie Romano. They met at the scene of a triple murder. He was the first officer on the scene. She was a junior detective. Even as they stood over the bodies of three murdered drug dealers, Eddie was charming and funny and a light that lit up even that grim crime scene. He reminded her of Tony Danza from *Who's the Boss?* She had always had a thing for Italian guys.

Marriage. House in Stone Mountain. Baby.

It all happened so quickly that Shay didn't notice or willfully ignored the warning signs. Eddie could be the life of the party, but he could also be the death of it. His moods swung wildly from the clouds in the sky to the depths of the ocean. You tend to overlook a lot of things when you're in love. When you have a child, however, motherly instincts take over. As she retreated from Eddie, Darron became Shay's world. Sometimes she thought they were the same person. He had come *from* her, after all.

"If you ever leave me, I'll kill you both." That's what Eddie said to Shay shortly before she did leave him. Darron was almost four years old. She had fought valiantly for her marriage and for Eddie's sanity, but it had come time to fight for their son.

Three days after Eddie had packed his bags and moved out of their Stone Mountain house, Shay awoke in the early morning hours to a room full of smoke. It was the smell that jolted her from her sleep. It was a toxic mix of melting plastic and burning drywall. It took Shay a moment to focus before she realized the house was on fire. She would always remember the strange sight of the fireplace going up in flames.

Shay made it to the upstairs hallway and tripped over what turned out to be a disabled smoke detector. She stumbled into Darron's room and followed the sound of his screams to find him hiding under his bed. It was on fire and so was he. She pulled him out into the open and used her body to smother him and extinguish the flames that had already badly burned his arm.

She carried Darron past a pile of burning stuffed animals, their plastic eyes melting in horror movie fashion, and lifted one of the windows open. The smoke funneled out, escaping into the dawn. Shay could hear sirens in the distance, and a group of neighbors were already gathering on the lawn. Two men struggled to put a ladder against the house, and one climbed up and carried Darron away.

Shay began to inch her way toward the ladder when she stopped. There was Eddie. He was across the street, sitting on the hood of his car with his arms crossed, looking at Shay like they were late for dinner. He had tried to burn them alive.

Darron got skin graphs and therapy, but for years after, Shay would be awakened in the middle of the night by his screams. When his friends would ask what happened to his dad, Darron would tell them he was "in hell. Where he belonged." He had probably heard this from Shay. Eddie had been sent to a psychiatric hospital, and the last Shay heard he was living in Arizona and keeping to himself. Until now.

Shay sat at the table on the back patio of Taqueria del Sol and looked across at her precious son. He seemed to be four years old again. They were a team. They always had been. She leaned in close and held her other hand against his chin. Look at me, she thought. Believe me.

"I'm going to protect you. I always have."

CHAPTER

14

Seven Days Before the Murder

KIRA

Kira's Mini Cooper was a great car for Los Angeles. It was compact and cool and perfect for fitting into tight parking spaces in the land where traffic was invented. It hadn't been quite so great for Atlanta, the land of SUVs and pickup trucks. Being small felt dangerous. She kind of wished she had a Hummer. On this day, however, as she searched for a parking spot around Chastain Park, the Mini was invaluable. It was small enough that she could make her own parking space on the end of a row in the overflow parking lot across the street and up the hill from the park.

She felt very Californian as she stepped out of her car and admired her handiwork. She thought about taking a picture to commemorate her outstanding parking job, but activity in a car in the lot below caught her eye. She looked down the hill to see a man sitting in a vintage convertible Jaguar. She would later learn he was Dan Milton, the husband of one of the Buckhead Betties. The top was down on the Jag and so were his pants. A pretty brunette was giving him a blow job and he seemed to be enjoying it as much as the perfectly sunny weather. Maybe even more. Just when Kira was beginning to think Atlanta was boring, she was thrown a curveball.

Kira left the couple behind and headed to the park. It was Family Day at CYB Baseball, and the park and fields were packed with players and their parents. It was a carnival atmosphere with balloons and banners and music playing. She made her way through all the baseball players to the furthest field, where the Vikings and their supporters were gathered. She wasn't eager to be there. She had work to do. But she wanted to be there for Kolt, even if he probably didn't care if she was there or not.

She approached the gathering just in time to see Coach Tupper hand Kolt a personalized Louisville Slugger bat. "Kolt Brooks, the best right fielder in the league," Anderson said. Kira doubted that was true, but it was a nice thing to say. Kolt smiled and that made her smile. The assembled parents, including the women she had met at the last game, applauded as Kolt shook hands with Anderson and his assistant coach, Marcus, and stepped aside for another teammate to get his bat.

Kira spotted her husband standing to the side with some other team dads. She couldn't help but think he was so out of place. Try as he might, and even with his khaki pants and Gucci loafers, he just didn't look like a southerner. He lacked the confidence and ease with people that, say, Anderson Tupper had. She looked over at Anderson and caught his eye. He smiled and she smiled back. When she turned to look at Kallan, however, he wasn't smiling at all.

Kallan left the dads and joined Kira. "You didn't have to come to this," he told her.

"I wanted to," she said. "It's Family Day."

"I don't think it makes any difference to Kolt."

"Well, it makes a difference to me," Kira told him.

Kallan didn't look at Kira. He kept his gaze firmly on their son. "I think you're putting too much pressure on him."

"By being his mother?" Kira was trying not to get upset, but Kallan was an expert button pusher. "We agreed that this was the right thing to do."

"You're asking a lot of him," Kallan said. "You're asking a lot of us all."

"I just want things to be normal again."

"That's impossible," he told her. "You're just going to have to accept that."

Kira was going to argue with him. She was ready to tell him that she didn't believe that. That everyone deserved forgiveness. She was maybe even going to say she was sorry for the ten thousandth time. Instead, she said nothing at all. She *was* sorry, but she didn't feel like she deserved forgiveness. She couldn't even forgive herself.

BIRDIE

Birdie watched Kira and Kallan Brooks carefully. She studied their body language and their faces. They didn't touch each other. There was no eye contact. They were more distant than strangers. At least strangers feigned smiles and pleasantries. There was nothing like that with this couple. Birdie wondered just how dysfunctional their dysfunction could be. She knew that Kira hadn't stayed behind in California to sell the house or work or whatever. That was ridiculous.

Birdie was going to have to put Freddie on the job. He would get the truth out of Kolt. Birdie saw Anderson smile at Kira and Kira smile back. "What's that all about?" Birdie said to no one in particular, even though she was standing with Sutton, Venita, and Amelia.

"What's what all about?" Venita asked.

"That Kira," Birdie said. "She's smiling at Anderson."

"How dare she!" Venita scoffed. "Seriously, Birdie, you don't even know her. It's too early to start hating her."

"Better too early than too late," Birdie declared.

Lamar Burrows joined them as they watched Anderson praise another one of his players and hand over another expensive, personalized bat. "Aren't you looking fine today, Sutton," Lamar said, singling her out. Birdie thought that from anyone else that would have been a compliment. But somehow, when Lamar said it, it sounded sleazy. Maybe because he was looking at Sutton like he wanted to devour her.

"What can we do for you, Lamar?" Amelia asked.

"Getting a lot of complaints from the other teams," he said. "They're giving out certificates and you're giving out expensive bats."

"Take it up with Anderson," Venita said. "He bought them."

"He should be watching his pennies," Lamar said.

"What do you mean by that?" Venita asked.

"Not a thing," Lamar replied. "You ladies have a nice day." He turned to Sutton before he walked away. "Chuck is one lucky man."

"He's so gross," said Sutton. "Why is he always looking at me?"

"Because your breasts are magnificent," Birdie told her. The praise seemed to settle Sutton down.

"What did he mean about Anderson watching his pennies?" Venita asked.

Amelia was silent, as Birdie knew she would be. "Don't pay any attention to Lamar," Birdie told Venita. "He thinks he's being cute." Birdie knew the truth. She knew Anderson was broke. She knew Amelia was broke. Birdie had a lot of faults but also had a few virtues. One of which was keeping secrets. Even though she knew Venita and Marcus had invested a lot of money with Anderson, she didn't feel it was her place to warn them about the state of Anderson's finances. That was their business. She was also kind of looking forward to the Wileys' inevitable fall. Birdie would one hundred percent be there for Venita, though, when it all came crashing down. That's what friends were for.

Birdie watched as Dan made his way between the fields. He stopped to say hello to a few people along the way and offered up handshakes and shoulder pats. He was like the unofficial mayor of Buckhead. After all, he had either represented or sued half the residents of Buckhead at one time or another. He was loved and hated but also respected. He also looked far too happy for Birdie's liking. Why was he in such a good mood?

Birdie caught sight of Kira again. The Californian was staring at Dan. Staring at Birdie's husband. It was one thing to flirt with Anderson. If Kira thought she could make a play for Dan, she had another thing coming. Like a swift kick in the ass.

CHAPTER

15

After the Murder

SHAY

SHAY AND DUB sat in the waiting room of the office of Dr. Lamar G. Burrows, gynecologist. There was a framed photo of the man hanging behind the reception desk. Shay thought his teeth were far too white. He looked like a doctor in a soap opera. Just the thought of "FU" Burrows being a gynecologist made Shay's skin crawl. She didn't like him from the moment he was rude to Dub at the baseball field. He had acted then like he was too good to talk to them. She was sure he would think even more of himself now that they were at his office.

"Is it weird to go to the gynecologist?" Dub whispered. He was reading a copy of *People* magazine he had taken from a rack in the corner of the office.

"Yes, it's incredibly weird," she told Dub.

"You know what's strange about this guy?" Dub asked.

"Other than everything?"

"When I interviewed the groundskeeper at the park, he said when he called Burrows to tell him about the murder, he was there minutes later," Dub told Shay. "Burrows said he was just coming back from the Steeplechase. After midnight."

"Birdie Milton said everyone left around nine."

Dub closed the *People* Magazine. "Yes, she did."

The inner office door cracked open and a young nurse in light blue hospital scrubs looked at Shay and Dub. "Dr. Burrows is ready for you."

"Oh, goody," Shay said as Dub put the magazine away and they followed the nurse past exam rooms to Lamar's office, where Burrows sat waiting for them. There was a diploma from the Medical College of Georgia on the wall next to a poster about genital warts. As they sat down, Shay wondered if gynecologists were better or worse in bed than laymen. Did they have inside knowledge of all the right spots to hit or did years of looking at women's vaginas take the fun out of it?

"Does this happen a lot?" Shay asked. She tried to look Burrows in the eye but was distracted by the stretched-out blue latex gloves on the desk between them. Where had those gloves been?

"Does what happen a lot?" Burrows asked.

"Do multiple people often threaten to kill your Little League coaches?" Shay asked. "I mean, we've kind of just started and we already have two."

"Well, Ms. Claypool—"

"*Detective* Claypool . . ." Two can play at that game, *Doctor* Burrows.

"Well, *Detective* Claypool, it happens more than you think," the doctor replied.

"I have a question about when we first spoke," Dub said. "The groundskeeper at Chastain said he called you right after he called the police that night."

"I'm chairman of the CYB board," Burrows reminded them. "I'm the contact person."

"He said you told him you had just been getting back from the Steeplechase," Dub continued. "That was around midnight. But we were told the Steeplechase ended around nine."

"Am I a suspect now?"

"Oh, everyone's a suspect," Shay remarked. That fact didn't appear to faze Burrows. He had the same look of condescension toward Shay and Dub he always had.

"I left the Steeplechase a little bit later than everyone else."

"What were you doing?" Shay asked.

"Just messing around. And then there was traffic and all." He fiddled with the Patek Phillipe watch on his wrist and polished its glass with the sleeve of his scrubs. "I was getting gas in Marietta around the time Anderson was murdered. You can check my credit card statement. And there's probably security camera footage from the station."

Shay nodded. You bet they'd be checking that. She wondered if he thought she was stupid enough to just take his word for it.

"I'm not the one you should be wasting your valuable time with," Burrows said. "I wanted to talk about what happened with Venita Wiley."

"Right," said Shay. "I wonder, did you think Mrs. Wiley was serious about her threat?"

"Well, you know how Buckhead Betties can be."

* * *

Shay drove her state-issued Dodge Charger up to the gates of Marcus and Venita Wiley's Buckhead mansion. "It looks like a hotel," Dub observed from the passenger seat. The house loomed in front of them at the top of a hill at the end of the long driveway.

"We should have had them come to the station," Shay said.

"And miss the chance to see Marcus Wiley's house?" said Dub. "Shoot, they could charge money to give tours of this place. Do you think they have the Heisman on display? Like in a glass case or something?"

Shay ignored Dub. She rolled down her window and pressed a button on the intercom at the gate. A phone rang for an annoyingly long time until Venita finally answered.

"Yes?"

"It's Detectives Claypool and Rattigan. Atlanta PD. We have an appointment."

They waited for a reply, but there was none. Shay looked at Dub and he shrugged. They finally got their answer as the gates began to open. They were decorated with a swirling wrought iron number 33. Any Georgia football fan, like Dub, knew that 33 was Marcus Wiley's number when he played there. Shay just kind of worked that out for herself as 33 separated into two threes and folded back as they drove through.

Shay pulled the car into the circular carport in front of the house. It wasn't surprising that the driveway was filled with brand new Fords. It was surely the perks of owning a Ford dealership. There was a Georgia Bulldogs red electric F-150 next to an orange Bronco with a Kensington Prep sticker on its back window next to a deep purple Mustang that looked like it could win the Daytona 500. It was a little more surprising that parked next to the "family" cars were a sexy Ferrari 812 Superfast and a Verde Mantis green Lamborghini Aventador that was imposing and futuristic and seemed on the verge of transforming into a robot and running away. Neither were made by Ford.

"I should have been a football player," Dub said as he eyed the perks.

"I should have married a football player," Shay countered as they approached the house. It was a two-story stucco mansion that did, indeed, look like a hotel. It was of chateau proportions and wouldn't have been out of place in Normandy surrounded by a maze of hedgerows. Shay eyed the majestic stone lions on either side of the oak front doors. Lions.

"We have a stone frog on our porch," Dub joked. "Debbie calls him Harold."

Before they could ring the doorbell, one side of the double oak doors opened, and Venita presented herself. She didn't smile. In fact, Shay thought Venita looked annoyed. Like this was an imposition. Like talking to someone about a *murder* was getting in the way of her probably going to the hairdressers for the fourth time that week or driving her Ferrari to the club for a light lunch and a spirited game of canasta.

"Please, come in."

The inside of the house didn't have any stone lions, but it was definitely the home of people who felt like they were at the top of the food chain. Everything was BIG. There was an overly overstuffed sofa in the living room below a mirror with an ornate gold frame that took up most of the wall yet was hung too high for anyone to gaze into. There was a massive fireplace that one could imagine Louis XVI warming his feet by but was so clean it appeared to have never hosted a fire. Above a dining table that could seat ten without adding extra leaves was a king-sized chandelier with all manner of dangling glass crystals.

Pictures of the Wileys' son, Wade, were on every available surface. Wade as a newborn baby swaddled in his hospital blanket with a pink and blue border. Wade as a toddler posing with Tigger at Disneyworld. Wade in his baseball uniform with a bat over his shoulder—the official baseball card photo every kid had taken at CYB. Among the many photos of the obviously adored Wade was a wedding photo of Venita and Marcus. It had pride of place on the grand piano no one probably even knew how to play. Shay lingered on it for a moment. They were so young and beautiful in the photo. So hopeful and happy. Neither of them could possibly murder someone. Of course, not many people looked like murderers in their photos. Except maybe meth addicts in their mugshots.

"Thank you for meeting with us," Dub said. "We appreciate it."

"I'm glad you could come to me," Venita said. "My husband . . . well, you know he's fairly well known. If I went to the station, people might talk."

"We're happy to come to you," Shay said, even though, truthfully, she was furious. It should have been their choice if they interviewed someone in the field or at headquarters, not the choice of a football player's spoiled wife in Buckhead. But they needed information and they had to take what they could get.

Dub seemed distracted, and Shay followed his gaze to a den off the end of the formal living room. Its walls were covered in wood paneling painted Egyptian blue like on the headpiece of King Tut, and she could just make out the first of what were probably several glass cases filled with awards and mementos from Marcus Wiley's football career.

"Trophy room, huh?" Dub asked. There was no hiding the fanboy in him. "Do you keep the Heisman in there?"

"Yes."

Yes? That was it. There was no follow-up question asking if Dub would like to see it. Who wouldn't want to see a Heisman Trophy? Except maybe Shay, but that wasn't the point. The nice thing would have been to invite Dub to take a look.

"You have some questions for me?" Venita asked impatiently.

"Is Marcus going to be joining us?" asked Dub. Shay loved that Dub was already on a first-name basis with one of his football idols.

"No. He's at work. I can answer any questions you have for him."

"We have questions for you both," Shay said. "Speaking to someone's wife isn't exactly the same as speaking to them."

"But speaking to someone's lawyer is," Venita countered. "I represent Marcus as both his wife *and* attorney."

"Well, then, I guess I'll get right to it," Shay said with more than a little attitude. "Did you or your husband kill Anderson Tupper?"

Dub raised his eyebrow. *That* was very direct. Shay stood her ground. If Venita was going to build a gold brick wall, Shay was prepared to drive a Brinks truck through it.

Venita smiled. She didn't appear to be worried about Detective Claypool or probably anyone else. "No. For the record, neither of us killed Anderson. Though, for the record, I thought about it."

"He was your friend," Shay said. "Where did it all go wrong?"

"He wasn't my friend. He wasn't my husband's friend. It's not like we went out for margaritas on Fridays."

"But your husband and Mr. Tupper coached together."

"This is Buckhead, Detective," Venita told her as if everything could be explained away by her zip code. "It's probably not the same where you live, but Little League here is all about making business contacts."

Not the same where Shay lived? How did this woman even know where Shay lived? Who did this woman think she was? There was nothing about Venita Wiley that Shay liked. Not her highlighted hair. Not her beige monochrome mansion. Not her French-tip fingernails and definitely not her stupid stone lions. Shay wanted to launch into a speech about being a single working mother and espouse the wisdom of shopping at Costco instead of Saks and her pride in having purchased her own home and decorating it herself. It must be nice to have so much money you can make your financial decisions at Little League games.

Dub seemed to sense that Shay wasn't exactly warming to Venita. They had been partners long enough to know when to step in for each other. "Why did you decide to invest with Mr. Tupper?"

"From what we heard, he had made people a lot of money," Venita said. "My husband and I are entrepreneurs. We appreciated that he was too."

"And, of course, he was a Tupper," Shay said, rejoining the conversation.

"And he was a Tupper."

Six Days Before the Murder

VENITA

Like most people in the country, the first time Venita Cummings saw Marcus Wiley he was on a football field. He was gaining fame, yard by yard, as the star running back for the University of Georgia. Venita was in law school and had reluctantly agreed to set aside her studies and attend a game. She wasn't a fan of football, but she couldn't help thinking it was beautiful the way Marcus ran. Like he was going places.

The second time Venita saw Marcus, he was at a Mexican restaurant near campus. He was with a group of other football players. Their large bodies were stuffed into a booth in the back, and they were facing the restaurant, like a table of mafia bosses on the lookout for anyone coming to shoot them. The most famous college football player in the country was having nachos, and he needed to be protected from the general public. That didn't stop Venita from approaching and making her pitch.

"Marcus Wiley, I want to be your lawyer."

Marcus later told her that he was sure she had said, "Marcus Wiley, I want to be your wife."

Venita was three years older than Marcus. She was a serious student. She already had a *retirement account.* Marcus grew up in Austell, a town west of Atlanta. He was raised in a trailer that sat on concrete blocks, down a county road that led to a dead end. His mother and father stayed around long enough to hand him off and then disappeared into a haze of poverty. He was brought up by an enterprising uncle who fed and trained him, like a prized bull at a state fair, to be a football player. He had never known what it was like to have a home that sat on a firm foundation or someone in his life who wanted to do something *for* him instead of get something *from* him.

Marcus and Venita started dating that very day in that Mexican restaurant near campus and never looked back. By the time Marcus won the Heisman Trophy, Venita had graduated top of her class from law school. She had job offers from all over the Southeast, but she was only interested in working for one client—Marcus Wiley.

Everyone knew Marcus would be the number one pick in the NFL draft, but not everyone knew Venita. The Buffalo Bills had the number one pick, but there was no way Venita was moving to Buffalo! It wasn't just because of the cold weather. It was because of the statistics. The average career of an NFL player was 3.3 years and some 78 percent of players went broke within three years of retirement. Marcus was a Georgia boy. He was a southern star. NFL or no NFL, he could do commercials for local car dealerships for the rest of his life. Venita wasn't going to let him go broke. Especially not in Buffalo.

Marcus signed as the number three pick with the Atlanta Falcons and played for exactly 3.3 years when a torn ACL ended his professional career. The end of his career as a running back, however, was just the start of his career being Marcus "The Coyote" Wiley. He did color commentary for football games on ESPN and motivational speaking for corporations. He starred in ads for Kroger and Coke. He happily plowed through trash cans in a Waste Management commercial and ran through Home Depot leaping over barbecues in another. He also did commercials for a Ford dealership. The one that he and Venita bought with the money they made from everything else. They named it Wiley Ford and the logo featured a cartoon coyote holding a football. It soon became the biggest Ford dealership in the Southeast, and just about every F-150 from Greenville, South Carolina, to Birmingham, Alabama, was purchased from Wiley Ford, located in Austell, near a dead-end country road where a trailer once stood propped up on cement blocks.

Everything in their lives was all going as Venita had carefully planned until one day she opened an envelope from Tupper Investments. They had a huge chunk of their money with Anderson Tupper, not only because he and Marcus coached Little League together but also because, if you wanted to make money, it seemed like a good idea to do it with someone who already had a lot of his own.

The envelope contained their quarterly statement with his investment fund. Anderson didn't send out monthly statements. He was old school. He also didn't keep anything online. He had told them that was a dangerous practice that could result in them losing their fortune to hackers.

As Venita stared down at the statement, however, hackers were the least of her worries.

Venita may have run a few cars off the backroads of Buckhead that day as she raced to Chastain Park. She arrived at the CYB fields in record time and parked her car in a handicapped spot. This was not the time for obeying laws. She slammed her car door with such force that it set off the alarm of the car next to her. The incessant screeching sound it made was the perfect accompaniment to her mood as she approached the field where Marcus was hitting pregame balls to the boys and Anderson was going over the lineup card.

Out of the corner of her eye, she saw Sutton wave from the bleachers. She was sitting next to Birdie. Birdie. Smug Birdie. She would secretly love this. That made Venita even more angry as she stormed across the turf toward Anderson.

Lamar stepped out of the stands and stood in Venita's way. "No parents allowed on the field on game day, Venita."

"Fuck off, Lamar!" Venita pushed past him and continued across the field. "Anderson. Anderson! I need to talk to you!" She was waving the statement from Tupper Investments around in the air before her.

Marcus seemed to recognize the look on his wife's face and realize there was a problem. He missed hitting a ball as his bat swung around, and he lost his balance and fell over. He scrambled to his feet and motioned with his hand for the kids to *take a knee*. All the boys except Wade dropped down to one knee. Wade sat all the way down in the grass. Evidently, he too must have recognized the look on Venita's face and knew he might be taking a knee for quite a while. From his place in the outfield grass, Wade looked in at Birdie's son, Freddie, squatting near second base. They appeared to share a moment of commiseration. The curse of having strong, opinionated mothers.

Marcus tried to cut Venita off at the pitcher's mound, but she was too fast even for him. He could only helplessly trail behind. "What's going on, Venita?" he asked. "What's wrong?"

Anderson already looked guilty before Venita even reached him. Panic registered across his face as his eyes widened and he quickly looked at the boys on the field as if he was thinking *let's not do this here*. "Venita, wait. It's okay," he said. "It's all a misunderstanding."

Venita reached Anderson and threw the statement at him. He fumbled to catch it, but it fell to the dirt at their feet. "Where's our money, Anderson?" she demanded. "Where's our fucking money? Where is it? I'm going to make sure you burn in hell. You will burn!"

Marcus put one of his big hands on Venita's shoulder, trying to calm her, but she pulled away. "He lost our fucking money, Marcus! It's gone!"

"What are you talking about?" Marcus asked as he looked over at Anderson, who suddenly seemed relieved that it was out in the open.

Anderson began mumbling something about "The money. Right, the money. I know. It'll all be okay . . . I'll fix it . . . It's just a liquidity problem . . ." and Venita began screaming something about "This is fraud . . . You will pay us back . . . We're ruined!" As they went about having their odd conversation, Marcus reached down and picked the statement out of the dirt. He dusted it off, almost in a daze.

There in black and white were numbers that had once been in the millions that were now in the thousands. Venita stopped yelling as she saw her husband's face change from confusion to anger to rage. Venita's husband was a man who prided himself on taking care of his family. They had both worked long and hard, and now their empire was reduced to a pitiful sum on a piece of paper with a fancy logo.

Venita knew what was about to happen, even if Anderson never saw it coming. Before she could stop him (and she wasn't sure she wanted to), Marcus slammed his very big fist into Anderson's very cut jaw. Marcus was suddenly all over Anderson with fists flying and limbs flailing. Venita could hear people yelling and just make out a small voice in the outfield saying, "Dad, stop!," but she didn't, or couldn't, bring herself to do anything.

It was a mercilessly long time before Lamar and some men from the bleachers ran in and pulled Marcus off Anderson. It took six of them. Anderson was now covered in dirt, and blood dripped from the corner of his mouth.

"My family . . ." Marcus muttered. "My family . . ."

Her family. Venita thought. Her family.

After the Murder

"So, you didn't threaten to kill him?" Detective Claypool asked.

"No, I did not threaten to kill him," Venita said calmly. Hoping someone burned in hell was very different from threatening to *kill* them. What happened in hell was out of Venita's hands.

"Where were you the night of the murder?"

"At dinner with Bubba Tyree." Venita could see Detective Rattigan's eyes widen a bit at the mention of the famous Bubba Tyree, Marcus's former college coach. She had encountered plenty of men like Rattigan. He was a Georgia boy who had never gone to the University of Georgia but revered their football team as if he had. Under any other circumstances, he would be asking her to get him an autograph.

Instead, Detective Rattigan asked, "Where did you have dinner?"

"Shanks Steakhouse. Call whoever you need to about that."

"Thank you. We *will*," Detective Claypool said pointedly. Like she wanted Venita to know she didn't believe her. Venita wasn't used to people questioning her in any way. She thought, *Don't these people know who I am?* And then she remembered—they knew exactly who she was. Her husband's fame didn't matter when it came to murder.

"Your husband was at the fields the morning after the murder," Detective Claypool said. "He wasn't coaching anymore. Why would he be there?"

"He wasn't a coach, but he was still a father," Venita told them. "Our son still wanted to play with his team. Marcus was just dropping him off for the game. No one told us it was canceled."

"You didn't know the coach had been murdered?"

"No, we didn't."

The detectives looked at one another, and Rattigan closed his notebook. They were through with Venita. For now. As Venita escorted them to the front door, Detective Claypool asked her one last (and Venita thought very inappropriate) question.

"How much money did you lose in Mr. Tupper's fund?"

"Sixteen million dollars," Venita told them.

Claypool nodded without emotion, and the two detectives left. Venita locked the door behind them. She wasn't sure why she did it. Maybe it was habit or maybe it was to keep the detectives from coming back and asking any more questions. Because even Venita thought that sixteen million dollars was a lot of money. Enough to kill for.

CHAPTER

16

SHAY

Shay watched as Tilly Tupper cried. It was a strange sight. Tilly had obviously had a good amount of plastic surgery and Botox, and as she cried, tears filled her eyes and her voice faltered, but the rest of her face betrayed no emotion whatsoever. Her plump lips didn't quiver. Her tight brow didn't furrow. Her tears struggled to fall over her cheek implants. Shay knew that Tilly was genuinely sad. What mother wouldn't be? But the lack of emotion on the woman's face gave the whole thing an air of theatricality rather than genuine grief.

Shay was in Deputy Chief Henderson's office, looking over his shoulder as he played a video on his computer of Tilly Tupper being interviewed by newsman Chris Odi. There was no mistaking why her boss had called Shay in to watch.

". . . if the Atlanta Police Department would do their jobs, I could get some closure," Tilly said on the video.

"You don't think they're doing their jobs?" Odi asked with overly dramatic sincerity.

"Of course they aren't!" Tilly said. "It's typical, isn't it? No one seems to care about us here in Buckhead."

Henderson paused the video and closed his laptop with a sigh. "Do we care?" he asked.

Shay wanted to say something sarcastic about the poor, unloved people of Buckhead, but she held her tongue. "Yes, we care."

"Every day that goes by makes it less likely that we find out who did this," Henderson reminded her.

"We're on it," Shay assured her boss.

"I know you are," Henderson told her as Shay headed out the door. "I'm nothing but grateful, Cousin Claypool. You and your team do the family proud."

Shay wanted to say something sarcastic about that too but kept walking toward the War Room. It was quiet when she entered. Farrell, Anthony, and Hannah were busy at work, or maybe just surfing the web. It was hard to tell since they were always on some sort of electronic device. None of them even looked up when she entered. She stood and stared at them, waiting for any reaction at all, but it was crickets. She finally turned around and slammed the door to the room so hard a gruesome crime scene photo of Anderson Tupper's bloodied body fell off the wall.

"Kids!" she said sternly as they all came to attention. "What the hell is going on? Why haven't we solved this case?"

Again, crickets.

"Anthony," said Shay, turning her attention to young Mr. Oakley. She had decided to go after them one by one. "Any progress breaking into Tupper's computer?"

"Not yet."

"Why is it taking so long?" she asked.

"Because I work for the Atlanta PD, not the CIA."

Farrell laughed, and Shay turned to him. "What about you? You come up with anything? What about Tupper's finances?"

Farrell looked up cautiously. Shay was playing Whack-A-Mole and he had been caught with his head sticking out. "Well, you know, it's pretty much a total clusterfuck." Shay shot him a disapproving look. "Sorry. It's a total disaster. Lots of debt. Lots of debtors. He owed so much money to so many people there was probably a line at his door of people wanting to kill him. This guy should not have been a financial advisor. He should have been . . ." Farrell looked at the driver's license photo of Tupper still on the wall. "He should have been a model or something."

"You think he was good looking?" Anthony asked.

"Yes," Hannah interjected.

"I thought this guy was rich," Anthony said. "Didn't he have a lot of stock in his family's company?"

"Yeah, why wouldn't he just sell it?" Hannah asked.

"The company's for sale," Farrell told them. "Maybe he was waiting for that."

Shay returned to her interrogation of her young charges, zeroing in on Hannah. "What about the cameras?"

"We're pulling footage from all the nearby residences," Hannah reported. "Door cams and stuff. Although some guy who lives right across from the fields won't give us his. Some old dude. Says we're infringing on his rights."

Shay didn't like it when people didn't do what she wanted them to do. No old man was going to impede her investigation. "Get a court order. Take the damn footage from him. Crocket and Tubbs wouldn't put up with this shit."

Anthony looked up from his computer. "Who are Crockett and Tubbs?" he asked. Shay was annoyed by Anthony's youth and chose to ignore him just as Dub came through the door with files under his arms.

"Crocket and Tubbs are only the coolest police detectives ever to work in Miami," Dub said. "We're a lot like them. Fighting crime and looking cool while we do it."

"Whatever you say, Tubbs," Shay said.

"I'm not Tubbs. *You're* Tubbs."

"Why?" Shay asked. "Because I'm Black?"

"Exactly."

Farrell picked up his computer and turned it toward the others. There was a picture of Don Johnson and Philip Michael Thomas, the original *Miami Vice* duo, on the screen. "Crockett and Tubbs," he declared.

"Still don't know," Anthony said.

"See this guy?" Shay asked as she picked up the crime scene photo of Tupper's body from the floor and showed it to the Kids. "Remember him? He was murdered. We're supposed to be finding out who killed him, and it wasn't Crockett or Tubbs."

Dub slid a file across the table to Shay. "I picked up a copy of the lawsuit Anderson filed against his brother. Interesting stuff. Also got a copy of Chatham and Amelia Tupper's divorce filing just for the fun of it. I'll tell you, these folks may be rich, but they sure are white trash."

Anthony turned his own computer around and showed the others a picture of the actors Colin Farrell and Jamie Foxx, both smoldering in dark sunglasses and serious scowls. "Google says *these* guys are Crockett and Tubbs. Boss lady is definitely Tubbs."

Shay continued to ignore Anthony and kept her attention on Dub.

"And guess who we heard from today?" Dub asked. "Chatham Tupper's lawyer. He said we aren't allowed to talk to his client. Not without him."

"Did he, now?"

"And even better," Dub continued. "Guess who his lawyer is? Dan Milton." Shay showed no sign of recognition, but then she wasn't used to dealing with fancy Buckhead lawyers. "Dan *Milton*," Dub said again.

"Mr. Birdie?" Shay asked. "We're going to have to pay Mr. Birdie and his client a visit."

"Can I go with you guys?" Hannah asked hopefully.

"No." Shay empathically shut that down. "No field trips until you guys find the killer." She looked at the Kids and then at Dub. "And, by the way, *I'm* Crocket. He was the cool one."

CHAPTER

17

Five Days Before the Murder

BIRDIE

Frances Abernathy Chipman was born at a Amoco filling station off Highway 441 in Dublin, Georgia. Her family was driving back to Atlanta from their vacation home on Sea Island when Dottie Chipman's water broke. This was an unexpected event that sent her husband, James, into a tirade. He was a judge in Atlanta and was due back that afternoon for a hearing. They were already late because their two young sons had run off in search of alligators that morning and weren't found until two hours later fishing off the sound-side docks. James blamed Dottie for this. "Your only job is to look after the goddamn kids," he admonished her. "It's not that goddamn difficult!" And now this. She couldn't have waited a few more hours until they got to Atlanta to have this goddamn baby?

James wasn't a bad man. He was just a loud man. He said what he said without filter and expected people to be strong enough to take it. It was a great quality for a judge but maybe not as great for a husband and father. What he lacked in subtlety, however, he made up for with generosity. He provided his wife with everything she desired, from a Philip Trammell Shutze mansion in Buckhead to their Sea Island "cottage" to luxury European vacations and no expense spared parties where top-shelf liquor flowed into the mouths of Atlanta's elite. It wasn't all paid for with his meager state judge's salary. Most of his wealth came from dividends collected from his family's Coca-Cola stock.

Baby Frances was called Frances for all of three minutes when one of her brothers declared that the child that had just been born in the back of the family Cadillac looked "all pink and wrinkled" like a newborn bird that had fallen out of its nest. From that moment forward, she would be known as *Birdie*.

Birdie's mother was a petite woman who was much more suited to having a name like *Birdie*. She was elegant and proper and only spoke up when she had a few too many cocktails in the evening, which she often did. Birdie was big and loud and much more like her father. For her third and final child, Dottie was hoping for a doll she could dress up and take to tea at the Swann House in Buckhead. Instead, she got a version of her husband and very quietly, with her small, sweet voice, spent Birdie's childhood letting her know that her daughter wasn't what she had ever wanted. "Bless your heart, you're so much like your father. If I hadn't been there when you were born, I'd wonder if I was even your mother." Mercifully for both mother and daughter, at age thirteen Birdie was sent away to boarding school in Connecticut, where she learned a lot about casual sex, cheap red wine, and bulimia and very little about anything else.

After four unexceptional years at the University of Georgia, Birdie took her marketing degree and headed home to Atlanta, where she got a job at Harry Norman Realtors selling houses. It was something she was terrible at. Sellers didn't like having someone tell them their house was ugly, and buyers didn't like having someone tell them they couldn't afford that ugly house. Birdie was already rich, with a trust fund filled with millions of dollars in Coke stock, and could barely be bothered to show up for open houses.

Dan Milton was from an unremarkable small town in Mississippi called New Albany. He had no Coke stock. No mansion. No pedigree of any kind. He wasn't southern aristocracy. He was one generation removed from a trailer park. He didn't have a lot of the things that Birdie had always been told were important. What he did have, however, was a brain that took him from that small town in Mississippi to Harvard Law School and to one of the top law firms in Atlanta.

On their first date, Dan laughed when Birdie berated a hapless server about the lack of salt on her French fries. When she was told there was a saltshaker on the table, she replied, "And I have a stove at home too, but I came here for you to cook for me!" Birdie was so unlike all the petite princesses he had always dated who were perpetually on a diet. He liked her even more when he realized she was not only one of Atlanta's elites but also the daughter of Judge James Chipman. Birdie already was everything Dan was planning on becoming.

They were married five months later at Trinity Church in Buckhead. Birdie quickly used her not-so-hard-earned real estate license to purchase a 1920 Neel Reid house on Habersham, one of the premiere Buckhead streets that may as well have been paved with Coca-Cola stock. It was a stately stone Georgian classic, and she purchased it for cash with the ease of someone buying a used Hyundai. With the right address, the right house, and the right wife, Dan had everything he needed to rise to the top. Which is exactly what he did. He moved from partnership to partnership until he had a partnership of his own.

The couple quickly had two sons, Chip and Al, who were both carbon copies of their father in looks and temperament and were both shipped off to boarding school, as Birdie had been, a few years after their third son, Freddie, came along. He was an unplanned surprise and, unlike his brothers, was every ounce his mother. That boy was now trying to hide his wide frame behind a thin, budding ginkgo tree as Birdie drove up the back road along the football field behind Kensington Prep. Freddie spotted his mother and scurried to her car.

"Where are the boys?" Birdie asked through the open window.

"They're coming now. They thought we were meeting in front of school," Freddie said as Kolt, Wade, Hampton, and Cash ran down a path behind the school with school bags on their backs and heavy baseball bags on their shoulders. "You're not supposed to pick us up here. It's against the rules."

"I didn't feel like waiting in the car line," Birdie told him. "It's like when the Socialists used to have to wait in line for stale bread in Poland. We're capitalists, Freddie. We don't wait in lines."

"Can I stay over at Kolt's house this weekend?" Freddie asked as he leaned in the passenger window toward his mother, trying to get on her good side. He smiled for maximum effect. Birdie was unmoved by his charms.

"We don't know his parents well enough," she said. "They could be ax murderers."

"Mom! They're not ax murderers."

"Well, they're from California. They could be swingers."

"What are swingers?" Freddie asked as he hung on the door. He had so much energy he was practically doing pull-ups.

"Kolt can stay over at *our* house any time he likes."

"You let me stay at Liam Walker's house and his dad was *arrested*," Freddie reminded his mother with an added degree of mom-shaming.

"That was for tax evasion. That's a victimless crime," Birdie said. "In fact, I kind of admired him for it." She checked her lipstick in the rearview mirror. It was her not so subtle sign to her son that she was through talking about sleepovers and illegal tax shelters. Freddie gave up and pushed away from the door with a frown.

The other boys huffed and puffed their way to the car and greeted Birdie with a barrage of "Hey, Mrs. Milton" and tossed their bags in the back. They all climbed over seats and each other to fill the car. Wade, Hampton, and Cash settled into the third row and Freddie and Kolt sat in the second. Birdie looked at the very open passenger seat.

"No one wants to sit up front?" she asked.

"We've got stuff to do," Freddie declared. "Game stuff." They pulled out their iPhones and were instantly in their own bubble. They were laughing and trash talking and completely absorbed in some shared game that had them chopping the heads off zombies on the streets of San Francisco. Birdie thought they all looked so cute (especially Freddie). They were at such a great age. They were still boys. It would be far less cute when they became men and were still playing video games.

* * *

Birdie pulled her SUV into the parking lot of a pleasant little Buckhead strip mall. It sat in the shadow of the St. Regis hotel and was populated by all the necessities of life: a juice bar, a med spa, a wine shop, and a spin studio, in front of which Birdie parked. It was called Flyte Time, and she could see the toned people of Buckhead riding their bikes to nowhere behind the windows of the studio.

"What are we doing here?" Freddie said as he looked up from his game and appeared surprised to see that they weren't at the baseball fields. "We're supposed to be at practice."

"I have something to take care of first," Birdie told him. "I'll be right back."

The hum of the flywheels on the spin bikes greeted Birdie as she entered the studio. Rows of trim women and men furiously peddled in place, sometimes lifting their very pert bottoms to gain extra speed. Even though they were stationary, Birdie marveled at how they all thought they were going somewhere special, when in fact they were all on the same journey as she was. To the grave. It was likely Birdie would beat them there. She would probably die from heart disease a few years before these people died from boredom. At least Birdie could say on her deathbed that she had never wasted her time spinning in place and had enjoyed every last pint of ice cream and loaf of bread these poor souls had denied themselves.

"Can I help you?" the sculpted young man at the front desk asked Birdie. She could see the look of disappointment in his eyes. Please don't let this size fourteen woman sign up for any classes. She'll ruin the illusion.

"I need to see Brit or Britney," Birdie told him.

"Sure thing. Hold on a sec."

The man walked away and a minute later an attractive young woman appeared. She was wearing a plastic nametag labeled "Brittani" and was the same woman Birdie's husband had been talking to in the parking lot at Chastain Park. Birdie had seen her from afar that day and up close she was even prettier than Birdie had remembered. Prettier and skinnier and younger. The sight of Birdie wiped the smile right off Brittani's face. She seemed rattled and stopped for a moment before proceeding with caution.

"Hi," she said tentatively. "Can I help you?"

"Yes," Birdie said. And then she slapped the woman so hard across the face that Brittani almost fell over. She held on to her now very red cheek as the hum of the spin bikes slowly died out and the riders stopped to stare.

Birdie left without another word. Her heart was racing so fast she feared she'd die of a heart attack right there in front of Flyte Time, which was too much to bear. She'd never give them the satisfaction. Wouldn't give *her* (Brittani with an "I" for Christ's sake!), the satisfaction.

As she approached her car, Birdie could see Freddie looking on with concern. With alarm. He had obviously seen what she had done. She got in the car and pulled on her seatbelt as if nothing had happened.

The other boys were lost in their game, unaware of anything and everything around them, as Freddie hung off the back of Birdie's seat and whispered to her from beside her headrest. "Why did you hit that lady?"

Birdie leaned in closer to her son and hissed an answer in his ear. "Because sometimes people deserve it."

CHAPTER

18

After the Murder

SHAY

SHAY AND DUB waited in Chatham Tupper's office in downtown Atlanta. It was on the top floor of a skyscraper, and all of downtown and the rest of Atlanta to Stone Mountain and beyond lay before them. It was a modern city with touches of the past that had risen from the ashes of the Civil War to rebuild again and again. Old buildings gave way to skyscrapers. Perfectly fine old stadiums were demolished for shiny new ones. Atlanta was forever discarding its wrinkled old wives for hot young mistresses.

"They own every tree out there," Dub said. "As far as you can see."

"Not all of them," Shay argued.

"Most of them." Dub conceded. "Your house is probably built with their lumber."

The door opened and Chatham Tupper and his lawyer, Dan Milton, walked in. Handshakes and dry pleasantries were exchanged, and they all settled into chairs. Chatham was wearing a Brioni suit and sporting a gold Rolex that was identical to the one his brother was wearing when he was murdered. Anderson's was engraved with a graduation message from his parents, and Shay assumed that Chatham's watch was a graduation present as well. She remembered getting a hundred-dollar savings bond when she graduated from college. She momentarily worried about what she would get Darron when he graduated. Definitely not a savings bond, but definitely not a Rolex.

Chatham was exactly what Shay thought he would be. He was the kind of guy who looked over your shoulder when he was talking to you to make sure he wasn't missing out on something better. In contrast, Dan Milton wasn't at all what Shay had expected. For some reason, when she envisioned Birdie's husband, the thought of Foghorn Leghorn, the bombastic cartoon rooster with a deep-fried Southern accent, came to mind. She half expected him to come in wearing a seersucker suit and smoking a cigar. Dan, however, was a handsome man with a soothing and measured demeanor. He was fit and trim and obviously worked out. Shay wondered what a man like this was doing with someone like Birdie.

"Thank you for meeting with us," Shay said.

"I just want to get this over so you can move on and find out who killed my brother," Chatham replied coldly. This man didn't seem to have a need to please anyone, detective or not.

"I promise you we're doing everything we can."

"I'm sure you think you are," Chatham said dismissively.

Chatham's assistant, a comely young woman whose skirt was, perhaps, a little too short, brought bottles of water for everyone. Everyone but Chatham said thank you.

Chatham opened his bottle and took a long sip. He seemed to like keeping people waiting. "So, what can I tell you?" he finally asked.

"Well, let's get the big one over with," Shay said. "Where were you the day your brother was murdered?"

Chatham looked to Dan Milton for a moment and got the go-ahead to answer the question. "I was at the Steeplechase most of the day, and then I was at home with my girlfriend."

"She'll corroborate that?"

"Of course."

"What's her name?" Dub asked. He had his trusty notebook at the ready.

"Heartlee Gilston."

"Mind if we give her a call?"

"My assistant can give you her number."

Dan Milton eyed Shay. He offered up a crooked smile as if to say—*so it's going to be like this, is it?* Maybe Shay had come on too strong. Maybe it was the pressure of coming up with a suspect. The victim's brother certainly was due a little more . . . finesse. "I'm sorry," she said. "I hope you understand that we're just doing our jobs."

"I want you to do your jobs," Chatham told her. Or maybe, *instructed* her.

"Do you have any thoughts on who may have killed your brother?"

"If I were to guess, I'd say it had something to do with money."

"Your brother was having some financial difficulties," Shay said.

"Always."

"But he had a lot of stock in the family company. Worth millions of dollars."

Chatham sighed and shifted in his seat. He seemed annoyed at having to deal with these detectives. "He did," he said. "He looked good on paper."

"I assume he was going to make a lot of money when you sold your company."

"A good assumption."

"Then why was he trying to stop the sale?" Shay asked.

"If only you could ask him that."

"I guess it'll be easier to go through with the sale now," Shay said. She let that hang out there for a moment.

"I guess it will," Chatham replied. He looked at Dan Milton, who tapped on his watch. They were already planning their exit. "My brother's financial problems weren't because of me, Detective. Believe me, my father and my mother and I had given him plenty of money over the years. He didn't want to work in the family company. He left Atlanta after college and opened a bar in Thailand. That failed. He started a venture capital company in Palo Alto. That failed. Then he tried a marijuana dispensary in Colorado and somehow even that failed. He came back here and started an investment fund that I hear failed too. There are plenty of people whose money he lost that you could look at. I'm not one of them."

"It doesn't sound like you liked him very much," Shay observed.

"Doesn't matter if I liked him," Chatham told her. "He was my brother. He was family. He didn't deserve to die for money or any other reason."

"Did you know that Anderson had given your ex-wife over two million dollars in the last year?" Shay asked.

Chatham no longer looked bored. It seemed like he was trying to hide the look of surprise on his face, but he failed. It was obvious that he had no idea what his younger brother had done. "I worked. My brother played golf. My ex-wife shopped. It doesn't surprise me at all."

Dub flipped through the pages in his notebook and jumped in with another question. "Did anything strange happen at the Steeplechase? The night he died?"

"The night he was murdered," Chatham said, correcting Dub. "Other than the general strangeness of being at a steeplechase at all, no, I don't remember anything unusual happening."

"What about the fight?" Shay asked.

"The fight?"

"We heard you two argued at the Steeplechase that night."

"We argued any time we were in the same room together," Chatham told her. "It was nothing."

Dan Milton appeared to decide this was the perfect time to bring things to a conclusion. "We need to finish up here," he said. "Mr. Tupper's answered plenty of your questions. I think your time would be better spent looking for the person who murdered his brother."

"What about you, Mr. Milton?" Shay asked, ignoring his efforts to end the meeting.

"What about *me*?" he asked.

"Where were you the day Anderson was murdered?"

"Am I a suspect?"

"No, we're just talking," said Shay. "You can have a lawyer present, but you know . . ."

"I was at the Steeplechase with my wife and then I was at work."

"On a Saturday?"

"You know what they say," Dan replied. "If you don't come in on Saturday, don't bother coming in on Sunday." Dan and Shay locked eyes. He seemed to be sizing her up as much as she was him.

"Your wife threatened Anderson with bodily harm," Shay said to Dan Milton before she could be pushed out the door and sent on her way.

Dan just smiled. If he was worried, he wasn't showing it. "My wife threatens to kill me on a weekly basis. She's something else, isn't she?"

Shay thought that both Mrs. *and* Mr. Milton were something else indeed.

"Well, thank you for coming here to meet with us," said Dan as he rose from his chair and Chatham followed suit. It was time for the detectives to leave. "I'm sure I speak for Chatham when I say we're grateful for all your hard work."

"Toni, would you get the detectives Heartlee's info?" Chatham asked his assistant, who was hovering by her desk, at the ready.

"Thank you for meeting with us," Dub said, putting his notebook away.

"Oh, do you mind?" Shay asked. "I'm going to get my water."

Shay quickly ducked into Chatham's office and returned with a water bottle, and she and Dub said their goodbyes and headed for the elevator. It was a relief when it came, and they escaped the Tupper Timber offices. Chatham gave Shay the creeps. Maybe because he kind of was a creep.

"He didn't seem too broken up about his brother being murdered," Dub observed.

"No, he did not."

Dub looked at the bottle of water tucked under Shay's arm. "Could I have some of your water?"

"No."

"No?"

"No," Shay said again. "It's not my water. It's Chatham Tupper's water."

"Ah, DNA sample," Dub said. "Smart. That's why you make the big bucks."

"I make two thousand dollars a year more than you," said Shay.

"Well, that's a lot."

As the elevator descended, Shay couldn't help but be struck by its opulence. Walnut wood paneling. Shiny gold floor buttons. Hidden speakers playing some jazz-tinged instrumental version of *Despacito*. Shay looked up at the crystal chandelier hanging over their heads. In a damn elevator. "Honestly," she told Dub, "I've never felt poorer."

CHAPTER

19

Five Days Before the Murder

BIRDIE

For their twentieth wedding anniversary, Birdie purchased her husband the car of his dreams, a classic Old-English-White 1966 E-Type Jaguar roadster with a red interior. In return, Dan got Birdie a month at a fat farm. It was disguised as the Canyon Ranch Spa in Tucson, Arizona, but Birdie knew she wasn't being sent there for a massage. "Since Freddie's our last kid," Dan said with a heart full of generosity, "you'll finally be able to lose that extra weight you've been carrying around." Birdie went to Canyon Ranch and came back three pounds heavier.

Birdie couldn't help but think of her stay at Canyon Ranch as chocolate ice cream dripped down the side of her wrist and fell to join other drips of Ben & Jerry's New York Super Fudge Chunk on the linen Maker&Son sofa in her living room. Birdie didn't care about the growing stain. Either her housekeeper would use her magic to clean off the offending spot or Birdie would have the sofa reupholstered. Maybe she would buy a new sofa. What did it matter?

Headlights flashed across the front of the house, and the sound of Dan's car rattled the room. It's noisy six-cylinder engine, which had once, to Birdie, represented Dan's virility, was now obnoxiously loud. Birdie continued to scoop out spoonfuls of ice cream and slowly transfer them to her mouth. She licked the spoon dry as the door opened and then slammed shut. Her husband was home. Hooray.

Dan was carrying an armload of files as he entered the room. Birdie thought that was a nice touch. He had been "working late" so, of course, he needed the files. Birdie laughed at him. It was a little laugh. A scoff, really. Did he really think he needed the files to keep up this ruse? He dropped the files on the table and quickly came across the room to his wife. He stood over her with one hand clenched tightly.

"How was your day, honey?" Birdie asked as she took another small scoop of the ice cream.

"You assaulted a spin instructor?" Dan asked in disbelief.

"I slapped *your* spin instructor," Birdie corrected him. "The one you're fucking."

Dan looked shocked. "I'm not . . . I'm not fucking anyone," he said.

"Least of all me."

"You think I'm sleeping with every woman I talk to. That's a bit of a cliché, Birdie. You're better than that."

"I'm not your wife, Dan," Birdie told him. "I'm your cash cow."

"You're my wife. You're my partner. I married you because I loved you. I still love you, but Jesus, Birdie, you can't go around hitting people." Birdie turned away and continued eating her ice cream. This only spurred him on. He began pacing back and forth in front of the sofa. He was appealing to a jury of one. "You're being paranoid, Birdie. You've done this before. You get down on yourself and you, you, you look for some way to lash out. But all you're doing is hurting me, the man who cares about you more than anyone else in the world." Dan sat on the edge of the coffee table across from Birdie. He reached over and took the ice cream from her and set it aside. He lifted her hand and slowly licked a drip from her palm then held her hand against his cheek. "I love you, Birdie. Only you," he said, teeming with sincerity. "You've been unhappy for a long time now. You haven't been my good old Birdie."

When Dan was sweet, when he smiled and spoke softly to her, he reminded her of the man she fell in love with. The man who loved her. Had she forgotten who he was? Had she been wrong?

"I think you just need a break, Birdie," he said gently. "You need to get healthy again. You should go back to Canyon Ranch. Maybe stay a little longer this time."

The fucker! Birdie wasn't going back to fucking Canyon Ranch. If she did, she would burn it to the ground!

She looked passively into his eyes, although he probably thought she was looking at him adoringly. "I'm sorry I slapped your spin instructor," she said. "I won't do that again." No, next time she just might slit the woman's throat!

"Good," he said. He patted her shoulder a few times like she was an obedient dog.

He really was a very good lawyer. He had talked his way out of dozens of speeding tickets. He had talked his way into her life and a seat at the head table in Atlanta society. He couldn't, however, talk his way out of this. Birdie had learned to see through Dan's lawyerly bullshit. She didn't have proof yet, but she knew the truth. She realized that she was, indeed, his cash cow. She had spent enough time in the cattle yard, however, to know when she was about to be slaughtered.

CHAPTER

20

Four Days Before the Murder

VENITA

Venita pulled two brown sugar cinnamon Pop-Tarts out of the toaster and placed them on a plate. Pop-Tarts. How many years had it been since she had made those? Was it in college? High school? She had certainly never made them for her son, yet here they were sitting on a plate getting cold while she waited for him to finish getting ready for school. She had tossed them in her shopping cart next to a bag of marshmallows and on top of an industrial-sized plastic container of cheese puffs. Whenever Venita was feeling down, junk food was her salvation. Now she wasn't sure there was enough processed cheese in the world to brighten her day.

Marcus fiddled with the Keurig at the counter behind her. He pushed the button to open the top of the coffee machine over and over, but it wouldn't budge. She could hear him huffing with frustration. Everything had been frustrating lately. Everything.

He finally got the machine open but dropped the small cartridge of Dunkin' Donuts vanilla roast (he had always been a

Dunkin' kind of guy) on the floor where it rolled under the edge of the kitchen island. "God damn it!" he said as he tried to retrieve it and it kept sliding out of reach. He finally snapped it up and returned to the machine. Now the cartridge refused to go into its slot. He finally smashed it in with his fist and exploded in rage. He grabbed his coffee cup off the counter and sent it flying into a nearby wall, where it shattered and scattered across the kitchen floor.

It had been like this lately. Since they found out Anderson had lost most of their money. Marcus had been in such a constant state of stress, Venita was sure he was going to have a heart attack. Anderson had promised to pay them back, but Venita knew that was highly unlikely. All she could see in their future were lawsuits and hearings and gossip.

"What are we going to do?" Marcus said. It seemed like he could barely look at Venita. Like he was embarrassed or ashamed.

"We're going to do what we've always done," Venita told him. "Fight."

Wade entered the kitchen with caution. "Is everything okay?" he asked.

"Everything's fine," Venita told him. "Have some breakfast." She handed Wade one of the Pop-Tarts. He looked at it like she had just given him a crack pipe.

"Pop-Tarts?" he asked.

This sent Marcus into a further rage. "Yes, Pop-Tarts!" he yelled at his son and at the gods. "It's all I ate when I was a kid. If they were good enough for me, they're good enough for you!"

"Marcus . . ." Venita said, gently admonishing him as Wade dutifully took a bite of the alien breakfast treat.

Marcus took a deep breath. He looked at his wife. She knew this wasn't him. She smiled and he smiled back. Marcus put his huge hand on Wade's shoulder. "Sorry, buddy," he told his son. "You didn't deserve that." He grabbed the other Pop-Tart off the plate on the counter. "I'm going."

"Where?" Venita asked.

"To work," Marcus replied. "Gotta make some money."

Marcus left his family in the kitchen as Venita got the broom and dustpan out of the pantry and worked to clean up the pieces of the shattered coffee cup. Wade pulled the trash can out from under the sink and helped her. He searched for the bigger pieces and threw them in the trash. He had always been thoughtful.

"Are we going to have to sell the house?" he asked. Sometimes he was too full of thought.

"No," Venita told him. "Why do you ask that?"

"Aren't we broke?"

"No, we're not broke."

They weren't broke, but they certainly were no longer rich. Truthfully, Venita didn't know if they would have to sell the house or not. She didn't know if they had a lifetime of Pop-Tarts ahead of them. She did know that her husband was filled with rage, and it was eating away at him, day by day. Their lives had changed. Her husband had changed. And she feared what he might do.

SUTTON

A call from her bedridden husband had Sutton making a stop at the Tack Room. It was a restaurant on the edge of Chastain Park that was favored by the locals for lunch and dinner but mobbed by Buckhead Betties for coffee and pastries in the morning. There was nothing like getting a flaky hot croissant before a rigorous walk around the park, followed by a chaser of laxatives.

The Tack Room was in a rustic-chic clapboard building that had once been a small store that sold goods produced on the farmland it stood upon. The current restaurant was now surrounded by multimillion-dollar homes and sold chai lattes rather than pickled onions and vine-ripe tomatoes. Sutton surveyed the long line of fit young women in jogging bras and chunky Loewe sneakers that stretched out the door and across the patio. Novices, she thought as she wormed her way past them, stopping to say an exaggerated "Hey!" to many along the way and apologizing that she was desperate to use the bathroom as she instead walked inside to the front counter like the Buckhead pro she was.

She spotted Kira at the front of the line. She was ordering a matcha tea and gluten-free banana bread. It was such a California thing to order, Sutton thought as she squeezed in next to Kira at the counter and greeted her like a long-lost friend.

"Kira!"

"Hi, Sutton."

"How's the writing going?"

"It's going," Kira said. "If I don't finish soon, I'm going to have to give them their money back."

Sutton had no idea what Kira was talking about but nodded along. "We should get together for coffee sometime."

"How about now?" Kira asked. "I'd love a reason to procrastinate."

"I can't. I have to get back to my husband." And she did. He'd already texted her five times since she left the house that morning. "Which reminds me . . ." Sutton said as she turned to the cashier. "I need an Americano and a *pain au chocolat*." The last part came out as *pain*, as in gain, instead of the correct pronunciation of *pan*.

"How's he doing?" asked Kira.

"You're so sweet to ask," Sutton said. "He's still alive."

"Always a good thing."

Sutton wondered if it really was but wasn't going to share that with Kira. "Yeah, it is."

The cashier put both Sutton's and Kira's orders down on the counter and asked if they were paying together. Sutton pretended to reach for her wallet but knew that Kira would insist on paying. Which she did.

"Thanks, Kira," Sutton said. "You're the best. I can't wait to read the new book." Even though she had yet to read the old ones. "Have a good day."

"You too."

Sutton was preparing to make a quick exit when she noticed Anderson sitting at a table in the far corner of the patio. A china cup filled with coffee (no paper cups for that boy, she thought) and a selection of pastries were on the table in front of him alongside an old-school paper copy of the *Wall Street Journal*. Buzzing at his side was a pretty brunette. She was impressively lean and toned from what must have been endless Pilates sessions and was about a foot taller than Sutton. Sutton hated her on principle.

"Anderson!" Sutton squealed as she approached his patio perch, planted a kiss on both his cheeks, and ran her finger across a red mark left over from his fight with Marcus. She thought it made him look rugged. Sutton had never made a secret of the fact that she had a teenage-girl-sized crush on him. He was one of the men she fantasized about most when she was having sex with her husband. Either Anderson or Lucius Malfoy. It must have been something with the hair.

"Good morning, Sutton," Anderson said in all his glorious blondness.

"I'll let you get back to your reading," the woman said with a come-hither smile. She finally turned to Sutton and chirpily said, "Have a nice day."

"You too!" said Sutton, out-chirping the woman. Sutton wiggled her way into a seat across from Anderson. "Are you sleeping with her?"

"Not at this moment."

"You'll have sex with her, but you won't have sex with me?"

"You're not my type, Sutton."

"What type is that?" Sutton asked. She had yet to find the man who didn't find her their type.

"The married type," Anderson clarified.

Sutton rolled her eyes. It was like Anderson had *accused* her of being married, rather than just stated an inconvenient fact. "So, are you going to the Steeplechase?"

"I'm on the board. I have to be there."

"Good. I like it when you dress up. Nothing like Anderson Tupper in an ascot."

"I'm not wearing an ascot."

"You're no fun anymore, Anderson," Sutton told him. "You used to be the kinda guy who would wear an ascot with, like, pastiche."

Sutton's iPhone dinged with a text message, and she looked down to see it was her husband. Again. She let out an exaggerated sigh of annoyance. "It's Chuck. I need to get him his chocolate croissant before it gets stale."

"Not exactly the thing someone who just had a heart attack should be eating, is it?" Anderson asked.

Silly Anderson.

"You only live once," Sutton reminded him. "I'll see you at the next practice."

"Make sure Cash doesn't forget his glove."

"Oh my God, you act like I'm his *mother* or something," she joked. Before Sutton left, she snatched a half-eaten croissant from the plate on Anderson's table. "The least you could do is go down on me," she said, joking again—or maybe not.

She pranced across the patio past the many preening Buckhead Betties. She didn't get to have sex with Anderson, but she still felt satisfied. A few minutes flirting with him was better than an entire evening with her hard to please, hard to be pleased *by* octogenarian husband.

As Sutton blew past the peons in line at the Tack Room and headed for the parking lot, she looked back and saw Kira now sitting with Anderson at his table on the patio. And Anderson was smiling. Why was Anderson smiling? He hadn't smiled when he was talking to *her*. Were they flirting? Kira should have known better than to flirt with Anderson. If anyone was going to have amazing sex with him, it was going to be Sutton.

Sutton suddenly thought that famous people could be so phony.

CHAPTER

21

After the Murder

SHAY

SHAY'S FEDORA HAD pride of place on the top of the dresser in her bedroom. She gently brushed it off every night before she went to bed so it would be good to go in the morning. Every Atlanta homicide detective was given a fedora upon completing their first investigation. Shay had forgotten hers that morning in her rush to get to the office and felt naked without it. As she returned home to retrieve it, her phone rang with a call from Dub.

"An arrest was just entered into the database," he said. "Amelia Tupper. Arrested for *assault*."

Shay was surprised, to say the least. Amelia was the last of the bunch Shay thought would be arrested for anything. Birdie Milton? That was a no-brainer. But Amelia Tupper? She was too much of a princess.

"Who did she assault?" Shay asked.

"Her ex-husband," Dub told her. "It happened on March 19th."

The date was three days prior to Anderson's murder. "Why are we just hearing about this now?" Shay asked as she got out of her car and walked toward her house. An assault on the victim's brother was noteworthy not just because it made for good gossip but because it could be integral to the case. It was an assault against a Tupper, and another Tupper was dead. Shay knew there were few coincidences when murder was involved.

"The arresting officer just logged it," Dub said.

Shay was about to explode. One of the things she really hated (along with animal cruelty and tailgaters) was sloppy police work. "Well, we could go talk to the arresting officer and spend all our time telling him what an incompetent loser he is, or we can just go pay Amelia Tupper a visit."

"I say we go see Amelia Tupper," Dub declared.

"I'll be back in twenty minutes," Shay said as she ended the call and let herself in to her house. She could hear music coming from Darron's room. It was something that was offensive to her ears by some new artist she wasn't familiar with, which could have been anyone who recorded music after 1992. She thought all the new songs sounded exactly alike and wondered if her parents thought the same thing about the music she listened to when she was a teenager. She also wondered if she was turning into her mother.

Hovering on the other side of Darron's door, Shay could also smell the stench of marijuana to go along with the objectionable music. She didn't like either of these things. She thought about knocking first but entered unannounced instead. Darron was on his bed, propped up on a bunch of pillows, reading his book.

"What the hell's going on in here?" Shay asked. She turned off Darron's Bluetooth speaker and brought the loud music to a merciful end. She stood before him with her arms crossed, then realized that's exactly what her mother used to do and uncrossed them. That felt uncomfortable. So she crossed them again.

"It's just weed, Mom," Darron said. "Just relax, okay? It's not like it's fentanyl or something."

They had had this conversation before, but that wasn't going to stop Shay from having it again. "It all starts with marijuana . . ."

"Don't, Mom . . ."

"First it's marijuana and then it's cocaine and then you're in a gutter with a needle stuck in your arm."

"That's so ignorant!"

"I am not ignorant," Shay said. "I've seen it myself. I've seen worse. You have no idea. Don't you call me ignorant."

"I didn't mean *you* were ignorant," Darron clarified. "I meant your opinion was ignorant."

"It's not an opinion. It's a fact." Shay gave Darron the once-over. He was wearing a T-shirt and sweatpants. Lounge wear! She noticed his toenails hadn't been clipped. For some reason this really bothered her. Her son was lounging around in his bedroom smoking pot and not cutting his toenails. It was all very postapocalyptic. "It's time for you to go back to school."

Darron almost fell off the bed. "Mommm, no!" he pleaded. "I can't. I can't concentrate there."

"Maybe you shouldn't be smoking pot . . ."

"It's not that," he said. He was whining now. "I don't know. I don't know how to explain it. I'm always on edge there. I'm always worried about, you know, about *him*. About him coming after me."

"Don't you think it's just as easy for him to come here?" she asked him. Shay sat down on the edge of the bed next to her son. She knew he had suffered real trauma, but she also felt that he was leaning into it rather than away from it. "Listen, Darron, I understand that something very bad happened to you. It happened to me too. Shit happens to everyone. Your shit may be worse than some, but it's also better than some. Now, I'm going to find you a therapist at school, and I'm going to make sure the police there know to look after you. You won't always be able to run away from the things you're afraid of. You're going to have to look after yourself."

"But Mom . . ."

"*We are not victims!*" Shay said firmly. It came from the depths of her soul and hung in the air for a good long moment. "Now, you need to book your flight back, okay?" She put her hand on his chest and said it again, quietly. "We are not victims."

CHAPTER

22

After the Murder

AMELIA

Amelia's house was off Blackland Road, in the heart of Buckhead and one mile and one zip code away from her old home with Chatham to the west. It was a seven-million-dollar 1920s faux-Tudor behemoth that she intended to remodel into a showplace that would make her former house look like a tract home in Des Moines. Those renovations, however, started and ended with the kitchen. It was somewhere between the lava stone countertops and the Carrara marble floor that she ran out of money. The circa 1999 Sub-Zero fridge that was still in the kitchen was a constant reminder her life was headed in the wrong direction.

A container of shredded parmesan cheese was in the middle of the kitchen island next to a bowl of salad with fancy lettuces like frisée and escarole. Amelia put the finishing touches on a serving dish filled with steaming penne pasta with pesto sauce and placed it next to the salad as Hampton, Poppy, and Auggie looked on. Auggie fidgeted on his tall barstool and threatened to topple over at any moment. He was only adding to Amelia's already frayed nerves.

"Everybody dig in."

Poppy looked at the plastic container of shredded cheese with disdain even as Hampton pulled the lid off and poured half the container on his pasta. "Is that from Target?" Poppy asked.

"Yes," Amelia told her daughter as she tended to Auggie and filled his small bowl with pasta.

"That's disgusting," Poppy declared.

"There's nothing wrong with Target," Amelia assured her.

"Clementine Tomlinson got her school backpack from Target this year," Poppy told her mother as she picked at her pasta, sweeping for landmines. "Everyone stopped talking to her."

"Well, that's ridiculous." Amelia tried to spoon some of the offending cheese onto Auggie's pasta, but he pushed her hand away.

"What's ridiculous is that we eat cheese from Target and live in 30342," Poppy said, continuing to offer up her best Veruca Salt impersonation. "I want to move back to 30327. That's where all the good people live." Even though both zip codes were in Buckhead, evidently among nine-year-olds in the know, 30342 just didn't cut it anymore. "Uncle Anderson lived in 30342. Look what happened to him."

Hampton had finally had enough of his snooty younger sister. "Don't be such a moron."

Poppy turned to her brother with death-ray eyes. "All my friends think you're ugly."

"Shut up!"

"Grow up."

Amelia stared down into her own plate of pasta. When her daughter was in this kind of mood, which was more often than not, she reminded Amelia so much of Chatham that Amelia would get a knot in her stomach. Despite Amelia's valiant efforts, Poppy was Chatham's daughter. Amelia could only take solace in the fact that Hampton was very much her son. Most of Auggie's life had been lived with his parents separated and at war. He had shown no signs of being like either Amelia or Chatham. Amelia thought he would either turn out to be the sanest one in the family or a serial killer.

Hampton looked across to his mother. He was always checking her emotional temperature. She depended on him for too much of her happiness. She knew that. An eleven-year-old boy shouldn't have to be his mother's rock, but he was just that. Sometimes she felt as if she had no one else.

Poppy, however, wasn't finished. She rarely ever was. She liked being the center of all drama. "Dad says he's going to take away our trust funds if we don't move back in with him." She pulled the pin on that grenade and watched it explode on the island before her.

"Poppy!" Hampton screeched. Amelia could tell by his tone that Hampton already knew this news.

"It's true," Poppy said. "And, honestly, Mom, I don't want to lose my trust fund. That would be a foolish financial move."

Amelia grappled with the news for a moment as little Auggie began to cry. She didn't know whether to tend to him or fire back at Poppy. She chose Poppy. "You're not moving in with your father. And legally, he can't take away your trust fund. That's what trusts are for. To keep parents' hands off the money!"

"Well, I still want to move in with him," Poppy said. She ate her pasta as if she'd said nothing at all.

"We're not moving back with Dad," Hampton told his sister.

"Fine. You can stay here. I don't care. I want to go."

Hampton and Poppy began arguing back and forth and Auggie continued to cry as Amelia sat silently. She already knew it had been decided. She wouldn't be able to keep Poppy from moving back in with Chatham. She wouldn't have been surprised if her daughter already had her suitcases packed.

Auggie's crying and Poppy's bullying finally pushed Hampton over the edge. He turned to his brother and screamed, "Auggie! What are you crying about?"

Tears ran down Auggie's red cheeks. He gasped for breath but somehow pushed it out. "I . . . don't want to lose my truss fun!"

"You don't even know what a trust fund is!"

This just made Auggie cry even more.

Hampton and Poppy traded jabs, and Auggie lamented the possible loss of a trust fund he didn't know he had. Amelia rubbed her eyes. She was exhausted. Maybe it would be better if they all went and lived with their father. Then she would be free to disappear. She could sell the house and buy a condo in some uncomplicated place like Traverse City, Michigan, or Boulder, Colorado. Some place no one knew her. She could shop at Target without being judged and live a simple life. Maybe she'd have a small garden. Maybe she would take karate lessons. Maybe she'd fall in love with a handsome sensei. He would be incredibly hot and ride a Harley. She would cook him steaks on a Green Egg on the back patio. They'd have sex, mostly in the missionary position, and he'd be satisfied. And she'd wear flip-flops. Not while having sex, of course, but every day during the summer. Maybe Amelia was secretly a flip-flop-wearing kinda gal.

Amelia's drift off into an uncomplicated world was interrupted by the sound of the doorbell ringing. She couldn't get up quick enough. Maybe it was the UPS man. That would be the next best thing to a Harley riding sensei from Traverse City.

Amelia opened the front door half expecting to see a dashing man in brown shorts. Instead, the large wooden door with its wrought iron handle swung open to reveal Detectives Claypool and Rattigan. Amelia's heartrate spiked. The appearance of these two at her door couldn't be good news.

"Evening, Mrs. Tupper," Detective Rattigan said.

"I didn't know we had an appointment," Amelia said, trying to remain calm.

"We didn't," Detective Claypool said in return. It was a power play to show up at Amelia's house. "We were just in the neighborhood and had a few questions, so we thought we'd swing by."

"My children are home. We're having dinner."

"It won't take long."

Amelia stepped out onto the front porch and closed the door behind her. She didn't want her children to be subjected to this intrusion, but she especially didn't want Poppy to know about it and tell Chatham. Despite her fantasies of a simple life in the Midwest, Amelia didn't need to give her ex-husband any reason to petition to take the children away.

Detective Rattigan consulted his notebook. Amelia wondered what juicy things were written in it. Things about her and her friends. About her and her enemies. She wondered what they had discovered about Anderson. "It's come to our attention that you were arrested for assault three days before your brother-in-law was murdered."

"I was arrested for assaulting my ex-husband," Amelia said. "But I'm sure you know that. I'm sure you also know that the charges were dropped."

"The report said you pushed your ex-husband down a flight of stairs," Detective Claypool said. "He's the brother of a murder victim. We wouldn't be doing our jobs if we didn't follow up on it."

"I didn't push him down the stairs."

"Would you like to tell us what *did* happen?" Rattigan asked.

Three Days Before the Murder

There was a game being played on every field at Chastain Park. Pint-sized Pee Wee players were hitting off a tee on the smallest of the fields, and fourteen-year-old boys were competing in the Bronco League on the Field of Diamonds, the premier, largest field. On a medium-sized field somewhere in between, the Vikings were facing the Bobcats, a team from out of town who had come to Atlanta on their spring break. They wore tiger-orange jerseys, and their white pants were stained with many games' worth of dirt. Most of the Vikings' pants were bright white. If the housekeepers of Buckhead couldn't get the boy's pants clean, it was an unofficial rule that the players should wear a new pair.

Hampton Tupper was on his eighth pair of pants that season. Amelia had purchased twenty pairs of the same white pants at the beginning of the year. The purchase fell under the "essential items" clause for the children in her divorce agreement. She had wanted to order forty pairs just to stick it to Chatham, but the store ran out of Hampton's size. Instead, she ordered a hundred pairs of socks and had him wear a new pair to every game and every practice. It was the little things that now gave her the most pleasure.

Amelia was on her usual perch halfway up the bleachers with Birdie at her side. They were both bundled up against the evening chill. Birdie wore her husband's ski jacket, and Amelia had on an old Herno puffer. Amelia liked the weeknight games under the field lights. The park was peaceful at night. The sounds of bats hitting balls and coaches calling out to their players carried farther in the night air, and it almost felt like being at a big-league game with the electronic scoreboard glowing in center field.

The Vikings trailed by one in the bottom of the sixth, which for this age in Little League would be the final inning. Hampton would be the first batter scheduled to come up. He was at the heart of the order and one of the team's best hitters. It was always a relief to the home team's parents when he came to the plate, with a good chance he would get on base. Amelia watched as Anderson gave Hampton a few last pointers. It was probably something along the lines of "just do your thing" or "you got this." Some form of encouragement.

"Oh, look, wave . . ." Birdie said as she executed a "royal wave" with her hand ramrod straight and turning gently like the rudder of a boat. Kira was waving at them from the bottom of the bleachers as she settled into a seat in the first row. "Does she think she's too famous to sit with us? I got one of her books. J. K. Rowling she is not. I could barely get through the first chapter. There was a dragon in it, for Christ's sake. Why the hell does every book have a damn dragon? It was in space! A space dragon!"

As Birdie complained about the space dragon and something about women from California all being bisexual, Amelia watched as Anderson hovered along the fence near Kira and the two chatted and smiled. Anderson flirted with every woman, especially the team moms, so it wasn't a surprise. Watching this new woman on the scene get attention, though, just reminded Amelia how she was yesterday's news.

Amelia's attention returned to the game with the swack of a bat solidly hitting a baseball. Hampton hit a double to left field. It whizzed past a shortstop who looked like he was sixteen instead of eleven and rolled to the fence below a sign advertising Land Rover of Buckhead. As the crowd in the bleachers voiced their approval with cheering and a few "Way to go, Ham!" calls, Hampton jogged to second base with ease. Amelia daydreamed for a moment that Hampton would someday be in the big leagues and would buy Villa Rosa back for her. Then she began to think about how she would probably hate his future wife and the daydream evaporated into the night air.

Next, Freddie walked up to the plate like he owned it (which, given the massive donation the Miltons had made to CYB, he kind of did). "You got this, Freddie!" Birdie screamed out. "Let's go!" As Freddie worked his way to a walk ("Just as good as a hit," Birdie declared), Amelia's daughter, Poppy, called up to her from the side of the bleachers.

"Mom! Mom, Auggie's game is over."

"Did they win?" Amelia asked as she looked over the side to see Auggie tugging at his pants and motioning toward the bathroom.

"I don't know," Poppy said. "Who cares? They're four."

"I have to pee!" Auggie said as he danced in place.

"Would you please take him to the bathroom?" Amelia asked Poppy.

"I'm not his nanny!" Poppy replied with her fine-tuned petulance.

"Please, Poppy." Amelia mustered as much patience as she could. "Before it's too late."

Poppy grabbed Auggie by the hand and dragged him toward the bathrooms as Amelia turned back to the game. Wade was now at bat. Amelia thought he looked a little more at ease now that his father was no longer the assistant coach. Instead, Lamar roamed the baselines as Anderson's second-in-command.

"Why is Wade still on the team?" Birdie asked.

"Just because Marcus quit doesn't mean Wade should miss out," Amelia said with a surprising amount of maturity.

"That's exactly why he shouldn't be playing," Birdie countered. "The only reason Anderson even drafted him was because of Marcus. He's so awful I'm not even sure he's Marcus's son. I think Venita may have been playing the field, if you know what I mean."

Amelia knew what she meant.

To everyone's surprise, Wade actually hit the ball and took off toward first base as Hampton headed for third and Freddie to second to load the bases. Wade claimed his base and smiled like he had hit a home run.

"There you go, Wade!" Anderson called from the dugout.

From the Bobcats shortstop, however, came a different kind of comment: "The monkey finally got a hit." He called it out in a joking way, like it was so obviously hilarious and everyone would congratulate him on his comedic genius. No one laughed.

Amelia wasn't sure she had heard that right, but Freddie, standing on second base, definitely did. He stepped off the base and began walking toward the shortstop. Even though the boy was much taller than Freddie, Freddie showed no fear. He was a Chihuahua nipping at the legs of a Rottweiler. "What the fuck did you just say?" Freddie spit out.

The shortstop didn't answer with words. Instead, he used one hand to grab hold of Freddie's head and pushed Freddie so hard he fell straight back onto his back in the grass. Before the umpire or coaches could even react, Hampton abandoned third base and ran across the infield, crashing into the shortstop. They both tumbled to the ground and began trading blows. Anderson stepped toward the field but was pushed aside as the bench of boys cleared behind him. Kolt and Cash led the charge as the Vikings ran out and met a contingent of Bobcats on the field. None of them really knew how to fight, but it made for an impressive brawl nonetheless, as hats and helmets and dirt and arms all mixed together to form the Little League melee of the season.

"Kick his ass, Freddie!" Birdie called out from the bleachers.

Amelia watched as Anderson and Lamar ran onto the field to stop the brawl. Anderson grabbed Hampton and swung him off the pile. Amelia looked at Hampton's pants. They were now filthy. Those would certainly be going into the trash. Hampton looked her way and she nodded, giving him the all-clear.

As things were sorted out on the field, Amelia turned toward the bathrooms to check on Poppy and Auggie. To her dismay, they were standing by the adjacent field with Chatham and his girlfriend, Heartlee Gilston, whom he had brought back with him as a souvenir from his stay at a sex addiction clinic in Wickenburg, Arizona. Heartlee looked so much like Amelia she could have been her sister. Her *younger* sister.

"Game!"

Amelia turned back to the field. "What happened?" she asked.

"I think the game was just called on account of racism," Birdie told her with glee. "We win!"

The umpire had, indeed, given the win to the Vikings. It was the usual custom after a game for both teams to line up on the field and acknowledge each other with high fives or low fives or no fives and just a "good game," but the Vikings were refusing to participate despite pleas from Anderson and Lamar. They silently packed up their gear and formed a protective semicircle around Wade. Anderson finally gave up and shrugged his shoulders at the Bobcats' coach, who was standing with his team in the middle of the infield.

"Let's get out of here," the visiting coach told his players, and they all shuffled off.

Amelia and Birdie and the other parents went down to the field to congratulate their little warriors. The boys were mostly somber. They were taking their cue from Wade, who had his cap pulled down low over his eyes.

Freddie dragged his equipment bag toward the women. He was filthy and bruised and resembled a coal miner coming out of a tunnel after a long day's work.

"Well done, Freddie," Birdie told her son with a hearty pat on his back. "But next time just kick 'em in the balls."

Kolt and Wade came off the field together and joined the waiting Kira. "You guys want to get something to eat?" she asked them.

"Can you just take me home?" Wade asked in return.

"You got it."

Kira smiled at Amelia as she escorted the boys away from the field. Amelia felt bad for not really liking Kira but not bad enough to try to like her. There was something off about Kira, and it was more than her being a stranger in a strange land. Kira was always uncomfortable. She was in a constant state of fidgeting, an awkward being who made Amelia nervous. Amelia would be relieved when the season was over, and she would no longer be forced to interact with this woman from California.

"Hi, Mom," Hampton said as he sulked toward his mother. "Sorry about all that."

"You have nothing to be sorry for," Amelia told him.

"Hey, Am," Anderson said as he greeted Amelia. He put his arm around Hampton's shoulder. "Mind if I talk to your mom for a minute?"

Amelia took a deep breath and steadied herself. She was pretty sure they weren't going to be talking about the snack schedule for the upcoming games. "Ham, go find your sister and brother and I'll meet you at the car. I'm parked up the stairs on Wieuca." She handed her car keys to her son, and he headed off through the tangle of parents and players in search of his siblings, looking back once to check on his mother. She smiled reassuringly and he continued on his way.

"The Wileys are going to sue me," Anderson told her, suddenly sending things in an entirely different direction. No more good ole Coach Tupper. His mood had darkened instantly.

"How much do you owe them?" Amelia asked.

"A lot."

Amelia was tired. She had tried to convince herself she was Wonder Woman fighting for justice. Now she was beginning to wonder if she had been Don Quixote all along. "Maybe we should just let Chatham sell the company."

"For half of what it's worth?" Anderson said. "I'm not going to let him screw us. Besides, I'd barely end up with enough money to get out of debt."

"Then what are you going to do?"

"I'll figure something out," he said. "I just wanted you to know that things may get rough."

"*Get* rough? It hasn't exactly been a picnic so far."

"Don't worry," Anderson told her. "I'll take care of everything."

At least Amelia could take comfort in the fact that things couldn't get much worse. "Good game," she said.

Amelia walked away toward the old concrete steps that led up to Wieuca Road and her Escalade. She decided to put all thoughts of her financial difficulties and her ex-husband out of her head. Just for one evening. She would take the kids for ice cream. They wouldn't worry about calories or sugar or financial ruin, and they would all pretend like everything was going to be okay.

And then she saw Chatham.

He and his girlfriend were now standing at the back of Amelia's SUV with the kids, and Chatham and Hampton were having an argument. Amelia couldn't hear what they were saying, but she could tell by her son's agitated body language that he was in distress. She quickened her pace and hurried up the steps.

Heartlee stood off to the side with Poppy and Auggie. This replacement Amelia was holding her children's hands and wearing the same kind of long, flowery dress that Amelia always wore. Like she was Amelia 2.0. Amelia wanted to lunge at her and gouge her eyes out. The thought lingered in her mind as she climbed the park's steps. Knoxville Amelia would have taken this bitch out! Buckhead Amelia, though, stayed composed as she reached the top of the stairs and stood protectively between her ex-husband and her beloved son.

"What's going on?" she asked in as calm a manner as she could muster.

"We're going to take the kids to Mellow Mushroom," Chatham said. Like it was a done deal. Which it wasn't.

"I don't want to go!" Hampton said. Like it was a done deal. And it *was*.

"Listen, son," said Chatham. He emphasized *son* like it was a curse word. "I'm your father and you do what I say."

"I do what Mom says. I don't want to go with you. Or *her*." Hampton looked at Heartlee for a fraction of a second, then looked down at the ground. He had made his point.

Amelia moved closer to Hampton. "You don't have the kids today," she told her ex-husband.

Poppy piped up from the peanut gallery. "I want to go get pizza."

"We're getting ice cream," Amelia told her, flat out, in a tone that meant there would be no argument. "You kids get in the car. Now. Let's go." Hampton grabbed Auggie by the hand and began loading him into his booster seat in the back of the SUV. Poppy lagged behind. She looked between her two parents, surveying the battlefield. The stern look on the face of General Mom, however, finally forced her to choose sides. She reluctantly climbed into the SUV next to Auggie while Hampton took his place of honor in the front passenger seat and slammed the door closed.

"You're poisoning Hampton," Chatham said, stopping Amelia as she began to head around to the driver's side of the car. "You've turned him against me."

"No," Amelia corrected him. "You turned him. He sees how you treat me. His *mother*. He sees what you've done. Mercifully, he doesn't take after you."

Chatham reached out and grabbed her by the elbow. She winced as his fingers dug in and circled her slender arm. "I saw you talking to Anderson." Anderson? Amelia flinched. Was this all about Anderson? "The two of you need to stop messing with my plans. Keep it up and I swear no one is going to remember either of you. Especially *my* kids."

Amelia pulled her arm away from Chatham. She tried to stand tall, to look formidable, but she knew she had very little power left in this superfund site of a relationship. "Anderson is looking out for the company."

"Anderson is looking out for himself, and he's taking you down with him!" Chatham was spittin' angry now. Amelia could see Heartlee from the corner of her eye. The young woman backed up a bit. Heartlee had signed up for the money and status, not all the ancillary drama that went along with it. "I'll have you in court every day," Chatham continued. "You'll be spending your Social Security checks on lawyer's fees."

"Don't you threaten me!" said Amelia. She stepped toward Chatham with her index finger waving in front of her. *You*! Don't *you*! She waved the finger but never laid a single digit on her ex-husband. Which made what happened next all the more shocking.

Strangely and unexpectedly, Chatham awkwardly fell to his knees and just as awkwardly rolled down the steps that led back to the baseball fields. He did this while screaming out a woeful "Nooo!" and grunting painfully at every turn, even though he was rolling at a snail's pace. Amelia would have laughed at the spectacle if she wasn't so alarmed by how odd it all was. Chatham rolled to a stop at the bottom, and Amelia and Heartlee shared the same confused expression. What the hell was *that* all about?

After the Murder

The detectives appeared to be as baffled by the story as Amelia was. It had been such a childish thing to do. Amelia remembered the sight of her former husband rolling around at the bottom of the stairs screaming out, "She pushed me! She pushed me!"

Luckily for Amelia, the many bystanders had clearly seen Chatham fall down the stairs all on his own and the charges against her were dropped. She wondered if the detectives believed her. Did they think she was the kind of person who resorted to violence? Did they think she was guilty of this or something more?

"I didn't push him down the stairs. And I didn't murder my brother-in-law either," Amelia added. "Just in case you were wondering."

As the detectives walked back to their car, Amelia noticed Claypool looking at the holes in the garden where Amelia's prized rose bushes had so recently been, before she was forced to return them to her ex-husband. Did the detective think Amelia had been practicing her grave digging? Honestly, she didn't care what they thought. Send her to prison. It sounded like a vacation compared to dealing with her vindictive ex-husband, her ferocious daughter, and her squealing bank account. Cuff me now. Take me away.

CHAPTER

23

SHAY

It was a late night of work for Shay and Dub. Usually, they would both already be home by this time of night. Shay would be finishing up a bath at her cozy cottage, and Dub would be sipping a beer and watching ESPN or reruns of *Modern Family* at his ranch house in Cumming. Tonight, however, they both felt the need to visit Chastain Park. A murder scene often brought clarity, but as they sat on the stone steps above the field where Anderson died—the same steps his brother had dramatically thrown himself down—Shay didn't feel a bit clearer about anything having to do with the Tupper case.

"It's funny how a murder ruins a place for you," Dub said between draws on the straw in his Chick-fil-A milkshake. "I'm never gonna drive past this park again without thinking about what happened." They both looked down on an empty baseball field. The field lights shone brightly. Someone had seen fit to light the place up at night to ward off any future murderers, electricity bill be damned.

"Remember the body we found in the water treatment plant?" Shay asked. "I think of that guy every time I take a bath or . . ." She held up her bottle of water and took a sip. "I can't even drink without thinking of a damn dead body floating in our water supply."

"Murderers suck," Dub joked.

"They really do."

Shay looked behind them where signs proclaiming "Free Buckhead!" and "Vote Buckhead Independence!" were stuck in the grass every ten feet or so along the road north of the park. The reminder of the Buckhead secession movement gave her an extra dose of anxiety. They needed to solve this case. "So, where are we at?" she asked Dub.

Most of the murder cases Shay and Dub worked on either had one suspect or no suspects at all. She wasn't used to having a plethora of people around a victim whom she felt were all capable of murder. She had to check herself, though, because of course all these people weren't potential murderers. Shay simply didn't like most of the citizens of Buckhead, and it was clouding her judgment. It was difficult to separate the evil from the asses.

"So, money or drugs or sex, right?" Shay observed.

"Right," Dub said, considering the options. "If it's money, we have a few possibilities. The brother, the lawyer, the football player. Although, I really hope it's not Marcus Wiley. I still haven't gotten over the whole O.J. thing." He moved the straw around in his milkshake and drank some more. "What about drugs?"

"GHB," said Shay. "That's a weird one. As far as we know, Sutton Chambers sells Adderall. It's a big leap from that to a date rape drug."

"Could tie in to our last motive," said Dub. "Sex."

Shay mulled it over for a long moment. "If it's sex, it could be anybody. One of the women. One of their husbands. The jealous boyfriend of someone Tupper had an affair with."

"But why here?" Dub asked. "Tupper lived a block away . . ."

"Which means it was premeditated," Shay said. "Someone lured him here because they knew any DNA would be swallowed up in a dugout that a hundred or more people traipsed through every week."

"So, he knew the person."

"He most definitely knew the person," Shay agreed.

"Which brings us to the phone calls," Dub said as he pulled a folded batch of papers out of his coat pocket. "She said she barely knew him."

"And yet Tupper called her ten times in one hour," Shay said. "We're going to need to talk to her again."

KIRA

Harper Cole stood on the edge of the Great Expanse. No one had ever returned from its vast wasteland of warped time and space. Some said it was where your soul went when you died. Harper had never asked to be a hero. She wanted to find Luke. After circling each other like twin stars dancing around a black hole, Harper finally realized that Luke was all that mattered. She loved him. She knew that now. He was somewhere out there in the Expanse, in the graveyard of the universe, and she was going to find him. She thought only of him as she took her first step into the darkness.

Kira closed the book she had been reading from, to the applause of fifty or so people, mostly teenage girls, sitting on chairs and on the floor or wherever they could find room, at the back of a Barnes & Noble bookstore in Buckhead. She had read the final chapter of *Star Runners—Paradox*, her second and best book, the one that had left everyone waiting for more, for the third book she was so late in finishing. She responded in the positive to every request for book readings or book signings that came her way to appease her very impatient publishers. It was a form of procrastination.

Her fans crowded around Kira. Some held out copies of her books to be signed, and some asked questions. "Are you almost finished with the next one?" a girl of about fourteen asked.

"Almost," Kira told her. "I'm very close."

"What's it called?"

"Well, that's a secret," Kira told the girl. "But just between you and me, it's called *Star Runners—Singularity*." She said the name of the book in a loud whisper. "But don't tell anyone."

Kira scribbled her signature across a page of a book being held out by a very excitable sixty-year-old man and looked across the store to see Detectives Claypool and Rattigan. "Um, would you guys excuse me for just a few minutes?" she asked her fans. "I just need to take a short break. I'll be right back."

Kira grinned her way through the crowd even as her heart began to race. Why were the detectives here? She had hoped her one interview with them was enough, yet here they were again. She doubted that their appearance in the self-help section was a coincidence.

"Hello, Mrs. Brooks," Detective Claypool said as Kira finally reached them. "We didn't mean to interrupt. We can wait."

"No, that's fine," Kira said. It wasn't fine, but she wasn't going to tell them that. "Just finishing up a book reading."

"We won't keep you long. We know you have to get back to your fans."

"I call them my *customers*. They pay the bills," Kira said. But enough about them. "What can I do for you?"

"We just have a few follow-up questions," Detective Rattigan said.

"Last time we spoke, you said you didn't know Anderson Tupper very well," Detective Claypool said.

"I didn't."

"We were wondering about March 20th?" Rattigan said. "His phone records indicate he called you ten times that evening."

"What?" Kira asked. She was trying to accommodate the detectives, but her fans were waiting for her. Kira didn't like to disappoint anyone. She could already envision the comments on social media about how she had kept people waiting at a book reading, which would inevitably lead to comments about how she had kept everyone waiting for the third book.

"Anderson Tupper called you ten times in one hour on March 20th," Rattigan continued. "That's a lot of calls."

"That is a lot," Kira said as she racked her brain for answers. Surely, she would have remembered talking to Anderson Tupper ten times. Then it dawned on her. "Oh, that was after practice. My daughter and I got our schedules mixed up. I thought she was picking my son up and she thought I was. Anderson . . . Coach Tupper . . . watched Kolt. I was working. My phone was off. I . . ." Kira stopped. She knew she was talking too much. She sounded nervous *and* guilty. "Coach Tupper was trying to get ahold of me."

Two Days Before the Murder

In California, it would have been a pool house. In Arizona, it was a casita. In Georgia, they called it a guesthouse. Whatever it was called, to Kira it was a prison. Or maybe an insane asylum. It was rehab without the support groups. It was home without a family. There was one big room with a kitchenette and a separate bathroom. A gilded, framed painting of a flower-filled vase hung above a king-sized bed. It was the kind of painting they used in staging a house for sale and was left over from when they bought the place. Kira had no say in its purchase. She was only allowed to pay the bill. Living in the guesthouse, she felt, was like living in a deluxe king room at a Hampton Inn in Oklahoma City.

But there *was* a desk.

It was in front of a big window that overlooked the pool, but Kira rarely noticed the view. All she noticed was her computer. It was through the screen in front of her that she would get lost in the world of whatever she was writing. Currently, that was the world inhabited by Harper Cole, the teenage heroine of her *Star Runners* trilogy. For now, though, it was the *Star Runners* diptych as Kira was already four months behind schedule for turning in part three. The practicalities of survival had gotten in the way of her writing schedule, and her editor was beside himself with worry. What if Kira never finished the book? Some days she just didn't care.

On this evening, she sat at her desk and did her best to come up with a fitting ending for the journey of Harper Cole. There would be adventure and romance and humor and heart, and she was certain her readers would be overjoyed at the conclusion of the story. If only she could get it out of her head and into the computer. It was so easy with the first book. She wanted to build an empire for her children to rule. The book poured out of her like it had already been written. She knew back then when she typed the final sentence that it was going to be a massive hit. And it was.

The second book was harder. Much harder. Sequels always are, and they usually aren't as good as the first. Kira, however, was a perfectionist. She was Type A (with a capital A!) and couldn't fathom being a one-hit wonder. She sat at that other desk, the one that looked out on another pool in California and worked so hard she often forgot to eat. She would sit down to write in the morning and the day would disappear into keystrokes and words. It would often be dark before she left her office. That was back when she still lived *in* the house with her family. Kira had always, her entire life, lived up to expectations. Book Two, *Star Runners—Paradox*, turned out even better than the first one and was an even bigger hit.

Between Book Two and Book Three, however, everything had changed. Everything. Kira sat at her computer, looking out onto the pool, in a guesthouse built for someone else's mother-in-law and marveled at the immensity of her self-inflicted misery. She didn't know how she was ever going to finish this book. She didn't feel like she even deserved to finish it. Doing that would mean she had succeeded at something, and Kira no longer felt like a successful person. She felt like a mistake.

She typed a sentence.

Harper Cole died and failed to save the universe. The end.

This, at least, made Kira smile, but it was not how her book would end. She was not going to disappoint all the young Star Runners out there. She had already decided Book Three would be called *Star Runners—Singularity* and was determined to write a triumphant, satisfying conclusion to Harper Cole's journey across the stars. She just wouldn't be writing it this evening. Kira pushed away from her desk and reached for her phone. It was turned off. She always turned it off when she wrote. It was endlessly distracting.

When she fired it up, she was met with a barrage of texts and missed calls.

"Oh, fuck."

* * *

Kira left her car running for a moment while she checked the address in the headlights. 435 Hillside Drive. It was an older ranch house that was one of the few left on the street that hadn't been torn down in favor of brick or stucco or brick *and* stucco large family homes with trampolines in the backyards and Teslas in the driveways. The house was close to Chastain Park, and the neighborhood was popular with Buckhead families with lots of little Buckhead kids.

Kira parked her car and hurried to the front door. She was out of breath as she rang the doorbell. It was from excitement, not fatigue. She noticed the white paint on the door was peeling away in places and that one of the tarnished brass lanterns on either side of the door was broken. She thought it odd that someone so rich lived in a house that reminded her of the one her great-aunt and -uncle lived in when she was a child. It was old like they were. This house, though, was owned by a young man. A young, rich man. Kira shook it off. He's a bachelor, she thought.

Anderson opened the door with a welcoming smile. Didn't he always have one ready for her? She smiled back. "Hi," she said. She was a little flustered. "I'm here! Finally, I guess. I'm finally here." She paused for a moment and gathered herself. "Sorry."

"Come on in," said Anderson as he held the door open for her. "We've just been playing some video games. Hope that's okay."

"Sure. Of course."

Kira stepped into the unexceptional living area of the house. It was dated, with wood paneling on the walls and shag carpeting on the floor. She could see a small kitchen beyond a dining room with a table that was filled with piles of mail and paperwork. It probably hadn't been used for actual eating on in years. The furniture looked as if it had been inherited from his parents, and it probably had been. There was a mix of antique cabinets and upholstered chairs from the seventies and a plethora of mismatched lamps with beige faded lampshades. The only new and expensive thing in the room was a giant big-screen television before which sat her son. He was playing a video game, something with guns and soldiers and explosions, and didn't even look up when she entered.

"Hi, buddy," Kira said. She hoped for a rousing reply but got nothing in return.

"We've been trying to save the world," said Anderson. "We've got the enemy on the run."

"Thank you for watching him," Kira told him. "I'm so sorry we weren't there to pick him up from practice. My daughter and I got our wires crossed and my husband was doing . . . I don't know." Her *husband*. Of course, he existed, but she had so far managed to never mention him to Anderson. She felt like she was cheating, but strangely she felt like she was cheating on *Anderson*.

"Would you like something to drink? Water? Coffee? I may have a Diet Coke."

"No, I'm fine, thanks," Kira said as she glanced around again. For a split second she imagined what it would be like to spend more time in this house. To live there *with* him? She could see the two of them cuddled up on the sofa watching *Emily in Paris* for the sixth time. She already had the imaginary key in her hand. "How was practice?"

"Good," Anderson said loudly. "Right, Kolt? I think we have a good chance in the playoffs. And Kolt, man, he's a great player. He just keeps getting better every day." Kolt remained silent and engrossed in his game.

Kira nodded like she knew all this. Like she and Kolt had long mother son conversations about every little detail of his life. Truthfully, what little she learned about what was going on in her children's lives she had deciphered from their social media accounts. "I'm sorry about Wade's dad. Are you okay after, you know . . ."

"I'm fine," Anderson said, brushing it off, even though a few cuts and bruises still marred his perfect face. "It was all a misunderstanding, but until we get it worked out, Lamar will stay on as assistant coach. He's like me. We're both trying to relive our Little League glory days."

He smiled that perfect smile again. This time it wasn't for Kira's benefit but seemed more of a wistful smile for times long past. She really wanted to ask him more. She wanted to talk to Anderson about everything that had happened in his life, about his hopes for the future and his regrets about the past. She wanted to know who he was. And then, after dissecting his soul, she really wanted to have sex with him. To make love to him or fuck him. She didn't care. She just wanted him.

Unfortunately, she needed to get home to her husband.

"Well, we've taken up enough of your time," she said as she shook off all (or most) thoughts of a carnal nature. "Come on, Kolt, let's let your coach enjoy the rest of his evening." Kolt didn't budge from the sofa. His hands were glued to the game controller. The light from the TV seemed to have hypnotized him.

Anderson stepped in to help. He switched to coach mode. "Kolt, let's go!" he barked. "Your mom's waiting."

Kolt dropped the controller and walked right past Kira without a word. He pulled open the front door and was gone in a flash, slamming it behind him. Kira was embarrassed by his behavior. "I'm sorry," she said as Anderson handed her Kolt's equipment bag and his school backpack. She slung them over her shoulders like a sherpa headed up Everest.

"No worries," Anderson said as he thoughtfully brushed off some of the dirt from the bag of bats so it wouldn't get on Kira. "I have to deal with these kids all the time. I've seen it all." Kira started heading for the door, but Anderson stopped her. "Are you going to the Steeplechase?"

"I'm not sure. I've donated a lunch, but I don't think that means I have to go, does it?"

"No, but it would be nice if you went," he told her. "It would be nice to have someone new to talk to."

"Well, maybe I'll see you there." She had unconsciously slipped into flirt mode and instantly pulled back. "Or anywhere. Like at practice or a game. Or the Steeplechase. Anyway, thanks again. And sorry again."

Rain began to fall as Kira drove Kolt home through the now-glazed streets of Buckhead. Lightning from a spring storm lit up the sky in the distance. How very ominous, thought Kira. The weather was conspiring with her moody son to cast a dark shadow over her evening. Kolt sat in the passenger seat. He was surrounded by an invisible, but very powerful, force field of silent fury. He said nothing. He was a possum playing dead.

The rain increased and the windshield filled with drops, but Kira didn't turn on the wipers. She was too busy trying to avoid the toxic waste dump in the passenger seat. After a minute of driving with little visibility, Kolt reached over and turned the wipers on. Kira was startled. It was an unwritten rule that should have been punishable by death that the passenger did not mess with the driver's controls. Never. Like ever.

"Don't do that!" she spat out at him. "I'm the driver!" She had finally had enough of coddling the little porcupine.

"You can't see!" Kolt spat back. "We're going to crash."

"We're not going to crash."

Kolt settled back down into his seat and stared straight ahead as the wipers swooshed back and forth across the windshield. Kira felt undeserving of his anger, at least on this night. "What's the problem?" she asked.

Kolt remained quiet, but it was obvious he wanted to say something. His lips quivered ever so slightly. He wasn't about to cry. He was about to explode. Finally, he erupted with a new level of anger that caused Kira to slide over in her seat as far away from him as possible.

"Where have you been?" Kolt asked. Almost spitting the words at her.

"I wasn't supposed to pick you up."

"Where have you been for like . . . for like forever?" Before Kira could even process that, her son brought down the hammer. "Were you drinking?"

And there it was.

She knew he had wanted to ask that question but was still surprised when it came out. It wasn't an unreasonable question. Unfortunately. It was actually a very reasonable question. It's one thing to be accused of something when you are guilty and trying to pretend to be innocent. It's an entirely different thing to be accused of something when you are innocent and still feel like you're guilty. Kira wanted to yell back at her son and make him cower in his seat, but instead she took a moment to find a more tactful approach.

"No, I haven't been drinking," she said softly in a monotone voice she had mastered in therapy. "I was working, and my phone was off. Like it always is when I'm working. I thought your sister was picking you up. I guess she thought I was picking you up. I don't know because, you know, she doesn't answer my calls or texts." As they waited at a stoplight, she took the opportunity to look at her son even if he wouldn't look at her. "Not everything is my fault."

When they got home, Kolt got out of the car and slammed the door. He went into the house, head down, and slammed the door to the house too. He left his equipment bag behind for Kira to deal with. Honestly, this wasn't unheard of. Kira sometimes thought of herself as Dobby from Harry Potter. It was the lot of most mothers. Weren't they all just a legion of house elves?

Kira entered the house to find her husband and daughter and son all in the den. Kallan and Iris were working side by side at a desk, poured over Iris's schoolwork. Kira could fault her husband for many things, but he was always helpful with Iris's studies. They both were on the scientific spectrum. They had the minds of engineers. Neither had an artistic bone in their bodies. Kira and Kolt were the dreamers, the artists, the inventors. The sensitive beings.

Kolt was already collapsed in a pile on a leather accent chair nearby. He sank in and glared at his sister. "What happened?" he asked.

"What?"

"You were supposed to pick me up from practice."

This appeared to be news to Iris. She glared back. "No, I wasn't. She made it very clear that she was picking you up from now on." She. That would be Kira. She was a "she" now. "You should have called me."

"I lost my phone."

"Again?" Iris said. Kolt had lost or destroyed eight iPhones in the course of his young life. Two went into the ocean. One into a lake. One ended up in the microwave. There was never any explanation for that one and the microwave was a lost cause as well. One fell out of his pocket in the bleachers at a Dodgers game and ended up smashed to pieces somewhere below. Two were stolen from school. One in LA and one in GA. And the last one, the latest one, was just gone. No one had made sure the Find My feature was turned on. Kira would have made sure, had she been there.

"I called you from Coach's phone," Kolt said.

"I don't pick up calls from strange numbers," Iris told him. He was looking at her like she had deliberately ignored him. "Why didn't you call your mother?" *Your* mother. Not her mother.

"I tried."

Kira decided it was time to jump in. She had never been one to stand on the sidelines. "I was working. I had my phone off."

"Convenient," said Iris.

This attitude irked Kira. She was getting tired of tiptoeing around her daughter. "I tried calling you. I texted you. You never pick up. It's rude that you don't."

"She's not being rude," Kallan said. He finally decided to speak up. Kira wished he hadn't. "You can't expect to come back in and have everything be the same. You've waltzed in here and disrupted our schedules."

"Your golf schedule?" Kira fired back. "Because I tried calling you—Kolt tried calling you—and you didn't pick up either. Because, I assume, you were playing golf. Like always."

"Dad was working!" Iris said. Kallan got to be "Dad." Kira was "She."

"*I* was working!" said Kira. "You were supposed to pick him up. That's why I bought you that car. Jesus, do you even realize how lucky you are?"

"Lucky?" Iris said. "Fuck you."

And with that lovely sign-off, Iris stormed off to her room. Kolt shook his head at Kira (shook his head!) and stormed off after Iris. That left Kira and Kallan alone in the room, something that made neither of them the least bit comfortable. He got up from the desk, sighed loudly, disapprovingly, and walked off in the general direction his children had gone. Kira now stood alone. She was in the middle of a cold war with her family. She felt like she now lived with the terrifying trio of Stalin and Lenin and Putin and she was powerless. There was nothing she could do to fight back, because in this Russian analogy, they may have been tyrants and dictators, but she was Ivan the Terrible.

CHAPTER

24

The Day Anderson Tupper Was Murdered

SUTTON

There were so many spangly, sparkly, sequined things hanging on the rods in Sutton's closet, Dolly Parton herself would have been right at home. For the Steeplechase, Sutton had chosen to wear a Barbie hot-pink jumpsuit. The top half was a halter that accentuated her breasts. They looked even more pert than usual and were impossible to ignore. The pants half of the jumpsuit flowed down to strappy pink and gold Valentino heels. These were going to be highly impractical at the Steeplechase, and Sutton knew she would be traipsing through overgrown grass and patches of dirt and the pencil-thin heels of the shoes would certainly be ruined. But they matched the jumpsuit. Sutton thought things should always match and would often dress her daughter to match whatever she was wearing, usually something pink.

To top it all off (literally), Sutton added an outrageously oversized pink hat to her ensemble. Its brim fanned out ten inches in every direction and pink and red tail feathers sprouted out of the top. She admired herself in the closet mirror and adjusted her boobs just so. She had no doubt that she would be the most photographed woman at the Steeplechase.

"Sutton! I need you!" It was Chuck calling from the bedroom. A few years before, Sutton would have gone running to fulfill his every need. Now she took her time.

Sutton entered the bedroom where Chuck was propped up in bed. Bottles of prescription medicines were on the nightstand along with half a glass of water and a box of Kleenex. Tissues littered the floor to the side of the bed. The television, with its volume turned up high for the hard-of-hearing Chuck, was showing a documentary on the Second World War. Ships were on fire in Pearl Harbor. Chuck loved World War II even though he was, surprisingly, too young to have fought in it.

"What the hell are you wearing?" he asked Sutton with a look of disgust on his face.

"I'm going to the Steeplechase," Sutton told him, knowing he would have forgotten all about it. "This is how they dress."

"That's how hookers dress," Chuck replied as he shifted uncomfortably in bed. Every movement he made seemed to exhaust him. "I need you to make me feel good before you leave."

Make me feel good. Sutton hated Chuck's euphemism for oral sex. Sutton wanted to tell him to "go fuck himself," which was her euphemism for masturbation. Instead, she decided to take advantage of his weakened position. "I don't have time," she declared.

"Then find the time!"

Sutton picked up a pink Chanel handbag off an armchair in the corner of the room. It took a lot of making Chuck *feel good* to afford the handbag, and she was going to show it off at the Steeplechase. "I have to go," she told him. "I can't be late. I'm on the auction committee." She began walking out of the room but didn't make it far.

"I think it's time we took another look at our prenup," said Chuck, stopping Sutton in her tracks. "Maybe even rethink this whole marriage business."

Sutton looked at her husband. He was so old and weak. So . . . useless. "We can talk about things when you're feeling better," she told him in a calm, mothering tone.

"I'm feeling just fine," Chuck said. He stared her down, daring her to leave the room.

Sutton accepted the dare. She turned on her high heels and walked out with a strut. The brim of her hat bounced up and down as she headed toward the main staircase. She knew she was inviting trouble. Chuck wasn't going to be happy with her, but she wasn't about to get her outfit wrinkled.

Sutton went downstairs and teetered into the kitchen to find Reyna supervising Ally as they made sugar cookies together. She eyed Reyna for a moment. Sutton had always suspected something was going on between Reyna and Chuck. Over the past year, he hadn't pestered Sutton as much about sexual favors. Sutton felt guilty about not enjoying the sexual part of her relationship with her husband, but she had grown to find him repulsive. Along with the aging of his body, he had become a tyrant and a bully, and she found neither quality the least bit attractive. Sutton was happy Reyna had taken on some extra housekeeping duties.

Still, it wasn't the perfect situation. How long until Reyna ceased being the housekeeper and became a candidate for Mrs. Chambers number four? The only thing tipping the scales in Sutton's favor was Chuck's not-so-subtle racism. Chuck had always said his Guatemalan housekeeper was only suited for cooking and cleaning. Anything else was "beyond their capability." He had, evidently, extended the list to cooking, cleaning, *and* sexual services rendered. Sutton was going to have to stay on top of the situation.

Ally exploded in a little cloud of flour when she saw her mother standing in the doorway to the kitchen. The hat! The feathers! The blingyness of it all! Sutton looked like one of Ally's school craft projects. All that was missing was glitter. "Mommy," she shrieked. "You look beautiful!"

"Thank you, bunny," Sutton replied as Reyna turned away and began cleaning up some of the considerable cookie mess. She couldn't seem to bring herself to look Sutton in the eye.

"We're making sugar cookies," Ally told her mother. She proudly showed off a plateful of cookies she was busy decorating with sprinkles and frosting. They were meant to be in the shape of animals but looked like amoebas.

Sutton picked one long, thin cookie up and examined it. "What's this?" she asked. "A penis?" She glanced at Reyna. Reyna ignored her and redoubled her cleaning efforts.

Cash came into the kitchen and gave his mother the once-over. "Why are you wearing so much makeup?" he asked.

"Wow, Mom, you look nice," she mimicked back to him.

"Sorry," Cash said, taking the hint. "You look good. You're just wearing a lot of makeup."

Cash was wearing an Atlanta United FC soccer jersey and was carrying a small gym bag. He was a good-looking boy. That was something Sutton took credit for. His hair, however, was an unruly mess, but Sutton had long ago given up on the hair-brushing battle. "Do you have everything you need?" she asked him.

"Yep."

"Did you pack a toothbrush?" Sutton asked. Cash deflated. There was no use arguing. "Go on. We're not savages. You're not going to a sleepover without a toothbrush." Cash turned without a word and headed back to his bathroom.

As Ally poured an entire jar of pink sugar on a single cookie, Sutton went to the sink where Reyna was dutifully scrubbing a bowl and trying her best to disappear into her chores. It was something that had always been easy for her to do since Sutton saw her as more of an accessory, like a Roomba or the microwave, than a person.

"Reyna, I was wondering if you could do something for me?" Sutton said as she pulled a crumpled hundred-dollar bill out of her purse. She smoothed it out on the kitchen counter next to the sink.

"Chuck needs some, um, servicing today, and I was hoping you'd take care of him for me."

Reyna looked down at the hundred-dollar bill and smiled. She looked back up at Sutton. Sutton thought Reyna must be relieved to know that she wasn't going to be fired. Grateful, even.

"Chuck pays me fifteen hundred," Reyna said. *Chuck*. Not *Mr. Chambers*.

Sutton felt the dynamic of power suddenly shift. She snatched up the hundred-dollar bill and crumpled it again in her fist. "The motherfucker..."

KIRA

What exactly was a steeplechase? Kira had to google that. A steeplechase was a horse race with jumps. It was like the Kentucky Derby with hurdles. She also googled Peachtree Steeplechases from years past to see what the appropriate attire was for such an event. What she saw horrified her. Women wore colorful cocktail dresses and outlandish hats. Kira was neither a fan of cocktail dresses nor of hats. She didn't look good in hats, or at least she had convinced herself of that. She felt that her head was bigger than normal, and hats made it look like a lollipop on a stick. This wasn't true. It was most likely her mother who planted that idea into Kira's normal-sized head. Still, she wasn't going to wear a cocktail dress or a hat. She opted instead for a straight-legged mauve suit and flesh-colored Marni wedges.

Kira admired herself in a mirror in the guesthouse/casita/leper colony. *Admired* may have been too strong a word. Kira rarely admired anything about herself. Instead, she stood before the full-length mirror that was on the back of the closet door and assessed herself. Suit made her look fat. Shoes made her feet look big. Hair lost in some Niflheim between haircuts. She checked her handbag prospects and came up with a flesh-colored Longchamp shoulder bag that matched well enough with the shoes. This was as good as it was going to get.

Kira came out of the guesthouse to encounter a pale orange cat meowing as it padded along the stucco wall that separated her property from the neighbors. "Hello, cat," Kira said as it slinked its way toward her, and she stopped to greet it. She offered her hand up to the cat, and it responded favorably, nuzzling its nose into her palm. "It's nice to know someone is happy to see me." She patted the cat on the head and they both moved on.

Kira made the walk of shame to the Big House. That's what she now called the main house where her husband and children lived without her. They lived in the Big House with its five and a half bathrooms, and she lived out back. She eyed the pool as she balanced in her high wedge heels. One misstep and she would be treading water. She wished they hadn't gotten another house with a pool. Pools, and water in general, worried her, but then just about everything worried Kira. There was peril around every corner. Cars ready to crash. Terrorists ready to attack. Criminals poised to pounce. The world was an unmarked minefield.

The Big House was quiet when Kira entered. Kallan usually had the television in the den on, tuned to either CNN or ESPN, but it was silent. She called out for Kolt, but there was no answer. She looked around the expanse of the place. It was much bigger than their California house and was, honestly, more house than a family of four (minus one, really, since Kira was kept in the dungeon) needed. Especially since Iris would soon be off to college. The place was also a mess. Shoes were left wherever they had been taken off and filthy socks were lying beside them. Jackets were thrown over the back of chairs. Dirty glasses were busy making rings on the coffee table. It was a clean-freak's worst nightmare. Kira began tidying up and then stopped herself. Cleaning was akin to criticizing, and Kira was in no position to pass judgment on how her family chose to live.

The front door opened, and Kallan came in from his morning run. His hair was matted to his head with sweat. For the first time, Kira noticed that Kallan's hair was thinning. He was a few years away from a bald spot. She knew that was going to happen. When she first met him, she was sure that Kallan had the kind of hair that would one day fail him. It would slowly thin away over the years until patches of hair existed only on the sides of his head. She knew this but married him anyway.

"You better hurry and get dressed," Kira told Kallan as he went through his post-run stretching routine.

"I'm not going."

"You said you were going. Coke has a hospitality tent there."

"I changed my mind," Kallan said coldly. "I don't think there's any reason for us to pretend, you know, that we're a real couple."

"I thought we decided to do this for the kids," Kira said.

Kallan ignored Kira and headed to the kitchen. She followed him and stood by as he made his postworkout *bulletproof* coffee, which was pretty much just coffee with butter and was disgusting. It became popular after men started reading the musings of male lifestyle guru Tim Ferriss. He wrote a book entitled *The 4-Hour Work Week*. It promoted an abundant lifestyle achieved through a work week that could be condensed into just four hours. There were days, when Kallan was unemployed and Kira was working all day at a publicity company and half the night writing the first *Star Runners* book, when she wondered if Kallan would ever achieve even one hour of work, let alone the four that Ferriss recommended.

"They don't care. They don't want us to pretend," Kallan told her as he watched the butter melt and rise to the top of his coffee mug.

"They want a normal family," Kira countered.

"They'll *never* have a normal family," Kallan said with a dollop of venom to go along with the butter. "You did that. My kids haven't been happy since what you did."

"*Our* kids."

"*My* kids," Kallan spit back. "I'm the one who protects them."

"Protects them?" Kira said. "Protects them from who? From *me*?"

"For a start."

"You know, where were you when they were growing up?" Kira asked. He was trying to take possession of her children, the ones she raised, and she wasn't having it. "Playing golf? Out with your friends? On some fucking male bonding survivalist bullshit trip on my dime? While I was taking care of them? While I took them to school every day *and* worked?"

"They don't love you, you know," Kallan said calmly. He didn't need to scream and curse. He could destroy Kira with one sentence. "Iris told me that. She said they don't consider you to be their mother anymore."

"That's not true," Kira said. She wasn't going to believe that. Kallan was just trying to get back at her for pointing out his years of unemployment. For so long he had been happy to live off her success and act like *he* had accomplished something. "I'm going to get them. I'm going to talk to them."

"They're not here. Iris took Kolt to the Miltons," Kallan said. "While you were sleeping or sleeping it off or whatever."

"I was *writing*."

"You're always *writing*."

"How do you think we paid for this house?" Kira asked. "You live here because of my writing."

"No, I live here because of your *drinking*," Kallan shot back. "I didn't want to move. You think I wanted to leave California to come *here*?"

"Aren't golf courses pretty much the same everywhere?" Kira said. She knew that was a low blow, but there was truth in it. Kallan had spent more time on the back nine than he ever did with his son and daughter. Certainly more than he ever did working.

"We want you to move out," Kallan said. Having dropped the guillotine blade, Kallan left the kitchen, bulletproof coffee in hand. He wasn't going to stick around to watch Kira's head roll around on the poured concrete floors.

Kira followed him as he walked through the house. "The kids don't want that," she said. "Things are better between us."

"They hate you!" Kallan screamed as he turned to face her. "They don't want you around. They don't want to see you. Especially Kolt. I have to *make* him spend time with you."

"You're just jealous. I was always closer to Kolt than you were. He's always been *my* son."

Kallan took a moment to calm down. He had never liked to fight. It wasn't in his nature. "He's my son too," Kallan said, softly this time. "He's *our* son. Iris is *our* daughter. And we need to do what's best for them. This isn't working, Kira. You find another place to live, or I'll find another place. The kids will split time between us. Okay?"

"So you want to get a divorce?" Kira asked. She had calmed down too. She didn't like to fight either, but it was how she was raised. She fought to survive. "I thought we were going to wait until Iris finished high school."

"What difference does it make?"

Kallan walked upstairs toward the bedroom, toward *his* bedroom, and it finally struck Kira. They weren't a family anymore, even though they had pretended to be. Kallan was a father. Kira was a mother. Iris was a daughter. Kolt was a son. But they weren't a *family*. She was surprised that she didn't feel devastated. Her marriage was officially ending. It was something she should mourn. Instead, she felt relieved. There was freedom in admitting failure. It left space to move on. Kira suddenly felt untethered from her past. She was free to drift for a while and find a new life for her and her children. Maybe even with Anderson Tupper.

BIRDIE

Birdie could hear Freddie and his friends playing video games as she walked by his room. They were trash-talking and cursing and sounded more like college students knocking back cans of Bud than preteen boys, but Birdie loved their rumblings all the same. It's said that a parent is only as happy as their unhappiest child, but Birdie was only as happy as Freddie. The moods of her older sons didn't sway her. She left their levels of contentment to her husband. Freddie, however, was all Birdie's, and listening to him good-naturedly call Hampton a "fucking loser" filled her heart with joy.

"Freddie, you boys need to go outside and play in the real world," she said through the partially closed door. Her son's lack of response caused her to call out "Freddie!" again in her sternest voice.

"Okay, Mom," he finally yelled back, though the video game marathon continued.

Birdie was wearing an outfit she had agonized over. It was a purple coat dress with lavender flowers and an Indian-inspired Nehru collar. She looked like the mother of the bride from a wedding reception at an airport Hilton rather than the rich Buckhead aristocrat that she was, but it was the only thing even close to appropriate for a steeplechase that fit. She had a matching purple hat custom made in the shape of a horse's head with a mane that flowed in an imaginary wind. It was a strategic move. Hopefully people would remember the hat and not the dress.

Birdie walked into the living room to find Dan attached to his iPhone with his thumbs tapping away on the keyboard. "Is that what you're planning on wearing?" she asked.

"Yes." He was wearing a sand-colored linen suit and a white linen shirt. Brown suede Loro Piana Open Walks adorned his feet and an off-white straw fedora with a brown and red striped grosgrain ribbon topped it all off.

"Are you off to Cairo to oversee a dig?" she asked.

Dan ignored Birdie's jibe and instead of retaliating, he kissed her. "Well, you look beautiful." Bullshit, she thought. She wondered how long he would go on pretending like he wasn't having an affair and how long she would go on pretending like she believed he wasn't. They were suspended in the bubble of a convenient mutual lie where neither had to face the messy truth of it all. "I'm going to drive myself to the Steeplechase," he told her. "I have to go to the office to work later. There's a lot of shit piling up."

"There certainly is."

The sound of the doorbell ended their marital pantomime. Dan headed upstairs, and Birdie went to the door to see which boy was now being dropped off for Freddie's sleepover. She opened it to find Venita and Wade on the other side.

"He forgot to pack a toothbrush," Venita said. "Do you have an extra one?"

"I do, but does it matter? They never brush their teeth anyhow."

The two women were nearly trampled as Freddie led Ham and Kolt in a charge out the front door, basketball in hand. "Come on, Wade!" Wade dropped his overnight bag at Birdie's feet and ran after the others. They all disappeared around the side of the house where a basketball hoop awaited by the three-car garage.

"Why aren't you dressed yet?" Birdie asked Venita. Venita was dressed in dark blue flare-legged jeans and towering high-heeled calfskin Celine boots. Although she looked amazing, she wasn't dressed for a steeplechase.

"We're not going to be able to make it."

"What about the auction?" Birdie asked.

"People sign their names on a piece of paper," Venita said. "You'll be fine without me."

"What's more important than the Steeplechase?" Birdie asked.

"Coach Tyree invited us out to dinner." Venita told her. "We can't miss that. Marcus idolizes him."

Sutton's Maserati pulled into the driveway and Cash jumped out and ran to join the other boys playing basketball. Birdie eyed the Pink Panther that was Sutton. "Jesus Christ, Sutton, we're going to the Steeplechase, not Hooters."

"Chuck's fucking the housekeeper!" Sutton declared as she adjusted her breasts in their halter top.

"And?" Birdie asked. She didn't find this news the least bit surprising.

"He's fucking the housekeeper *and* he's paying her more to have sex with him than he pays me."

"Chuck pays you for sex?" a shocked Venita asked.

"Doesn't Marcus pay you?"

"No!"

Sutton turned to Birdie. Birdie could see that Sutton's entire worldview was crumbling before their eyes. "Does Dan pay you for sex?"

"I pay Dan for sex," Birdie joked, though in a way she felt she did.

"Good luck with the auction," Venita said as she went to her car. She was driving the Ferrari Spider today. It was painted gold, or Giallo Modena as Ferrari called it. "I'll see y'all later. Let me know how it goes."

"She's not coming?" Sutton asked as Venita got in her Italian sports car and roared away. The sound of the powerful engine shook the quiet streets of Buckhead.

"No," Birdie said. "And I'm glad. Marcus sucks the air out of every room. It'll be nice not to have to compete with him for attention." She looked down at Sutton's perfectly round breasts. "Though I guess we'll all be competing with *them*."

"It's just how God made me, Birdie."

"No, it's just how Doctor Bohi made you," Birdie corrected her, referring to Atlanta's go-to plastic surgeon and the man responsible for saving countless Buckhead marriages. "Your tits are your greatest asset. What would you do without them?"

KIRA

The glorified hat show that was the Peachtree Steeplechase. The entrance to Crabapple Plantation was past a mile of white picket fencing and a pecan tree–lined gravel drive, at the end of which stood a genteel antebellum mansion. It had a front porch that ran the width of the house and a lacquered black door with a gold knocker in the shape of a pineapple.

Kira joined a line of race fans, all decked out in their steeplechase finest, past stables to fields where white tents were set up along a racetrack carved out of the red Georgia clay. Bars, manned by bartenders in crisp white shirts, were aplenty, and signs marked each of the hospitality tents. Some were for sponsors, like Coca-Cola and Home Depot, while others were set up with high-top tables for eating and drinking or had booths with attendants ready to accept bets on the day's races. All for charity, of course. The proceeds of the gambling and drinking were to go to an Atlanta children's hospital. Charitably deductible sin.

Kira followed signs to the Silent Auction tent. She wasn't eager to see how few people had bid on having lunch with her, but she didn't want the inevitable news that no one cared to come as a surprise. She entered the tent to find round tables set up with bidding sheets on which patrons wrote their top offer for things such as luxury vacations to Iceland or Hawaii, private boxes at Braves games, and cooking lessons from Top Chef Kevin Gillespie. The current highest bid, of sixty-three hundred dollars, was for a Marcus Wiley signed University of Georgia game-worn jersey.

On the last table, Kira came across the auction that offered *Lunch with Best-Selling Author Kira Brooks*. There, below a picture of the cover of her first book, was an empty sign-up sheet. No one had yet bid on lunch with her. She hadn't wanted to be part of the auction for just this reason. It brought up bad memories like not being picked for the second-grade production of *The Wizard of Oz* or being dumped by Bill Hydon in college.

Kira contemplated bidding on herself and putting down a fake name, but this was for *charity*. Maybe she could sneak away or say she had been suddenly stricken with some virus from North Korea or had been attacked by Civil War hobbyists in a battle reenactment or anything other than be there for the embarrassing moment everyone realized that no one in Atlanta wanted to have lunch with her.

"I'm thinking five thousand dollars," came a voice from behind her. Kira turned to find Anderson Tupper, pen in hand. He slid in next to her and wrote his name and that very amount of money at the top of the bid sheet. "If someone outbids me, I hope you'll still have lunch with me."

"I doubt you'll be outbid," she said. "I'm not sure these people are really my readership." She stared at him a moment longer than she probably should have. What was it about Anderson Tupper? It was like the sun was suddenly shining only on Kira. Just standing next to him, she felt warm in all the right places. "Congratulations on making the playoffs, by the way. Sorry I didn't tell you that before."

"Thank you. We couldn't have done it without your son." Anderson shifted the conversation to a more serious track. "How are you and the kids doing, by the way?"

Kira wanted to tell him that her children hated her. That they didn't want her around. That she lived in the guesthouse in quarantine and sometimes felt the only time she saw them was through the windows of the Big House. Instead, she said, "Good."

Anderson nodded. He seemed to sense that "good" didn't really mean good. Mercifully, he didn't delve further into her dysfunctional relationship with her family. "So, interesting steeplechase attire," he said, alluding to her hatless pantsuit ensemble. "Bold move."

"I don't look good in hats. Big head."

"I like your head," he said.

He *likes my head*, she thought.

Anderson reached out and touched Kira's hair. He gently brushed a section back behind her ear. "You're right not to cover up such nice hair."

It was a simple act of intimacy that just about knocked Kira off her feet. Her husband had never done such a thing. It was so personal and such a deliberate journey into Kira's space that she couldn't possibly interpret it as anything other than a declaration of attraction. A feeling of guilt started to simmer, but Kira suddenly realized she had nothing to feel guilty about. Her husband had ended their marriage. Just that morning! She wasn't cheating. She was flirting! She was free to take this as far as it could go.

Just as Kira was about to dip her toes into the flirting waters, Birdie entered the tent. She was dressed in all her aubergine glory with a truly terrifying horse head hat topping it all off. "Hello, Kira," she said, eyeing Kira with a sneer, like she disapproved of Kira being alone with Anderson. "Hello, Anderson."

"Hello, Birdie," Anderson said in his charming way.

"What are you two up to?" Birdie asked.

"Not much," Anderson told her. He smiled at Kira. "I've got to go show my face at the sponsor's tent. I'll see you later." Kira wondered if he meant it. She wondered *how* he meant it. Was it *I'll see you later* as in they'd nod to each other in passing or was it *I'll see you later* as in he would rip off her clothes and fuck her on top of a bale of hay? She hoped it was the latter. He wandered off before she could get a sense either way, and she was left with the company of Birdie and a smattering of racegoers come to check out the auctions.

Kira hovered over the table touting cooking lessons with the Top Chef. She thought about bidding on it even though she hated cooking. Anything to cut the tension between them. "Thank you for inviting Kolt to the sleepover," Kira finally said. "We'd love to have Freddie stay over some time."

"I don't think so."

She didn't think so? "Is there some sort of problem?" Kira asked.

"No, no problem." Birdie stood by the auction table that offered lunch with Kira. She stared down at Anderson's name alone atop the bidding sheet. "Are you married or aren't you married, Kira?"

So, there *was* a problem. Kira hated passive-aggressive people, and that included herself. "What does that have to do with Kolt having Freddie over?"

"Kolt mentioned that you live in the guesthouse. That's a little strange. I don't want Freddie to be exposed to unconventional lifestyle choices."

It had never occurred to Kira that anyone would think the fact that she lived separately from her family was unconventional, though she now realized that it could be seen that way. She was only trying to be close to her children and now this woman, this *Birdie*, was judging her. People who live in glass houses shouldn't throw stones. They may get the shit kicked out of them.

"My husband and I are separated," Kira said in as calm a manner as she could muster. "I live in the guesthouse so we can raise our children together. I guess that is a little unconventional. It would probably be more acceptable if I lived in the main house, and we all pretended that everything was fine. Like your family does." Kira, after all, had seen Dan Milton getting a blowjob at Chastain, and it wasn't courtesy of his wife. With that, Kira retreated from the tent. She hadn't planned on starting a war with Birdie, but she couldn't help herself. Kira never knew when enough was enough. Now she had swatted at the Queen Bee of Buckhead, and she could only expect she'd eventually get stung.

AMELIA

Amelia had recycled one of her old Etro dresses to wear to the Steeplechase. It was a creamy floor-length number with ruffles along the hem and large orange chrysanthemums snaking up and around the torso. The dress was a relic from her life with Chatham, and she was sure she had never been photographed in it before. If she had, some awful Atlanta Instagram troll would surely point it out. She wore a brown rabbit-felt Hermes Faubourg hat with a monochrome brown ribbon that was boho chic and European and a fuck you to all the other women there. Amelia could still pull off wearing a Hermes cowboy hat. It didn't matter, though. Not the dress or the hat or the Birkin bag on her arm. She was at the Steeplechase, with the anybody who was anybody of Atlanta, but she was no longer Mrs. Chatham Tupper.

As she walked toward the racetrack, Amelia saw Anderson deep in a contentious conversation with Dan Milton. This couldn't be good news for either Anderson or her. Dan was right in Anderson's face with his veins bulging and his eyes wide with anger. Amelia thought back to the good old days, when she was newly married and the Tuppers and the Miltons vacationed together at Sea Island. There was always drinking and laughter. Now Chatham and Anderson were at war and Dan was her ex-husband's attack dog. It didn't matter that they had all been friends or that Dan was married to her best(ish) friend, Birdie. Not where money was concerned.

Amelia was due to relieve Birdie at the auction tent but stopped to watch the horses instead. Birdie could wait. The course of the Steeplechase took horses and their riders around an imperfect circle of straightaways mixed with hurdles of fences or hedges the horses had to jump over. It seemed cruel to Amelia. She didn't think, left to their own devices, that the horses would run around and jump over hurdles they could easily avoid. She thought about sneaking over to the stables and letting the horses run free. That's what they were meant to do. They would probably get hit by cars on the highway, though, and Amelia would be blamed for it. She had already given people enough to talk about.

"Run away with me."

Amelia turned and peered out from beneath her Hermes hat to find Anderson approaching along the track. "Where would we go?" she asked him.

"Oh, I don't know. How about Mexico?"

"Too hot."

"Canada?"

"Too cold."

"Scranton?" he said, referring to the oft-maligned Pennsylvania city that was home to the Dunder Mifflin Paper Company in the TV show *The Office*. "We'll pack the kids into the old minivan and make our escape to paradise," Anderson continued. "Maybe get a Weimaraner."

"Mr. and Mrs. Anderson Tupper living a suburban life in Scranton," she said. "What a disaster that would be." She only half believed that. It couldn't be more of a disaster than having been Mrs. Chatham Tupper, and the thought of creating a scandal by marrying her ex-husband's brother was appealing. Now, as they stood together, she could already see people looking their way. She couldn't hear them but could imagine what they had to say. There had been rumors in the past about Amelia and Anderson, that they had had a torrid affair with liaisons that stretched from Sea Island to Highlands and that Hampton was actually Anderson's son, not Chatham's. Despite the rumors, though, they hadn't really spent any meaningful time together in the years they had known one another, not until Anderson approached her with his plan to keep Chatham from selling the company out from under them. She had always thought that Anderson was the master of superficiality. Everyone loved him, even if no one really knew him.

Anyway, Amelia's fantasy involved a simple life with a Harley-riding everyman in Traverse City, not a complicated one with her ex-brother-in-law. The thought of the kids having to decide whether to call Anderson *Uncle* or *Dad* was reason enough.

Amelia waited for the horses to finish their race before she asked Anderson, "What were you talking about with Dan?"

"Bad news, I'm afraid."

Wasn't it always?

"Chatham's issuing a capital call," Anderson continued.

"What does that mean?"

"It means all the shareholders have to put more money into the company or we forfeit our shares. He can buy us out at book value."

"How much money do we have to put in?"

"What does it matter?" Anderson asked as he shook his head at the absurdity of it all. "It could be a hundred thousand or a quadrillion. Either way, neither of us has it."

Amelia was stunned. She had fought so hard for so long she had forgotten what it felt like to live in peace. Now all her suffering had amounted to nothing. Chatham would pay her a pitiful few million dollars for what she knew was worth much more. He had screwed her again.

"So, he wins. I'll have to sell him my stock."

"No. We're not doing that," Anderson told her.

"Anderson, I'm running out of money. I can't do this anymore."

The sunny "let's run away together" Anderson suddenly disappeared. He practically glared at Amelia. His gaze was direct and cold. "You have to do it. Don't mess with my plan, Amelia. I've done a lot for you . . ."

"I know."

"If you had sold him your shares, like you wanted to, you'd have already blown through that money by now. You'd be fucking back in Knoxville working in a fucking dental office or something," he said. "I need this money. I need to get the fuck out of here. You owe me, Amelia." Anderson seemed to catch himself. He sighed from what must have been the stress of their shared misfortunes. "I'm sorry, it's just the pressure, you know?"

"I know."

"I have a plan," Anderson continued. "I'm going to declare bankruptcy. That way a judge will have to look into everything and there's a chance he won't let Chatham sell the company for less than market value. At the very least, it'll stop the capital call and slow them down. I just told Dan."

"I bet he didn't like that."

"No, he did not."

Anderson's phone rang. Venita Wiley's name was on the screen. "Speaking of people looking for money."

"You take it. We'll talk later," Amelia said as Anderson stepped away to answer the call.

Amelia took her hat off and looked toward the sun to warm her face. She hadn't counted on the chill in the air.

BIRDIE

Birdie looked down at the bidding sheet for the chance to win lunch with Kira. She fiddled with the pen in her hand, twirling it around and around like a tiny baton. In a moment of rare introspection, Birdie questioned why she hated Kira so much. The hatred felt cancerous, like a tumor pressing against whatever part of her brain processed rationality. She knew that at the root of it, she was jealous. Kira had made her own success. She hadn't inherited it or received it as a stipend from her husband. Birdie had done well to manage the money her family had given her, to guard it from stupidity and indulgence, and she had been an unparalleled mistress of the manor. She knew, however, that she had benefited from the help of nannies and cleaners and a bottomless bank account. She didn't want what Kira had, but she hated her just the same for having it.

"Hello, Birdie," church lady Laura said as she entered the tent. She was dressed in some god-awful chartreuse quinceañera outfit and sported a straw hat with plastic flowers that she must have stolen from a chorus girl in a local production of *Easter Parade*.

"Hello, Laura."

Laura glanced down at the placard on the table. Lunch with Kira Brooks. "Are you going to bid on that?" she asked.

"Hadn't planned on it."

"Poor Kira," Laura said. "Bless her heart."

"Why do you say that?" Birdie asked.

"It's nothing," Laura said but continued on. "It's just that I heard from her neighbors that she sleeps in the guesthouse. I think that's kind of strange, don't you?"

"Oh, I don't know," Birdie replied. "You can't believe everything you hear. For instance, I heard from someone that you gave Pastor Cranley a hand job during the Christmas carol concert last year."

"That's not true!" Laura looked grief-stricken.

"Of course it isn't," Birdie continued. "But rumor is he really belted it out during *Joy to the World*!"

"Who said that?"

"You know, actually I might have heard that from Kira. Probably not. I mean she wasn't even living here then. Anyhow, don't worry, most people don't believe it."

"I have to go help out at the . . . the sponsor's tent," Laura stammered. "I have to go."

"Okay, nice seeing you," Birdie said as Laura quickly made her exit. Birdie had made up the entire story. There was no rumor, though she thought maybe she'd start one. She looked down at Anderson's name alone atop the bidding sheet for Kira's auction. That just wouldn't do. She crossed his name out and wrote Laura's in its place.

Birdie gave up waiting for Amelia to relieve her and left the auction tent behind, stepping out into the waning sunlight. One of the races had started, and she could see the horses speeding around a far turn and over one of the hurdles. She hadn't gone more than a few steps when Sutton joined her, wiggling in her high heels and trying to keep up as Birdie made her way to the track.

"Do you think Chuck's going to divorce me?" Sutton asked.

"Probably. You blew it, Sutton. All you had to do was make him happy until he died. Which should be any minute now."

"I should have hired an ugly housekeeper."

"It wouldn't have mattered," Birdie told her.

"Then I should have hired a male housekeeper."

"Still might not have mattered," Birdie said. They reached the edge of the track near the finish line as the horses and their jockeys raced closer. "The good news is, you're still young and bouncy. You have time to find another rich guy. But next time pick someone older. Preferably someone already on a ventilator."

"Hello, ladies," Dan said as he approached Birdie and Sutton. "Nice hat, Sutton." He said "nice hat," but Birdie knew he really meant "nice rack" as he glanced down the plunging V of Sutton's jumpsuit.

"Thanks, Dan," Sutton said as she adjusted her cleavage instead of her hat. It was a good thing that Birdie didn't consider Sutton a threat to her marriage. It wasn't because they had a particularly close friendship as much as it was that Sutton knew Birdie would beat the hell out of her if she ever made a play for Dan.

"I'm going to have to leave soon," Dan said. "I have some stuff to catch up on at work." Birdie nodded, and Dan kissed her on the cheek. "I'll see you later tonight."

Birdie watched Dan walk away and promptly step in a pile of horse shit. How appropriate, she thought. He wiped his shoe off in the grass and headed for one of the hospitality tents.

"Dan works on Saturdays now?" Sutton asked. "Is that some new thing?"

Oh yes, Birdie thought. Dan was definitely doing something new.

AMELIA

The hem of Amelia's dress brushed the red clay as she walked along the dirt pathway leading to the portable bathrooms. These were not the port-a-potties of Amelia's youth. Not the rank smelling, filthy outhouses that lined the perimeters of music festivals where you squatted above fly-filled holes and held your nose in the darkness. These toilets were large and bright with several spotless stalls and clean white sinks with Le Labo hand soap at the ready. The air had a hint of lavender that was evocative of peeing in Provence.

Amelia entered the bathroom and was relieved to find it empty. She quickly locked herself in one of the stalls, pulled the lid down to make a seat, and began to cry. It was a quiet, dainty cry with very few tears and no theatrical sobbing. She didn't want anyone to hear her, and she didn't want to ruin her makeup. The thought of people thinking she was upset about anything was overwhelming. Amelia wondered how many hours she could sit there before she could sneak away. She listened to the muffled voice of the track announcer in the distance. Maybe she would wait for one of the top races and leave when everyone was at the track. Maybe . . .

"Amelia?"

An unfamiliar voice came from the other side of the stall door. Amelia looked down to see the woman's feet. Her toenails were painted a subtle shade of blue that matched the strappy high-heeled shoes she was wearing.

"Amelia? It's Heartlee. I was wondering if we could talk?"

"I'm a little busy right now," Amelia replied.

"I can wait."

So much for riding it out in the bathroom. Amelia got up and flushed the toilet. She hadn't even used it but thought it would be strange to exit the stall without flushing. She came out to come face-to-younger-face with her ex-husband's girlfriend. She was surprised to see that Heartlee was wearing a floral one-sleeved Ulla Johnson midi-dress that Amelia instantly recognized.

"Are you wearing my dress?" she asked Heartlee as she looked her up and down.

"Uh, I don't know," Heartlee said, then immediately gave in and fessed up. "Actually, yes, I am. You left it in one of the closets at the house."

"Because it was out of fashion," Amelia said dismissively as she washed her hands in one of the porcelain sinks. Even though she didn't have to. She looked in the mirror at Heartlee behind her. The young woman seemed nervous and kept shifting her weight from one foot to the other, rocking back and forth. The two had barely ever spoken. Their longest conversation had been about Ham getting a rash from poison ivy when he was with Chatham and Heartlee at the family farm in south Georgia. That conversation mostly revolved around the word *calamine* and was thankfully brief. They had never actually been alone in the same room together. "What do you want?" Amelia asked.

"I need your help."

"Help with what?" Amelia reached for a stack of thick paper towels embossed with the Peachtree Steeplechase horse head logo. Heartlee beat her to it and handed some to Amelia as she declared:

"I'm pregnant."

It's incredible how many thoughts can race through your mind in a matter of seconds. The words had barely exited Heartlee's mouth before Amelia was already worrying about dealing with her children having a stepsibling. She would probably have to include the little tyke on family outings and listen to Auggie complain about not getting enough attention. "Congratulations," she said, reluctantly coughing up the word.

Amelia pushed past Heartlee toward the door, but Heartlee blocked her way. "I hate him. I don't know how you stayed married to him for so long. He's an asshole."

"I agree," Amelia said. "If you'll excuse me . . ." Amelia tried to leave again, but Heartlee grabbed her by the arm and pulled her back.

"He wants me to have an abortion," Heartlee said. She was wide-eyed now and on the edge of panic. "I told him I wouldn't do it. But he said he'd never let me have the baby. What does he mean? Like, what would he do? You have to help me."

Amelia remembered what it felt like to realize her husband was the enemy. There was something terrible in the way his feelings for her turned from love to hate. She felt loathed and abandoned, then hunted and tortured. She understood that Heartlee was now probably feeling some of those things, but she had suffered enough fighting her own battles with Chatham. She couldn't take up this young woman's cause as well.

"I'm sorry," Amelia finally said. "I can't help you."

"Maybe I can help *you*," Heartlee said in a conspiratorial tone, low and ominous. "I know what Chatham is doing to you. I know what he has planned. We can work together. If I have to go to court to fight him, you can testify for me. You can tell everyone what he's like. We both win."

"The only way I can help you is by telling you to get the abortion," Amelia told Heartlee. She no longer hated this woman who was seeing her ex-husband. She pitied her. "If you have this baby, you'll be tied to the Tuppers forever. And trust me, everything you think you're going to get isn't worth the price you'll pay for it."

SUTTON

Sutton could feel the eyes of every man on her as she walked into the main hospitality tent. Married or single, straight or maybe even gay, she knew she could get any one of them in bed if she made even the slightest effort. Of course, she would never have an affair unless she knew for sure Chuck was going to cut her loose, and she would never have an affair with a married man unless he was very, very unhappy with his current wife. But weren't they all unhappy? She couldn't remember the last time she had a conversation with a man that didn't start and end on her breasts. Not that she didn't enjoy the attention. She wanted to be desired. She also wanted to be loved. Chuck didn't love her, and it seemed he could desire any woman. Maybe his dalliance with the housekeeper was the universe's way of telling Sutton she needed to move along.

The Steeplechase had progressed from racing to dancing, and couples filled a temporary parquet dance floor and boogied away to a cover band playing a serviceable version of the B-52's "Rock Lobster." Sutton surveyed the scene like she was perusing the offerings at an all-you-can-eat buffet in Vegas. Some older men danced with their younger partners. They were like the prime rib being carved to order, expensive and rare, but something Sutton had tired of. There were younger men who were out of shape and boring, like stale macaroni and cheese, and men who were slick with their ponytails and Tom Browne sports jackets, who were the shaved brussels sprout salad of the evening, new and interesting but not something you wanted every night. Then there was Anderson Tupper. He was the buttery bowl of mashed potatoes in the center of the buffet. The thing you really wanted. That you craved. That you would choose as your last meal before you were executed.

Unfortunately, the mashed potatoes were dancing with Kira.

"God damn, Sutton, nice outfit," Lamar said as he came up behind her. On the buffet, Lamar would be the last of the zucchini casserole, stuck in the corner of the pan, crusty and unwanted. "Does Chuck know how good he has it?"

"Not sure. Hopefully." Sutton moved to put some space between her and Lamar, but he moved right along with her and his shoulder, encased in a customary blue blazer, rubbed against her bare skin. Although the blazer was made of wool and linen, it felt slimy. Sutton couldn't bring herself to tell Lamar to leave her alone. Her need to please, and please men in particular, kept her by his side even though she felt repulsed. Thankfully, the cavalry appeared in the form of Amelia, who came across the dance floor and wedged herself between the two.

"Your wife's looking for you, Lamar," Amelia told him.

"Oh, fuck," he said as he immediately stepped away from Sutton and went in search of the Mrs. without so much as a "catch you later."

"Thank you," Sutton said to Amelia.

"My pleasure."

"Amelia, are you and Anderson sleeping together?" Amelia looked shocked, and Sutton instantly realized that maybe she had overstepped her bounds. "I mean, no, right? Of course not."

"*Of course* not."

"It's just, I've always had a crush on him, and I didn't want to, you know, get into anything with him if you were interested."

"Okay, first, he's my brother-in-law," Amelia said. Sutton didn't know why that had anything to do with it, but she heard Amelia out. "And second, he's my children's uncle. I would never. *He* would never. And, as a matter of fact, he would never with *you*. Not as long as you're married to Chuck."

"Well, I may not be Chuck's wife for much longer. I'm thinking about leaving him," Sutton said. It was a lie, of course. *He* was thinking about leaving *her*, but Sutton didn't want that version out in the world. It was one thing to tell Birdie, who for all her awfulness always protected Sutton, but a completely different thing to tell Amelia, who was divorced herself and may have been eager for someone else to suffer its indignities for a change.

"You know, Anderson doesn't have any money," Amelia added.

As if it was about money!

"That's not why I like him," Sutton tried to convince Amelia. "But he probably will have money some day when his mom dies. Not that it matters!" She watched Anderson and Kira dancing together. Anderson had moves, for sure. There was rhythm in them thar hips. "It really would be all about the sex. Which I hear is amazing."

Birdie joined Sutton and Amelia on the edge of the dance floor. She had a stack of auction bidding sheets in her hand. She passed one to Amelia. "The auction is officially closed. Congratulations, you won the trip to Maui."

"I bid a hundred dollars," Amelia said.

"Somehow that was the highest bid," Birdie told her with a wicked smile. Sutton thought that was nice of Birdie. Amelia could never afford a luxury trip to Hawaii. Not anymore. There *were* perks to being Birdie's friend.

Laura left the bar behind them, holding a glass of red wine. Sutton thought it was probably all the church lady drank as it somehow brought her closer to Jesus. Maybe she had herself convinced that she really was drinking his blood.

Birdie stopped Laura as she passed by. "Oh, Laura, good news, you won the auction," she told her as she handed her a bidding sheet. "Enjoy your lunch with Kira Brooks."

Laura looked down at the sheet with confusion, then looked back up at Birdie, who sported a big, fake smile. "Very funny, Birdie." She handed the sheet back and went on her way.

"The bids are binding!" Birdie called after her as she turned back to Sutton and Amelia. "Actually, Anderson won the auction to have lunch with Kira. He bid five thousand dollars."

"Jesus," Amelia said as they all turned their attention to Anderson and Kira as the two now danced closely together. They playfully bumped their hips against one another as the band now played "Celebration" by Kool & the Gang. They were all laughter and smiles, and it irked Sutton to no end.

"You know, she's an alcoholic," Birdie said as they watched the pair dance.

"You don't know that, Birdie," Amelia chastised her friend.

"Actually, I do," Birdie declared. "That's what her son told Freddie. That's why she didn't move at the same time as her family. She was in rehab."

Sutton thought sometimes it was a chore to like Birdie. She was too often a social sniper, firing off shots with little regard for those she killed. Sutton was happy, however, to hear that Kira wasn't the perfectly put together woman she appeared to be. She wasn't so special after all.

"So, who wants to help me inform the lucky auction winners?" Birdie asked.

"I'll do it," Amelia offered as she took half the bidding sheets from Birdie. "I guess I better earn my trip to Hawaii."

Sutton looked back toward the dance floor and saw that Anderson was now catching his breath and chatting away with some of the other single men in attendance, none of whom rated Sutton's attention. She noticed that Kira was now in line at one of the bars. Sutton didn't know whether Kira's past problems with alcohol, or her stay at what Sutton guessed was a star-studded rehab facility someplace glamorous like San Diego, were true. It would be easy enough to find out, though, by seeing what Kira ordered, so she joined her in line at the bar.

"Kira!"

"Sutton, hi," Kira said. She was dewy with sweat from all the dancing and her hair was a tangled mess. For the first time, Sutton looked at Kira and thought she was sexy. She seemed to have shed her shyness and uncertainty.

"It looked like you were having a good time out there," Sutton said as she gestured toward the dance floor.

"This is so much fun!"

"It is, isn't it? Hey, by the way, where's your husband? I haven't had a chance to meet him yet."

Sutton waited as Kira pondered her reply. Sutton was sure she had her, that Kira would remember she was a married woman and stop flirting with Anderson Tupper, Sutton's top choice for replacement husband. Instead, Kira said, "Actually, we're getting a divorce."

"Oh my God, I'm so sorry," said Sutton with feigned sincerity.

"It's fine," Kira told her. "We tried, but it just didn't work out. We're friendly. I mean, you know, we want what's best for our kids, but we kind of decided that what was best for them was for us to be apart. So, next week I'm going to start looking for a place to live."

"I know a great real estate agent," Sutton offered. "Nancy Earle. She's the best. I'll text you her info."

"That's so nice. Thanks."

"Go dance with Anderson," Sutton said. "It looks like you're having so much fun. I'll get your drink."

"That's okay, I can wait."

"No, I insist," said Sutton. She was so helpful. "I'm standing here anyway. What do you want?"

"A Pepsi would be great."

"A Pepsi?" Sutton asked. She was hoping Kira was going to order a double shot margarita.

"Oh, right," Kira said. "This is Atlanta! I'm not supposed to say the word 'Pepsi,' right?"

Oh, yeah. "Right."

"I'll have a Coke, thanks," Kira said, correcting her potentially offensive error of ordering anything other than the liquid gold of the South. "With extra ice."

Sutton waited almost five minutes in line to order Kira's drink. She made sure to get extra ice. She also made sure to add some GHB she had gotten as a bonus gift from her Adderall supplier. Of course, Birdie must have been right. Birdie was always right. Kira was an addict and was hiding it from everyone—including Anderson. Only Sutton could expose the truth. Someday, Anderson would be grateful.

BIRDIE

Birdie gripped the steering wheel with both hands so tightly that her knuckles began to turn white. She sat in her car in a dirt field that had been made into a parking lot for the Steeplechase. Most of the cars were still in the lot, and Birdie could see the racegoers in the distance and hear music from the band. Everyone seemed so very happy. They were all far too busy with their own revelry to hear Birdie as she began to *scream*. It was a tortured wail that seemed to linger long after the air in her lungs gave out. She began banging on the steering wheel as tears poured from her eyes. She wasn't one to cry, and the sudden appearance of the tears surprised her. She wiped them away as she regained her composure and checked her makeup in the rearview mirror.

Birdie got out of the car and opened the tailgate. She pushed away baseball bats and gloves and canvas shopping bags from Fresh Market to find a box from Amazon buried beneath. She opened it and pulled out a collection of items from the Spy Masters, a company specializing in surveillance equipment used by private investigators, the FBI, and suspicious spouses everywhere.

She looked at the row of cars behind her where Dan's vintage Jaguar was parked. The top was down. Dan liked to drive with the wind flowing through his abundant head of hair. The only time he put the top up was when he knew a storm was approaching. He obviously hadn't foreseen the one headed his way as Birdie carried the box of spy gadgets toward his beloved car.

SUTTON

The festivities at the Steeplechase were winding down. The band had begun to only play slow tunes in an effort to ease people off the dance floor. An offkey version of John Legend's "All of Me" was bringing things to an end as the caterers began packing up bottles and pulling wine-stained cloths off tables. A few couples were still on the dance floor, including Kira and Anderson. They were both glassy-eyed and only still standing because they were leaning against one another. Every so often, Anderson would whisper something in Kira's ear, and she would explode in a shriek of laughter, and he would giggle along with her.

Sutton sat alone at one of the tables, finishing off a glass of white wine that was now warm, and watching Anderson and Kira. She had been pleased as Kira drank from the GHB-spiked Coke. She was less pleased when she saw Kira share the same Coke with Anderson. They had both looked exhausted from all the dancing and that Coke must have really hit the spot. About twenty minutes or so later, they began dirty dancing, then tried in vain to start a conga line, then finally settled into a slow dance long before the band had started to play slow dance music.

"I know what you did last summer," Lamar said as he sat down next to Sutton.

If he was trying to be charming, it wasn't working on Sutton. "Where's your wife?" she asked him, hoping that would make him scurry away again.

"She already left. Had to get back to the kids." He laid his arm across the back of her chair and caressed her shoulder even as she squirmed. "I saw," he whispered in her ear.

"What are you talking about, Lamar?"

"You spiked that drink." Sutton sat perfectly still as if Lamar was a bear and if she didn't move, he would lose interest and leave her alone. Lamar wasn't going anywhere, though, and he leaned in closer and the hand that wasn't on her shoulder began sliding up her thigh. "Everyone knows you sell drugs. Everyone but your husband. I don't think he'd be happy about it, do you?"

"That's not true," Sutton said with little conviction. It was worth a try.

"It is true. But I can be persuaded to not only keep quiet, but also reassure Chuck that his pretty wife would never do anything to embarrass him."

"What do you want, Lamar?"

"I just want you to be nice to me."

"Fuck you!" That didn't come out of Sutton's mouth, although she had wanted to say it. It came from the dance floor where Anderson was no longer dancing with Kira but was now facing off against his brother. Heartlee stood behind Chatham and Kira stood behind Anderson as the two brothers began arguing even as the band played their final song of the evening, Kenny Rogers's "Lady."

"I can declare bankruptcy if I want," said Anderson. "I can dance if I want! I can fuck up your plans if I want!" He poked his finger sharply into his brother's chest. "I'm a Tupper. I can do anything I want."

Chatham pushed Anderson away and he stumbled to the ground. Chatham looked down on his brother, as he probably always had. "Dad and I built our company. You just fucked around. You lost all your money and everyone else's. You're a fucking embarrassment to our family!"

"Embarrassment? Me?" Anderson asked as he struggled to get up. He finally got back on his feet and faced his brother. "There was a story in *Vanity Fair* about your divorce! You fucked prostitutes in your wife's bed. Come on, dude! *I'm* the embarrassment?"

"You're drunk."

"You're an asshole," Anderson said. "And I'm going to take you down. The next story on you is going to be in the fucking *Wall Street Journal*. I'm going to lay out every fucking one of your misdeeds."

Chatham surveyed the tent. All eyes were on them. He reached out and straightened the collar of Anderson's shirt and patted him on the shoulder. "Enjoy your irrelevance." With that, he took Heartlee by the arm, and they left the tent.

Sutton watched as Kira and Anderson stumbled out of the tent together and off into the night. Sutton's plan to embarrass Kira and drive her and Anderson apart had failed. She had only succeeded in driving him into her arms.

"Look what you did," Lamar said as his lips grazed her earlobes. His breath was rancid, a combination of pulled pork and whiskey. "You've been a bad girl. A very bad girl."

CHAPTER

25

After the Murder

SHAY

ATLANTA'S HARTSFIELD-JACKSON AIRPORT was, in most years, the busiest airport in the world. It was a crossroads for planes traveling around the globe and, as Shay discovered from conversations with taxi drivers in London, the place they all had passed through on family trips to Disney World. The airport itself was the perfect representation of Atlanta, a mix of race and privilege and old and new. Shay both loved and hated Hartsfield-Jackson. She loved it when she was going somewhere. When she was flying to London for vacation or to Boston on her way to visit Darron at Dartmouth. She hated it when she was returning home or, like today, when she was dropping Darron off. On days like this, it was not only the busiest airport in the world, but it was also the saddest.

"You don't have to walk me to security, Mom," Darron told Shay as they snaked around a tour group from China headed to catch a plane to Orlando. Darron was moving at his usual languid pace. It was a gait common to young men. Shay wondered how he ever made it to class on time.

"I just want to make sure you get on the plane," Shay said.

"Mo-om, come on."

Shay smiled. She loved it when her son said the word *Mom* like it had twenty-three syllables. "I just want to spend as much time with my son as possible."

"I can always stay."

"Well, that *would* give us some time to talk about your choice of major," Shay told Darron as he trailed behind her and his wheeled carry-on trailed behind him. "I really think you need to come up with something more useful than Humanities. I don't even know what that is, but I'm pretty sure you can't make any money doing it."

"Oh, it's definitely time to go," Darron said as they reached the entrance to the security lanes.

Shay searched her son's face for clues to his mood. She was certain that his entire trip home was as much about a need to get away from the rigors of academia as it was about any fear of his father's return. Darron had never been as strong as she was, and she had to remind herself that, although he was now taller than her, he was still so young.

"It really is going to be okay," she assured him. "Every law enforcement officer in New Hampshire knows they'll have to answer to me if anything happens to you." Shay stood on her tippy-toes to embrace him. Her head nestled just under his shoulder, and she held on for dear life. "Love you."

"Love you too," Darron said. He pulled out of the hug. It was time to go. He was out of sight too quickly.

In truth, Shay didn't know for sure that Darron would be okay, but his father visiting him and possibly harming him was just one thing on an endless list of things Shay worried about. Shay often couldn't sleep thinking of all the *what ifs* that could befall her precious child. The biggest one of all was—What if he stopped loving her?

The irrational *what ifs* of a loving mother would never go away. Not as long as they were both alive and no matter how old either of them got. Shay thought back to when she taught Darron how to ride a bike. It was a harrowing affair filled with tears from Darron and cursing from Shay, but eventually he got the hang of it. She remembered his laughter as he rode, emboldened by his newfound power to pedal along. Always trailing behind him, though, was his mother. Shay was there to steady him and ready to grab ahold of the bike before he ever toppled over. She would always be there.

CHAPTER

26

KIRA

AND. And?

A... n... d? And. Kira sat at her desk and stared at the computer screen. She typed in AND again. It was the only word on the screen. She wondered where this three-letter word that people probably used hundreds of times a day had come from.

Time to google.

Where did the word "and" come from?

The explanation referenced *ampersand*. Of course. Love & Hate. Life & Death. Her web search went on to say something about Latin, and Kira gave up her quest. She often went down these rabbit holes when she didn't feel like writing. She could always find a thousand other things to do. There was laundry waiting or emails to return or linguistic journeys on the derivation of words to go on. She found she could waste an entire afternoon searching the internet for Christmas presents even if it was June. Anything other than finishing her book, because as long as it remained in her head and not on the page, it could still be a masterpiece, rather than the disappointing third part of a trilogy she feared it was.

In the days after Anderson's murder, Kira had found it difficult to do much of anything at all, let alone write. She veered from sadness for the death of the man she barely knew but had hoped to get to know better to fear that a serial killer was roaming the streets of Buckhead and would find a woman living in a secluded guesthouse to be a prime target. Most concerning, however, was the void at the center of the Steeplechase. All her memories of that night had disappeared into it. This had happened to her many times before and always after drinking. Alcohol was the only explanation and the thought that she had started drinking again, and didn't even know it, was more frightening than the murder of a man she barely knew.

Kira shook off her worries and got back to her procrastination. She was about to go on the ultimate time waster, eBay, when a calendar reminder popped up on the corner of her screen. *Nancy Earle—1:30 PM.* She got up and put on her shoes. This was a *scheduled* procrastination, and it deserved her immediate attention. She grabbed her keys and her Paul Smith handbag only to catch a glimpse of herself in the mirror. She was already wearing a busy striped shirt and it clashed in the worst way with the busy striped Paul Smith bag. She went to the closet and pulled out the Longchamp handbag she had taken to the Steeplechase. Admittedly, she had chosen it that day not only because it matched her outfit but also because the Longchamp logo was of a horse. It had been very appropriate for the occasion, even if, once she had arrived at the Steeplechase and saw all the women with their sparkly little handbags, she had felt instantly out of place. In any case, she transferred her wallet to the Longchamp bag and hurried out the door.

Kira was locking the door to the guesthouse when a voice startled her.

"Excuse me, but have you seen our cat?"

Kira looked around and finally saw a neighbor peeking over the wall that separated their two properties. "Hi," she said warily to this man whom she had seen several times but never met.

"I'm Matthew Woolsey, your neighbor."

"Hi, Matthew, I'm Kira. I know your cat. He's very sweet."

"He's a *she*. Her name is Valentine."

"*She's* very sweet. But I haven't seen her today."

"You spend a lot of time out here. In the guesthouse," he said. He didn't seem to care about the cat anymore.

"I work out here. I'm a writer."

"You must write a lot."

Kira had had enough of the neighborly inquisition. "I'm sorry," she told him. "I'm late for an appointment. I'll let you know if I see your cat."

Kira couldn't walk away fast enough. Was the neighbor looking for his cat or looking for gossip about the eccentric writer who lived in the guesthouse next door?

* * *

"This is a top neighborhood. Very kid friendly," Nancy Earle told Kira as they drove down Lake Forest Drive toward Chastain Park. They were in Nancy's white BMW 5 Series sedan. Kira thought it was the perfect car for a Buckhead real estate agent. It was expensive but not intimidating and aspirational without being condescending. Nancy was an impeccably put together woman. She was the kind of person who took the time to curl her hair every morning and wore bright lipstick and uncomfortable designer shoes. She had a pleasing southern tone that Kira noted was particular to Atlanta. It was just pronounced enough to send a strong message that the accent belonged to someone who was proud of their place in the world. Nancy's accent reminded Kira of Birdie's. She was a little bit afraid of both women.

Kira looked at the Chastain baseball fields as they drove past. It had been less than a week since Anderson Tupper was murdered, but life in Buckhead had already returned to normal. They had canceled all the games for her son's age group but none of the others. Too many parents complained when they were told the season was going to be cut short. What would little Timmy (or Grayson or Bradford or Aldwych) do if they missed a season of baseball? A space on the shelf was already cleared for the participation trophy.

As Lamar told the CYB board of directors: "What happened to Coach Tupper was unfortunate, but let's not overreact."

Play on.

Kira was lost in thoughts of Anderson as they turned onto a street she had driven down before. It took her a moment to get her bearings and then it hit her. It was the same street Anderson lived on. Or had lived on. In fact, they were headed right for his house. Was it already for lease? Was Kira going to have to walk through a murdered man's house? Mercifully, Nancy Earle pulled into the driveway of a newly renovated house directly across from Anderson's ranch house, and she and Kira headed for the front door. On the other side of the street, crime scene tape was still strung across Anderson's porch. One end of the tape flapped in the breeze. It looked like it was there as a decorating choice, like crepe paper at Easter. It was a macabre reminder for the neighborhood children that the nice man who used to live there was now *dead*.

As she unlocked the door to the rental house, Nancy noticed Kira was looking at the home across the street. "Oh, don't worry about that," the realtor said. "Someone was murdered, but it didn't happen in the house. There's nothing to be concerned about." She suddenly looked at the house with what seemed to be renewed interest. "Although, if you decide to buy instead of rent, we may want to look into the situation with the heirs. We could probably get a really good deal on it. People tend to be skittish about things like murder."

Kira followed Nancy into the house, but she was finding it difficult to concentrate. She could feel her temperature rising so fast that her ears began to burn. The house's new herringbone patterned hardwood floors and farmhouse chic wood beams could not distract her from the proximity she had found herself to Anderson's house.

"It's just going to be you and your children, right? You have two?" Nancy asked as she waited for any kind of reaction from Kira.

"Yes," Kira said. "A son and a daughter. My daughter will be leaving for college next year, but I still want bedrooms for them both."

"Of course," said Nancy as she steered Kira toward the kitchen. "I'm sure they'll love this house. You can walk to Chastain Park. And the yard—"

"Can you excuse me for a second?" Kira said, interrupting Nancy. "I really need to use the bathroom."

The realtor pointed to a door off the hallway. "There's one there. You go right ahead. The house has three and a half bathrooms. That's the half. Let me know what you think."

Kira felt like she was on fire and was going to burst into flames. Burst into flames or vomit. Neither was a comfortable feeling as she hurried to the bathroom and locked the door behind her out of habit. She dropped her handbag on the counter and leaned over the sink as she took a few deep breaths. The bathroom was newly decorated with an industrial flair and had black fixtures and Moroccan-themed tiles that were all the rage in design and probably the same as every other newly renovated home in Atlanta. Even in her state of nausea, Kira couldn't help but think it was already a bit dated.

She looked in the mirror. She had aged so much in the past year and even more in the past week. She was looking at someone she didn't recognize and wondered how this woman in the mirror had taken over her life. She turned on the tap and was ready to splash water on her face and wash this other woman away when she noticed something on her handbag. There were dark brown spots splattered across the side of the bag. She picked it up and looked closer. They weren't dark brown spots. They were dark *red* spots. It was blood.

Kira dropped the handbag and it fell to the floor. Her wallet came out and a tube of Clinique lipstick rolled across the tiles. She quickly gathered everything up and put the handbag back on the sink. She pulled at a roll of toilet paper over and over, rolling a bundle around her hand, wet it under the faucet, and began scrubbing away at the spots. As Kira worked to wipe the bloodstains off the leather of her bag, she searched the database in her brain for an answer. Had she cut herself? Had she set the handbag down at an abattoir and forgotten?

She finished wiping the bag off and threw the tissue in the toilet, flushing it away. She watched as it swirled down and then flushed it again just to make sure. She stood paralyzed for a moment. Should she flush the handbag down the toilet too? No. It was just blood. It could be her blood. But it could also be Anderson's blood. What had happened after the Steeplechase?

Kira came out of the bathroom but looked like she had just come out of a sauna. No amount of straightening her hair or clothes made any difference.

"Is everything all right?" Nancy asked.

"I'm just a little hot."

"Well, luckily they just installed a brand-new air-conditioning unit!" the agent said as she continued with her tour of the home.

Kira looked through the windows at Anderson's house across the street and suddenly got the chills.

At least she wasn't hot anymore.

CHAPTER 27

VENITA

Venita hated school meetings. She was jealous of parents who were never called into meetings because they had perfect children who never caused trouble or were elected class president or started charities to send gently used iPads to Third World countries. She didn't know any of these mythical parents, but she knew she wasn't one of them.

Accept others for who they are. Not for who you think they should be.

That was the poster tacked on the board outside the counselor's office. Venita thought back to when she was in school. The posters then were of the presidents or the periodic table. Now walking through a school was like visiting a New Age retreat in Sedona. *Dream Big. Be a friend. Dare to be Kind. Be the change you want to see in the World. Think Less—Do More.* How about think *more*? How about work hard? Venita wondered if the country was raising a generation of remarkable mediocrities.

Wade was sitting in a burnt orange cushioned armchair in a corner of the counselor's office. He was reading one of the books from the counselor's bookcase. It was called *Be the Best You*, and

Venita wanted to rip it out of his hands and beat Brené Brown over the head with it but instead said, "Hey, baby."

"Hey, Mom," Wade said as Venita stepped into the office.

The school's counselor, Mrs. Rowen, rose from her desk to greet Venita. She had been with the school for six years and had always been kind to Wade. Venita had a soft spot for the counselor. Two years earlier, at the school's Disco Dancefever fundraiser, Birdie had had more than her fair share of piña coladas and lifted the skirt of Mrs. Rowen's sequined outfit to reveal the three layers of shapewear she was wearing beneath. It was humiliating for the counselor, and the flowers that Birdie sent her the next day didn't come close to healing the wound. Mrs. Rowen was forever after known as *Mrs. Spanx.*

"Hello, Mrs. Wiley," the woman said as she shook Venita's hand. "Please sit down. Wade, why don't you join us?" Wade sat next to his mother in one of the two chairs in front of the counselor's desk. He brought the book with him and kept reading it as they talked. "Well, it's been a little bit of a challenging day, hasn't it, Wade?" Mrs. Rowen asked. Wade didn't look up from the book, and Venita reached over and took it away from him.

"Yes, ma'am."

"You want to tell your mother how you're feeling?"

Wade shook his head.

"What happened?" Venita asked. Enough of this *feeling* crap.

Mrs. Rowen looked to Wade, but he was closed for business. "Well, it seems that Wade was triggered by something in science class."

The word *triggered* triggered Venita, and she immediately raised her hand up to stop Mrs. Rowen from speaking. "We don't use that word. Triggered. That's a curse word in our house."

The counselor nodded her head gently. This wasn't her first rodeo with Venita. "Okay, well, Wade was upset about a lesson Mrs. Winningham was teaching in science class."

"What was it, Wade?" Venita asked. "What happened?" Wade remained silent, and Venita looked to the counselor for more information.

"They were studying geology and Yellowstone National Park."

Venita was confused. She looked at her son again. His chin was still firmly pointing south. "We've been to Yellowstone. We had a great time. We saw a moose. We ate s'mores. What could possibly be wrong with Yellowstone?"

"It's a volcano!" Wade suddenly announced like he was having a flashback to 'Nam. "The whole place is a giant caldera. It's the top of a volcano and we *went* there! It's overdue for an eruption. Millions of tons of rocks and ash will be, like, shot into the sky and cover, like, the entire country! It'll be a nuclear winter!"

"I don't even know what that is," Venita told him.

"It'll be a species ending event!"

"We're more likely to die in a car crash on our way home, Wade."

Mrs. Rowen looked at Venita with wide eyes. That might not be the best argument. "Let's just take a breath," Rowen said. "Wade and his friends, the boys on the team, have been through a traumatic experience with what happened to their coach. And I think it might be a good idea if the other boys, and Wade, saw a therapist."

"The boys are from Buckhead," said Venita. "They were issued therapists at birth." She paused for a long moment. She was trying to be like some of the other mothers she had encountered, the touchy-feely ones who coddled their children, but she just didn't have it in her. She mistakenly thought they were having a rational conversation. She turned back to Wade. "We don't even live close to Yellowstone."

"It doesn't matter," her son said wearily. "We're all going to die."

A bell rang, and it seemed to punctuate Wade's ominous prediction.

"Wade, honey," Mrs. Rowen said in her soft, caring manner, "why don't you go to assembly and let me talk to your mother for a few minutes?"

"I'll see you after school," Venita told him as he left the room, but not before he took one last look at his mother as he went. It was hard to tell if he was more afraid of her or of the Yellowstone super-volcano.

"Wade's under a lot of stress," Mrs. Rowen said after he was out of earshot. "He's always been a sensitive boy, but now with his coach being killed and the rumors about his father . . ."

"About Marcus? What kind of rumors?"

"It's just, well, a lot of the kids have been saying things about your husband and Anderson Tupper. I don't know, things like—"

"Like his father is a murderer?"

"Things like that."

Venita was annoyed before. Now she was hoppin' mad. "Which kids are saying that?"

"We're not going to go on any vendettas against children," Mrs. Rowen warned. "Or their parents. This won't last forever. Kids can be cruel. Parents can be cruel. We just need to focus on Wade, who needs some extra love and attention right now."

"How are his grades?"

Mrs. Rowen appeared to be caught off guard by Venita's sudden pivot to academics. "His grades? His grades are great. Like always."

"Then he'll be fine. Thank you, Mrs. Rowen. I appreciate your time," said Venita.

With that, Venita got up and left the room. The hallways were now filled with children moving toward their lockers, the din of their chatter rising to a deafening pitch. Some children looked at Venita as she passed by. Parents were always an alien presence in the corridors, but Venita thought that wasn't the only reason they stared. She wondered which ones were gossiping about her family. What had their parents whispered in their ears? She wanted to grab one and smash them up against a locker and beat the information out of them, but she was an upstanding citizen of Buckhead. You can have impulses, but you can't act on them. At least not in this case.

BIRDIE

Birdie's car was number ten in the line of cars idling in front of Kensington Prep that stretched across the parking lot and down the street. She had resigned herself to participation in the soul-destroying exercise known as the school run. The security cameras had recorded her picking up Freddie and his teammates behind the school, and she had been fined for her disobedience. She decided to withhold her donation to the school's annual fund in protest. She would sit like one of their puppets in the car line, but they would pay in the end.

A knock on her window startled Birdie. It was Venita. Birdie rolled her window down, and Venita practically crawled through it. "Have you been telling people that Marcus murdered Anderson?" Venita asked with a discomforting amount of anger.

"No," Birdie replied calmly. "But that's not a bad idea. Maybe if I did, they'd stop thinking I killed him."

"Seems like there are a lot of rumors going around."

"And a lot of detectives," Birdie said. Birdie hadn't discussed the fact that the detectives had interviewed her with any of her friends. She suspected that she wasn't the only one. "Have they talked to you?"

"Of course they've talked to me. What about you?"

"I think I had the honor of being the first one they interviewed."

"What did you tell them?" Venita asked.

"That I did it, of course," Birdie said sarcastically. "It's so ridiculous. We all know Anderson was probably killed by some guy who was upset that he was fucking the guy's girlfriend."

"Is that one of the theories the detectives have?" Venita asked, fishing.

Birdie didn't have a chance to answer as she was interrupted by someone now tapping on the passenger window. It was Sutton. Birdie rolled the side window down. "Hey, y'all. What do you guys plan on wearing to Anderson's funeral?" Sutton asked.

Leave it to Sutton to be worried about that. "It's a funeral, Sutton," Birdie told her. "No one cares what you wear."

"Of course they do," Sutton told her. "I mean, the press is going to be all over it. I want to look good. We're going to be in paparazzi shots and stuff." Birdie wanted to argue with Sutton, but Sutton was right. The press would be there. They'd be eager to take pictures of the rich and powerful murderers of Buckhead.

Amelia walked up from her car, which was parked somewhere down the line. Birdie could see that all eyes were on them. "What's going on?" Amelia asked.

"Oh, we're just talking about murder and stuff," Birdie replied.

"Have the detectives visited you guys too?" Amelia asked.

"Visited?" Birdie said. She felt she had been one-upped by her old friend. "*They* came to *you*? I had to go to them. I wonder if that means anything?" Amelia suddenly looked uncomfortable, which was just what Birdie had intended.

"We're talking about what we're going to wear to Anderson's funeral," Sutton said from her side of the car. "I think I'm going to wear Chanel."

"I don't even want to go to the damn funeral," Birdie told them.

"If you don't go, you'll look guilty," Venita announced, like she had thought a lot about this already.

"Do any of you even care that Anderson is dead?" Amelia asked.

"Of course we care that Anderson is dead," Venita said. "Someone killed him, and it could be someone we know."

"It could be one of *us*," Sutton said ominously. Birdie pressed a button on her door and the passenger side window slowly rolled up, shutting Sutton out. The school doors opened, and students began heading to cars and joining their mothers and nannies and the smattering of stay-at-home dads. Venita, Amelia, and Sutton returned to their cars to await their boys. Things had changed in

Buckhead since Anderson's murder. There was a general unease. A nervousness. The silent inquisition had begun.

AMELIA

Amelia returned to her car to wait for Hampton. Auggie was strapped into his car seat in the back, sound asleep after a long day of preschool and whining. Auggie was cutest when he slept. That's the way Amelia liked him best. She was relieved that Poppy was going to a friend's house and that she wouldn't have to pick her up from the all-girls school she attended on the other side of Buckhead.

Hampton came to the car with his head down and slammed the door behind him as he climbed into the passenger seat. Auggie stirred but mercifully didn't awaken. Hampton's cheeks were flushed and his eyes watery. He hadn't been crying, but he was close to it.

"What's wrong?" she asked.

"Nothing."

"Something's obviously wrong. Come on, Ham. Fess up."

"Do you promise not to do anything?" he asked.

Amelia thought about that for a moment. She wasn't prepared to give up her parental right to overreact, but she wanted her son to tell her what was wrong. So she lied. "Yes."

"Nicholas said that Dad killed Uncle Anderson," said Hampton. Nicholas Cho. Pious Laura's little dick of a son. He had always been mean to Hampton, even back to their days in preschool.

"That's ridiculous," Amelia told him. "Nicholas's just being a jerk. As always."

"He said Dad killed him because he found out that I'm Uncle Anderson's son, not his."

That fucking rumor. "Your father didn't kill your uncle," Amelia said. "People are just jealous because you're a Tupper."

"I don't want to be a Tupper!" Hampton screamed out. "I hate the Tuppers! I hate Dad. I hate Poppy! I hate them all!" Hampton broke down in tears and buried his head in his lap so no one would see. He was heaving with sobs, and Amelia was beginning to seethe.

Nicholas Cho, a boy who was short for his age and in possession of a permanent smirk, came out of the school and made his way toward his mother's car. Amelia watched as he joked with another boy and laughed like he didn't have a care in the world. He was laughing so hard he didn't see Amelia as she got out of her car and headed his way.

Amelia was on autopilot as she intercepted Nicholas before he could get to the safety of his mother's SUV. Amelia wasn't a confrontational person. She didn't like drama. Fighting drained her, which was probably why she had been so destroyed by her divorce. The endless fighting. Something in her, however, had finally snapped.

"Hey, you little shit," she said as she grabbed the strap on Nicholas's backpack. "Don't you ever say anything to my son again, got it? Don't talk to him. Don't talk about him. Don't even look at him. I swear to God, if you mess with him again, I'll rip your fucking head off."

Nicholas was stunned and frightened. Amelia had actually wiped the smirk right off his face. The other parents looked on, astonished. Laura jumped out of her car and ran toward Amelia and her beloved Nicholas.

"What's going on?" she said as she pulled her son away from Amelia.

"He got it from you, didn't he?" Amelia said. "You've been spreading rumors about me and Anderson. You better hope that Chatham didn't kill him. He didn't like his brother, but he hates you. If he's a killer, you're top of the kill list, Laura." Amelia looked at everyone who was looking at her. She wanted to attack them all. She wanted to drop a bomb on the whole damn place. She turned back to Laura. "Keep my family's name out of your twisted mouth. Understand?" She then looked down at the cowering Nicholas. "And that goes for you too, you little prick."

As Amelia walked back to her car, she caught sight of Birdie still waiting in line. Birdie slapped both her hands against her cheeks like Macaulay Culkin in *Home Alone* and looked on in amazement. Amelia had just done a very Birdie-like thing and knew her friend would be immensely proud, even if she herself felt like she was going to throw up right there in front of Kensington Prep.

CHAPTER

28

SUTTON

Sutton was wearing a strappy Chanel little black dress and towering Tom Ford stilettos. She thought it was an understated look and proper for a funeral when in fact she looked like a high-class hooker hovering near a Pai Gow poker room in Macau.

She click-clacked across the living room at Azalea and out the French doors to the back patio. Chuck was in the yard practicing his short game on his personal putting green. Sometimes he would spend hours there knocking around a little white ball and grumbling when it failed to do his bidding. Sutton hated the putting green but loved that it occupied Chuck's time.

"Chuck, you shouldn't be exerting yourself," Sutton chastised her husband from the edge of the green. "You don't want to have another heart attack, do you?"

"I'm fine."

"The kids and I are going to Anderson's funeral. Don't you want to come?" She said it like she was asking him if he wanted to get tacos.

"Why would I want to go to that spoiled brat's funeral? His family gave him all that money and he pissed it away." Chuck lined up a putt and gently hit his golf ball. It stopped tantalizingly short of the hole. "God damn fucking cunt!" he yelled in frustration.

Sutton wasn't sure if he was talking about her or the ball but wisely took that as her cue to leave. "Okay, well, we'll see you later on." She turned to walk away, but Chuck wasn't quite finished.

"We need to talk."

Uh-oh. Those were some of the last words you wanted to hear in a troubled marriage.

"I want a divorce," Chuck said. Those were the other words.

"Well, I don't want one."

"Well, I don't care."

Sutton's mind raced as fast as it could. Was he serious? He looked serious. Should she get angry? Make threats? No. Those were losing propositions. She needed to use the tactic that had gotten her to this mansion in Buckhead in the first place. She stepped onto the green gingerly, trying to keep her pointy heels from sinking into the grass, and moved toward Chuck with her most alluring bedroom eyes.

"Chuck," she said in a seductive whisper. "You're just having a bad day. I can make you feel good." She started to slide her hand into the front of his comfort waist khakis, but he pushed her away.

"Is that what you did for Anderson?" he asked. "I've heard the rumors."

"I never did anything with Anderson."

"Did you sell him drugs? Is that what the autopsy's going to show? That he was high on coke or some shit from China?" Chuck may have been old, but he was still bigger than Sutton and he was holding an iron stick in his hand. Sutton stumbled backward as her heels sank into the grass and Chuck turned red with fury. "I bet I'm the laughingstock of Atlanta, married to a slut who sells drugs to the neighbors."

"I don't—"

"I've heard all about it! Hell, everyone at the damn country club knows! This is exactly the reason I put a morals clause in the prenup. So I could protect my good reputation!"

Sutton decided it was time to fight back. "*Your* reputation? What do you think all your friends at the PDC and all the good people of Buckhead will think when they find out you were fucking the housekeeper?"

Chuck was quiet for a moment. He calmed down. Sutton was sure she had him until: "You'll have a hard time proving that considering she's on a plane to Nicaragua or wherever the hell she's from. She won't be coming back."

Oh, shit. Sutton was blindsided by Chuck's sneak attack. Reyna's one day a week off, it turned out, was going to be permanent. She couldn't let Chuck see that victory was within his grasp. She needed time to think. She needed a new plan. She needed to get the hell off the battlefield. "We can talk about this later," she said with as much nonchalance as she could muster. "I'll see you tonight." She pulled her heels out of the grass. The tips were covered in dirt. Damn, another thing to worry about. Sutton walked off with a confidence that wasn't real. She looked like she was strutting but felt very much like she was crawling away.

SHAY

Shay and Dub sat in their car in the parking lot at Trinity Presbyterian Church. It was a 1940s American Greek Revival style building with a coffee cream-colored spire that rose to a point above the surrounding trees and was the day's setting for Anderson Tupper's funeral. They had come, they would tell anyone who asked, to pay their respects. In truth, they had come to see all the pieces together on the chessboard.

The lot was filled with expensive cars, most of which had stickers on their back windows or bumpers proclaiming the driver's affiliation with one of the private schools of Atlanta. There was the green and white sticker for the Westminster Schools, the burgundy one for Holy Innocents Episcopal School, the blue one for Lovett, the oval one that looked like a European country code sticker for the Atlanta International School, the Pace Academy sticker with its majestic sword, and the royal blue lion passant of Kensington Prep. These were the modern-day heraldic coat of arms of the wealthy.

"Reminds me of Colonial Williamsburg," Dub said as they got out of the car and headed toward the church. "We went there when I was a kid. I got my picture taken in one of those torture things. You know, where you stick your head and hands in holes, and they lock you in."

"A pillory," Shay informed him.

"Oh, like when you're *pilloried*? Like ridiculed. So that's where that came from."

"Yep. We should consider bringing those back."

News vans were parked on the road outside the church. The press and a pack of photographers were keeping a respectful distance, but that didn't keep them from taking pictures of every mourner who walked by, including Shay and Dub. Shay pulled her hat down to shield her face. She could hear the sound of dozens of shutters clicking away. She knew it really didn't matter. No one was interested in boring shots of detectives. Those would be deleted in favor of photos of the grieving Tuppers or Marcus Wiley.

Singing could be heard from inside the church as they walked past four Greek columns to the entrance. Dub opened the door for Shay, and they removed their hats. The nave was large by Presbyterian standards, but Shay thought it must have seemed tiny to Dub, who attended one of the Baptist megachurches in the Atlanta suburbs. They joined the end of one of the last pews. Dub sang along without picking up a hymn book, as Shay took a look around. Sutton Chambers was there. She appeared to be wearing a cocktail dress. Her mini-me daughter was beside her. The little girl was uninterested in singing and used the time to look at the adults around her. She caught Shay's eye and smiled. Shay smiled back. Birdie and Dan Milton were on the aisle of a pew close to the front. Birdie was singing loudly. Even from the back Shay could hear her booming voice. A perpetually nervous looking Kira Brooks was near the middle, not far from Lamar Burrows. Amelia Tupper was in the first row. Her daughter stood next to her, looking bored like any nine-year-old would be, and her small and squirmy younger son was standing on the bench, pretending he knew the song but singing out random words at the top of his lungs. Across the aisle sat Chatham Tupper, his young girlfriend, Heartlee, and the family matriarch, Tilly Tupper.

At the front of the church was Anderson Tupper. Dead. In a closed coffin. It was surrounded by elaborate displays of white lilies and roses that cascaded in tiers. Shay thought flowers were a waste of money. All they did was die. Here was a dead man surrounded by dying flowers. Why even bother? In general, Shay didn't see the point of funerals at all. She wanted her loved ones to throw the party of the year when she died. She didn't want people to be happy *that* she died, she wanted them to be happy she had lived, and she wanted them to eat chocolate while they told tall tales of her fabulous crime-fighting life.

The hymn ended after what seemed to be about two hundred refrains and the attendees sat back down. There was a loud thud and all heads swiveled toward Marcus Wiley. He had dropped his hymn book. He held his hand up in a gesture that seemed to say "my bad" and sat down next to Venita. For a man accustomed to having all eyes on him, he appeared to be struggling with the attention. He was visibly sweating and shifted in his spot in the pew like he was slowly being burned alive beneath a magnifying glass. Shay noticed, however, that Venita Wiley showed no emotion whatsoever. Venita must have honed this particular skill while watching her husband struggle with injuries on the field during his career.

An elderly female pastor with gray curly hair and a kind face offered the benediction. She said it with passion, but she didn't say anything new. It may have been the funeral of Anderson Tupper, the prince of Buckhead, but there were no magical words to send him on to the afterlife or comfort his loved ones. Death was the great equalizer.

Then, just as Shay was about to whisper to Dub about her disappointment at the ordinariness of Anderson Tupper's funeral, the bagpipes began.

Bagpipes.

The doors to the church opened, and a lone bagpiper made a slow march down the center aisle. He was wearing a red and blue tartan *kilt*! He had on a dark blue coat and a matching blue cap and was making the most god-awful racket Shay had ever heard. The music (was it music?) echoed off the walls of the church. It was deafening.

As far as Shay knew, the surname Tupper was German or maybe French. It was not Scottish. (She would learn later that the Tuppers had flown in the bagpiper who played every evening for guests at the Sea Island Golf Club. He flew private.) The bagpiper concluded his journey at the foot of Anderson's coffin and six men, one of them Chatham, raised it on a wheeled bier and pushed it gently up the aisle. Shay could see Tilly Tupper wipe tears from her eyes.

"Oh, Jesus Christ," Dub whispered. He wasn't praying. Shay followed his eyes to a corner of the church where a door opened and the twelve young baseball players from the CYB Vikings filed into the chapel. They were wearing their uniforms and solemnly held their caps over their hearts. The bagpiper led the coffin and its attendees up the aisle as the boys followed behind. It was meant to be poignant, a team bidding farewell to their beloved coach, but to Shay it was exploitative. This wasn't a school play. They weren't pantomime miners mourning over the casket of a princess in a school production of *Snow White and the Seven Dwarfs*. They were *boys*.

"I want to wear *my* uniform!" Amelia Tupper's little son yelled out as his brother and the team passed by. His sister nudged him to quiet him down and he hit her. They jostled back and forth until Amelia admonished them both and put an end to it.

As Chatham escorted the coffin out of the church, he noticed Shay and Dub in the pews. He stared at Shay for an uncomfortably long moment. Maybe they shouldn't have come, after all. Shay watched as the boys passed by. She recognized some of the names on the back of their jerseys. Brooks. Wiley. Milton. Chambers.

Tupper. This was cruel. This was child endangerment. This should be illegal. Shay looked around the church at their parents and wondered what other crimes they had committed.

The congregation of mourners flowed out of the chapel. Tilly and Chatham stood outside the doors accepting condolences from people as they left. It was mostly the standard "sorry for your loss" with a sprinkling of "heartbreaking" and "shocking" thrown in.

From behind Shay came the familiar voice of Birdie Milton. "Detectives!" she said. "Here to make some arrests?" Dan turned away and struck up a conversation with the couple next to him. He seemed to shrink in the presence of his wife.

"We're just here paying our respects," Shay said as politely as possible.

"The Atlanta PD. Full-service organization. Do y'all do weddings too?"

"Nice to see you, Mrs. Milton," Shay said, as the Miltons joined the queue. Ahead of them, Shay watched as Amelia kissed Tilly's cheek. The old woman showed no emotion or acknowledgment. It must have been like kissing a rock. Tilly was much warmer toward her grandchildren. She hugged them and scooted them on their way. Amelia nodded to Chatham though Shay wondered if she might not just end up punching him right there in front of the church. *That* would make for a good funeral.

Shay and Dub kept to the sidelines. In the distance, Shay could see the boys from the team messing around on the lawn. They kicked pinecones back and forth as they waited for their parents. She watched as Kira came for the boy wearing number seven, her son Kolt. He barely acknowledged her and seemed to accompany her to the parking lot with reluctance. Shay could tell that something was broken in that relationship but then caught herself. Darron was difficult at that age too. Still, something was off. Kira Brooks was off.

The detectives watched as the rest of the line moved through to pay their respects. Birdie made an inappropriate joke about how Anderson would have loved being the center of attention, and

Sutton tried to comfort the Tuppers by telling them Anderson's death was "all part of the Universe's plan for us all." It was the Wileys, however, who really got the party started.

"Sorry for your loss," Marcus said to Tilly. Venita nodded her head in agreement at his side.

"Thank you so much," Tilly said as the Wileys moved along past Chatham, who offered only a scowl.

Shay could hear Tilly ask, "Was that the caretaker from the farm?"

"No, Mama," Chatham told her. "That was Marcus Wiley."

"It wasn't!" Tilly said as she stepped away from her son and followed the Wileys. They were retrieving their son from the group of boys when Tilly came up behind Marcus and tapped him sharply on the arm. "You assaulted my son!" she said. Her neck was so clenched she lost a few wrinkles. "Did you kill him too? Did you kill my son?" Marcus refused to engage. Venita took her son by the hand, and they all walked toward the parking lot as Tilly continued to scream after them. "Did you kill my son? Did you?" Shay could hear the clicks of camera shutters as the photographers chronicled the encounter from their perches on the road. This was not the press coverage Marcus Wiley was used to getting.

Chatham rushed to his mother's side but not before pausing along the way to zing Shay and Dub. "If you would do your goddamn jobs, we wouldn't have to deal with this shit. Find out who killed my brother." He didn't wait for a reply from the detectives and went on to console his hysterical mother.

"Maybe we shouldn't have come," Dub said to Shay.

"And miss the bagpipes?" Shay asked as the back of the hearse carrying Anderson Tupper's body slammed shut behind them. His murderer had probably been in that church, thought Shay. Chatham Tupper was right. They needed to do their goddamn jobs.

SUTTON

Cash was already pulling his baseball jersey off as he and Ally and Sutton returned from Anderson Tupper's funeral. He tossed it onto the laundry room floor and kept moving. Sutton had been so proud of how grown-up he'd been at the service. She also thought he was the best-looking of all the boys and should have been at the front of the coffin instead of behind it.

"Cash, I thought we'd order from Fellini's tonight. We can get whatever pizza you want. What do you think about that?" she said as she held on to Ally's hand and they both trailed behind Cash as he stomped down the hallway.

"Why did you make me do that?" he yelled at her. "We looked like idiots walking behind his coffin! Like it was some show or something. People were laughing at us."

"No one was laughing. It was a nice thing to do."

"That was so fucking stupid!" Cash said. He ran down the hall and stomped up the back stairs.

"He said *fucking*," little Ally said in her little voice. The word almost sounded cute coming out of her mouth.

"Why don't you go upstairs?" Sutton told her daughter. "Mommy will be up in a minute." She watched as Ally followed her brother up the stairs. Sutton stood still with her thoughts for a moment. She wasn't too concerned about Cash. She knew that pizza would make everything better. She had other things to worry about. She had her husband to deal with. Sex was now a useless weapon in her arsenal. If Chuck could just pay for it, he could get it from any woman. The fact that she was his wife, and the mother of his children, was irrelevant. It was all laid out in the prenuptial. Fifteen years and she would get five million dollars. She had come up short.

Sutton absolutely loved Hilary Mantel's historical fiction audiobooks and had also watched every season of *Outlander* three times and worshiped the bodice-ripping *The Tudors*. She always wondered why people in the *olden days* seemed so eager to die. Duels were beyond silly. Why would someone just stand there and be shot at? She was mystified by the death of her heroine, Anne Boleyn. Henry VIII's wife number two of six supposedly went quietly to her beheading, saying, "Good Christian people, I am come hither to die, for according to the law and by the law I am judged to die, and therefore I will speak nothing against it." What was that shit all about? If Chuck was going to cut off Sutton's head, he was going to have to drag her kicking and screaming to the executioner.

The light was on in Chuck's office as she approached. Sutton steeled herself for battle. She thought of all the things she would tell Chuck. How she was going to hire the best lawyer in Atlanta. How the prenup would be shredded into confetti. How she would take the house *and* the kids. (Or maybe just the house because she knew Chuck didn't care that much about the kids and would be happy to be rid of them.) As for the *morals clause*? Chuck had cheated on her with their *housekeeper*! And he had also cheated on his last wife with *her*! Who was he to talk about morals?

The office door was ajar, and Sutton peeked in. She noticed there was paperwork strewn across the top of his desk. The desk was a copy of the Resolute Desk, the one that Queen Victoria gave to President Rutherford B. Hayes. Chuck's second wife had purchased it for him on their anniversary two months before he left her for Sutton. He got the desk in the divorce. Wife number two got millions.

"Chuck . . . ?" Sutton pushed the door open, but it stopped after just a foot and wouldn't budge. She looked behind it and jumped back with a gasp. Chuck was face down on the floor, his eyes open only a slit. Drool ran from the corner of his mouth to form a little pool next to his head. He was breathing, but it was shallow and came in fits and starts. He let out a weak, gurgling moan. The last smoking embers of a dying man.

Sutton took a steadying breath, stepped past her husband, and sat down at his desk. A copy of their prenuptial agreement was fanned out before her. Chuck had obviously been working on it and his chicken-scratch notes filled the margins. Sutton took off her heels and massaged her sore feet. It had been a long day. She really needed to take a bath and have a good soak. She looked down at Chuck and he looked back at her. His eyes appeared as desperate as hers were passive. Sutton gathered the pages of the prenup and picked up her shoes. They dangled from their straps in her hand and swung back and forth as she stepped over Chuck's twitching body. She turned the lights off and slowly pulled the door closed.

Good old Chuck. She vowed then and there to give her husband a bigger and better funeral than Anderson's.

CHAPTER

29

SHAY

SHAY PEERED BEHIND the door of the refrigerator in the lunchroom at headquarters. There were lunch sacks with names written on them in Sharpie, and plastic containers full of dark and scary things that had been in the refrigerator so long they had taken on a life of their own. She retrieved her own plastic container. Her name was on it, along with a warning that said *YOU TOUCH YOU DIE*.

As she pulled the top off her lunch and sat down to join Dub at one of the tables in the room, Shay realized that no warning was necessary. The contents of her container were so healthy no one would want to steal her lunch. She looked across at the spread Dub had unpacked. It was a box of Bojangles fried chicken, complete with two biscuits and sides of macaroni and cheese and French fries. He didn't even get coleslaw. "Jesus, Dub, you might as well eat a shaker of salt."

Dub took a gander at Shay's so-called lunch. He sniffed the air. "I'm not even sure *that's* food."

Shay poked her fork at the mess of quinoa and micro greens and only God knew what else. "I'm not sure either. But at least I'll live long enough to find out." Shay's phone dinged with an alert. She looked at it and wasn't sure what to make of the news. "Chuck Chambers is dead," she informed Dub.

"Sutton Chambers's husband? Did she kill him?"

"Heart attack. She probably spiked his Metamucil."

Farrell entered the room and sat down at the table with Shay and Dub. He helped himself to some of Dub's French fries and was otherwise silent and mysterious. Shay thought he was an odd kid but could put up with quirkiness so long as it showed up on time.

"Want a drumstick?" Dub asked Farrell, holding up that very thing.

"Fries are fine, thanks," Farrell said as he grabbed a few more.

"Is there something you've got to say?" Shay finally asked as she continued to poke at her "salad," searching for anything recognizable, like a cucumber or tomato.

"I have news."

"Lemme guess," Shay said. "Chuck Chambers is dead."

"He is? Seriously? Did his wife kill him?"

"Why don't you say what you were going to tell us."

Farrell held his tongue for an enticing moment. Whatever he knew, it was good. He wanted this to be suspenseful. "Kira Brooks was arrested. It was last year. In California. Someone tried to bury it, but of course I can find anything."

"You want to tell us more?" asked Shay.

"The charges were dropped," said Farrell.

"Jesus Christ!" Shay exclaimed. "Why do these rich women keep getting let off? Is it just me or is this a thing? How does this shit happen?"

"Well, then, you're really not going to like this part," Farrell continued. "She was originally charged with *attempted murder*."

CHAPTER

30

Eight Months Before the Murder

California

KIRA

*K*IRA SAT ON *one side of a table being interviewed by two detectives in an interrogation room in California. Her hair was a Medusa's tangle of knots that hung down around her puffy, vacant eyes. She was slumped in her chair with a coat wrapped around her shoulders over a filthy T-shirt that was stretched at the collar. She looked as if she had been pulled out of a washing machine and hung over the chair to dry.*

"Witnesses on the beach said you were trying to drown him," one of the detectives said. He wore a suit and a stern expression.

"I wasn't trying to drown him. I was . . . we were . . . we were just trying to stay above the water."

"Why don't you tell us what you think happened?" The detective wasn't doing a very good job of hiding his disgust with the woman sitting across from him.

Kira knew there was nothing she could say that would ever make any of this sound anything other than monstrous. She wasn't even sure what had happened. She thought for a moment. She tried to organize the events in her mind. How had she gotten in the water? How had she gotten in this chair? Where were her children? She was alone now. Wasn't that what she wanted all along? She coughed lightly. She could still taste the salt water in her mouth. Kira told stories for a living. It was time to tell another one.

* * *

Kira thought the ocean looked beautiful that morning. A storm off the coast and a strong onshore wind had churned the Malibu surf into swells of gray waves topped with white foam. She watched as the waves crashed on the rocks offshore and geysers of water spouted into the dark sky. Kira never liked heat. The sun depressed her. The clouds and gray had shown up to try and save her after a summer of relentless sunshine and blue skies.

They had come to save her. But they had come too late.

In a manic period, sometime after two glasses of wine and before a half bottle of tequila, Kira had decided to rent a beach house for the summer. She justified the extravagance by thinking she would be inspired to finish her third book in a new location west of their home in Studio City. Kallan could still commute to his office at Coke in downtown Los Angeles, Kolt could be a proper beach rat before school began in the fall, and Iris could tell everyone at school that the family had spent the summer in Malibu. Her bragging would go perfectly with her tan. Friends could come visit and bask in the glow of Kira's status as celeb author extraordinaire, and Kallan would see that Kira didn't have a drinking problem. She had a life problem. A sea breeze would blow all their problems away.

Kira thought she was clever. Obviously, she wasn't an alcoholic, though she did hate the way Kallan looked at her when she had a drink, and decided it was better to hide any bottle that might cause an argument. It wasn't the alcohol. It was the judgment. She hid airline size mini bottles of Tito's vodka in her tennis shoes in the closet and 350ml bottles of Casamigos tequila under the seat of her car. Whiskey was tucked behind the homeowner's architecture books on the bookshelves, and bottles of wine had pride of place in the back of the dishwasher where no one else would ever find them since she was the only one who cleaned up. Kira wasn't an alcoholic. She was just very good at hiding things.

Kira had abstained from alcohol until her thirty-eighth year. She had never had a sip and had resisted every temptation, even when she was in college and everyone was drunk at least four nights a week. Kira's mother had been a terrible alcoholic. For most of her life, Kira didn't realize this. She thought all mothers had to be tiptoed around for fear of provoking their rage or that they all left their children on street corners for hours because they forgot to pick them up or that they all forgot entire conversations. It wasn't until she was fifteen, and after the death of her father, that Kira realized that keeping gallon jugs of vodka under the kitchen sink behind the Cascade was not what all mothers did.

Kira could trace her mother's steps through the house by the ting-ting-tinging of ice in a glass of vodka, and she could monitor the amount her mother drank by the number of glasses stained with pink or red lipstick on the rims. For years after, the sight of lipstick on a glass repulsed Kira, as did the sound of ice clinking in a cocktail, so Kira never wore lipstick, and she never drank alcohol. Until she did.

When her mother died, Kira went to Encino to clean out the small apartment her mother had lived in. Lived in was not the right term. It was the apartment in Encino that she died in. The kitchen sink was filled with dishes encrusted with food. The recycling bin was overflowing with wine and liquor bottles. The entire place stank of cat urine and the litter box was full of cat shit. Kira never found the cat.

The bathroom hadn't been cleaned in months and smelled of the perfume her mother used to mask the smell of everything else. One drawer in the bathroom, however, was neatly lined with unopened boxes of Clinique lipstick. Kira didn't know why her mother had so many and could only guess it was because she forgot she had bought them so would buy them again. For some reason, even though almost everything else went in a dumpster in the alley, Kira kept the lipstick.

It wasn't long after her mother died, on one morning when Kira was feeling a sadness that often crept up behind her out of the dark crevices that ran through her life, that Kira put on lipstick for the first time. She opened one of her mother's Clinique boxes and pulled out a silver tube of lipstick aptly named Red Alert. She carefully applied it to her lips, trying her best to keep within the lines of her mouth, and rubbing it in gently with her fingertip. She looked at herself in the mirror that day and saw someone else. She saw her mother.

Kira had spent her entire life trying not to be like her mother. She wouldn't succumb to her mother's depression or her delusions. A lifetime of holding back the darkness, however, had left her exhausted. She now saw an easy out in a glass of wine. With that first glass of wine, Kira discovered what her mother had so cleverly figured out long ago. There was a way to relax and a way to silence the incessant noise in her head. An orchestra of stories and characters rattled her brain along with whispers of failure and imperfection. She could now keep her mind quiet. She could fail. She could be imperfect. She could drink. The lipstick stained the rim of that first glass as it would the rims of countless glasses to come.

There were times when Kira thought she could feel the earth turning as it moved around the sun, effortlessly traversing its space in the solar system. She would be caught in one of her inherited bouts of depression and suddenly remember she was on a giant rock rotating in a vast universe, that she was nothing more than an ant on that rock, and for a brief moment, as she felt the phantom sensation of her home planet turning, she didn't care about anything or anyone. She felt like a redundant cog in the great mechanism of the universe. The world would turn with or without her.

On this morning in Malibu, with Kallan at work and Iris at a sleepover and as clouds formed and the world turned, Kira felt an overwhelming desire to throw herself off the edge of the planet and float away into space. She tried to drown the feeling with alcohol. She finished off the vodka in her tennis shoes and the tequila in her car. It was when searching for the bottle of Johnnie Walker hidden on the bookshelves, however, that the ultimate solution to her battle with life presented itself. There, next to a Dan Brown thriller, was a copy of Virginia Woolf's 'A Room of One's Own'.

Of course. Virginia Woolf.

Virginia Woolf was a respected writer, admired in her own time, with a supportive husband and an enviable life, who filled her pockets with stones and waded into the River Ouse and drowned herself. It was a sign. Right there next to the bottle of whiskey was the answer Kira had been looking for. She had been given the blueprint to build her death.

Kira found a puffy red Moncler ski jacket hanging among a storehouse of sporting goods in the garage. It was meant to keep someone warm on top of a mountain in Telluride and was certainly not beach attire. It was appropriately heavy, however, with pockets on the inside and out and it fit the bill. She pulled a small dumbbell off a shelf and stuffed it into one of the pockets. She found a wrench on a tool bench (or a pair of pliers—she wasn't sure) and put it in an inside pocket. It was a good start.

In the kitchen, she poured a jar of change into the top pocket. She missed a few pennies and dimes, and they spilled out and rolled across the kitchen floor. Normally, Kira would have dutifully picked them up. She decided, just this once, she didn't have to be so conscientious.

Kira pulled cans of soda out of the fridge and found room for them in her strange collection of items in the ski jacket. The weight began to pull her shoulders down. She then found the perfect addition to her après ski outfit. It was a stone mortar and pestle that sat on the counter next to the stove. They were dark gray, almost black, and both primitive and stylish at the same time. Kallan had gotten her a similar set one Christmas. It was a subtle nudge to up her cooking game. She had never used them. Now she saw that such things had purpose. After a bit of rearranging, she was able to fit the mortar and pestle in a large pocket that was meant, perhaps, for ski goggles or a Subway sandwich to eat atop a snowcapped mountain.

She finished off the bottle of whiskey as she worked on what was to be her final literary work. It wasn't her book or a short story. It was her last letter to her children. How could she sum up all the feelings mixing like a deadly potion in her mind? How could she both make them understand but also assure them that they had no blame in what she was about to do? How could she tell them she loved them so much she was leaving them? She tried to come up with the right words, but much like the third book in her trilogy, she couldn't manage to finish. In the end, she scribbled down all that mattered.

Kira slowly walked the letter down the hall to the room Kolt was staying in. The ski jacket really was heavy. She felt strangely proud of herself for doing such a good job with that. She cracked the door open a few inches to find Kolt asleep in a room that was usually occupied by a young girl. It was pink and purple and filled with all things flowered and sweet. Too many frilly pillows littered the floor, and Kolt himself was splayed out, all arms and legs, atop a comforter covered in rainbows.

She slipped into the room and quietly made her way to the foot of the bed. She took one last look at Kolt. Her son. He was so kind and timid. A quiet, nervous little guy. He reminded her so much of herself at that age. Which was even more reason to untether herself from their world. Her departure would save him. Iris would be fine. Kira could already feel her daughter pulling away. Maybe that's just what happened naturally or maybe she had been a terrible mother. Probably the latter. Kolt, however, would struggle. She knew that. They were so close. With her gone, though, her son could be more like his father and his sister and less like her. He might hate her for a long time, but he would surely someday realize that she had sacrificed not only for herself but also for him. She placed her final letter, brief as it was, on the foot of the bed and tried to sneak away. One of the soda cans in her pockets, however, fell and made a clanging sound loud enough to cause Kolt to stir. He shifted in the bed but didn't wake. Kira closed the door.

When Kolt finally awakened later that morning he would find a note with two words written on it.

I'm sorry.

Atlanta

There was screaming. It was the kind of screaming that rang in the ears long after it had ended. High and piercing and fierce. Kira remembered that much. That, and the sensation of her arms coming down with great force. It had come back in flashes in the days since the Steeplechase. She had glimpses of something horrible. Of the screaming and of blood. The flashes were always accompanied by a feeling of fury mixed with a chaser of guilt. There was always guilt.

Kira sat in the interview room at police headquarters. Detectives Claypool and Rattigan were talking to her, but her mind had drifted off. Detective Claypool repeated her question.

"Mrs. Brooks? Why didn't you tell us about your arrest in California?"

California? That caught Kira off guard. She was ready for them to ask her about the night of the Steeplechase. The night that was haunting her in fits and flashes. How did they know about California? "Those charges were dropped."

"But didn't you think they were worth mentioning to us? This is a murder investigation."

"They were *dropped*."

Detective Rattigan opened the screen on a laptop computer and slid it across the table toward Kira. There, frozen in time from months before that felt like moments before, was her daughter Iris. She was sitting in a police station in Malibu talking to an unseen interviewer. She was being filmed by a camera somewhere above, and her voice in the tinny audio sounded as small as she seemed to be as she sat slumped in a chair, pale despite a summer tan and exhausted.

"*How long were you on the beach?*" *asked the disembodied voice of a police officer.*

"*Just a few minutes,*" *Iris said.* "*I had just gotten home from a friend's house.*"

"*From what you could see, what did you think your mother was doing?*"

Iris looked up at the camera for a moment like she knew Kira was watching. "*I think she was trying to kill him.*"

Detective Rattigan paused the video, and both he and Detective Claypool looked to Kira for some acceptable explanation. She could see they were judging her. And rightfully so.

"I wasn't trying to kill him," Kira said.

California

It began to rain as Kira walked down the wooden steps to the beach. How fitting. It never rained in California (or so the old song went), but now the distant storm had come ashore to greet her. Perhaps it was another sign. It was easier to do this in the gloom, she thought, since it was a very gloomy thing to do. It also made the ski jacket more appropriate for the occasion. On a bright and sunny day, wearing a ski jacket to end your life on a Southern California beach seemed akin to wearing white after Labor Day. People who cared about such things just wouldn't approve.

As a last concession to the small comforts of life, Kira had slipped on her Teva flip-flops before heading to the beach. Now, as she trudged across the sand toward the water, she thought how odd she must look in the red Moncler ski jacket and jeans and flip-flops. She was relieved that no one was yet on the beach that morning to see this spectacle. When you spend your entire life worrying about being judged, it didn't seem a lot to ask to be able to die without comment.

Kira stepped into the water and met a wave as it unfolded on the shore. The waves broke with a snap that sounded like the ocean's own version of thunder. The wind blew the caps off the waves and the water hit Kira's face. She plowed forward and was soon thigh high in water. Her left flip-flop came off and popped to the surface. It was instantly carried off by the receding water and sucked into a bigger wave that crashed just before Kira and momentarily lifted her off her feet. She dug the toes of her left foot into the sand and propelled herself forward even as the waves kept pushing her back.

It was soon apparent that the Moncler ski jacket was water resistant, not waterproof, as the salt water began to soak through the outer layer and saturate the goose feathers within. Kira had to hold the jacket tightly together with one hand to keep the waves from pulling it off her body. She regretted not having zipped it closed before she entered the water. Rookie mistake. Maybe next time.

Kira felt purposeful as she headed out to sea. She had a task, and she was a task master. Every hard-fought step into the waves felt like a mighty triumph against life itself. Fifteen feet from shore she stepped into a trough and suddenly the water was nearly to her chest. The waves had their way with her, tugging her this way and that, lifting her up and pushing her down as seaweed swirled around her and the rain attacked from above. And then it happened. One fierce wave came to knock her off her feet, and a second more formidable wave crashed into her and sent her floating for a moment, lying across the surface of the water, before she sank like a woman in a weighted down ski jacket should sink. Successfully.

She was only a few feet below the surface, but that was enough. Kira opened her eyes and looked toward the water churning above her. She barely noticed the sting of the salt water and watched passively as her second flip-flop floated above her and was carried away. It was all just what she had imagined it would be. In that moment, while she still had air in her lungs and while her body had yet to begin its involuntary battle for survival, she felt nothing but relief.

And then the other thing happened.

Kira felt something tug on her arm. She watched as her arm raised up and then saw another arm. Then another. Then, hovering above her like an angel in a mismatched set of pajamas, was her son. He was there and then he was gone. Had he really been there? Was she dying? Kolt. She remembered she loved him. Suddenly, her body lifted from behind and she twisted along the pebbles at the bottom. Her arms pulled back and her shoulders strained at an uncomfortable angle. Had she understood what was happening, had she not been drowning and had she realized Kolt was real and not some sea serpent, she may have tried to stop him as he struggled to pull the ski jacket off her body. Just as her oxygen ran out and she began to breathe in water instead of air, she popped to the surface like one of her flip-flops.

She took in a great gasp of air as Kolt surfaced next to her and did the same. He reached out and grabbed ahold of her arm and pulled himself toward her. "Mom! Mom! Come on! We have to go back!" He wrapped his legs around her like he used to when he was smaller, and she was happier. Like when they would go to the beach and she would carry him out just far enough to make it exciting but not far enough to make it scary. He didn't seem scared now. He seemed terrified.

Kira looked at her son's skinny arms now wrapped around her neck. He kept screaming, "Mom! Mom!" but she wasn't listening. She had felt at peace for that moment underwater and now she was back in a swirling pool of chaos. The waves were loud. The wind was loud. Kolt's screams in her ears were piercing. She became overwhelmed with a need to escape back under the surface. Kira worked to pry Kolt's arms off her neck and literally get him off her back. He was holding on for his life and hers.

As Kira spit up salt water and struggled with her son, she came back to the world in a panic. She felt like she was drowning in oxygen. It wasn't the water that was killing her. It wasn't the world below. It was the world above. She clawed at Kolt's arms. Her nails dug into them deep enough to cause open wounds. Blood mixed with salt water and ran in channels down his arms and down her chest. She finally escaped his grasp as a wave crashed into them both. They were pulled apart and Kira tried to swim out farther, but Kolt grabbed the end of her shirt and had her in his grasp once more.

Kira turned and grabbed both his shoulders and pushed him down beneath the water. She just wanted him to stop. Even as he struggled against her force and tried to surface, she didn't think she was doing anything other than trying to survive long enough to die. After too long a moment, his hand broke the surface and seeing it was almost like being slapped by it. She let go of her hold and he rose from the ocean, coughing up sea water and desperate for air. His eyes locked on hers as they both bobbed in the water. It was as if he had been baptized in the Pacific Ocean and born again as someone else's son. An unspoken pact between mother and son and parent and child had been broken. She was no longer his protector. She could see it in his eyes. She had become someone new to him, a stranger who had tried to drown him.

Kira was instantly sober.

Atlanta

"Any plans to try and kill yourself again?" Detective Claypool asked.

Kira liked the detective's directness. A lifetime of tiptoeing around difficult subjects had led her to appreciate it. "You can't think about living without thinking about dying. That's six months of rehab and therapy talking, by the way. I highly recommend it."

"Did you leave the Steeplechase with Anderson Tupper?" Detective Rattigan asked.

"Not that I remember."

Claypool cut to the chase. "Were you drinking that night?"

"Not that I remember," Kira said again. "But the fact that I don't remember makes me think that I might have been."

"Mr. Tupper's autopsy indicates that he had taken GHB that night."

"The date rape drug?" Kira asked. "I didn't see that. I mean, I didn't give it to him, if that's what you're wondering."

"Do you think you could have been drugged?" asked Detective Claypool.

"Well, now I do."

Detective Rattigan flipped over to a new page in his little black notebook. It concerned Kira that he was taking notes on everything she said. "Do you remember how you got home that night?"

"Promise not to arrest me?" Kira asked.

"No," Detective Claypool said.

"My car was in the driveway the next morning. So I assume I drove it home from the Steeplechase."

"Under the influence?"

"Under the influence of something," Kira told them. Kira wasn't a murderer, was she? But she had driven home and didn't remember it. What else had she done that she didn't remember?

CHAPTER

31

SHAY

Drowning seemed a terrifying way to die. Most men committed suicide by shooting themselves. Most women took pills or slit their wrists. Drowning was an odd choice, though Kira was an odd person. Shay herself had never contemplated taking her own life. Not once. Not after the fire or the divorce. Not when she struggled to pay the bills. Not when she struggled as a single mother. That option never even occurred to her. She had spent the whole night thinking about Kira. She was a woman of accomplishment, a mother, who had more money and success than she knew what to do with but had waded out into the Pacific Ocean in the hopes it would swallow her whole. Did life mean so little to Kira that she had to think of an eccentric way to end hers?

Kira occupied Shay's thoughts as she waited for the elevator to take her to her office. Shay tried to build the case in her mind. Kira had been drunk or high. She and Anderson Tupper had gone to the fields that night for a romantic rendezvous that went awry. Anderson Tupper had rejected Kira's advances. They fought. She had attacked him . . .

No.

Maybe it was Mr. Brooks. Shay knew there was a Mr. Brooks, but he had, until now, been a footnote in her investigation. Maybe Mr. Brooks—Shay couldn't remember his first name—caught his wife and Anderson *in flagrante* and killed Tupper in a jealous rage. Maybe . . .

Shay's phone rang and rescued her from all the *maybes*. It was Dub. "Where are you?" he asked. "I've got some news."

"You want to just tell me over the phone?"

"That's no fun," Dub said.

"I'm waiting for the elevator. I'll be there in a minute."

Their call ended just as the elevator door opened. Before Shay could get in, however, she was interrupted by the appearance of Deputy Chief Henderson. He bounded through the metal detectors at the front entrance to the building, all smiles and back-slapping brotherly love, and strode toward Shay with his ramrod posture and protruding pecs.

"Cousin Claypool," he called out. "Let's talk."

Shay took a deep breath, steeling herself for his onslaught, and held the elevator door open. Instead, Henderson beckoned for her to follow him. "Let's take the stairs."

Their offices were on the tenth floor. Of course Henderson wanted to take the stairs. He was a take-the-stairs kind of guy. Shay suddenly knew how Dub must have felt when she got on him about his poor dietary choices. She decided she'd lay off Dub for a while. She didn't want to be a Henderson.

"So, I just got back from meeting with the governor," Henderson said, as he opened the door to the stairwell and bounded up the first flight of stairs. Shay did her best to keep up, but she hadn't run in three days and stairs were a level of exertion she tended to avoid. "Nice man. Misunderstood, I think. He's a Republican, you know?" Yes, Shay knew. "We tend to demonize people because of their politics, don't we?" Henderson continued. "There really shouldn't be political parties. It divides us. We should be a united people. Atlantans. Georgians. Americans."

Earthlings? Let's get past all this kumbaya bullshit and get to the point, Shay thought, as her legs began to falter somewhere around the third floor.

"Anyhow," Henderson said as he took the fourth floor *two steps at a time*. Asshole. "The governor was wondering where we're at on Tupper. I'm wondering that too. The Buckhead vote is coming up and people are nervous."

"Well, sir, we're making progress," Shay said as she tried to catch her breath and Henderson waited for her on the fifth-floor landing. "We have suspects. We have leads."

"How close are we?"

"Close."

"Who do you think did it?" Henderson said, getting down to business and starting his climb again. "I won't hold you to it. Just wondering what your gut says."

"At this moment, I'd say Marcus Wiley is our top suspect," Shay told him. "There's not enough evidence yet to charge him, but that's what I'm feeling."

Henderson stopped again, and Shay used the handrails to slowly pull herself up to the sixth-floor landing to join him. As she tried to look cool, to look like her lungs weren't screaming and she didn't need to call for oxygen, Henderson smiled and put his hand on her shoulder. "I think it would be good if, maybe, you got a different feeling," he told her. "We really don't want it to be Marcus Wiley. That's not a good look for Buckhead or Atlanta."

With that, Henderson turned and ran up the remaining floors. Shay sat down on the stairs and caught her breath. *Not a good look?* Did Henderson just deliver a message from the governor to eliminate a suspect because he was a football star? Shay understood the ramifications of Marcus Wiley being a murderer. He was the favorite son. The gridiron hero. The governor was just a governor. Governors came and went. Marcus Wiley was an icon. Shay took the message for what it probably really meant. Not that she shouldn't arrest Wiley if he was the killer, but that she should be damn well sure that he was before she did.

By the time Shay made it to the tenth floor, with sweat running down her back and her lungs shredded, she had forgotten that Dub was waiting for her with news. She found him standing by the elevators, and he was surprised to see her when she came up behind him looking like a tourist who had just climbed the Spanish Steps in the middle of July.

"What happened?" Dub asked.

"I took the stairs," Shay said. "For exercise. I think we should start doing it every day."

"If you keep this up, I'm asking for a new partner," Dub said. He was probably only half joking.

"What did you want to tell me?"

"DNA results from under Tupper's fingernails came back."

"And?"

"It's a match. To his brother," Dub said. "Not that we know that officially. We didn't have a warrant for that sample."

It was true. Shay had taken Chatham Tupper's water bottle without his knowledge. He hadn't agreed to it. He hadn't been arrested for a felony, which would have given them the power to take a DNA sample, and they hadn't gotten a warrant for it. Sometimes, as detectives, you stretched the boundaries of the law in order to do your job. Sometimes you had to.

"It doesn't stop us from talking to him," Shay said.

"What about his lawyer?" Dub asked.

"What if we just happen to run into Chatham Tupper?"

"Just happen to be wherever he is in Buckhead?"

"Sure," Shay said. "I like hanging out in Buckhead. It's growing on me."

AMELIA

This was once her fiefdom. Her personal Moon Base Alpha. The Peachtree Driving Club was where Amelia reigned. She used to saunter in, right past whichever lackey was manning reception, and hold court like the Empress of Buckhead that she was. Women would take note of what she was wearing and hightail it to Tootsie's the next day to copy her style. Men would seek to charm her with flattery in hopes that she'd put in a good word with her husband. To be Mrs. Chatham Tupper at the PDC was a very good thing.

After her divorce, Amelia checked Emily Post's etiquette book to navigate the rules on how a divorced woman should be addressed. It said she could choose her maiden name or she could keep the Tupper surname. What she could no longer be was Mrs. *Chatham* Tupper. She could be Mrs. *Amelia* Tupper. And now that Chatham had revoked her country club membership, Mrs. Amelia Tupper was standing at the reception desk like any other peon.

"You're meeting Mrs. Dan Milton?" the woman in a black blazer at the desk asked. She acted like she didn't know Amelia, when in fact she had worked there for ten years and had dealt with Amelia hundreds of times before. Amelia had tipped her a thousand dollars every Christmas. She had gotten Chatham to write a college recommendation for the woman's son and vouched for her when she wanted to join the Junior League. Now the woman was looking at Amelia like she was a homeless person who had wandered in off the street looking for a bathroom.

"I'm here to see Birdie," Amelia said, trying to keep her cool. "She's waiting for me in the dining room. Can I go through? I remember the way."

"Of course. Enjoy your dinner, Amelia."

Amelia took a few steps, then turned back around. "You can still call me Mrs. Tupper." Emily Post said so.

Amelia found Birdie sitting at one of the prime tables in the PDC dining room. The elite of Buckhead were at the tables surrounding them. Delicate porcelain plates topped with buttered saltine crackers were on each table, an amuse-bouche that the PDC was famous for, as if to say, *we're just common folk*. Every one of those common folk stared as Amelia sat down with Birdie. Word had now traveled to the farthest reaches of Buckhead, all the way to Brookhaven and Brookwood Hills, that the members of the Peachtree Steeplechase auction committee had all been interviewed by the police. If they had become an object of fascination in the school car line, here it felt like they were on the stand at the Salem witch trials. Amelia wondered if they were preparing a pyre on which to roast them in the ballroom.

"We could have met somewhere else. There's a new restaurant in Chamblee that's supposed to be good," Amelia said.

"Chamblee?" Birdie said with mock indignation. "I'm not even sure they have paved roads there, let alone good restaurants. Besides, it's fun to mess with everyone. Let them think we killed Anderson. Let them worry they might be next."

Birdie looked across the dining room where Laura was sitting with some other women. They had been whispering and stealing glances at Birdie and Amelia, and now Birdie stared them down. She didn't divert her gaze until Laura wilted and turned away.

"I don't like people thinking we've done something," Amelia said.

"Well, maybe we have. I mean, I can absolutely make a case for Sutton having murdered Anderson."

"Birdie . . ."

"Come on, don't tell me you haven't thought it. I mean, it's even money that she killed Chuck, even if it was just by withholding his meds or something, so it's not out of the realm of possibility that she did in Anderson when he spurned her advances."

Amelia scoffed at Birdie's hypothesis. "You don't really think so."

"No," Birdie admitted. "Though it is fun to imagine. Little Sutton luring Anderson to Chastain with her feminine wiles. Then beating him to death with one of Chuck's golf clubs." She let that hang out there for a moment. "I'm *joking*. He was probably killed by loan sharks. You know what a fuckup Anderson was." Birdie stopped and seemed to realize she had, once again, gone too far. "I'm sorry," she told Amelia. "I shouldn't make fun. He was your brother-in-law."

"He was my brother-in-law *and* a fuckup."

The sommelier approached the table with a wine list, but Birdie stopped him before he could say a word. "Just bring us whatever Mr. Milton got last time he was here," she told the man, and he scurried away to the wine cellars. She turned back to Amelia. "That way, depending on which wine he brings, I'll know if Dan's been here without me."

"What's going on with the Dan situation?" Amelia asked, even if she wasn't sure she wanted to know.

"Let's just say I've been binge-watching a lot of *Snapped* lately," Birdie said.

All eyes turned to the front of the room, and Amelia looked to see Chatham and Heartlee enter. Just what she needed. She hadn't been to the PDC in five months, and now, when she finally decided to show her face, he had decided to come on the same night. Amelia wondered if the black-blazered woman at the reception desk had called him and told him to run over to further humiliate his ex-wife.

Chatham was stopped by at least a dozen people as he and his girlfriend made their way across the room. "Chatham, we're so sorry about Anderson." "What a tragedy . . ." "We're all hoping they find out who did this terrible thing soon." "Has there been any progress in the investigation?" Chatham and Heartlee were consoled all the way to the only table in the dining room even better, even more prestigious, than Birdie's. The table next to her and Amelia.

Amelia did her best to ignore her ex-husband's presence so close to her and to avoid Heartlee's gaze. She wondered if the young woman had gotten the abortion. Amelia had regretted telling Heartlee to get one. She wouldn't have ended her pregnancies, even if she had known what her husband was really like, so why had she told this woman to do it? Maybe if they ran into each other in the restroom later, Amelia would be kinder to Heartlee. Or maybe she'd just let it go. It wasn't her problem, after all.

The sommelier brought a bottle of wine to the table and displayed the label for Birdie to approve. She rolled her eyes when she saw it. "Jesus, how pedestrian," she said. "Take that swill away. Bring us a bottle of the 2018 Silver Oak Cabernet." The sommelier took the offending bottle away leaving Birdie looking pissed, and not in the drunk way. "Fucking Dan. Fucking fucking fucker. He brought her here. I know it."

"Come on, Birdie, let's just leave," Amelia pleaded. "Let's go get drunk in the parking lot."

For a moment, Amelia thought she had Birdie convinced. She could see that Birdie was contemplating it. The thoughts of Dan in the same room, and probably at the same table, with another woman would have lit what was becoming an increasingly shorter fuse. Amelia was about to reach for her Hermes bag to make a quick escape when she looked back across the room to see Detectives Claypool and Rattigan headed their way. *Here*, she thought. They came *here*. It was one thing to show up unannounced at her home, but now they had invaded the PDC. A sacred space. And in front of *everyone*. Detective Rattigan smiled at her as they came closer. Why was he smiling? What did they want? Amelia felt like she was in middle school and the principal had come to her classroom to take her away. When the waiter returned with the bottle of Silver Oak, he couldn't fill her glass fast enough.

Then, at the last moment, the detectives turned and approached the table next to Birdie and Amelia. *Chatham's table*.

"Good evening, Mr. Tupper," Claypool said. "Mind if we join you for a moment?"

"What are you doing here?" Chatham asked. He seemed as confused as Amelia. "How did you know I was here?" He looked around the room for a moment. Yep, all eyes were on him.

"Your assistant was kind enough to tell us," Claypool said. "Can we sit?"

Amelia looked at Birdie. She was watching the unfolding encounter with a joyful expression. Nothing had happened and it was already the best show in town. Birdie raised her wineglass in a toast toward Claypool, but the detective didn't acknowledge her or Amelia.

"I think, maybe, you should speak with Dan Milton," Chatham said softly. He kept the volume down, but his every word could still be heard in the hushed dining room. People leaned in.

"We just have a few questions," Claypool said. Loudly. "I'm sure you want to help out in any way you can, right?"

Chatham reluctantly motioned for the detectives to take seats at the table. Heartlee looked frightened. She was already out of her element, and this couldn't have helped ease her nerves.

A server, apparently unaware that this party of four was unusual in any way, deposited a plate full of saltines in the center of the table. "The butter crackers," Rattigan said. "It's true. Mind if I try one?" Rattigan didn't wait for permission and took a cracker. Amelia observed that the detectives were acting differently than they had with her. They were more aggressive. She wondered what this meant.

"Are you here to share some information about my brother?" Chatham asked.

"Well, I guess so," Claypool told him. "We were able to obtain some DNA from your brother's body. From under his fingernails. It seems he might have scratched his killer during the attack."

"That's helpful," Chatham said, unconvincingly.

"And we were wondering if you might have any thoughts at all about whose DNA that might be?"

"I have no idea."

"No idea? Are you sure?" Claypool asked as Rattigan took another cracker and devoured it in one bite. "Maybe you'd like to submit a DNA sample, just to give us a clean slate. You know, my boss likes for us to narrow down all possible suspects."

"I'm not a suspect," Chatham said coldly.

"Then help us out."

Chatham was silent for a moment. When Amelia first met him, she took these bouts of wordlessness as signs of his intellect. When he grew quiet, she thought he was coming up with grand plans. It was only later, when he was lying to her about threesomes with prostitutes and secret bank accounts used to hide his assets, that she realized that these pauses were something else. Time spent to come up with lies.

"There *was* something," Chatham finally admitted. "During our fight that night."

"At the Steeplechase," Claypool said. "I thought it was an argument."

"There was the fight after the argument," Chatham told them. "We got into, I guess you would call it a *scuffle*, outside the tent after we argued."

"A *scuffle*?" asked Claypool.

A *scuffle*, thought Amelia.

"It was nothing really," Chatham continued. "We pushed each other around a bit. I don't know. It's possible he scratched me then. I mean, I had some minor scratches. So, I guess, there's a small chance that my DNA could be under his fingernails."

Birdie finished off her glass of wine in one large swig and Amelia followed suit. There had been no talk of a fistfight that night between the brothers. But then, Amelia never had a chance to talk to Anderson again after that night. All she could think was what an idiot Chatham was being. Without Dan to watch over him, it seemed he'd say anything.

"We had worse fights when we were kids," Chatham said. "It was harmless."

"Did anyone else see this fight?" Claypool asked.

"No," Chatham said. "No one was there." He suddenly seemed to remember something. Or seemed to catch himself. He looked at his girlfriend. "Except Heartlee. Heartlee was there, weren't you?"

Heartlee looked lost. Like she had been caught using the salad fork for the main course. She stared back at Chatham, then glanced at Amelia. All Amelia could think was *don't bring me into this*. Heartlee turned back to the detectives and coughed up a barely audible "Yeah."

"Is that a 'yeah' for the record?" Claypool asked.

"Yeah."

The detective turned her attention back to Chatham. "Anything else we should know? Was there a scuffle *after* the scuffle *after* the argument you want to tell us about?"

Chatham seemed to finally come to his senses and remember that he was Chatham Fucking Tupper, and they were on his turf. "I think any more questions should be reserved for my lawyer," he said. "Just so we don't have any misunderstandings."

Claypool nodded. "No, we don't want any misunderstandings." She stood up from the table, which prompted Rattigan to do the same. "Thank you for your vital assistance. We'll be in touch." With that, the two detectives departed. A low din of conversation returned to the room, and Amelia knew that the diners weren't talking about the previous night's Braves game.

Chatham. Could he have killed Anderson? It had never occurred to Amelia, but now she could think of nothing else. She had always thought her ex-husband was capable of anything. He had never ceased to surprise her with the depths of his viciousness. Once, during a particularly rough round of sex, Chatham had choked her until she passed out. That was all in the name of pleasure. But was murder pleasurable as well? Amelia shook it off. Chatham couldn't be a killer. She couldn't have married a killer. Her children couldn't be the children of a killer.

Could they?

Birdie poured herself another glass of wine. "Aren't you glad we stayed?"

CHAPTER

32

SHAY

"One time, my brother broke two of my fingers," Dub said as he pulled on a light overcoat. Spring had turned to winter again for a few days. He and Shay were in the War Room. They had been discussing the Tupper vs. Tupper fight when Dub had decided it was time to pick up some lunch.

"That's just kids being kids," Shay told him.

"No, that was at Thanksgiving two years ago. Remember?"

Shay had a vague recollection of Dub complaining that his fingers hurt. Yes, brothers did fight. Sisters too. Shay was an only child. All her battles were with herself.

"I'm going to pick something up at the salad place," Dub told her. "You want anything?"

"Are you going there before or after you go to Chick-fil-A?" Shay asked. Dub just smiled. It was obvious he was only going to the salad place if she wanted something. "I'm fine, thanks."

Dub left the War Room and left Shay alone with her thoughts. She had a million of them and she was trying desperately to organize them all in her head. Marcus Wiley was nagging at her, but Chatham Tupper was screaming for attention. He had failed to mention the physical altercation with his brother. He was smart not to offer more information than he had to, though stupid to admit to the fight without his lawyer present. He could have been lying, but there was the pesky matter of a witness. She was the same witness who said she had been with Chatham the entire evening. Girlfriends of rich men, Shay found, were notoriously unreliable.

Chatham Tupper or Marcus Wiley. Shay didn't have enough evidence to arrest either of them. Besides, Henderson and the governor didn't want the killer to be either of them. They wanted it to be a loan shark seeking payment or a jealous boyfriend seeking revenge. It couldn't be someone notable, not one of Buckhead's leaders or a beloved football star. And it shouldn't be someone from the other side of the tracks. Not a drug dealer or a gang member from South Atlanta. That would just prove the Buckhead secessionists' case: that although they paid the lion's share of the taxes, they got the lamb's share of the policing.

Find us a *convenient* killer.

"Lt. Claypool, I have something," Farrell said as he entered the War Room and sat in the chair next to Shay. He always had something. His eagerness, which was sometimes annoying, was also sometimes endearing. Shay remembered when she used to be excited about every little found clue or new evidence in an investigation. She wondered how many murders she had investigated before she had become jaded.

"I've been digging around the secretary of state's office, looking into this corporate stuff with the Tupper company," Farrell told her, almost breathlessly. "You know it was for sale?"

"And Anderson Tupper wasn't happy about it."

"Well, a company called Oconee Concepts had an offer in," Farrell explained.

"Never heard of them."

"That's because they only exist on paper," he continued. "They were incorporated six months ago. Oconee, in turn, is owned by another corporation called Buckhead International that's owned by *another* corporation called Tupelo Holdings."

"And?"

"Tupelo Holdings lists its director as none other than Dan Milton."

"Mr. Birdie?"

"Mr. Birdie," Farrell confirmed. "Sounds like Mr. Birdie and Chatham Tupper had some sweet side deal going on. Make a lowball offer to buy the company and then flip it later for more money."

"And screw all their shareholders, including his ex-wife and his brother. Anderson was making that very hard for them," Shay said as she looked at the photo of Dan Milton that had been added to the wall of suspects and a new thought began to take shape. Maybe Chatham Tupper. Maybe Dan Milton. Or maybe Chatham Tupper *and* Dan Milton.

"If you don't come in on Saturday, don't bother coming in on Sunday," Shay said.

"I have to come in on Saturday?" Farrell asked. He seemed genuinely alarmed by this.

"No," Shay told him. "It was something Dan Milton said. Has anyone confirmed that he was at his office that night?"

"We're still working on the warrant."

"Well, maybe you *should* come in on Saturday," Shay told Farrell. She was annoyed now. But also fired up. She grabbed her hat and her bag and headed for the door. "I'm going to go to Milton's office myself. Sonny Crocket wouldn't wait around for a warrant."

"I thought you were Tubbs."

"I am not Tubbs!" Shay declared as she exited the War Room to the pulsating Jan Hammer *Miami Vice* theme music that was playing in her head.

* * *

The Law Offices of Goodman, Roberts, Milton & Goizueta were in a luxury mid-rise office building in the heart of Buckhead. Peachtree Road squeezed through the small commercial district, and traffic in the area could be a nightmare. In fact, traffic everywhere in Atlanta could be, and usually was, a nightmare. Shay often had gruesome fantasies about road rage vengeance. She thought that if she should ever be diagnosed with terminal cancer, she would spend her final days crashing into cars that cut her off. Atlanta would be her end-of-days demolition derby. It was a nice thought to pass the time in a traffic jam.

Shay maneuvered through Buckhead traffic and parked in the porte cochere at the front of the building. A parking attendant jogged from the valet stand waving his hands in alarm. With a Bentley SUV and several shiny sports cars out front at the ready, Shay's Dodge ruined the image the landlords were trying to promote. Shay set the attendant straight by pulling out her badge and waving it back at him.

With her trusty Dodge wedged between two Porsches, Shay took the elevator to the eighth floor, one of three floors the law firm occupied in the building. The elevator doors opened on two twelve-foot-tall wooden doors with the law firm's name printed in stately block letters across the front. There was an intercom, and Shay noticed a keycard reader next to it. You couldn't just walk in off the street and gain access to this place. This wasn't a personal injury law firm. They didn't chase ambulances. Not unless they were filled with millionaires.

"Can I help you?" The pleasant and officious voice of a young woman came through the speaker at the intercom. Shay was surprised since she hadn't even pressed the button yet.

"Detective Claypool, Atlanta PD," Shay said as she looked around for hidden cameras but couldn't find any. The door buzzed and opened automatically. Shay entered to find the young woman from the intercom sitting at a long desk alongside two other young women. They all had on headsets and were answering an endless inflow of calls that they then transferred to the offices behind them.

"Hello," the intercom woman greeted Shay. "Are you here to see someone?"

"Actually, yes, I am," Shay said as she flashed her badge. "I was hoping I could speak with whoever it is that handles your keycard system."

"That would be Derek Kerr from IT." In a flash, she called Derek from IT and asked that he come to reception. Shay was waiting for her to ask for a warrant or court order or even a sticky note from the boss saying this was okay, but she didn't question Shay. "He'll be out in a sec."

Shay looked around the offices as she waited. A small army of people worked behind glass walls, on phones, ferrying paperwork, meeting in hushed clusters. After her husband tried to roast Shay and Darron alive, she still ended up having to fight him for custody in court. It was then that Shay gained a grudging appreciation for lawyers. They didn't care about feelings. They cared about facts. Lawyers were the rational custodians of the irrational. During the only time in her life when Shay felt unhinged, her lawyers reined her in. This place was filled with the same kind of people. These, however, were the expensive ones.

"Detective?" came a voice from behind Shay. She turned around to find a man who was much younger than she expected. Anyone who worked with technology, Shay remembered, was going to be younger than her. "I'm Derek Kerr," he said, shaking her hand. "You wanted to talk about our keycard system?"

"Yes, I was wondering if you keep a log of when people enter and exit the offices."

"Yeah, it's all stored in the system."

"Do you think you could pull up a particular day for me?"

Derek looked a little uncomfortable. "Uh, I think I'm supposed to ask if you have a warrant," he said with uncertainty. He was an IT guy, after all, and not a lawyer.

"I'm here informally," Shay said. "I'm not requesting any documents." That had nothing to do with a warrant, but it sounded good.

And it did the trick. "Okay, great," Derek said. "Follow me."

The IT guy led Shay through a maze of hallways to his small office in a far corner next to a supply closet. It was filled with computer servers and mysterious equipment with blinking lights that probably did amazing things and were run by artificial intelligence.

A laptop computer and a ham sandwich were on a small desk that was surrounded by Atlanta Braves bobbleheads. The heads of the sports figurines jiggled back and forth as Derek sat down and began navigating his computer.

"What date were you looking for?" he asked. He was so helpful. Shay really hoped he didn't get in trouble for this later.

"March 22nd."

"A Saturday," he noted. "Won't be as much action on a weekend."

Shay watched as Derek searched the system. A commemorative Hank Aaron bobblehead nodded at her from beside him. "I see you're a Braves fan," she said, hoping to bond with the young man.

"Massive," he replied. That was obvious from the bobbleheads. "What about you?"

"Not me," Shay told him. "But my partner's a diehard fan. Honestly, it's a little annoying."

"Yeah, we can be that way for sure," Derek said as he stopped typing. "Here you go."

Shay looked over his shoulder and saw the log for March 22. It was a simple list of names, with entry and exit times. There were more people than she thought there would be for a Saturday. This was a hard-working law firm. She scanned over the names. Even though at least thirty people had come into work that day, it didn't appear that any of them were Dan Milton. "Is this it?"

"That's it. Last person out that day was Mr. Goizueta. He left at 8:49. Early night for him."

"Is there any way someone can get in or out of here without it being logged?" Shay asked.

"Maybe if they rappelled off the roof, but other than that, no way."

"Okay, well, thank you, Mr. Kerr," Shay said. "I appreciate your time."

"No problem."

"Oh, one more thing," Shay said as she pulled out her iPhone. "Would you mind if I took a picture of your bobbleheads? My partner would love to see them."

"Yeah, go for it," a proud Derek said as he got out of the way, and Shay took a picture of the desk with its baseball memorabilia—*and* the computer screen with the information on the key cards.

"I can find my way out," Shay told him. "Go Bravos!"

BIRDIE

Chip Milton's bedroom was a time capsule circa 2015. There was an old Sony PS4 on a shelf next to a collectible Groot figurine from *Guardians of the Galaxy* next to a collection of Rick Riordan's *Percy Jackson and the Olympians* books and dozens of *Doctor Who* action figures. The room had been preserved intact from the time Chip went away to boarding school and never really came back. He went on to Notre Dame and then a job in finance in New York and hadn't spent more than two weeks at home in Buckhead in almost ten years. He and Birdie weren't close. She had never been shy about telling Chip and his brother Al that she liked Freddie best. "Every parent has a favorite," she would say. "They just won't admit it because they're liars. At least I don't lie to you."

Ever since Chip had declared he would be spending future Christmas holidays with his girlfriend's family skiing in Whistler, Birdie had been planning to turn his childhood bedroom into an extension of her closet. Her weight had fluctuated so much over the years that she found herself with six different sized wardrobes, from her all-time high size 18, to her current 14, and all the way down to size 8.

Samples of paint were taped to the wall, and swatches of fabric and wallpaper were piled on Chip's twin bed, all for Birdie's perusal. This wouldn't be an ordinary closet with shelving systems purchased at the Container Store. This would be a custom closet with built-in cabinetry, heated floors, and expensive wallpaper from France, because Birdie wasn't one to cut corners. She sat on

Chip's bed and imagined the room's future. The organizational possibilities made her heart soar.

"What are you doing?" Dan asked as he stepped into the room and spoiled her revelry.

"I'm turning Chip's room into a closet." Obviously.

"Shouldn't we keep it like it is for when he comes home?"

"He's made it very clear that he doesn't intend to spend much time here."

Dan sat on the end of the bed and began sorting through the fabric swatches. He wasn't looking at them as much as aimlessly thumbing through the choices. He glanced up at Birdie. She had yet to look at him directly. Instead, she busied herself with the wallpaper, taking each choice and holding it up against the window to see how it looked in the light.

"I have something I need to talk to you about," Dan said. Birdie still refused to look his way. She had been expecting this conversation. He was going to ask her for a divorce. This was the moment she had been planning for. He would ask for a divorce and she would refuse to give him one and then she would spend the rest of her life making him so miserable he would wish he had never brought it up in the first place. Birdie was a big believer in marriage, even if it meant living unhappily ever after. Her own parents' marriage had set the example. As her father said in a speech at one of their anniversary parties: "Dottie and I have had ten happy years together—which ain't bad considering we've been married for thirty."

"The police want to talk to me," Dan told her. "I think they know I lied about where I was after the Steeplechase."

Birdie finally looked at Dan. He seemed so timid and weak. "Lied? Where were you, Dan?"

"I was just driving around," he said, unconvincingly. "I was driving around thinking about us. Where we are. What our future is. We're not as happy as we used to be."

"No shit."

"I need your help, Birdie," Dan continued. "I need you to tell the detectives that I was with you all night."

"Why don't you just tell them the truth?"

"Because they won't believe me."

"Because it's all bullshit?" Birdie asked. "Because you were actually with your mistress?"

Dan dramatically threw his arms in the air. "Birdie! How many times do I have to tell you? I'm not seeing anyone else."

Birdie couldn't hold her rage for another second. She reached for the closest weapon she could find, Chip's *Doctor Who* figurines, and began launching them at her husband. Daleks and Cybermen and different versions of the Doctor began flying through the air. One after another, Birdie pitched them, fastball style, at Dan as he cowered. "I'm not fucking stupid, Dan!" she screamed at him as he fended off the projectiles. "Just say it! Just say it, Dan! Admit that you're fucking that woman! Say it! Say it! Fucking say it!"

"We broke up!" Dan finally said as a blue Tardis crashed into the wall next to him and fell into pieces on the floor. "I broke up with her after the Steeplechase." Birdie had almost wished Dan had kept on lying. That way she could at least pretend that it wasn't true. Dan reached out to touch her, but she recoiled. "I'm sorry, Birdie," he said. "I made a mistake. We were having problems. I fucked up, but it's over. I told her I loved you. You. You're the one that I love." He reached out again, and Birdie slapped his hand down harshly.

"Now you want to touch me? I know what you think about me, Dan. I know! You sent me to a fucking fat farm!"

Dan began to grovel. It wasn't an appealing quality in any man, but it did appeal to Birdie's need to be the one calling the shots and he probably knew it. "It wasn't a fat farm. It was a spa. I wanted you to have a chance to relax. You were so unhappy—"

"*You* made me unhappy," she told him. Accused him. "You made me unhappy when you stopped loving me."

"I never stopped loving you," Dan said, switching to a tender tone. He cautiously approached Birdie again. Her face flushed red with anger. She raised her hand again, to slap Dan or to push him away, but he grabbed it in midair and held on to it. He pulled her in closer, into an awkward embrace, and held her hand to his cheek. "I left her because she's not you. No one ever could be." He kissed her and she began to thaw. He had always had a power over her.

Birdie tried to shake him off. She tried to pull away, but Dan held her tightly. "Why don't you just have that woman tell the police you were with her?" Birdie asked. "What does it matter?"

"Because I left her house at *ten*."

"You didn't get home until after midnight. Where were you?"

"I left her and, like I said, I was just driving around—"

"You drive around a lot," Birdie said. "I don't believe this shit. Why do you think the police will? Where were you, Dan? With another woman? Do you have a second fucking girlfriend? A third? Where the hell were you?"

"I was at Anderson's house." Dan said. "I went by to talk to him about selling the company. I knew if I could see him again, I'd have a chance to talk sense into him."

"What did you do, Dan?"

"Nothing!" Dan assured her. "He wasn't there. I waited, but he was probably . . . probably already dead in the park by the time I got there. I didn't kill Anderson, but I don't want anyone to think I did. It would ruin my reputation and our family. I need you to help me protect us. Think about Freddie. What would his life be like if people thought his father murdered someone? I need you, Bird. You need to help me."

The only thing worse than Dan being a murderer was having people think he was a murderer. Birdie could live with an unhappy marriage. That was easy. She couldn't live with the gossip. If anyone thought Dan killed Anderson, the Miltons may as well pack up and move to Mississippi. The shame of it all.

Birdie felt the power shift back her way. Dan had dared to stray? She would bring him in line. "I'll tell them you were with me," she said. He looked relieved. He was hanging on to Birdie for dear life. "But you will never see that woman again. And we aren't getting a divorce. Ever. I'm your wife. For *life*." Now she grabbed a hold of him. She kissed him, forcefully, and moved one hand down into his pants. He wasn't aroused but soon would be. If there was ever a time to rise to the occasion, this was it. She pushed him down on the bed as they kissed with all the passion of two actors faking it for a movie sex scene. It may not have been real, but this is what the job called for.

SHAY

Shay and Dub sat in their shared office in front of their computer screens. Having a shared office worked because they both knew when to be quiet. There were times for important conversations and times for conversations about the mundane, but most often they sat in silence and left room for their own thoughts. Shay had once shared an office with a junior detective who talked as much as he breathed and did both loudly. It was a dysfunctional situation that always had Shay on edge. She and Dub functioned perfectly, like an old married couple who had settled into a life of comfortable nods and grunts instead of words.

Hannah came to the open door and knocked softly. "The Miltons are here," she said.

"Hannah, did Bubba Tyree get back to confirm he was with the Wileys the night of the murder?" Shay asked.

"Yeah, he said he was."

"Did we confirm with the restaurant?"

"I mean, no, I don't think so," Hannah admitted. "Why would we need to?"

"Coach Tyree isn't going to lie," Dub said. Of course that's what he thought. Coach Tyree. Marcus. They were his heroes.

"This is a murder investigation," Shay said. "We don't just take people's word for it."

"I'll check on it now," Hannah said.

"Why don't you concentrate on getting the surveillance camera footage from the guy who lives across from the park," Shay said as she got up from her chair and Dub followed suit. "I'll take care of the restaurant."

Shay and Dub left Hannah behind and made their way through the maze of cubicles on the detective floor toward the small interrogation room on the other side.

"Why are you so eager to believe that Marcus Wiley is guilty?" Dub asked Shay.

"Why are you so eager to believe he's not?"

"You know how you think I'm obsessed with Chick-fil-A?" he asked. He didn't need to wait for the obvious answer. "I think you're just as obsessed about the Wileys. It's a little irrational."

"Do you ever plan on giving up your chicken sandwiches?" Shay asked him.

"No."

"Well, I don't plan on giving up on my belief that the Wileys aren't telling the truth. Our job is to find the murderer. Not appease Georgia fans."

They reached the interrogation room and opened the door to find Birdie and Dan Milton sitting on opposite sides of the table. This was unusual since it was common knowledge to anyone who had ever watched a crime drama on television that detectives sat on one side of the table and suspects on the other.

"Mr. and Mrs. Milton, thank you for coming in," said Shay. Dan rose from his seat when the detectives entered the room, but Birdie stayed put, making no effort at all to change sides. "Mrs. Milton," Shay finally said. "It's customary that the detectives sit on one side, so if you could move . . ."

"Oh, of course," Birdie said as she made a show of changing sides to sit next to her husband. Her chair scraped across the floor as she got up. She gathered her handbag from the floor next to it and then scraped her new chair across the floor, set her handbag down, rearranged its placement, and finally settled in to face Shay and Dub as they sat down. Dub pulled out one of his trusty notebooks and prepared to take notes.

"I'll remind you that you can have a lawyer present. Someone other than yourself," Shay told Dan.

"I understand my rights, thank you."

"Well, let's get to it," Shay said. "Previously, Mr. Milton, you told me and my partner that you were at your office at the time Mr. Tupper was killed. Do you remember saying that?"

"I may have said that," Dan told them. "It's been a difficult time for all of us. Memories can be affected by stress." He looked at Birdie for a moment. She nodded with an exaggerated frown on her face.

"Some information has come to our attention," Shay said. "We have reason to believe that you weren't at your office that night."

"If I said I was there, I was mistaken."

Mistaken? Oh, Shay loved to hear those kinds of words. Mistaken. Confused. Muddled. Distracted. All the words liars used.

"He was at home with me," Birdie finally piped in.

Shay was pleased Birdie had joined the conversation. Although she may not be truthful, at least she would be entertaining. "Why didn't you tell us this before, Mrs. Milton?"

"Y'all were so busy insinuating I was a murderer, I must have forgotten."

"Birdie, come on . . ." Dan said quietly.

"Oh, just tell them the truth, Dan." Birdie placed her hand on top of his in a seeming gesture of reassurance. She turned back to Shay. "We were on a cocaine bender that night."

Dub stopped taking notes, midsentence.

"You know . . ." Shay stammered, "you know that cocaine is illegal, right?"

"Not quite as illegal as murder," Birdie declared. "To be honest, we've been having some marital issues, and we thought a little dabble might spice up our sex life. Right, honey?"

Dan said nothing. Perhaps because his wife had said more than enough. Shay got the feeling that whatever story the Miltons had agreed on when they entered the room wasn't the one Birdie was telling now. Shay half expected Dan to admit to Anderson's murder just to escape his wife. He had seemed so powerful and confident when Shay first met him. Now, as he sat next to Birdie, he was disappearing before Shay's eyes.

"Anything else?" Birdie asked. "Do you want specifics?"

"No, not about that," Shay said. The last thing she wanted to know about was this couple's sex life. "But I do have another question."

"And we have nothing but answers," said Birdie.

"I don't know much about financial things," Shay told them, "but it seems to me that you, Mr. Milton, as the lawyer for Tupper Timber, had a lot to gain from the sale of the company and, again, this isn't my area, but I imagine that it's going to be a lot easier to sell the company now that Anderson Tupper is dead."

"Anderson being dead doesn't make anything easier," Dan said coolly. "It's a terrible thing for all of us."

"Have you ever heard of Tupelo Holdings?" Shay asked. She searched Dan's face for any signs of discomfort, but he showed none. "It's a corporation that lists you as the director."

"I set up a lot of corporations for my clients."

"And who would they be?" Shay asked. "The ones who own Tupelo?"

"They prefer to remain anonymous."

"I'm sure *they* do," Shay said pointedly.

Dan smiled. Shay smiled back. They were smiling for different reasons. "I think, for the sake of everyone concerned, it would be better if you referred any additional questions to my lawyer," he finally said.

"So, lawyers *do* have lawyers?"

"We do."

"We really need to get going," Birdie told them. "So many bodies to bury . . ."

"I apologize for my wife's macabre sense of humor," said Dan.

"No, please, she's so funny," Shay said as she stood up. "Thank you both for coming by. I'm sure we'll meet again."

Birdie and Dan left the room. They were holding hands like the happiest of couples. That cocaine must really have done the trick. Not that Shay believed their story.

"Well," Dub said as he closed his notebook. "There you go."

"What do you think?" asked Shay. "One of them killed Anderson Tupper? Both of them?"

"I can see him killing Tupper over some business dispute," Dub said. "But I can see her killing him just for the heck of it."

BIRDIE

"Well, that was a shit show," Birdie said to Dan as they walked to their cars, parked side by side in the police department's parking lot. "Jesus, Dan, even I'm starting to wonder if you killed Anderson."

"I didn't."

"You were stupid enough to make it seem like you did. If I hadn't jumped in, you'd be in handcuffs right now."

"Everything's going to be okay." Dan tried to comfort Birdie, but she brushed him away.

"Let's not do this here," she said. "We can talk about it at home."

"I have to get back to the office," Dan said. "I have a meeting in thirty minutes." Dan kissed Birdie on the cheek. "I'll see you tonight." He put AirPods in as he climbed into his little convertible. It was dwarfed by Birdie's SUV. She got into her car and imagined driving over the Jag and crushing it like she was driving a monster truck.

Installing the spy gear in Dan's car at the Steeplechase had been easier than Birdie had thought it would be. She planned on giving her purchase a positive review on Amazon. With the device hidden under the driver's seat in his Jag, all Birdie had to do was call it to activate its eavesdropping capability. The number was already programmed into her speed dial, and she selected it from the list on the digital screen of her dashboard. Birdie didn't feel guilty as she waited for it to connect. She just hoped it would work.

After a moment, the sound of traffic noise and the revving of the Jag's engine as it changed gears sounded from the speakers in Birdie's car. She could hear Dan talking. It was his side of a phone conversation, and Birdie struggled to hear him above the sounds of the traffic.

"It was a disaster," she heard Dan say. "They're suspicious. They know I wasn't at work and that's a problem. We just have to get through this. There's so much money involved. We're so close. Birdie wasn't helpful at all. She was her typical bitchy self. I just need to make this money so I can get the hell away from her."

He was probably talking to Chatham. Matters of money and murder often sounded the same. They had definitely been planning to screw Anderson out of his fair share of the sale of the company. That was just business. But had they gone further? It had taken Birdie a long time to believe that Dan had the guts to have an affair. To believe he was capable of murder? Well, she honestly didn't think he had it in him. The wuss. She waited for Dan to say something incriminating or exonerating. Instead, he said, "What are you wearing?"

He hadn't been talking to Chatham after all. At least, she hoped not.

"I won't be there for thirty minutes, and I need something to occupy me while I'm driving . . . fuck, yeah, keep going, keep talking . . . you're so fucking sexy . . . just suck on that stick shift, baby . . ."

He was talking to his mistress. Birdie punched her finger at the dash touchscreen and disconnected the audio. Jesus, she thought, Dan was even a dumbshit when he talked dirty.

* * *

Birdie drove her car slowly down a street named Amalfi Way. Many of the streets in Alpharetta, the commuter suburb north of Atlanta, were filled with new subdivisions named after places in Italy, like Sorrento or Bellagio. The names gave the cookie-cutter neighborhoods a kind of old-world cachet. Amalfi Way was in Little Tuscany and was lined with two-story townhomes. Some flew American flags from their small front porches, and some had signs on their lawns that promoted the children of the family within, like *HOME OF AN ALPHARETTA HIGH SENIOR* or *CONGRATS ASHLEY! CENTENNIAL CHEERLEADER!* Birdie was a stranger in a strange land of Marshalls and T.J.Maxx.

Dan's Jaguar was parked in the short driveway of one of the townhomes. It was next to a bright-blue older Jeep Wrangler. It had a *SPIN QUEEN* sticker on the back window and one of those obnoxious *26.2* marathon stickers on its bumper. Birdie gagged a little when she saw it. She parked across the street, wedging her Suburban between a contractor's giant Ford F-250 and a small, dented Nissan Sentra, and walked past a budding crepe myrtle to the front door of the townhome.

A wreath made of twigs and dried flowers hung on the door. It was the kind of thing you purchased at Hobby Lobby, and it had a small sign glued to it with *grateful* painted in pink swirly letters. Birdie had always thought Dan was secretly a redneck, and the wreath hanging on his mistress's door only confirmed her suspicions. Everything Birdie hated in the world came with this wreath. It was tacky and cheap and common, and it hung on the door of the woman fucking her husband.

Birdie pulled the offending wreath off the door and carried it back to Dan's Jag. This car once represented her love for her husband and now, like the wreath, it represented her hatred for him. She pulled a lighter from her handbag. It was one of the long-necked lighters she used to light the pizza oven on her back patio, and it was no accident that she had it with her. Birdie wasn't in any way spontaneous. This was premeditated. She fired up the lighter and held the flame under the disgustingly positive wreath and watched as it slowly ignited. Flames crept up its sides, engulfing the small flowers and charring the edges of the *grateful* sign, burning through until *ate* was all that remained.

She tossed the wreath onto the passenger seat of the Jaguar. She thought how stupid Dan was to leave the convertible top down. She had warned him about that so many times. The fire from the wreath soon spread to a pile of legal files on the floor and then set alight the new "old-stock" carpet Dan had ordered from a car restorer in Oldbury, England. Birdie was pleased that new old-stock carpet burned the same as old old-stock carpet.

The entire car was going up in flames when Birdie decided it was time to go. If she stayed much longer, she might get stuck in afternoon traffic.

CHAPTER

33

SHAY

Shay's gut feeling that the Wileys were hiding something brought her to Shanks Steakhouse on Piedmont Road in Buckhead. She had left Dub behind at the office. She didn't want to hear any more from him about how irrational she was being about the Wileys, even if maybe she was being just that. Venita Wiley said that she and Marcus had been at Shanks with his old football coach on the night of the murder, and the coach had confirmed that. Perhaps Shay would be less irrational if she could confirm things for herself. She had an itch she needed to scratch.

Shanks was a gin-and-tonic, old-school, expense account mecca of privilege. A wedge salad, which was basically a slab of iceberg lettuce with some blue cheese and bacon thrown on top, cost sixteen dollars. A twelve-ounce filet would set you back over seventy dollars. Everything was eye-wateringly expensive, though money didn't really matter. If you were at Shanks, chances are you were either a politician or a lobbyist and someone else was picking up the tab.

Shay had never been to Shanks. She had never even thought of going there. In her mind it was akin to going to Sri Lanka. You knew it was there and people had good things to say about it, but it seemed like an awful lot of money and effort to actually make the trip. Now she stood at the edge of the bar in the restaurant and regretted never having been. It really was a good-looking place with its walls filled with local art and photographs of homegrown celebrities, tables with white cloths, and deep-red leather chairs in dark wood-paneled rooms. It was all so tastefully done.

The restaurant didn't open for another two hours, which made Shay wonder why it was taking the maître d' so long to come out to meet with her. When he finally showed up, he did so with a pleasant smile and a firm handshake. "I'm Montgomery Lang," he said with a strong, old-timey Southern accent, like a plantation owner might have had. "How can I help you?"

Shay presented her badge and introduced herself. "I was wondering if I could ask you some questions about some guests you had on March 22nd?"

"I can check our reservations system," Lang said. "Who were you looking for?"

"Marcus Wiley," Shay told him. It was barely perceptible, but Shay could see the man's face tighten ever so slightly. "I was wondering if he dined here that evening and if you remember when he left."

"Yes, he did," the man said without looking at the reservations.

"You remember him?"

"He's Marcus Wiley. Of course I remember."

"You don't even want to check?"

"I don't need to check."

"Would you mind if I looked for myself?" Shay tried to look at the computer on the podium that held the reservations, but Lang blocked her.

"Actually, he was in the private room. We don't keep that on the system. We try to keep it discreet."

"Do you know what time he left?"

"I couldn't really say."

Shay looked to the wall behind the desk where autographed photos of famous Atlantans hung in matching frames. Ludacris. Usher. Ted Turner. Ryan Seacrest. In the center of them all was a photo of Marcus Wiley. A football was tucked under his arm as he hurdled a hapless defender in the SEC Championship game. He signed the photo: *To Monty—My brother from another mother! Marcus Wiley.* Personally, Shay didn't see the resemblance, but the picture was clear enough. Montgomery Lang may not be the most reliable of witnesses.

"Thank you for your time, Mr. Lang."

"If you ever need a reservation, please give me a call," he said as he handed her his business card. In normal circumstances, this would have been cause for celebration. Shay suddenly had an "in" with the maître d' at the best steakhouse in Atlanta. If Dub had been with her, he just might have fainted.

Shay left the restaurant and was about to get into her car when she noticed a young man in a white apron smoking a cigarette at the loading dock behind the restaurant. She approached him with her badge out. "Hello, I'm Detective Claypool with Atlanta PD. Can I ask you a few questions?"

"I'm just having a smoke."

"You have nothing to worry about." The young man nodded. Ask away. "I'm assuming you work here?" He nodded again. "Do you know who Marcus Wiley is?"

"Sure. That's like asking if I know who God is, right?"

Shay smiled. "Right. I was wondering if you might remember if he was here on March 22nd. It was a Saturday night."

"He wasn't here."

"Are you sure?"

"Pretty sure. We were closed. Water main break. Shut down the whole street. I remember nights when I don't get tips."

Shay didn't know whether to feel happy that she had uncovered the Wileys' deception or disappointed that they had deceived. In any case, she would be paying another visit to the Wiley mansion with its stone lions and monogrammed security gate to clear things up. She thanked the young man and began walking away, then turned back. "I have a tip for you," she told him. She was a motherly type and he reminded her of Darron. "Smoking is bad for your health."

He took a long drag off his cigarette and exhaled a great plume of smoke. "So is being a cop." He snuffed out the cigarette and went in the back door of the restaurant. Yes, he reminded her a lot of her son.

VENITA

Venita's spacious walk-in closet was organized like a high-end boutique in Miami and wallpapered with the same green palm fronds pattern that was at the Beverly Hills Hotel. Venita and Marcus had stayed there once when they were in Los Angeles for the ESPYs, the sporting world's equivalent of the Emmys. Venita had fallen in love with both the hotel and its wallpaper and was on the phone to her interior decorator within minutes of checking in. The closet was Venita's sanctuary. It was her version of a she-shed, which was a term she thought was ridiculous, as if a woman's domain was some sort of outhouse in the backyard.

At the very back of the closet, behind silk curtains with small pink and green tassels that matched the wallpaper, Venita stood in front of a large gun safe that held no guns. Instead, it was filled with important documents like birth certificates and wills, hard drives with backups of every picture they had ever taken of Wade, Marcus's original Heisman Trophy (the one in the trophy room was a copy), and Venita's jewelry collection, which she was currently perusing.

Marcus was hopeless when it came to picking out clothing, either for himself or for Venita, but he had the eye of a De Beers diamond merchant when it came to choosing jewelry for his wife. At the beginning of their relationship, when Marcus was a famous but poor college student, then barred from accepting any kind of money or favor despite already being a star who brought in millions for his school, he would buy her jewelry from Zales. On sale. Venita still had the delicate (i.e., thin and cheap) gold chain with a single, infinitesimal diamond that he got her for their first Valentine's Day. As years passed and money came in, the chains got thicker, and the diamonds got bigger. He never failed to get his wife a piece of jewelry every year on Valentine's Day, Mother's Day, Christmas, their anniversary, and her birthday. He once even got her a ring on St. Patrick's Day just because it gave him an excuse to buy her an emerald.

Venita pulled out velvet lined drawers and surveyed her choices. She was already wearing her wedding ring. As the cliché goes, it was big enough to choke a horse. She opened a drawer toward the bottom of the safe. A seven-row diamond and gold choker from Van Cleef & Arpels sparkled under the halogen lights. It cost $165,000 and was a recent gift from Marcus, not for any special occasion but to thank her for anything that was to come. "Call it a down payment on my future love for you," he said when he presented it to her. The necklace wasn't something she would wear other than, say, going to the Academy Awards or to a royal wedding, but it was the necklace Venita chose to wear now. On this day she felt she needed to look as rich and powerful as possible.

"Venita, I put her in the trophy room."

Venita turned around to find her housekeeper, Annie, standing at the entrance to the closet. She was a little older than Venita, but the years had not been as kind and showed on her wrinkled face and in her rounded shoulders. She was Marcus's third cousin. Venita hadn't wanted to hire her as a housekeeper, but Annie needed help and refused to accept charity. She worked around the house a few days a week and Venita paid far above the going rate.

"Thank you, Annie."

Annie smiled knowingly when she saw Venita's choice of necklace. "Pulling out the big guns, huh?"

"Too much?"

"Never too much," Annie said. "I took care of some of the laundry. It's folded in the laundry room. I'll do the rest on my usual day."

"Thanks for coming today," Venita told her. "I appreciate it." Annie left and Venita looked at herself in the closet mirror. She felt so silly showing off and wearing her expensive jewelry and having her housekeeper come in on her day off. It was something Sutton Chambers would do. She was such a Betty. Venita wasn't. Of course she wasn't.

Armed with killer jewelry from the gun safe, Venita headed down the hallway to meet her guest. She paused at the doorway to Wade's room. She turned to look at a framed document hanging in the hall opposite his doorway. It was a print of a speech by Theodore Roosevelt titled "The Man in the Arena." Bubba Tyree had given it to Marcus before the NFL draft.

The motivational speech ended with "if he fails, at least fails while daring greatly, so that his place shall never be with those cold and timid souls who know neither victory or defeat." Venita had hung the antiqued parchment print in a place where her son would see it every day when he left his room. She hoped that someday it would mean something to him but knew he had never once glanced at it. Wade was eleven. He wasn't concerned about his legacy.

Venita knocked lightly and pushed Wade's door open. "Hey, buddy." Wade, still in his school uniform, was at his desk working on his computer. "Getting your homework done?"

"Yes," he said, drawing out every letter like he was in pain. "I'm getting my homework done."

"Let's drop the attitude," Venita warned him. "But keep up the good work."

Venita moved to leave, but Wade stopped her. His tone was a tad more pleasant now because he wanted something. "Mom, can I stay over at Cash's house after his dad's funeral?"

"You know, you don't have to go. I think two funerals in one month is a lot to ask."

"We're all going," Wade told her. "We should be there for Cash. And we're going to play video games afterward. You know, that's what Cash wants." Now it made sense. Wade would go to a funeral every weekend if he could play video games.

"I'll call Mrs. Milton to see if you can go with them," Venita said.

"You and Dad aren't going?"

"No, we have an important meeting to go to," Venita told him. "But you can stay over."

Venita left Wade behind and walked down the long hallway toward the living room. She reminded herself to watch her posture and she pulled her shoulders back. The posture, combined with the high heels she was wearing, made her look fierce. She strode into the trophy room where her husband's awards were displayed and where the detective was standing waiting for her.

"Detective Claypool."

"Mrs. Wiley," the detective countered. Neither of the women moved to shake hands. A nod was going to have to do.

"Did my housekeeper offer you anything to drink?"

"She did, but I'm fine. Will your husband be joining us?"

"Unfortunately, he's unavailable."

"We really would like to speak with him."

"So many people would. The hazards of being a celebrity. Would you like to sit down?" Venita asked. She motioned toward the cerulean blue upholstered chairs in the center of the room. She watched as Detective Claypool sat down and was immediately thrown off balance. The detective didn't know that the chair both rocked *and* swiveled and almost tumbled over. Venita gracefully took the seat across from her. She swiveled ever so slightly toward the (replica) Heisman Trophy. She chose these chairs especially so guests could swivel 360 degrees to take in the walls full of Marcus Wiley memorabilia. It was designed for shock and awe and the reason she had the detective brought here, unlike the last time when she hadn't invited the detectives into the room. She wasn't taking things seriously then. She was now.

"I'm sorry my partner didn't have a chance to see the Heisman," Claypool said in what appeared to be a deliberate dig at Venita for not letting the man look at it before. "He's a big fan."

"I'll get him an autograph."

The two women sat in the chairs, facing each other but saying nothing. It was Frost and Nixon facing off or a standoff in the Bravo studio but without Andy Cohen moderating. Venita crossed her legs and let her Bottega Veneta–clad feet dangle in front of the detective. Venita looked down at Claypool's own shoes. She couldn't make out the brand because they were obviously from some place she didn't shop. Like Nordstrom Rack. Or Payless.

"So, you have some additional questions?" Venita asked, breaking the ice.

"I wanted to ask you a little more about your dealings with Mr. Tupper."

"Sure."

The detective leaned in closer to Venita, closing the distance between them. Venita knew this was just the detective's effort to show that she didn't fear Venita and felt comfortable invading her space. Venita, though, could tell that the woman across from her felt anything but comfortable. "You're trained as a lawyer?"

"I am a lawyer," Venita said. She held her position and her eye contact.

"And you're suing Mr. Tupper's estate?"

"We lost a lot of money."

"It must be devastating to have come so far and lose it all."

"We haven't lost *it all*, Detective Claypool," Venita said. "But we have come far. My husband and I have always been on the move. My family made sure I knew how to take care of myself, and my husband's family gave him no other choice. We did it before and we can do it again. We're always headed up."

"That climb's a lot easier when you're married to a Heisman Trophy winner," Claypool said as she finally sat back in her chair with an arrogant look that Venita wanted to wipe right off her face.

It was one thing to be suspected of murder. It was something far worse to be suspected of being a gold digger. Marcus may have been the running back, but Venita sure as hell dragged him over the goal line. "You're not poor because I'm rich, Detective."

"I'm not poor."

"What do you want, Detective?" Venita asked.

"You and your husband weren't at Shanks the night of the Steeplechase," Detective Claypool said, getting down to business. "You told us you were having dinner with Bubba Tyree?"

"I believe that's correct."

"Shanks was closed that night," the detective told her. "Maybe you could consult your calendar again for us." The detective casually swiveled back and forth in her chair as she read through her notes. "You called Anderson the day he was murdered."

"I'd have to check on that."

"No need to check. It's in his phone records."

"I had a lot of conversations with Anderson that week," Venita told her. "I was trying to come to some kind of accommodation with him."

"Did you?"

"No."

"Were either you or your husband at the baseball field the night Mr. Tupper was murdered?"

"That would mean that we either saw who murdered him or that we murdered him," Venita replied. "And neither of those things are true."

"Then where were you?" asked Detective Claypool. "It's a simple question."

"And one I choose not to answer at this time," Venita said as she stood up. It was time for the detective to go. "I think we're through here. Thank you for stopping by."

"I don't think you're doing yourself any favors by acting like you're too good for this," the detective said as she reluctantly stood up. "I still have questions about a lot of things, including your financial situation."

Venita had had enough of treating this woman like she was a guest in her home when she was an intruder. "My financial situation is obviously better than you want it to be," Venita told her. "My husband and I belong here because we earned it. He got his head bashed in on a weekly basis so we could afford to live in a nice house and send our son to private school. And I worked hard right alongside him. We deserve to be here. And you know what? So do our neighbors. We all worked hard for this or work hard to keep it. I don't know what the word is for someone who judges another person because they have money, but it's some form of prejudice. You want to ask me questions? Charge me with murder. Otherwise, get out of my big fine house."

SHAY

Shay sat in her car in front of Venita's "big fine house." She had to take a moment to check her emotions before she started driving. There was too much possibility of road rage for Shay to be released on the general public without a pause to reflect.

"I'm not prejudiced," she said to herself. "Or a socialist or whatever. Oh, what the hell is it?" Shay took out her phone and pulled up Google. She typed in TERM FOR SOMEONE WHO HATES RICH PEOPLE and hit the search button. The first entry was: POOR. She scrolled down to find different answers from BIGOT to SNOB to AVARICIOUS. She didn't know the meaning of the last word and didn't even like the way it was spelled.

It wasn't the fact that Venita Wiley was rich that bothered Shay. Of course not. It was the fact that she was uppity. She thought she was better than Shay and everyone who lived in South Atlanta or anywhere else that wasn't Buckhead. If Shay had the kind of money the Wileys had (or used to have!) she'd live in Buckhead too, but she wouldn't be a Buckhead Betty like Venita and she wouldn't have big stone lions in front of her house either. That was just tacky as hell.

Shay finally calmed down enough to start her car and was pulling away from the estate when she glanced up at the house and saw a figure of a man looking out from an upstairs window. He was gone by the time she looked again, but he sure did look an awful lot like Marcus Wiley. Just then, the heavens opened and a torrent of rain began to fall from the thick clouds that had been circling Atlanta. It was a true southern rainstorm, a real soaker, and it would finally, once and for all, wash away all the pollen and clear the air.

CHAPTER

34

AMELIA

CHATHAM HAD MADE it very clear to Amelia that he didn't want Hampton going to Chuck Chambers's funeral. He had made it so very clear in a tense phone call in which he called her a "terrible mother," a "drama queen," and a "martyr." She, in turn, called him an "asshole" and hung up. Chatham thought it was too much to ask a boy to go to two funerals so close together, and she agreed. Ham's desire to be with his friends, however, trumped all else. He had begged her to let him go. Amelia didn't have a lot of people left on her side. One was even murdered. She wasn't about to lose her son too. If he wanted to be with his friends she was going to let him, no matter what her ex-husband had to say about it.

Poppy was with her father, and Auggie's former nanny had picked him up that morning. He would spend the day with her. Amelia could no longer afford a full-time nanny for the children and was grateful that the woman agreed to babysit on occasion. The nanny, the cleaner, the beach house, the private jet. All gone. Somewhere in the loss of everything else, however, Amelia was gaining something new. Her grandfather would have called it *gumption*. Her mother would have called it *moxie*. Little by little, Amelia was growing up.

"Ham, let's go!" she said as she left her bedroom and headed downstairs. She was wearing all black, as a funeral dictates, but had managed to dig a different black dress out of storage than the one she had worn to Anderson's funeral. The old Amelia would have bought something new, like she was sure Birdie had done, but the new Amelia was the kind of girl who economized. If wearing a five-year-old Balmain dress meant she would survive another day, so be it.

Amelia turned into the kitchen and jumped back with a start. There, slumped over the island, was Heartlee. One arm rested on the counter while the other was wrapped around her abdomen. Mascara, soaked by tears, ran down her cheeks and mixed with the blood that was seeping out of a nasty slash across her chin.

"Heartlee?" Amelia said with concern and some alarm.

"He beat me up," Heartlee told her, barely coughing it out. "When I said I wouldn't get the abortion. He beat me." She looked at Amelia with pleading, wounded eyes. "He beat you too, didn't he?"

Amelia's non-answer was answer enough. She went to the sink and soaked a kitchen towel with water. She handed it to Heartlee and the young woman held it against her chin.

"How did you get in?" Amelia asked.

"I stole Poppy's keys. She hates me, you know."

"She hates me too."

"I don't have anywhere else to go."

Before Amelia could debate the etiquette involved with the new girlfriend seeking refuge at the former wife's house, Hampton came into the kitchen. He looked at Heartlee and then at his mother.

"Don't worry," Amelia said. "She's just . . . had an accident." Amelia put her arm around Heartlee's shoulder and led her to the living room where she sat her down gently on the sofa. "Do you think you need to go to the hospital?"

"I'm just sore," Heartlee said. "I just need to lie down for a while. Is that okay? Can I just hang out here? Please."

"We have to go to a funeral," Amelia said.

"I'll be fine. As long as I can stay here, I'll be fine."

"Okay," said Amelia. "Just try not to bleed on the sofa. It's from Roche Bobois, and I'll never be able to afford a new one." She caught herself. She was being the old Amelia. "I'm sorry. You bleed all you want. Take a bath. Raid the fridge. Whatever you need. We'll be back tonight."

"Thank you."

"Of course."

Amelia started to walk away, but Heartlee pulled her back. "Amelia," she whispered as Hampton looked on from the kitchen. "I lied. To the detectives. I lied about what Chatham was doing that night."

CHAPTER

35

SHAY

SHAY HAD ALREADY dutifully put her phone in her handbag as she approached the metal detectors at headquarters. She knew the drill. As she said good morning to the guards on duty, she was surprised to see roving reporter Chris Odi in the lobby on the other side of security.

"Detective Claypool!" Odi said with far too much enthusiasm. He always looked like he knew something that Shay didn't, which was a great quality to have when you were trying to talk someone into giving you information.

"Who let you in?" Shay asked as she kept walking and Odi kept following.

"It's a government building," he told her. "And I'm a tax-paying citizen of the great state of Georgia."

"You don't pay enough taxes to go upstairs with me," Shay said as they reached the elevators and she pushed the button. She hoped the reporter would go away, but he was still right there next to her.

"I just want to know if you're planning on arresting Marcus Wiley."

Shay tried her best to not look surprised by his question. Had he followed her to her meeting with Venita? Had Venita spoken to him? "I'm not planning on arresting anyone today," she said, then she turned and looked him in the eye. "Unless they really piss me off."

Odi smiled but didn't budge. "It's just that he's giving a press conference over at the stadium in ten minutes and I thought you might be able to tell me why."

Shay couldn't conceal her surprise this time. "A press conference? Why aren't you there?"

"Only sports reporters were invited. I've never been much of a football fan."

The elevator finally arrived, and Shay hurried in. The reporter tried to follow, but she held up her hand and stopped him in his tracks. "Don't make me shoot you," she said as the doors closed.

Marcus Wiley. Was he going to confess? Was he going to turn himself in for the murder of Anderson Tupper? Shay was disappointed if that was the case. Not that she didn't want it to be the Wileys. She was convinced that it was Marcus or his snobby wife. No, she was disappointed because Marcus Wiley was stealing her thunder. He was robbing her of the chance to arrest him with cameras flashing and reporters screaming out questions. An arrest was her version of a touchdown.

Shay reached her floor to find most of the detectives and activity in the lunchroom. The television there was usually reserved for news or sports. On this day, it was a bit of both. A small group gathered to watch the press conference of former football star and local car dealer Marcus Wiley. Shay pushed her way through the other detectives and joined Hannah and Farrell, whose eyes were fixed on the television that was mounted on the wall above the coffee machine and an overflowing container of pink Sweet'n Low packages.

On the television, a view of the press room at Mercedes-Benz Stadium, home of the Atlanta Falcons, was being broadcast. Shay watched as Marcus came to the podium and stared down at the microphone before him. He was flanked by men, some of whom Shay thought might be former players, and by Venita. She had her head down, and when she looked up dozens of flashes went off from the photographers assembled in the room. Shay could see that Venita was uncomfortable. In fact, she looked close to tears.

"Man, he was great," one of the other detectives, a big man who looked like he had once played football himself, said from the back of the group. "He's a legend."

"Well, he's a murderer now," Hannah declared.

"He hasn't even said anything!" Farrell chastised her. "Let's wait and see."

"Wait and see that he's a murderer."

On the television, Marcus cleared his throat. He looked out at the reporters in the room and then over to Venita for encouragement. He seemed to gather strength from her as he began to speak. "Thank y'all for being here. I appreciate it. And I appreciate the Falcons organization for setting this up for me. They've always been good to me and my family. And I'd like to thank my wife, Venita, for standing by me all these years through the good times and the bad. A man never had a better wife."

"Or a better accomplice?" Hannah added.

"Shush!" Shay admonished her young colleague as Marcus continued.

"I was blessed to have a great career," Marcus said. "First at the University of Georgia—Go Dawgs—and then with the Falcons. Couldn't have asked for anything better than to play in the state I grew up in and the state I love. I've been a very lucky man." Marcus paused for a moment. He seemed to be on the verge of breaking down, but he reeled it back in. "There's been a lot of talk going around. A lot of speculation. It hasn't been easy on my family. So I think it's time I put an end to the talk and come clean."

Shay felt like she was watching a drama with actors on television. For a moment, she forgot that these were real people. Television could do that. Reality television made you think the Real Housewives of Poughkeepsie or wherever weren't real or that the

Starks of Winterfell were. Shay still hadn't gotten over Ned's death.

"A few weeks ago, something happened that changed the course of my life," Marcus continued as his voice broke for a moment. "Changed the course of my family's life. Two weeks ago, I was diagnosed with amyotrophic lateral sclerosis. Y'all probably know it as ALS. Lou Gehrig's disease."

"What's that?" Hannah asked. "What does that mean?"

"It means he's fucked," Farrell said.

"It means he probably didn't murder Anderson Tupper," Shay said. "And it means I'm a huge asshole."

At the stadium, Marcus continued to talk and then to take questions from the press, but Shay had already tuned him out. She had hoped that Marcus was the one who murdered Anderson Tupper. She had hoped that Venita had helped him. She also knew in her heart that she had hoped these things because she didn't like Venita, and she knew she didn't like Venita because she was jealous of her. Shay had to reckon the person she thought she was with the person she really was. At least in this case. She felt she had let herself down.

Shay was startled as Deputy Chief Henderson put his hand on her shoulder. She hadn't seen him watching the press conference from the back of the room. He had a fatherly look of disappointment on his face. And it wasn't because Marcus Wiley was out of the running for Heisman Murderer of the Year. "Maybe now we can move on from the football hero," he told Shay. He didn't even call her cousin. She felt chastised. He walked back to his office without another word.

"He still could have done it," Hannah said. Her arms were crossed like a petulant child's. Hannah was a lot like Shay. She didn't like to be wrong.

"ALS affects your muscles and stuff," Farrell told Hannah. "I seriously doubt the guy could beat someone to death. Or that he'd want to. He has more important things to worry about than murder."

As Farrell schooled Hannah on the horrific and debilitating effects of ALS and Marcus's voice continued to play from the television above, Shay began to make herself coffee. She didn't even want coffee. What she really wanted was to go back in time and have been a nicer person when she interviewed Venita. She tried to console herself with the fact that she had no idea what the Wileys had been going through and tried to justify her actions with the fact that Venita was, regardless, rude to her. Or *was* she? Maybe Shay had been acting more like a Buckhead Betty than Venita.

Anthony came into the lunchroom and walked right past the arguing Hannah and Farrell. He didn't stop when Farrell tried to share news of Marcus's ALS diagnosis. He only wanted to get to Shay. He was holding Anderson Tupper's laptop in his hands. It was open and he fumbled with it as he slid next to Shay at the coffee station and spoke in a whisper.

"Hey, boss, I finally broke into Tupper's computer," he said with a seriousness she was unused to from him. Anthony held the screen up for Shay to see and pushed the spacebar. Shay stared down at the screen and tried to make sense of what she was looking at. Confusion quickly turned to alarm. She looked up at Anthony. He shared the same shocked expression.

Shay was stunned by something far more unexpected than the news from the press conference she had just watched. "We need to get Kira Brooks in here."

Eight Months Before the Murder

California

KIRA

Kolt was drowning in the Malibu surf. He bobbed up and down in the waves alongside a discarded bottle of Mountain Dew. It floated. He didn't. His lungs were now filled with sea water, and every time he came up for air, he coughed up sprays of it. His slight body—he had always been skinny and lanky and long—was no match for the Pacific Ocean.

Kira may have been drunk and suicidal and depressed, but she was, above all things, the mother of Kolton Terence Brooks. The familial contract she had signed with the universe when her children were born stated that their lives were all that mattered. They were more important than her husband's life or her life or the lives of anyone else on the planet.

Even as the waves tried to knock her back toward shore, the same waves she had tried to succumb to minutes before, Kira fought her way toward Kolt. She was driven by centuries of DNA passed from one woman to the next. It was Darwin's survival of the fittest. Strong mothers kept their children alive so they could make even stronger mothers in the future.

After what seemed like hours—but was probably less than a minute—of fighting, Kira made one last lunge through the waves and was just able to grab Kolt with her fingertips, capturing enough of his pajama top to secure a hold and pull him to her. She reeled him in and turned toward shore. She remembered the days of her own childhood when a friend's mother would drive a group of girls to the beach and Kira would spend hours bodysurfing in the Pacific. She would be in the water so long she could feel the motion of the waves long after she was back in the Valley in her bed. She could feel the push and pull of them, as if she had become a part of the ocean itself.

Whatever was left of that relationship with the sea reemerged in Kira, and she used the power of the waves to push her and her son toward the beach. They came crashing down with one last wave and were slammed onto the shoreline. They were both coughing up sea water. Both exhausted. Before Kira could take another breath, though, someone was suddenly upon her. The salt water cleared from her eyes just in time to see it was her daughter. Iris began beating Kira with her fists. She was screaming at her, cursing her, but Kira chose to listen to the waves instead. Kira didn't defend herself against the blows from her daughter. She deserved them. After too long but truthfully not long enough, Iris fell back into the sand and crawled to where her brother sat soaked and shivering on the beach. She wrapped her arms around him, and they both stared back at their mother. *The sea monster.*

After the Murder

Atlanta

Kira stood among moving boxes in the guesthouse. She had finally unpacked everything and now it was almost all packed and labeled and ready to move again. She had taken a lease on a cottage in the Vinings area of Atlanta, near Kolt's school. It was a community close to Buckhead and reminded her of the homes in Los Angeles that were marketed as "Beverly Hills adjacent." Close to Beverly Hills, but not quite there. Zip codes were just a state of mind, though, weren't they?

Now that she was going back in to meet with the detectives, however, she was sure she would never have a chance to move into the new house. She was probably going to prison. She didn't remember killing Anderson, but she didn't remember *not* killing him. She had blacked out before. Most of those times she had sworn the next day that she hadn't had much to drink. Sometimes she even believed it.

There's a theory in quantum mechanics known as Schrödinger's cat. It says that if you place a cat and radioactive material in a box and seal it, the material will ultimately decay and kill the cat. But until you open the box, you won't know if the cat is dead or alive. As long as the box is sealed, the cat is, in effect, both dead *and* alive. Both outcomes are true. Kira was like Schrödinger's cat. In this moment, at least, she could have been either guilty or innocent. Someone just needed to open the box and see.

Kira left the guesthouse behind and headed to the Big House. It really was big. It was also nice. It was a dream house. Kira had never doubted she would have a house like this one day. She had planned on it. She had worked for it. When she finally got it, though, she couldn't even live in it. It was like having a pair of expensive shoes that didn't fit. Beautiful but useless.

Iris was in the family room when Kira entered. She was lying on a Restoration Hardware cloud sofa and had sunk so far into its cushions that it looked like it might swallow her. She was on her iPhone. Not talking (heavens, no, who *talked* on a phone?) but aimlessly scrolling through TikTok videos.

"Iris, could you pick Kolt up from the Chambers's house after the funeral?" Kira asked her daughter. Iris lifted her head just enough to look very bothered.

"Why can't you? I thought you liked doing that stuff now."

"I really don't want to argue about it," said Kira. She really didn't. "Can you just do it? Amelia Tupper is taking him. I just need you to pick him up. Please."

"Fine."

Sometimes Kira wondered if Iris had wished her mother had drowned that day in Malibu. She was sure the thought must have at least crossed Iris's mind. Had it lingered there? Did she imagine finding Kira's body tangled in a mess of seaweed? Was she momentarily relieved by the thought? It didn't matter. Kira would be gone one way or another.

Kira moved on to find Kolt at the kitchen island eating breakfast. He was using a large spoon meant for stirring sauces to shovel great quantities of cornflakes into his mouth. It looked like he was trying to eat it all before it suddenly disappeared. He was already dressed for Chuck Chambers's funeral and was wearing the same pants he had worn to his fifth-grade graduation the year before. They were slim and black but now tight and about two inches too short.

They didn't speak to each other as Kira pretended to be interested in pouring herself a cup of the coffee Kallan had already brewed that morning. Kira didn't know what to say. She had been on pins and needles with her son for so long that she was sometimes afraid of saying anything at all. She looked at his tie. It was a red and blue plaid tie from his old Episcopal school in California. It hung loosely around his neck. He had never mastered the art of tying it. It was something Kira had always done for him. She took it as an opening.

"Want me to do your tie?" she asked with hesitation.

Kolt stopped eating long enough to reply. "Sure." He swiveled his barstool around and faced Kira.

She pulled apart what work he had done on the tie and began to sort it out. She took her time. She wanted to enjoy every last second with her son. She wove the tie around and around. The rabbit went through the rabbit hole and on its journey. She looked at Kolt's face. She was sure he had aged a year overnight. Where had this little man come from? Of course, boys always looked older when they wore ties.

"I know what you're going to say," Kolt told her. "That I need to learn how to tie a tie."

"Oh, who cares?" Kira said. "It's just a tie. And you know what? They actually sell ties that are already tied that you just clip on. And probably by the time you're old enough to work in an office, men won't even be wearing ties anymore." Kira surprised herself with all that. In times past, in California, she would be on Kolt every morning before school about tying his tie and tying his shoes and buttoning and tucking his shirt. All that now seemed to be so much nonsense.

It was just a tie. It wasn't the end of the world.

Kira finished with the tie and was about to start crying. Crying for what she had done and for what she was going to miss. Crying because she had lost her children in a bottle of tequila. She smiled a fake smile and headed toward the front door.

"Aren't you going to Mr. Chambers's funeral?" Kolt asked.

"I can't," she said. Then she turned back to him and said, "I'm sorry."

"For what?"

For trying to kill myself? For almost killing you? For killing your coach?

"For, you know . . ." Kira said as she left the house, and her children, behind.

SHAY

Anderson's computer was on the table between Shay and Kira. It was like a gun loaded with a single bullet for a game of Russian roulette. It just might kill one of them. Despite what some people thought of detectives, they didn't relish this part. At least Shay didn't. She wasn't eager to present evidence. To accuse someone of something heinous. It was just another step in the journey of a crime. The original act wasn't the thing that caused the harm. News of the crime was the real culprit, as it passed from one person to another, filling each with blame and guilt and sorrow. No, a crime was never a singular act against one person. It was an assault on everyone who knew the victim.

Shay thought that Kira's eyes were vacant. She was lifeless, with her hands folded politely in her lap and her shoulders hunched forward. Were her shoulders bowed from the weight of guilt or was it simply resignation? Did she know what Shay was about to say? Did Kira know what Shay was about to show her? People had their stories. They had their narratives of what their lives were like and how events unfolded. The stories were often lies, but just as often they were fantasies. People created new realities so they didn't have to deal with the messiness, and sometimes the trauma, of the inconvenient truth of their lives. Video evidence of a crime, however, left little room for fantasy. Presenting someone with the truth, not their story, either necessitated the invention of a new story or the acceptance of reality. Either an alibi or a confession.

"Are you sure you wouldn't like to have someone with you?" Shay asked Kira.

Kira looked down at the laptop. "No."

"I just want you to know that this isn't something I take pleasure in doing," Shay told Kira as she opened the computer. The light from the screen lit up Shay's face and reflected off her eyes. "What I'm going to show you is . . . disturbing."

Kira nodded solemnly. It *was* resignation.

Shay took a deep breath. She, too, felt like a victim of this crime. Her fingers hovered over the laptop's keyboard. Pushing a key was the simplest of acts but fraught with enormous implications. There was nothing but cruel suspense to be gained by waiting, however, and Shay finally pressed a key and turned the laptop to face Kira. She slid it closer as a video began to play. Mercifully, the audio was silenced.

Shay watched as the light from the screen now played across Kira's face. She appeared confused at first, as her eyes darted back and forth, looking from one part of the screen to another, as if she was trying to make sense of what she was seeing. Then she suddenly sat up straight in her chair and gasped. Her hand involuntarily moved to her mouth and covered it, as if her hand was holding back a scream. She slammed the laptop closed and looked to Shay for answers. Or maybe for help. It wasn't a look of guilt. It was a look of horror.

Shay pulled the laptop back toward her and held on to it. She crossed her arms over its surface like she was keeping it from opening again on its own.

"Did you know that Anderson Tupper raped your daughter?"

Shay already knew the answer to that question from the look on Kira's face. Kira had no idea. Like a virus, the crime had first infected Kira's daughter. Then it infected Shay. Now it had infected Kira.

"I don't understand," Kira said. She really didn't seem to or really didn't seem to *want* to understand. "What is that?"

"It's Anderson's computer," Shay told her. "It's a video he took about a month ago. It looks like he drugged your daughter and then assaulted her. We found communications between the two of them. It seemed to start innocently and then escalated to rape. He threatened to expose compromising pictures of her if she said anything. He said it might affect *you* negatively."

"It's on his computer?" Kira asked. "He kept it on his computer? It's real?" Kira seemed to be looking for a story she could live with.

"He shared it on the dark web," Shay said. "There are other videos. Not just of your daughter. Other young women too." Shay was trying to be professional. Trying to stick to protocol. Regardless of the guilt of the victim for his own crimes, he had still been murdered.

"Do you think your husband knew about this? About the rape? Maybe he did something about it."

"No," Kira said without hesitation. Then, "I don't know."

Kira pushed her chair away from the table and stood up. She looked around the room like she didn't know where she was or how she had gotten there. She wasn't the same person who had walked in. They had played Russian roulette and Kira had lost.

"I have to go," she said. "I'm going. I'm going."

"What about your husband, Mrs. Brooks?" Shay called after Kira as she left the room. "Do you think he had anything to do with the murder?" Shay was going through the motions of being a good detective. The mother in her, however, knew that nothing else mattered now. Not murder. Not Anderson Tupper. All that mattered was a teenage girl somewhere in Buckhead.

KIRA

Kira's hands were shaking as she drove toward Sutton's house on Tuxedo Road, and for once they weren't shaking because she was drunk. She was fueled by guilt and rage but also by purpose. Only she could fix this. Certainly not Kallan. She had tried to call him a dozen times, but he never picked up his phone when he was playing golf. And he was always playing golf. Had he been playing golf as Anderson Tupper raped their daughter? Did he know? Had Iris confessed her secret to her father and not to her? Had Kallan taken matters into his own hands? Maybe Kira was no longer the only guilty parent.

There were dozens of cars, including Iris's BMW, lining the street in front of Sutton's house, and a valet stand was set up at the entrance to the driveway. Kira didn't have time to weigh the merits of having a valet service for a wake and handed an attentive young man her keys at the stand without waiting for a ticket.

Kira rang the doorbell at the house over and over again. She could hear the sound of the bell coming from inside. It was a long melody that rose and descended in dramatic tones as if it were signaling that a duke or duchess was waiting at the palace gates. Kira had no patience for the pretense of doorbells. The front door was unlocked, and she pushed it open and let herself in. She didn't care if it was rude. She only cared about finding her daughter.

A somber crowd of well-dressed people mingled in the large living room at Azalea. The men wore dark suits. They were mostly older golf buddies or business associates of Chuck's, and Kira could hear snippets of their conversations as she passed between them. They told stories of Chuck's temper on the links and marveled at his stamina with his now widowed (and available) young wife.

It was surprising to Kira how few women were there. Other than the odd trophy wife, the absence of women gave the event more of the feeling of being an afternoon at a private men's club than a wake after a funeral. In the back of the room, huddled in a small group away from the others, Kira found the few women who belonged. Birdie and Amelia were there to console Sutton. They sat with her by a window overlooking the backyard. Kira could just make out their conversation.

"I'm going to spread Chuck's ashes on his putting green," Sutton told the others as she nodded toward the window. "That way, Chuck will always be able to play golf and he'll always be home."

"That's a nice idea," Amelia said.

"How fitting," Birdie commented. "Chuck sold fertilizer and now he's going to *be* fertilizer."

"Is my daughter here?" Kira asked as she approached the women. She could feel beads of sweat running down the back of her neck, and she was sure her cheeks were red. They were burning.

"I think she's in the basement with the boys," Birdie said with some attitude. "I'll get her for you."

Birdie! Kira didn't want anything from Birdie. "No, I'll get her," Kira said, cutting Birdie off. Kira quickly surveyed the room and spotted the staircase to the basement. She left the women behind and cut her way through the mourners toward the daughter she needed to save. Iris was at the bottom of the stairs somewhere and she was hurting. Kira could make everything right.

Kira tore down the stairs and followed the boys' voices. She moved through the finished basement past shelves filled with sporting equipment and muddy winter boots and stacks of board games and past the gym where Chuck Chambers used to work out with the family housekeeper. A hallway lined with framed family photos of the Chambers children led to a game room with a ping-pong table, pool table, half-empty wine refrigerator, and the five boys, including Kolt. They were playing video games. They held game controllers in their hands as they sat before a television of movie theater proportions. Chips and soda cans were strewn across a dark wood coffee table that had probably once been upstairs but had been relegated to the basement as times and fashions changed.

She saw Iris sitting in a plaid chair in the corner. She realized that she hadn't liked her daughter very much since Kira had joined the family in Buckhead. It's difficult to like someone who hates you. An immense feeling of love, though, washed over Kira now as she looked at Iris, slumped in a chair with her legs dangling over the side and her head buried in her phone. Kira was a woman. Iris was a girl. Still just a girl.

That girl looked up and was surprised to see her mother in the doorway. Kira nodded and motioned for Iris to join her. Iris sighed dramatically and got up to join her mother. As she came closer, however, and as they retreated into the hallway, Iris seemed to sense that this was no normal visit. She approached with caution.

"Iris," Kira said softly. It was almost as if she didn't want her daughter to hear her. She knew that the conversation they were about to have would be cataclysmic. The tsunami was coming. The boys continued to play their video game. Formula One cars raced around a circuit in Bahrain as virtual spectators cheered from the grandstands and the boys themselves talked trash around the old coffee table. "We need to go home now," she told Iris. The Chambers's basement wasn't the place for *this* conversation.

"Why?" Iris asked, though she seemed to know.

"We have to go," Kira insisted. "Get your brother and let's go home."

"You're here now," Iris said. She was deflecting. "You can take him home. I'm going to go out with my friends." Iris began to walk away. She headed toward the stairs and a quick escape, but Kira stopped her. She grabbed ahold of her arm and held tight. Her grip was probably too tight, but she wasn't going to let go. Not now.

"I know about Anderson Tupper," Kira said in a whisper. "I know what he did to you."

She didn't mean to do it in Sutton's basement, in a house full of strangers, but she didn't feel she had a choice. She *did* know about Anderson, and it was a secret that was killing her and probably her daughter too. "The police have his computer. They have a video."

Tears began to run down Iris's cheeks faster than she could wipe them away. "Do they think I killed him? I didn't kill him. I didn't kill him!"

It hadn't even occurred to Kira that Iris could have killed Anderson. She pulled her daughter in and held her, even as Iris began to sob. Kira wanted to protect her. To heal her. "Of course they don't think that," Kira said. "Of course not."

"We didn't mean it," came another voice. Kira hadn't noticed that the sounds of the boys playing their video game had ended. She turned to see Kolt standing behind them. The other boys stood behind him. "It was an accident. We didn't mean to kill him."

Kira released her grip on Iris, and both mother and daughter looked at Kolt and the other boys. The boys all looked sad and shameful and a little relieved. Unburdened.

"We were just trying to warn him to leave Iris alone," Freddie said. He was their leader. He would give the debriefing. "We were going to scare him. It just . . . it just happened." Freddie looked like he was about to cry, but he held it in.

"You killed him?" Iris asked in shock and disbelief. Freddie nodded, and Iris, rather than being horrified, gratefully hugged the boy. She looked at the others and at her brother. Of course he had defended her honor. The boys all looked to Kira for a sign of punishment, for consequences, but she was in too much shock to move beyond the moment. Kolt began to sob uncontrollably, which caused Hampton and Cash to begin crying even as Freddie and Wade were too scared to flinch.

"I don't want to go to jail!" Kolt cried out. "I want to die! I just want to die!"

This brought Kira roaring back to life. She looked at the boys. They *were boys*. They were innocent boys and Anderson was an evil man. She grabbed Kolt and pulled him toward her, and he gripped on to her with equal intensity. He held on to her like the child he was, not the young man he was becoming. Kira held his face in her hands. She looked at the other boys and then at her son. "I will never let anything bad happen to you ever again," she declared. "Do you understand? *Never.*"

CHAPTER

36

THE TEAM

It was a flirtation that had started innocently enough. Iris would pick her brother up from games or practices and linger to talk to his handsome coach, who seemed to have nothing but smiles and time for her. Talk of the best pizza in Atlanta or the latest Taylor Swift song (he knew all her music; he was old but not that old) slowly turned to things more personal. Iris told Anderson about the trauma of a day on the beach in Malibu, and Anderson told her about his sadness that he no longer got along with the brother he had idolized. They were both disappointed in their parents. They were both damaged souls who needed friendship. And maybe love.

She snuck out late at night to meet him at his house. It wasn't hard. Her dad barely noticed she was there. Her mom wasn't there. Iris and Anderson would watch movies together, usually classics from his own youth like *The Day After Tomorrow* and *National Treasure* (which they watched three times), order in Thai food, and just talk. Until the talking turned to something more.

Iris, Anderson would soon enough learn, was a virgin. It was something he told her he respected. Until he didn't. After first getting her to send him chaste pictures that may as well have been from her high school yearbook, he convinced her to send him nude shots. Iris wasn't alarmed. Just about every girl she knew sent naked pictures to guys. This guy just happened to be older and her brother's Little League coach.

On the evening that her prince turned into a frog, Iris and Anderson had started to watch *Talladega Nights* but didn't finish before they began making out on the worn-out sofa in Anderson's living room. They were drinking wine that night, something (along with smoking pot) that Iris had done before. She may have been a virgin, but she wasn't a prude. It wasn't long, however, before the movie and the wine seemed to blend together into a haze and the next thing Iris remembered was waking up in Anderson's bed, naked and sore, with a camera on a tripod pointed her way.

All Anderson could say was, "You woke up too soon."

It all changed in an instant. They went from friends and confidants to adversaries and enemies. Iris threatened to tell her father, but Anderson reminded her that he had pictures of her. And a video. And she had come over willingly. Many times. Imagine the stories in the news. The daughter of a writer who wrote books for teenagers sending naked photos to an older innocent man. What would that do to her mother, who was struggling through rehab on the other side of the country? What would that do to her career? Hadn't she already tried to kill herself?

So Iris kept it a secret, and it remained one until one night when no one picked Kolt up from practice and he used his coach's phone to call his mother. While holding Coach Tupper's phone, a notification came up on the screen from *Iris Brooks* on the Signal app. "Why did you do this to me?" it said. Why did he do *what* to her? And why were his sister and his coach texting each other on Signal, a private messaging app?

Kolt confronted his sister and she quickly confessed all. Kolt and Iris had grown uncommonly close. They had been forged together in the fire of their mother's dysfunction. His sister's story was more information than an eleven-year-old should ever have to hear, but Kolt had dealt with worse in his short life. Iris begged her brother not to tell anyone, and he promised her he wouldn't. That promise lasted until the next morning when he saw Wade at school. How could he not tell Wade? They had become best friends.

Even though Wade agreed not to tell anyone else, he felt he had to tell *someone*. Wade thought he should at least tell his parents, but he knew they had enough to worry about. Something was wrong with his father, and his parents seemed always on edge, no matter how well they hid it from both Wade and the world. Wade had no idea then what ALS was and what it would eventually mean for his family. He didn't know then that he was lucky that he would not turn out to be a great football star like his father and have his head smashed in game after game. That glory and that pain would never be his legacy.

Instead of his parents, Wade unburdened himself of what he now knew in the halls of Kensington Prep, to Cash and Hampton. They had all been friends since preschool. They had never confided with each other about their deepest secrets and desires, but they knew them all the same. Wade was crushed under the pressure of being his father's undeserving son. Cash's father had other sons and a former life that was more important to him than Cash and the life they lived together at Azalea. And Hampton? Well, they all knew that his dad was a "dick." They all had difficult relationships with their fathers. Fathers were inherently pals. They were guides to the wild places in life. They were models on how to be a man. Cash and Hampton lacked those role models even as Wade struggled to fit the very large mold his father had formed for him. But what about their mothers? That was another matter. Boys love their mothers in a different way than they love their fathers. Mothers are fearsome creatures, but they are also mighty protectors. Wade and Cash and Hampton sometimes hated their mothers, but they knew that those flawed and complicated women would always be there for them. Kolt and his sister had come to Atlanta without their mother, and Iris had been picked off from the herd.

The secret that Wade had told Cash and Hampton stayed a secret for the length of the school hallway, when they joined their fearless leader, Freddie. No secret was safe from him. His mere existence, a boy filled with spit and vinegar and oozing confidence, begged lesser beings to spill their guts.

The four boys made it as far as the Kensington Prep cafeteria and its organic salad bar and locally sourced chicken nuggets before they collectively spilled the secret to Kolt that they knew *his* secret. They would take care of this problem together. An attack on Iris, one of their sisters, was an attack on them all. Seemingly every bit of inspirational jargon they had amassed from years of Little League Baseball and Pee Wee soccer and episodes of *Daniel Tiger's Neighborhood* was coming through. They all had each other's backs. They would always be there for each other. They would never let each other down.

In the end, it was Freddie's plan. He was their team captain and the strategist of the group. Kolt would engage the coach in a video game battle online, then invite him to meet at the Chastain fields after dark. All communication would be through the Xbox. There would be no record of a phone call. Once he was at the park, all the boys would confront their coach and blackmail him. Either he would leave Iris alone and delete the video of her or they would tell their mothers what they knew and it would then be only a matter of minutes until the whole world knew. Even though Ham began to waiver and Wade expressed his doubts, they proceeded with the plan. *Teamwork makes the dream work.* Wasn't that something Coach Tupper himself had told them?

At the last moment, on the night of the Steeplechase as they snuck out of the Miltons' house and headed for Chastain Park, Cash grabbed a wooden bat off the wall in Freddie's room. It was one of the Louisville Sluggers that their coach had given each of them. Cash thought they might need a bat for protection. They were going to Chastain Park at night. No one went to Chastain Park at night. People were always being murdered there. At least that's what his mother had told him to keep him from even thinking about going out at night on the mean streets of Buckhead. Little did he know then that he would become part of a cautionary tale that would be told to the children of Buckhead for generations to come.

The boys could pinpoint the moment it all went wrong. There was a lot of cursing (mostly from Freddie) and bluster (Freddie too) and threats (again, Freddie), but Coach Tupper, who was unsteady on his feet and seemed drunk to the boys, showed no signs of backing down. He told the boys no one would ever believe them because, he insisted, it just wasn't true. That Iris was a "vulnerable girl" prone to "exaggeration" and "was obviously depressed." That he was *Anderson Tupper*. That he "ran Buckhead" and that the boys were "little idiots" who would be "laughed out of school." Then he went after them one by one. Kolt's mom was "a pathetic alcoholic." Wade's mother was "a bossy bitch." Cash's mom was "a drug-dealing slut." Ham's mother, Anderson's former sister-in-law, was a gold digger who'd be "living in a trailer park in Tennessee" if it wasn't for the Tuppers. And Freddie's mother? Coach Tupper zeroed in on the team captain as Freddie stood defiantly before him. "Your mother is the most hated woman in Buckhead," he said. "Even your father doesn't want to sleep with her." Coach Tupper talked and talked and then—he talked too much. "Don't blow this out of proportion, Freddie. *Don't be like your mom.*"

But Freddie was just like his mom. So much so that he was offended that anyone would think there was anything wrong with that. Freddie grabbed the wooden bat out of Cash's hands. In games he struck out more often than not. Now, though, he had a chance to defend both his mother's honor and Iris's. This time, he was swinging for the fences. Wade was sitting on the bench in the dugout with his head down as the others argued with the coach. He didn't see Freddie swing the bat and hit their coach on the back of his head, but he heard it. It was the unmistakable crack of a home run. Coach Tupper stumbled in the dirt as he felt the blood running down the back of his head. Then he fell to his knees and finally to the ground where he lay motionless.

"Did you kill him?" Cash asked.

"I don't know."

"What if he gets up?" asked Wade. His mother had handled their family's image like a public relations pro. Wade seemed to know that the optics weren't good on this. "He'll tell everyone."

"What if he's dead?" Ham asked. It was his uncle, after all, even if they had never been close.

"He should die," Kolt said. "He deserves to die."

Freddie stood over their coach's body with the bat still tightly gripped in his hand. He turned to Kolt and held the bat out toward him. "It's all of us," he said. "We're a *team*."

Kolt took the bat from their captain, raised it over his head, and brought it down on Anderson's head with such force it was like he was unloading every fear and frustration he had experienced in the last long year. Coach Tupper didn't move at all. It was a good bet that Freddie's first blow had ended his life. Everything now was in the name of comradery. Cash took the next hit and Wade the one after that. He passed the bat to Ham. Ham hesitated for a moment, then struck his uncle's body with one last weak and inconsequential blow.

It was done. They all looked at Coach Tupper's lifeless body. He was an evil opponent they had defeated, but unlike a character in one of their violent video games, they couldn't reset him back to life.

Cash kicked at Tupper's body. There was no movement. "I think he's dead," he said.

"Good!" Freddie declared.

* * *

"I said it was good. Like you told me, Mom. Sometimes people deserve to be hurt."

Through fits of sobbing, the boys had finished recounting their tale to their mothers. They were all at once repentant and unapologetic. They were certainly more worried about getting in trouble for what they had done than for actually having done it. Venita had joined them now and along with Kira, Sutton, Amelia, and Birdie had listened to the tale silently. It was a lot to process. This moment wasn't in any of the child psychology books any of them had read. They didn't go over it at the Mothers Monday Meditations at church or at school orientation. The closest Kensington Prep had come to preparing them for such a thing was the school's recent parent seminar on the dangers of drugs, which was funny because that was exactly what they all could have used at that moment.

"We took his wallet," Freddie said, filling in that one final detail. "So it would look like a robbery."

Amelia was ashen. She looked at her son, bewildered. "Ham, how could you?" she asked him. "He was your uncle." Ham just looked at the floor. He had no acceptable answer.

"What did you guys do with the wallet?" Venita, ever the lawyer, asked the boys.

The other boys looked on sheepishly as Cash said, "It's in my locker at school."

Sutton almost started hyperventilating. "Oh my God, Cash! What were you thinking? Oh my God. Oh my God!"

Birdie tried to ignore Sutton's meltdown and got to the big question. "What did you do with the bat?"

"We burned it in the pizza oven at our house," Freddie said.

CHAPTER

37

THE TEAM MOMS

THE PIZZA OVEN at Birdie's house.

It was all the fashion for a brief moment in time. Birdie had it installed when they renovated the patio. For a solid month, the family ate nothing but pizza. They started off with the classic margarita with fresh basil from Fresh Market and graduated to a rather elaborate barbecue duck pizza that Freddie refused to eat and whose ingredients cost five times what it would have cost to simply order a pizza from Fellini's. It was then used sporadically, sometimes for cooking pizza and more often for Freddie to burn random things like Legos or his old stuffed animals. Now Birdie used barbecue tongs to pull out what was left of a wooden baseball bat. It was a charred chunk of the barrel.

"I just made flatbread in there on Tuesday," Birdie said with a shudder as Amelia, Sutton, Venita, and Kira looked on.

"It's not funny. You shouldn't joke about this," Venita chastised Birdie. "A man is dead."

Birdie turned to face Venita. She was dead serious. "I wish I had killed him myself."

"Why don't we just say it was an accident?" Sutton offered. "I mean, it *was* an accident."

"It doesn't matter if it was an accident or not," Birdie said. "Our boys' lives will be ruined. *Our* lives will be ruined. Jesus, can you imagine what they'd say at the country club? Those gossips live for this shit at the PDC."

"The country club?" Venita asked. "This would be the lead story on *Sports Center*. Remember who my husband is?"

"Yes, Venita, everyone remembers who your husband is," said Birdie.

"Those detectives are going to keep looking," Sutton said nervously. She was sweating despite there being no fire in the oven. "I mean, Chuck just died. What if they think that's suspicious?"

"Why would they think that?" Amelia asked.

"I don't know," Sutton said defensively. "People are just dying all around us."

Kira studied Sutton for a moment. She had a terrible poker face. Kira didn't know these women. She didn't know if she could trust these women. She did know, however, that only one thing mattered. Her entire world, her complicated marital situation, the deadline for her book, the whole drinking thing—it had in one afternoon reached its own singularity and condensed down to a single point—her children.

"I'll say I did it," Kira blurted out.

"Oh, my God, don't be a martyr," Birdie said.

Kira was determined. She had taken all of thirty seconds to decide this was the best course of action. "I was with Anderson that night. Everyone saw us leave together. I have to do this. I've got to protect my kids."

"It's a little late for that," Birdie told her.

"How about I tell the police that your son took the first swing?" Kira shot back.

"Do that and they'll have another murder on their hands," Birdie said, right in Kira's face. Like they were prizefighters facing off before getting in the ring. Everyone was looking at everyone else. Suspicious glances passed between them. They were mostly friends. Sometimes enemies. Sometimes confidants. Sometimes betrayers. It was hard enough for one person to keep a secret. But five? Or eleven if you counted the boys and Iris. But this wasn't just any secret. The truth could destroy all of their lives and the lives of their children.

"I know we don't all always get along," Venita said in a low and measured tone. A serious tone. She turned to Birdie and Kira. "I know you don't necessarily like each other. But it's time to stop being such goddamn Buckhead Betties and get with the fucking program. We're stuck with each other. For life." She looked at each woman in turn. "It's not about you, or you, or you, or you. It's about *us*. From now on we're a family. And families protect each other."

They were all quiet for a good long moment. This was rare. Kira looked around at each of the other women's faces. She hadn't thought of them as a contemplative lot, but here they were, all silently thinking. Kira was fairly certain that Sutton wasn't thinking as hard as the others, but the look of consternation on Sutton's face at least gave the impression she was trying.

"We need to find a viable suspect," Venita declared, breaking the silence. She said what the others were probably thinking. They needed to start pointing fingers at someone.

"I have an idea," Amelia finally said. "I know what we can do."

CHAPTER

38

SHAY

"CHATHAM TUPPER, YOU are under arrest for the murder of Anderson Tupper. You have the right to remain silent. Anything you say can and will be used against you in a court of law. You have the right to an attorney. If you cannot afford an attorney, one will be appointed for you..." Shay recited the *Miranda* rights as two uniformed officers jostled with a seemingly shocked and indignant Chatham at the door to Villa Rosa and cameras clicked and flashed as questions were shouted by the contingent of press surrounding them.

Touchdown.

"Are you fucking kidding me?" Chatham screamed at Shay. "This is crazy. I didn't kill my brother."

The charred remains of a baseball bat were found in a firepit in the backyard at Villa Rosa, and Anderson's wallet was found hidden in a box of sex toys in Amelia's former closet. The one Chatham had turned into a makeshift sex dungeon. Shay thought it odd that Chatham hadn't done a better job of getting rid of the evidence. Maybe he was so arrogant he didn't think he needed to even try.

At first, Deputy Chief Henderson and the mayor and the governor weren't thrilled that Shay planned on arresting Chatham for the murder of his brother. It would be a high-profile case that would invite national scrutiny. Not as high-profile, however, as if Marcus Wiley had done it. That would have resulted in an *American Crime Story* limited series starring someone like Idris Elba instead of a Lifetime movie starring some C-list version of Bradley Cooper as Chatham Tupper. In any case, Henderson and the lot of Georgia bigwigs got over their reservations about the arrest when the Buckhead secession vote failed. The Atlanta PD could hardly be blamed for Anderson being murdered by his own brother. No amount of taxpayer-funded police protection could have stopped that.

Tilly Tupper rolled up the driveway in her black Mercedes. She was in a tizzy. She hadn't even had time to have her hair styled before heading over to deal with this mess. "Don't you worry, Chatham," Tilly told her son as he was loaded into the back of a squad car like a common criminal. "I'll get this sorted out." Tilly made a beeline for Shay like a mama grizzly bear, all snarly and ferocious. "This is you, isn't it?" she asked with the wave of a finger in Shay's face. "You people. You people hate us. You're trying to punish us. It's like the French Revolution! Kill the rich! Well, this isn't Paris. We're not going to let it happen! You're going to pay!" With that, Tilly pulled out her mobile phone and began barking orders into it as she disappeared into Villa Rosa.

Shay looked back at the house and noticed that all the rose bushes were dead. They were shriveled up and brown and hardly better than weeds. It seemed to Shay that they were a fitting representation of the Tupper family in general.

CHAPTER

39

HEARTLEE

HEARTLEE KNEW THAT Amelia would help her. Of course she would. They had shared so much. Chatham's bed at Villa Rosa. Chatham's indiscretions. Chatham's twisted sexual proclivities. And with the birth of Heartlee's baby, their children would share his DNA too. Yes, Amelia would help Heartlee. All Heartlee had to do was recant her statement to the police and tell the truth. She hadn't even been with Chatham when the murder occurred. That night they had picked up a prostitute after the Steeplechase and taken her back to Villa Rosa. Although they had enjoyed liaisons with prostitutes together before, Heartlee had sat this one out. She was pregnant now, and there was a baby to think of. She had let Chatham have his every which way with the woman, and then she dutifully drove the prostitute back to a dark corner in South Atlanta. Heartlee thought Chatham was sleeping at home at the time of the murders, but she wasn't there so truthfully couldn't be sure. He could have killed Anderson. He really could have.

The Buckhead Betties, it turned out, weren't the scary women everyone made them out to be. Amelia paved Heartlee's way into

Atlanta society and introduced her to all the important people worth knowing. Venita was kind enough to find Heartlee one of the best attorneys in Atlanta and made sure Heartlee got a generous settlement from the Tuppers with more than enough money for her and her unborn baby. She also offered her a discount on a Ford. Heartlee didn't really see a Ford in her future, but thought it was incredibly nice all the same. Kira gave Heartlee autographed first editions of her books and promised to name a character after her in her next one! Sutton Chambers—well, Heartlee knew they would be best friends. Even Birdie, who was like the Brownie troop leader of Buckhead, welcomed Heartlee into the fold by sponsoring her membership to the Peachtree Driving Club. Thus, Heartlee Gilston became a platinum card–carrying member of the Buckhead Betties.

AMELIA

Sometimes you love something so much you can't let anyone else have it. That's how Amelia felt about her David Austin roses. Her garden at Villa Rosa was the showplace of Buckhead and the envy of anthophiles everywhere. She had carefully selected roses from the Austin catalog. *She* had. Not Chatham. She had chosen the Thomas à Becket shrub roses for the property line and the Tess of the d'Urbervilles climbing roses for the trellis by the garden shed. The soft apricot colored Roald Dahl roses lined the front walkway, and pale yellow, aptly named, Teasing Georgia roses burst out of the beds beneath the windows at the front of the house. It was all part of her masterpiece. The mise-en-scène of her life.

Amelia loved those roses so much that on the night of the Steeplechase, she killed them. After the race, she dressed head to toe in Black Ops Chanel, from the leather loafers on her dainty feet to the vintage cashmere sweater hugging her slender neck, parked around the corner, and snuck through the neighbor's yard to her former mansion. She lugged a gallon of herbicide with her and quietly went about pouring poison on every single rose bush.

Eventually, after the rose bushes had died and the dust had settled in Buckhead, Amelia sold her house and moved with her children to Traverse City, Michigan. She bought a nice little tract house in the suburbs, enrolled her kids in public school, and began dating the UPS man. He had great legs and always insisted on paying for dinner. Usually at the Olive Garden.

BIRDIE

The day Birdie burned her husband's beloved car to a crisp wasn't the first time she had been to his love shack in the suburbs. After the Steeplechase, she followed the GPS tracker she had installed in her husband's Jag and drove to Alpharetta. She crouched beside a barbecue on the back deck of Brittani's townhome and watched as Dan and his mistress made love on the sofa in the living room while HGTV played on the television and cast a blue light across their naked bodies. Brittani was so skinny. That's all Birdie could think. She was skinny and she wasn't Birdie. How pleased Dan seemed to be with it all. By the light of *House Hunters International*, Birdie could see a look on Dan's face that she had never seen when he was with her. It was a look of contentment. She hadn't torched his car on that evening, but the match was lit then.

For Birdie, revenge was a dish best served *hot*.

Birdie and Dan remained unhappily married. She had stood by his side, after all, when his client was charged with murder. It wasn't a good look for the family that Dan was entangled with Chatham Tupper. Dan's law firm lost a lot of business. It was a lot less business lost, though, than if his son had committed murder. But Dan would never know that. That was Birdie and Freddie's secret.

SUTTON

Around the time Anderson Tupper was meeting his fate on a baseball field in Buckhead, Sutton Chambers was in room 301 of a

Comfort Inn off interstate 75 in Marietta. There was an Outback Steakhouse next door, but Sutton was too busy having sex with Doctor Lamar Burrows with a U (or, appropriately in this case, as Detective Claypool would have put it—a "fuck-u") to partake of the blooming onion on the other side of the shared parking lot.

Lamar had threatened to tell his golfing buddy, Chuck, about Sutton's side hustle dealing drugs. "Spend the night with me and I'll keep quiet," he told her. He also told her how Chuck had bragged about everything from the breasts he had purchased for her to the threesome he and Sutton had once enjoyed when they were in Las Vegas for a fertilizer convention. Sutton had hit the jackpot with that one. That cost Chuck ten thousand dollars. She didn't know how much he paid the prostitute who had joined them.

Lamar was sleazy and a colossal asshole, but Sutton had to admit that he was good in bed. Maybe it was the fact that she had only had sex with Chuck for the previous thirteen plus years (not counting the Vegas prostitute) or maybe it was the budget Comfort Inn with its forbidden aura of sexual seediness, but she hadn't had such a good lay in years.

Sutton eventually decided to dig up Chuck's putting green and replaced it with a covered patio and outdoor pizza oven. Just like the one Birdie had. She didn't know what happened to her dear departed husband's ashes. They were an unfortunate landscaping casualty.

Sutton, the most likely of the Buckhead Betties to spill the beans, turned out to be a fortress of silence. If anyone started asking questions about Anderson Tupper's murder, they might start asking questions about Chuck's death. Sutton had gained too much. She wasn't about to go to jail or go back to Alabama.

KIRA

She killed the neighbor's cat.

It came back to Kira later in bits and pieces. She hadn't left the Steeplechase with Anderson. He abandoned her at the Steeplechase, and she had driven herself home and stumbled to the guesthouse in a stupor. She was searching for her keys when the neighbor's cat suddenly jumped off the retaining wall next to her. In the haze of the waning effects of the GHB, Kira swung at the cat with her Longchamp handbag and connected with it in midair, launching the poor animal into the wall where it tragically died of blunt force trauma. That wasn't Anderson's blood on her handbag. It was Valentine's.

After a hopeless effort to administer CPR to the poor animal, Kira put Valentine in an old Amazon box and tossed the body into a recycling bin at the curb. She thought that recycling was akin to reincarnation and perhaps that little extra effort to dispose of the cat in an environmentally friendly manner might one day earn her some redemption for having killed it in the first place.

Or maybe she just made all that up. An addict's version of events usually bore little resemblance to reality.

Kira had been accused of trying to kill her son so it was ironic that it was murder that finally restored her relationship with her children. They shared the great secret. It was a secret they had to keep from everyone, including Kallan.

Kolt and his teammates never got to finish the baseball season. They never went to the playoffs. But they remained a team long after baseball ended. They would always be the Vikings. They would always be warriors for each other.

Iris decided to go to college at New York University's campus in Shanghai, China. It was about as far away as Iris could get from Atlanta. Kira took the nineteen-hour flight with her daughter to drop her off and get her settled. Mother and daughter toured the city, ate soup dumplings, bought cheap souvenirs to bring back to Kolt, and acted like a day at the beach in Malibu and a night on a baseball field in Buckhead never happened.

VENITA

Venita wasn't committing any kind of crime on the night of the Steeplechase. She was tending to Marcus after a day at the hospital where he was definitively diagnosed with ALS. The realization that the end of his life would be more like its tough beginning than its triumphant middle had sent him into a deep depression. Venita loved Marcus even if she wasn't sure she had the strength to deal with what was to come.

Venita, however, couldn't be absolved of guilt. She had made Amelia's idea to frame Chatham for his brother's murder work. Heartlee was already susceptible to taking her baby daddy down. The Betties just needed a plan, and Venita had done nothing but plan her entire life. She had mapped out her husband's post-football career and her family's rise to the top of the Buckhead ladder. Framing someone for murder was just another chore on her to-do list.

Venita didn't feel bad about setting up Chatham. She was sure that Chatham would have killed Anderson if he thought he could have gotten away with it and that he would surely hire enough high-powered lawyers to ensure he was never convicted. It would let just enough time pass to make any other suspects recede into the background. Whether he did it or not, everyone would always think that Chatham was a murderer, and the overburdened and understaffed Atlanta Police Department would move on.

The Buckhead Betties weren't guilty of murder. But they *were* guilty.

CHAPTER

40

SHAY

SHAY WALKED ACROSS the floor of the detective's unit like a lioness. She was filled with pride for having solved the Tupper case and was carrying a new handbag to celebrate it. It was a Paul Smith tote, much like the one Kira Brooks owned. Shay always purchased herself something special when she finished a case. She found this multicolored beauty on eBay for a suspiciously low price. It was almost certainly a fake, but no one would know that. It was better a fake than nothing at all.

Shay entered the War Room to find it being disassembled by the Kids. Hannah and Anthony and Farrell were busy taking down the wall of suspects and sorting papers into files and files into file boxes. Shay felt a sense of satisfaction and also of relief. Unsolved cases were a menace, forever nagging at her, and she had sleepless nights fretting over missed clues or errant witnesses. The Tupper case was being wrapped up with a big pink bow.

"Hey, boss," said Anthony. He put a lid on a file box and marked it with a thick black Sharpie. *Tupper #3.*

"How's it going, kids?"

"Almost done," said Hannah as she sat down at her computer.

"You guys were very helpful," Shay told them in a motherly way. "I have to admit, I'm going to miss you."

Farrell pulled Anderson's photo off the wall. It was the last one. "Hopefully some other rich guy will get murdered so we can do this again."

Dub joined them with a down home "Hey, y'all." He looked around at the War Room, which was quickly returning to the conference room it had once been, and then looked at his partner. They shared a moment of satisfaction. "All paperwork complete," he said. "Chatham Tupper is officially in the hands of the DA."

"I brought you something," Shay said as she opened her new fake Paul Smith bag and pulled out a paper sack from Chick-fil-A. She handed it over to Dub with some reverence.

"You didn't . . ." Dub looked like Shay had just handed him a puppy that was riding Pegasus through clouds made of cotton candy. He took the bag and tore in with gusto.

"Lt. Claypool," Hannah said from behind her laptop. "That redneck dude who lives across from the baseball fields finally gave up his security footage. He dumped like thirty-three megabytes on us. Should I just send it over with everything else to the prosecutor's office?"

"That would be lazy of us, wouldn't it?" Shay told her young comrade.

"We're being moved over to the Johnson case," Anthony interjected. Which meant Shay was going to have to finish up all things Tupper. She never half-assed anything and she wasn't going to start now.

"Fine," she told Hannah. "Forward the footage to me. I'll take a look."

As the Kids packed up and Dub ate his celebratory chicken sandwich, Shay went to the office they shared and sat down behind her computer. She moved aside a copy of *Animal Farm* that was next to the keyboard. A Barnes & Noble bookmark stuck out of the top of the book. She was determined to finish it before Darron returned home for the summer.

She fired up her computer and found an email from Hannah at the top of her inbox and clicked to a file Hannah had humorously labeled *RICH OLD DUDE*. It took Shay a few minutes to work her way through the file to find the day in question. It was easier than she thought, and she was disappointed in Hannah for not making the effort to go through the footage herself. As millennials or Gen-Zers went, her Kids weren't that bad, but she noticed they didn't have the same work ethic she and Dub had, though to be fair, not many people did.

Several different angles from several different video cameras at the old man's house were displayed on Shay's computer screen. There were six boxes with black and white views of the front door, the back door, the backyard, the driveway, and the street in front of the house. The footage wasn't crystal clear, but it was good enough. Shay moved the computer's cursor along a bar at the bottom of the screen and scrolled through the day. She fast-forwarded past the daylight hours, when the old man who lived in the house put a letter in the mailbox and raised the flag. She watched as cars and walkers and bikers passed by and as the mailman came and went and the old man came back out to retrieve his mail. It all whizzed by as Shay fast-forwarded to that night.

She slowed the video footage down and kept a sharp eye out for Chatham's car but none of the passing cars were of note. She began fast forwarding again as the time stamp moved past ten o'clock and then ten-thirty and ten-forty-five. She scrolled even faster, speeding up past eleven o'clock. The footage was flying by in a blur and Shay had almost lost interest when something flashed past on the box in the upper right-hand corner of her screen. She paused the footage. She wasn't sure if she had seen something different or if it was just another passing car.

Shay scrolled the video feed back to 11:22.06 and leaned in closer to the screen. It wasn't a passing car. There were figures on the sidewalk in front of the house and across from the park. Five figures that flickered across the screen. She scrolled back again and paused the video. There, frozen midstride, were five boys from Tupper's team. They looked like the devil was chasing them. Freddie Milton led the way with a baseball hat in his hand, and Kolt Brooks brought up the rear, looking back over his shoulder, back toward the fields. Even in the darkened video footage it was plain to see the panic on their faces.

Shay had stopped breathing for a moment, and now she gasped. It wasn't Chatham. He hadn't killed Anderson. She had thought that was too easy, but she had been happy to believe it was him. Now, though, the truth was there before her. The boys had done it and she knew why. It was the answer she hadn't been looking for. Her palms began sweating. She could feel a chill creep up her spine as the shock of the truth began to charge through her body. The boys, she thought again. The *boys*.

A strong nuclear interaction is said to be the most powerful force in the universe. It is responsible for binding together the particles that form the cosmos and is trillions of times more powerful than gravity. Yet any woman knows it pales in comparison to the supernova of a mother's love for her child. It's God-like. Birth is a miracle. Only the Lord and mothers give life. The power of both is beyond physics and sometimes beyond reason.

Shay's hand hovered over her keyboard. She was a creator and a protector. She had the ability to warp the fabric of space and time and to make things disappear. She was a mother. Shay pushed a button and deleted the video.

THE END

ACKNOWLEDGMENTS

THIS BOOK PASSED through a thousand hands on its long and perilous journey. I'm grateful to all who helped in big ways and small. To my life team: Johnelle, Lisa, Laura, Nancy and Jenny. I am honored to be your Captain. To Nancy and Bill for shelter in all storms. To Derek and Debbie who help me navigate rough seas. To Annie, my sister and my metamorphic rock. To Paul and Brian, consiglieri and fratelli. To Debby, my faithful unpaid life coach. To Ilyssa, who keeps hope alive. To Sandra and Margo for being friends who are also family. To Ellen, Cynthia, Adam, Nick, Stephen, Alisa and Ally for being family who are also friends. To Aunt Ann, for representing both the family and my father. To Farrell for everything. I would kill for any of you. But please don't put me in that position . . .

Thank you to everyone at the Seymour Agency and all at Crooked Lane for helping shepherd this book on its journey and to my amazing editor Holly Ingraham for talking me out of bad decisions and guiding me to good ones. And a final Godzilla-sized thank you to my agent Lesley Sabga. Tenacity. Dedication. Kindness. I could go on, but I gotta keep this under 100,000 words! This book exists and my dream came true because of you.